THE
FRIEND
OF THE
FAMILY

FRANKENSTEIN SERIES

Prodigal Son · City of Night · Dead and Alive · Lost Souls · The Dead Town

MEMOIR

A Big Little Life: A Memoir of a Joyful Dog Named Trixie

THE
FRIEND
OF THE
FAMILY

DEAN
KOONTZ

THOMAS & MERCER

Text copyright © 2026 by Dean Ray Koontz and Gerda Ann Koontz, as Trustees of the Koontz Living Trust dated July 11, 1994

Published by Thomas & Mercer, Seattle
www.apub.com

Amazon, the Amazon logo, and Thomas & Mercer are trademarks of Amazon.com, Inc., or its affiliates.

EU product safety contact:
Amazon Media EU S. à r.l.
38, avenue John F. Kennedy, L-1855 Luxembourg
amazonpublishing-gpsr@amazon.com

ISBN-13: 9781662533297 (hardcover)
ISBN-13: 9781662533303 (paperback)
ISBN-13: 9781662533280 (digital)

Cover design by Jarrod Taylor
Interior illustrations by Edward Bettison
Cover image: © New Africa, © alialam1, Suzanne Tucker / Shutterstock

Printed in the United States of America

First edition

*Every life is meaningful. Every life has
the potential to lift others by example.
This book is dedicated to
Canine Companions for Independence,
to all the employees and volunteers,
to the puppy raisers, to those who
bravely face their challenges with
the help of assistance dogs, and to
the beautiful, unforgettable dogs.*

From childhood's hour I have not been
As others were—I have not seen
As others saw.

—Edgar Allan Poe, "Alone"

Part One
1930

"Dear child, be not afraid." So it begins with a voice that is melodious and comforting—a dream in shades of blue and eerie light. Visitors of fantastic forms and faces descend a staircase invisible, with the moon above and stars diamonding the darkness all around. In the waking world, some of these people would be thought beautiful, others horrific, though to me, the sleeper, they are equal to one another and no more or less than enchanting.

They descend into my room and gather around my bed. Although I have not once awakened, I have been aware of them arriving. No fear troubles me when, one at a time, they enter my mind as if passing through a door. Each succinctly tells me of his or her life with powerful images and emotions that require no words to convey deep understanding. Although they come to me in a dream, they are not figments of my imagination. They are people as real as I am. They are not just the Ghosts of Christmas Past but of all the ages of mankind, outcasts like me, having come out of time immemorial to comfort me, to say in essence, "Yes, I know."

—from a letter by Alida, April 17, 1927

ONE

For much of my life, I had no last name. During those years, I never felt at home or loved. I was called Alida, a name under which I lived in miserable circumstances with unusual companions.

Everyone called Forest Farnam "Captain," which was how he billed himself. He had never been a captain of anything, and his real name was not Forest Farnam. Although he claimed to be six feet tall, he would have been five nine if he'd taken the two-inch lifts out of his boots. A person of ample dimensions, Captain wore three-piece tweed suits even on the hottest days, but he perspired no more than a penguin dwelling in the Antarctic. He remained perpetually pale regardless of how much time he spent outdoors, as if he were immune to natural light just as he was inoculated against respect for natural law.

McKinsey Shows, the country's largest traveling carnival, which owned all its rides and select other attractions, also leased midway space to entrepreneurs. The shooting gallery, the high-striker, the mouse-in-the hole scam, the various winner-every-time games, and the grab joints that offered eat-while-you-walk fare were all owned by individuals who made an excellent middle-class living. The Captain operated a popular ten-in-one, an attraction that put on display ten "human wonders," which he called "freaks" in private. Each of the ten had his or her stall along a sawdust-carpeted viewing corridor that wound from one end of the tent to the other. Outside, luridly illustrated banners provided a backdrop to the pitchman—often Captain—who ballyhooed the passing crowd, swearing on his mother's grave that the experience of a lifetime awaited them inside.

In Captain Farnam's Museum of the Strange, as it was called, most of the "biological oddities" were less wondrous than the rubes had been promised. The man with the "iron throat" was actually just a sword swallower, a former vaudeville performer from Pittsburgh. At four hundred pounds, the bearded lady was said to be the fattest of her kind in all the world, which maybe she was or maybe she wasn't, but at least the beard was real. Rubberman was double-jointed and capable of seemingly impossible postures, though he could not shake hands with himself behind his back as boldly depicted on the banner outside. The littlest person on display was Miss Cora Wallingham, an achondroplastic dwarf with shortened extremities and a large head. Cora was a buoyant, witty woman. While many of her fellow performers refused to converse with the marks, Cora enjoyed answering questions from them, charming even the most boorish individuals.

Conrad Heinz, a kindly man cursed with a mean face and a third eye in his forehead, gave the customers more of what they expected. Although the orb was milky white and blind, it rolled in its shallow socket, seeming to focus on this or that face among the crowd. When he growled, most women and more than a few men recoiled in fear.

In spite of all that Conrad had to offer the morbidly curious, I was the main attraction in the Museum of the Strange. Onstage, I wore only the bottom of a two-piece bathing suit. No one was likely to entertain erotic fantasies about me. I was minimally clothed for the sole purpose of exposing my unique nature so that the paying customers would feel they had gotten their money's worth.

Most of the time, I sat on a padded stool, though twice an hour I was required to "parade," as Captain called it, moving about the small stage, which had a mirrored back wall so that the marks could fully appreciate how different I was from them.

I had learned to deafen myself to everything they said to one another and to me. I rarely glanced at them, and when I did, they looked like wide-eyed fish peering through the wall of an aquarium, nothing but silence issuing from their open, moving mouths.

Judge not lest you be judged. That is one of the principles by which I live as best I can, although I am not always faithful to my intention. When I was very young and first put on display, I watched the rubes as they watched me. I saw among them dark souls who took pleasure in the sight of me for whatever reasons, and others who clearly found me disgusting. Sometimes there were men with pity in their eyes and women unable to hold back tears, but their compassion was no more meaningful to me than the contempt and sick delight of the others. Whatever sympathy they felt for me was insufficient to inspire them to take action that might free me from enslavement. Although I wasn't old enough to attend grade school, perhaps they convinced themselves that I enjoyed a variety of options and had considered all paths forward and had chosen a life of servitude and degradation. I forgave them. Day by day, year after year, I forgave them and wished no ill upon them. I ceased to hear the marks and ceased to see them except as a blur of faces, because it was easier to forgive them en masse than as gaping, goggling individuals.

Judge not lest you be judged. I was incapable of forgiveness when it came to Captain Farnam. I judged him. I imagined a place in Hell awaited him, that in fact it was Hell from which he had come into my life.

He claimed that my mother—of whom I had no memory—was his sister and that she supported his adoption of me when I was two

7

•

years old. He possessed a thick sheaf of legal documents to support his contention. I was nine before I began to suspect his official-looking paperwork was a sheaf of forgeries. However, in 1922, child welfare wasn't a big concern of authorities, who had finally passed a law restricting child labor only six years earlier. If a crusading lawyer took my case, Captain knew how to buy his way out of any kind of trouble. If he retained custody of me following a legal skirmish, he would make my life even more miserable than it had been.

Besides, I had no money or skills with which to support myself. A penniless "biological oddity," alone in the world, seemed certain to fall into the hands of some monster more vicious than Captain. At least my current keeper never beat me or exhibited the slightest sexually perverse interest in me.

The nine other oddities in the Museum of the Strange were contract performers, as was usually the case in freak shows. They prospered, receiving a slice of the box office. In the offseason, mid-October through mid-March, they retreated to their homes in Gibsonton, Florida, a small town that welcomed carnies and even oddities from McKinsey Shows and all other carnivals in America. Those with the strangest deformities could live relatively quiet lives in that community.

I had no contract, no slice of the box office. To all intents and purposes, I was *owned* by Forest Farnam.

The Captain shunned Gibsonton. He had purchased a property on the Southern California coast, where he intended to build his dream home upon retirement in twelve years.

By that schedule, when eventually he closed or sold the Museum of the Strange, I would be in my twenties. At night, lying awake, I sometimes wondered what might become of me on the day that Captain no longer needed me. Would I then be sold to the owner of another ten-in-one? Having enslaved me all my life while pretending to be my guardian, he might worry that, once he relinquished control of me, I would find an advocate with the dedication to pursue him and bring him to justice. More than once, I dreamed that Captain drove me along a lonely, unpaved back road in the high desert on a bitter winter night and abandoned me to the mercy of coyote packs and deadly cold. He wasn't by nature a violent man, though he could no doubt conceive of a dozen largely passive ways to dispose of me such that my death would be less than a featherweight on his conscience.

In the interest of fattening his net worth, Captain remained busy during the offseason, and I continued to be the property that he peddled. In his black and boxy Ford Model T, and later in his Cadillac V-8 town car, we traveled the West and South to engagements in those elegant speakeasies catering to a monied and sophisticated clientele.

In public beyond the grounds of the midway and when not in the company of carnies, I dressed in lace-up boots, gloves, and a long, roomy robe with wide sleeves and a hood. I had no need to cover my face, of which I had reason to be proud. I'd been called pretty by those who were able to see only my face. My hair was thick, silky, and the color of spun gold. Mother Nature sometimes bestows a grace on those she otherwise disfigures and makes grotesque. I was given the consolation of my face and my mind. I have a very good mind.

When touring, I rode always in the back seat. We often traveled a hundred miles or more without exchanging a word. Captain thought of me less as a person than as an object. I suspected that, though he was the most callous person I had ever known, he was troubled by the fact that I was intelligent, a truth that conversation would force him to consider. He wanted to believe that I was little more than a trained dog with a repertoire of tricks, but the smartest of dogs does not read Louisa May Alcott's *Little Women* or the novels of Jane Austen and Charles Dickens.

In those days, books were my salvation, a window on the fullness of life that I would never otherwise know. Indeed, books remain so precious to me that I am unable to put into words how I feel each time that I open a new one to begin the tale it offers. In the back seat of the car, I had a lot of time to read.

In spite of his hard heart, Captain acquired books for me. He never bought them. His larcenous nature and related skills enabled him to visit libraries and bookshops along the way and walk out with a volume or two under his coat. He was never caught.

We stayed in "motels," which was a new word in those days. Often the establishment was a collection of small cabins arranged in an L or semicircle. I was always provided with my own room or cabin. Captain brought my favorite foods from local restaurants. As he said without irony, "A good farmer would never starve those animals he intends to bring to market."

If anyone caught sight of the Gothic figure I presented in my hooded robe, the Captain explained that I was a nun excused from the monastery to be taken to the bedside of our father, who was in his last days on this Earth. Or he said I was his sister, tragically disfigured in a fire and mortified to be seen in my diminished condition. He was a natural-born liar, and his native talent for deception was polished to a high gloss by years on the pitchman's platform, conning the marks into paying out their dimes—and later quarters—for the experience of a lifetime.

That autumn, Captain and I left the carnival when it was still in season, with the nine biological oddities having agreed to look after the business, allowing us to undertake a longer and more ambitious road trip. And so it was that on Thursday, September 4, in my seventeenth year, we motored south from Los Angeles to San Diego, after three weeks of engagements at clandestine supper clubs in the City of Angels from which Captain had profited greatly. The Cadillac V-8 provided a roomy and almost plush back seat compared to that of the previous Ford Model T. The smooth ride was ideal for a reader who wanted nothing more than to remain happily submerged in William Makepeace Thackeray's *Vanity Fair*.

We were booked into twenty-nine speakeasies operated by the same syndicate. Our tour had begun in San Francisco. After we had completed two performances a night for five nights at a place called Blue Mood in San Diego, we would move on to Texas, Arkansas, and Louisiana, finishing in New Orleans.

However, that wouldn't be the end. Loath to remain idle through the month of February, Captain had arranged a shorter second tour at upscale speakeasies in Mississippi, Alabama, and Tennessee.

Those were among the states where bootlegging and gambling were controlled from Chicago by the Capone gang. Al Capone was reputed to be making sixty million dollars annually, an almost incomprehensible fortune in those days. One year had passed since he solidified power in the St. Valentine's Day Massacre. Captain admired the gangster and hoped that, if audiences responded well to us, we'd be booked throughout Capone's territory when the forthcoming carnival season ended and winter was again upon us.

Being exhibited in Captain Farnam's Museum of the Strange with nine other biological oddities was so degrading that I wouldn't wish it on anyone, but that was nothing compared to the indignities to which I was subjected on many speakeasy stages. In movies featuring these secret supper clubs, lead characters and their friends are often lighthearted fun-loving individuals who are merely rebelling against government oppression in a spirit of adolescent naughtiness. I never took the stage in front of a crowd as innocent as that, although I'm sure there were a few such people among the rabble.

On Friday, September 5, my first night on display in Blue Mood, I endured lacerating and prolonged humiliation more painful than any beating could have been. Throughout the ordeal, Captain never came to my defense. The exuberance of the audience excited him, because he thought it guaranteed a booking with the same syndicate for the following year and at a much higher price.

Although I sometimes longed to be done with this life, I never considered suicide. Because of books, especially those written by the wonderful Mr. Dickens, I believed this was a made world with profound meaning. I kept faith that each of us has a purpose and that if we fulfill it, we will rise from even the lowest position as surely as a night mist rises from a lake in the morning sun. After my two sets on the Blue Mood stage, however, after Friday became Saturday, as I was lying abed in my room, I spent time contemplating how one might kill oneself in a painless fashion.

Six years were to pass before Mr. F. Scott Fitzgerald would write, *In a real dark night of the soul it is always three o'clock in the morning.* When I read those words in 1936, I was conveyed by a vivid memory to that motel room in San Diego.

Long before Blue Mood, I had read *The Great Gatsby.* The novel was too acerbic for my taste, but I identified with Gatsby. He might have been a shady character, even a bootlegger, but I sympathized with his yearning to be accepted in a higher social strata than the one into which he was born, to be thought respectable.

In the real dark night of the soul, where I found myself at three o'clock on that San Diego night, I thought of the ill-fated Jay Gatsby. His problem was that he tried to lift himself with the wrong hoist, by accumulating wealth and mimicking the attitudes and fashions of those who presumed to be his betters. He did not believe this was a made world with profound meaning or that he had a purpose greater than his own needs and desires if only he could find it. Had he believed as much, he would have understood that the only chance we have of being lifted ourselves is by lifting others.

Although I was a biological oddity, a freak, I had been waiting all my life for the opportunity to lift others and thereby rise with them. That dismal California night, I could not know that my purpose was soon to be placed before me and that the challenge of fulfilling it would be the work of a lifetime.

TWO

In Blue Mood, two crescent-shaped tiers of tables stepped down to a small dance floor that fronted the stage. A white cloth dressed every table. Each place setting featured a blue charger, flatware in an Art Deco motif, and short-stemmed glasses that would be filled with ice water as soon as the diners settled in their chairs. The lighting was romantic but not dim.

The menu featured everything from pasta Bolognese to lobster, and the food was priced below cost. Those who ate a filling meal tended to have a greater capacity for liquor than those who came only to drink, and this establishment was in business to mint money from alcohol. A single shot of rye sold for a dollar. Prohibition had made booze more profitable than drugs. The wines here were not the sixty-day bottled-in-the-basement *vin ordinaire* served in less elevated joints, but fine vintages. If that was what you wanted, you'd better bring a fat wallet.

No less so than in the Roaring Twenties, the clientele arrived well attired, men in suits and ties, women in high heels and the smartest dresses. Soon Blue Mood was busy with conversation and laughter. From Lucky Strikes and Pall Malls, ribbons of smoke unraveled into a general haze.

The collapse of the stock market, dubbed "Black Tuesday," was one year in the past, unemployment was soaring, banks were beginning to fail, and the Great Depression was underway. Yet in the United States of America as in all countries throughout history, regardless of the form of government, some prospered while many suffered in times of economic disaster. Blue Mood catered to those who had suffered very little or not at all.

As in all of these more elegant venues, the night was divided into two seatings, the first from five o'clock to nine, the second from nine until two in the morning.

Two seatings meant two performances.

An elevated island to the left of the stage accommodated the nine-piece band. A lone pianist provided dinner music for the first hour, followed by an hour of easy-listening dance music by the full band. The floor show usually lasted an hour and a quarter, including two fifteen-minute opening acts.

Captain and I were always the second act, though *"act"* was too grand a word for the tommyrot and vulgarity that he was peddling. If I'd been nothing more bizarre than a three-eyed girl, we would never have been booked anywhere. Conversely, if I had not been attractive from the neck up, if my head had been as shocking as the rest of me, many in the audience might have left in disgust or fled in horror, or at least parted ways with the dinner they had recently eaten. It was that dichotomy, the contradiction between face and body, that made me a creature of fascination, a bargain-basement star in the bootlegging bottom of the culture.

A stagehand wheeled me into the spotlight in what appeared to be the upright coffin of a mummified pharaoh, which had been shipped from our prior engagement in Los Angeles. The closed box was carved and painted with an ornate Egyptian motif, although what Egypt had to do with me or Captain or anything else in the act was never explained.

Captain thought it would intrigue the audience, establish a sense of the exotic and mysterious even before I appeared.

To the audience, he spoke of mermaids and centaurs and Gorgons, although I wasn't like any of those half-human half-animal and fully mythological beings. He recounted how adventurous missionaries happened upon me in a Brazilian jungle, though I had never been in Brazil and had never met a missionary. Thirty-two years earlier, Mr. H. G. Wells had published *The War of the Worlds*, and throughout the first two decades of the new century, his work inspired numerous stories of alien encounters both on Earth and on distant planets. Captain wished to play to the public interest in science fiction by teasing the audience with the possibility that I was not a child of this world.

When on cue I opened the lid of the Egyptian casket and stepped onto the stage, the audience responded with a collective gasp. Some issued cries of distress. Others stood up from their chairs, not in alarm but to get a better view of what had come before them. I was perplexed about why a supper club audience always reacted with more excitement and apprehension than the marks showed when they reached my stall in the Museum of the Strange. Perhaps it was because the carnie pitchman prepped the rubes to expect a dash of horror with the wonder and because a carnival was a venue where grotesqueries were more expected than in a speakeasy catering to the upper crust.

If some patrons thought that I, though apparently almost naked, must be cleverly costumed, their misapprehension was soon dispelled. For one thing, a nightclub accommodating two hundred is an intimate space, much more so than the average movie theater. Furthermore, willing members of the audience were brought onto the stage to have a closer look, to touch me.

My job was first to condone their goggling and their questing hands. You might expect that those who came forward at Captain's invitation would be the most boorish in the audience, and you would be right. They were mostly men, but when women stroked and prodded me, they were usually less respectful of the sanctity of my person than were their male companions. Captain insisted I smile at them as they touched me, but I would not be that gracious.

However, I did forgive them for their cold indifference to my feelings, for their rudeness and crude remarks. They had visited Blue Mood to become inebriated, and by the time the floor show began, they'd achieved that condition. Indeed, they were descending to an even lower level of cognitive impairment. When sober, they might have been better people. Even saints on their long journey toward canonization often stray from a righteous path.

When the touching and poking ended and everyone had returned to their seats, Captain and I followed a script he had written and we'd memorized. Our dialogue was stilted and stupid, but it didn't seem to matter. It was the kind of hokum that the marks—whether poor or rich, educated or not—always believe because they *want* to believe it, because it spices their lives with mystery and wonder that they haven't known since Sunday became just another day of the week. In telling my fabricated story, I was required to be coy while seeming to let slip intriguing details that suggested I might be concealing a terrible or at least shocking truth about my origin.

The performers who preceded us were often magicians, though sometimes it was a juggler, perhaps a pair of acrobats who could astonish with their tumbling and balancing feats, or a performing dog and his master. They never gave me any grief. However, in the interest of encouraging repeat business, management wanted to send customers home in a pleasantly besotted condition with a memory of laughter, so the main act in a five-star speakeasy was always a comedian. Funnymen could be trouble. Of those who watched me from the wings rather than waiting in a dressing room for a call, some saw me as rich material. They rushed onstage before we could leave, before the master of ceremonies announced them.

Like many of his kind, the stand-up comedian at Blue Mood that year, Buddy Beamer, specialized in vulgar, smutty jokes for which the audience had prepared by dumbing down on whoopee water. With a well-rounded body like that of Oliver Hardy and Charlie Chaplin's mustache, wearing a windowpane-plaid suit straight out of vaudeville and a hat that was too small for his head, Buddy looked as much like a cartoon as like a comedian. The first night that he appeared ahead of his intro and fanfare, he crossed the stage while daubing at his eyes with a handkerchief, as though my appearance evoked in him such pity that he could not repress his tears. He went to one knee beside my chair and posed a few questions that any genuinely compassionate person might have asked, although his manner was so unctuous and his voice so fulsome that it was apparent he regarded me as a figure of fun. The faux compassion soon evolved into impudence and mockery. No matter how I responded to him—solemnly or with a wisecrack or with stony silence—he had a comeback that was crude but also amusing. Although he was a heartless creep, he was quick witted; I'll give him that much. At first the audience reacted with subdued, nervous laughter. Perhaps they thought this was part of our act and well rehearsed, because they soon threw off whatever misgivings they might have had, rewarding the funnyman with hearty laughter and occasional applause. When he asked why I was wearing briefs but was otherwise naked, I knew we were descending to depths that comedians in other clubs had not dared to plumb. Buddy wanted me to take off my pants so that, as he said, "we can see what all the boys on Mars are talking about." All my life, humiliation after humiliation had been piled on me, but it was only at that moment in Blue Mood that I felt as if I might break under the weight of it all.

Whenever a comedian intruded on the end of our act and kept me onstage for an extra five minutes, Captain Farnam welcomed it. With rare exception, the response of the audience was enthusiastic, and happy customers ensured a happy club manager. What was I, after all, but a performing dog, and what more should a dog expect than to be provided with food and a dry, warm place to sleep?

That evening, between the first show and the second, I schemed to make Buddy Beamer appear to be a fool and a bully. I assumed he would intrude again, repeating those questions and punch lines that drew the biggest laughs in the prior show. I crafted counterpunches wittier than anything that he had said earlier. For the first time, I looked forward to being exhibited to a crowd of hooch hounds.

Nothing went as I anticipated. The comic had a quicker wit than he'd revealed in our first encounter. As I hoped, my practiced lines drew laughs at his expense, though his ripostes were funnier. To my chagrin, the audience assumed that our exchanges were as scripted as the conversation between Captain and me, that for a few minutes the funnyman and I were a comedy team.

I didn't know how I could endure eight more shows at Blue Mood, with Buddy Beamer watching from the wings like a vampire who fed not on blood but on the emotional and mental resources of his victims.

Whatever I once had been, whatever I became in the years after that ordeal in 1930, whatever I might yet become as I write this, I have never been nor ever will be a prophet. The future doesn't bloom before me in a crystal ball, and I cannot interpret the language of the lines in my palms or yours. I dare to hope I know my ultimate destiny when this body withers and I rise from it, but the years before me on this world are a mystery that I can marvel at—but never solve—as clock hands carry me forward day by day.

On the afternoon of September 6, 1930, ensconced in a stained armchair in a seedy motel room, I tried to leave my time and place and worries by immersing myself in the nineteenth-century England of Thackeray's *Vanity Fair*. Whenever I read, I see the novel's scenes vividly in my mind, in full color and three dimensions. However, on this occasion, and to my dismay, Buddy Beamer repeatedly appeared in the drama, as anachronistic as a caveman. He posed as a member of the Crawley family, now as one of their servants, and yet again as a visiting friend, always with a sinister smile, togged out in a windowpane suit and a too-small hat.

I finally had to put *Vanity Fair* aside and steel myself for the evening's first floor show at Blue Mood.

THREE

On that second night of our engagement at Blue Mood, Buddy Beamer interrupted our act earlier than before. He was accompanied by the two topless showgirls this time. Previously, they had joined Buddy only after Captain and I left the stage. The comedian panted around those beauties as if he were a dog in heat. He took off his hat and held it over his private parts, pretending he had an erection so evident that it embarrassed him—and then he turned to me. He started in the gutter and quickly descended into a drain that sloped precipitously down into moral darkness.

After all these years, what I remember most clearly is not any of the rancid jokes that he told and not the meanness of the man who told them. What still haunts me is the raucous laughter with which the audience rewarded him, such pitiless laughter ripe with contempt for those who, like me, were weak and less blessed by Nature than the Blue Mood patrons in all their finery. Arrogant laughter born from vanity and ignorance is no less frightening than the shrieking and shouting of an enraged mob bearing torches and pitchforks.

Perhaps that was the experience that eventually cured me of the assumption that their indifference to my mortification was largely a consequence of drinking too much alcohol. To believe that the human conscience can guarantee a stable and worthy society is akin to the delusion that the arc of the universe bends toward justice. Forever expanding in all directions, the universe has no arc, and in many people the human conscience is as atrophied as their appendix. Mass murderers and thieves sleep as soundly as people who have done the right thing every day of their lives. If a conscience functions at all, it does so mostly—although not reliably—in those who believe in a higher power of some kind and who fear a judgment more profound than anything courts and magistrates can impose.

As for my guardian, Captain Farnam, the highest power he could imagine was the almighty dollar, which he chased with devotion. He laughed as heartily as anyone in the audience. When Buddy Beamer finished with me and segued into his own act, as I hurried off the stage with Captain close behind, the crowd broke into applause, as though I'd come there seeking their approval and would be gratified by their ovation.

In the dressing room, shaking violently and unable to calm myself, I put on my long johns and hooded robe as Captain enthused over Buddy's interaction with me. He fantasized that our contract with Blue Mood might be extended indefinitely and at a much higher price. The comedian would surely demand that club management retain us. Eventually we could link up more formally with Buddy, offer a two-act combo, and go on the speakeasy circuit indefinitely. Captain could find a new freak for his ten-in-one and turn over day-to-day operations to Bruno Hiscuss, the pitchman who ballyed the show to the marks passing on the midway.

I listened with growing despair, for it seemed my chances of escaping a life of debasement and humiliation were fast fading.

Long had I dreamed of being rescued, though not by a fairy-tale prince. My deformities ruled out a future as a bride to the ruler of a kingdom. Instead, I hoped for a compassionate doctor like the one who freed John Merrick, the Elephant Man. Merrick had suffered from an extreme case of neurofibromatosis and had been exhibited as a freak in the 1870s and '80s. Although his affliction was not the same as—and worse than—mine, I'd read and reread a book about Dr. Frederick Treves, the man who ransomed Merrick from a squalid and inhumane existence, giving him years of safety, peace, and dignity.

I made my own dignity, and I found some peace in the escape books provided, but there was no safety, no security, in the life I'd been given to live.

There in the dressing room at Blue Mood, as Captain babbled on about a two-act package with Buddy Beamer, I began to abandon all hope that an equivalent to Frederick Treves would come into my life.

Then someone rapped insistently on the door.

When Captain responded, a well-dressed and handsome couple with an air of authority pushed past him and into the room as if on an urgent mission. The man's face was flushed, and the woman appeared distraught. "What is this girl to you?" the man asked Captain, his voice taut with restrained anger. "Is she your daughter, your niece, any relation at all?" Captain expanded his chest and stood taller, letting it be known by his posture and his haughty expression that this intrusion was an affront to his dignity. However, nothing about Captain suggested that he was in any way dignified. Exasperation only made him look more rotund, straining the seams of his tweed coat. His perpetually pale face paled further, and by contrast the whites of his eyes were revealed as more bloodshot than previously had been evident. Captain was a patron as well as an employee of the speakeasy. His demand that the two intruders leave or be violently removed by bouncers, expressed with the bombast of a carny pitchman, failed to intimidate them.

"No one is throwing us out," the woman said, as a muffled roar of laughter rose from the showroom. "When we spread a few C-notes around, the thugs took off their brass knuckles and went away to write letters to their mothers. Who is this child? What gives you the right to exploit her? You have no such right. No one has."

The Captain fancied that he was not just a showman but also a thespian equal to the great John Barrymore. He contorted his face into an expression of indignation so exaggerated that an illustrated banner bearing such a portrait in front of his ten-in-one tent might have been titled *The Angriest Man in the World*. "Madam, her name is Alida, and she is not a child. She is seventeen and my daughter. Without any help from you, Alida possesses the mental capacity to choose how to make her way in this cold and unkind world. Do you think this poor child of God can land a job as a secretary? Looking like she does, would she be hired as a waitress, a shopgirl selling cosmetics, a nanny with children in her care, perhaps a chanteuse crooning romantic ballads? She's *chosen* to be displayed for the wonderment and education of the public, and she makes a very good living for herself."

"From what I saw on that stage," the woman said, "I suspect she makes a very good living *for you*, while she lives little better than an organ grinder's monkey." She was Loretta Fairchild, as I would soon learn, and I will never forget how she looked that night in her elegant, silky hyacinth-blue dress and string of pearls. She was the picture of self-assurance. In her righteous anger, she appeared fearless, and I'm sure she would have been no less resolute if Franklin, her husband, hadn't been with her. "You claim to be her father, but a claim made by the likes of you is meaningless. You'd claim to be your own father if there was anything in it for you."

Captain was not able to sustain the role of innocent, affronted Christian. His faux exasperation hardened into genuine wrath, and his moon face became a sight fit for Halloween. "I have papers to prove Alida is mine. If anyone says she isn't, I'll sue them into the poorhouse. You want trouble, you'll get a kisser full of it."

I had read *Little Women*, *Jane Eyre*, *Pride and Prejudice*, and other novels in which strong women triumphed over adversity and took on every challenge with confidence. I was not, however, easily able to speak up on my own behalf. Convinced someone like me could not make her way in the world alone, I indentured myself to Captain Forest Farnam, trading my self-respect for food, lodging, and the protection provided by a well-rewarded keeper. That might have been a convenient excuse for retreating from the struggle required to find a better station in life, but there was also hard truth in it. Every culture in the world, throughout history, has valued beauty above all things other than wealth. Even though by most standards my face was quite attractive—flawless skin, blue eyes, golden hair—I would never win a pageant with my looks. In spite of the daily humiliation that wore on my heart as surely as a flowing river wears a channel in the earth, I counted myself fortunate to be an asset of such value to the Museum of the Strange that I would not be beaten or starved and would be given books that nourished me—for now if not forever.

When this handsome couple weren't daunted by Captain's threat, I dared to think my fondest wish might be true: that in real life there were people as honorable as the better characters in novels. That possibility, as slight as it seemed, nevertheless buoyed me so much that, to my surprise, I spoke up for myself. "Captain bought me from my mother. I have no memory of her, but he bought me from my mother." It seemed that maternal treachery as heinous as that must not be true, but I never was able to convince myself that it was a lie. Such is the world.

"A price so high," the Captain said, "that I've yet to make a profit. She eats twice what a child her size should eat, and she's so often sickly that her doctor bills alone have prevented me from putting away anything for my retirement."

At that point in my life, I dared to take a measure of pride in only two things. I possessed a mind sharp enough for the reading of books.

And in spite of my fragile appearance, I was always in good health. "I've never had one cold," I objected. "I've never needed to see a doctor. I've never missed a day in the Museum of the Strange during carnival season or a night on the speakeasy circuit."

Captain was stunned that I would contradict him, and I was no less astonished than he. Although he had never beaten me or even just slapped me, I knew as surely as I knew anything that Foster Farnam was capable of violence if ever his little money machine ceased to know her place and defied him. Until that moment in the dressing room at Blue Mood, I had always cautioned myself to treat him with respect, with deference. In novels, the timid characters sometimes are inspired to acts of courage by the bravery of others. Perhaps it was the example set by this couple that gave me the pluck to correct Captain's lie.

FOUR

In their early twenties, Franklin and Loretta had been dreamers with limited resources, but they also possessed vision and ambition. With enough discipline to work seven days a week, they carved out a place for themselves in a new industry with a bright future—moving pictures. Those were the days of silent films. Mary Pickford. Harold Lloyd. Fatty Arbuckle. Charlie Chaplin.

Although I was seventeen when Franklin and Loretta found me, I'd never seen a moving picture. Their home contained a screening room. In addition to a library of all the productions of Fairchild United, their company, they possessed copies of numerous films made by their friends, including many comedies. During my first month in Bramley Hall, I laughed more than in all my previous years combined.

For so long, laughter had been my best defense against the desire to be done with this world, but it had always been tainted by bitterness or keen anger. Now I discovered that laughter could be an expression of pure joy.

Franklin and Loretta were producers. He directed. She wrote the scenarios and composed succinct and witty copy for the flash cards that guided the audience through the plot and conveyed essential dialogue that, in those days, could not be captured on film.

In the beginning, they were wise enough to choose actors whose careers were stalling short of major stardom, who could be hired for modest fees while still bringing name value to the project. Broncho Billy Anderson's days as a star of Westerns were fading as William S. Hart, who had once been a real cowboy working cattle drives, was captivating audiences with his gravitas.

Over time, while still making their own movies, they invested some of their profits in co-financing deals with the studios that were on the rise and would one day be multibillion-dollar companies. In 1923, Paramount's *The Covered Wagon* was one of the biggest hits to date, and they owned a piece of it. The brightest new star of the year was a handsome German shepherd named Rin Tin Tin. Franklin and Loretta, dog lovers, had a special reason to love Rinny. Their money helped finance Tom Mix Westerns and much else.

On September 5, 1930, not yet having met my emancipators, I had no hope that I would escape the cruelties and indignities that were as much a part of my life as air and water. I hadn't surrendered to despair, but I had resigned myself to a life of mistreatment, loneliness, and imprisonment.

That Friday, Franklin and Loretta set off on a much-needed vacation, leaving their children in the care of a nanny. They didn't go far—only down the coast to San Diego, to stay at the fabled Hotel del Coronado and enjoy the city's Little Italy, East Village, and Gaslamp Quarter.

Not surprisingly, they were combining pleasure and business, for they were never quite able to indulge strictly in the former.

Prohibition had been in effect for a decade. Bootleggers flourished and quickly metastasized into the organized gangs that thereafter plagued the country. The empowerment of the gangs and the related corruption of politicians that followed struck them as promising material for a film.

In those dry days, the Gaslamp Quarter, though famous for its beautiful Victorian architecture, was known as well for its brothels and the easy availability of demon rum. Some speakeasies were dim and dirty places that provided sports betting and card games. Others were stylish supper clubs that did business under the protection of city hall.

Blue Mood was the most elegant of such establishments in the Gaslamp Quarter. It occupied a former garment factory on a back street. There was no sign or parking lot to call attention to the place; customers curbed their vehicles on surrounding streets or taxied to and from this fountain of forbidden brews.

The windows had been infilled with bricks, and an effort had been made to soundproof the walls. Nevertheless, muffled music could be heard a block away, because Blue Mood employed a nine-piece band that accompanied some stage acts and provided dance music.

Occasionally a member of the Temperance Union or Anti-Saloon League filed a complaint with authorities. They were told that the garment factory had been repurposed as a recording studio and venue for big bands to practice, a legitimate enterprise.

If those who complained were to doubt that explanation, they might discover that water and power were no longer provided to their residences. This reliably proved to be a billing error, and it was regrettable that two weeks or more passed before the mistake could be rectified. Fate meddled in the lives of the complainers with impressive creativity, visiting a variety of misfortunes on them until they convinced themselves that, indeed, the old garment factory had been repurposed as a recording studio.

On Saturday, September 6, on their second night in San Diego, Franklin and Loretta went to Blue Mood for a steak dinner, superb wine, and research. This was not the first speakeasy they visited over the past decade. However, in the higher social circles, Blue Mood had a singular reputation for its elegance, fine cuisine, and risqué entertainment, which suggested that this was the place most likely to provide two filmmakers with colorful material for a movie.

The maître d' sported a tuxedo, and every waiter wore black slacks and a white shirt. Members of the band, excellent musicians, were dressed alike in black slacks, powder-blue sport coats, and black neckties. There was a comic who relied on blue material. There were two gorgeous chorus girls, resplendent in sequined and feathered costumes; they shared the stage with the funnyman and acted as his foils, and both were topless.

Franklin and Loretta were sophisticated. Neither the foul-mouthed comic nor the topless beauties shocked them. However, they weren't prepared for a thing like me or for the humiliation to which I was subjected—or for the laughter and applause with which the other two hundred well-heeled patrons responded to every indignity that I was forced to endure.

FIVE

Loretta's anger was hot, but her voice was ice cold as she repeatedly stabbed Captain's chest with a forefinger to emphasize her words. "No one has the right to buy another human being. You don't have—no one has—the right to force a child to endure a crucible like that disgusting so-called stage act of yours, to endure it even once let alone over and over again."

Captain's usual bluff and bluster deflated like a punctured tire. He retreated from Loretta until he backed into a wall. "I have papers. Papers signed by her mother. Adoption papers approved by a court." He drew himself up in a pretense of righteous indignation. "If you don't get out of here right now, I'll summon the police."

"Summon?" Loretta said. "Should we refer to you as your royal highness? Your majesty? Sure, all right, *call* the police. You think they'll storm into a speakeasy that they've been paid to pretend doesn't exist? And if they do, after the raid, will management just break your legs or maybe put a bullet in your head?"

Until now, Captain had viewed the world as a planet of rubes, marks to be bamboozled. This couple that had invaded his domain were neither hicks nor gullible sophisticates. They could not be cowed by threats, intimidated by pompous attitude, or snowed by an avalanche of words. Captain suddenly realized that his usual feints and bold flourishes would not win the day. His customary high self-regard melted like stage makeup under too many hot lights, and something of the boy he had once been came into view. His round face swelled with petulance and, for the first time in my experience, he glistened with sweat. There was anger in his eyes, but also confusion and fear. Any difficult child looked like this as he worked himself into a tantrum. His lower lip trembled. He made a fist of his right hand.

Franklin shouldered past Loretta and seized her would-be assailant's wrist below the fist. With his other hand, he clutched Captain's throat and pressed him so hard against the wall that my keeper's ever-pale countenance flushed a shade of red that I found satisfying. "Just settle down, Farnam. Don't be stupid. It's over. You know it. We don't need to see your papers. No court would allow a man who's not a relative—a carnival barker or whatever you are—to adopt a child as afflicted as this girl and put her on exhibit."

"You have no damn idea what a judge will do for money," Captain declared, spittle springing from his lips. "People like you have no damn idea."

Now and then the band played a few bars in support of whatever Buddy Beamer was doing onstage. The music seemed to come from far away, from another world.

Franklin's anger didn't put an edge on his voice, as his wife's anger sharpened hers. He sounded like a prosecutor calmly laying out the case against a defendant. "Even if some judge was pitiless and corrupt enough to sell out to a piker like you, he'll have scrubbed it from the public record. So the charge is kidnapping. They fry you for that, Farnam. But if you're smart, it won't go to court. As much as we'd like to see you locked up, we can't allow this girl to be splashed through the tabloids so the knuckle-dragging readers of those rags can gape at her and get a dirty little thrill."

31

Captain was certain of my dependence on him and of my inability to take the risk that ordering my life in a new way would be better than what he provided. He could have tried to pry Franklin's hand from his throat, but he didn't. Maybe he was afraid he'd be unable to do it. He tried to shake off Franklin with a sneer of contempt and a pitchman's bravura. "You see Alida onstage for a few minutes, and you think you know all about her. You really get my blood up, you really do, you snotty high-hatters, you snobs. Black Tuesday meant nothing to you, millions out of work and worse ahead, but you slide through untouched, so then you think you know everything about everything. Well, you know nothing about this girl here. This girl gets her purpose and meaning from being onstage. She isn't ashamed of her difference. She likes the attention, how they marvel over her. She gives them an education just by showing herself, teaches them about the whims of Nature, and that's honorable work."

"I hate it," I said. "I die a little bit every time. The only reason I'm not dead for real is because I figure you'd pickle my corpse and go on showing me in a big jar, wouldn't need to buy me food or provide a place to sleep, more profit for less effort. I won't give you that chance."

They were all staring at me—Captain with keen vexation and disbelief, Franklin and Loretta with sympathy and a lovely anguish that made me feel as if, after years onstage, I was truly seen for the first time.

Loretta said, "I'm so sorry, honey, so very sorry."

No one had ever spoken to me with such affection. I'm not sure why I pulled off my hood to let my hair fall around my face. Perhaps I wanted to remind her there was a part of me anyone might find easy to love if what my robe concealed could be put out of mind.

"You ungrateful little bitch," the Captain said. "After all I've done for you, all the trouble I've gone to. If I'd never come along, your mother would have strangled you and thrown your lifeless body in a garbage dump to feed the rats." He had more—and much worse—to say. My longtime keeper might have indulged in a lengthy, vicious tirade, but after maybe half a minute, Franklin let go of Captain's throat in order to punch him in the face.

Although I am a peaceful person, I will admit that, in this case, the sudden violence warmed my heart.

Captain had no inclination to defend himself if a face-to-face confrontation was required. I suspect he preferred retribution of the knife-in-the-back variety. With one hand over his bleeding nose, unsteady on his feet, he sidled along the wall to a straight-backed chair that protested the sudden burden of his bulk.

His voice hollowed by the need to pinch his nostrils shut to diminish the bleeding, he said, "That was assault and battery. You can go to jail for assault and battery."

"After we resolve the matter before us," Franklin said, "I'll drive you directly to police headquarters so you can have me booked for assault and battery while I have you booked for violating this state's child welfare laws and other crimes against a minor."

"You broke my nose."

"I didn't break it," Franklin said. "I punished it a little. Anyway, it wasn't your best feature, the way it stuck out too far."

"If you insist on having the whole story told," Loretta warned Captain, "there will be outraged people standing in line to break your nose every day of the week."

Franklin said, "Well put, darling."

"Thank you, Franklin."

Belatedly parsing what Franklin had said immediately after the assault, Captain asked, "Resolve what matter?"

"The future of this girl," Franklin said. "Birth certificate—"

"There is no birth certificate."

"Then tell us the place of birth."

"On the road, in a carny bus, between one county fairground and another. Who bothers with a birth certificate for a thing like her?"

"What is her mother's name?" Loretta asked.

"She had a dozen of them. I never knew her real name. I think even she didn't know it anymore."

"Do you have any idea where she might be?"

"Somewhere dead and buried, the way she lived her life."

Loretta glanced worriedly at me, and Franklin asked Captain, "Lived it how?"

"She was an alcoholic. Loved her hashish. Laudanum. Ayahuasca. You name it. Good-looking woman. Had two occupations, if you want to know." Captain lowered his hand from his nose and looked at me. "She danced in the hootchy-kootchy show and whored herself to anyone who had seven dollars in his wallet."

"You wretched sonofabitch," Loretta said.

Captain shrugged. "You wanted to resolve the matter before us."

Loretta came to me where I sat on the vanity bench with my back to the makeup table and mirror, and she put a hand on my shoulder. "You shouldn't have had to hear that, honey."

I met her eyes. They were a lovely shade of green. "It's okay, ma'am. There are truths that can hurt you and truths that free you. All that he said was just the second kind."

She got down on one knee and took one of my gloved hands. "You're amazing, aren't you. Everything changes now, sweetheart."

I was about to ask *how* everything would change, which was when Franklin said, "If she wants to, the girl's coming with Loretta and me. What will it take for you to just walk away?"

Captain stared at his bloody fingers for a long beat. "I never let go of what's mine. I hold fast to it."

"She isn't yours. She never was. You can explain yourself to the police and make an argument for keeping her—or you can tell me how much you want to stay out of her life forever."

"People like you think you can buy anything."

"We're not buying her. We're paying ransom to her kidnapper, ransom to bring her home where she belongs."

Captain looked up. There was a terrible meanness in his eyes. His lips glistened with blood that oozed out of his nose. I'd read Bram Stoker's *Dracula*, a compelling though fanciful novel that, just at this moment, didn't seem so fanciful after all.

He said, "You can't kidnap what the mother didn't want, what the mother would have thrown away. If you save a dog from the pound before they put it down, that's no crime."

"So it's the police, then," Franklin said. "You're that sure of yourself, are you?"

"I didn't say police. I'm just laying my cards out so you can see it's not for sure a losing hand. There's potential in it."

"Name a price."

Grimacing, Captain said, "I'm not some mark who can be conned into paying a fiver for an emerald bracelet made from bottle glass. Negotiations start with the one who wants what the other has."

After studying Captain for perhaps a minute, as if somehow he could measure the depth of the man's greed, Franklin said, "You walk out of here tonight, alone, before the midnight show, and we never see you again. Is that what I'm getting for my money?"

"That's it—unless you want me to throw in an emerald bracelet to sweeten the bargain. Just don't insult me with a low-ball offer. Whoever you are, however you got your money, you want to keep the tabloids and the rest of the press out of this as much for yourself as for the kid. Personally, I love the tabloids. That's my kind of news, my kind of people. As far as I'm concerned, bring 'em on."

"Thirty thousand dollars." Franklin looked to his wife.

She nodded without hesitation, as if he'd said "ten dollars."

I almost didn't believe my ears. In those days, a cup of coffee cost but a nickel. When we were on tour, staying in a motel, Captain brought me food. Just last week, it was from a nearby Automat. Two nickels would open the little glass door so you could get a nice serving of macaroni and cheese. Three nickels would buy an egg-salad sandwich. Three for a slice of berry pie, two for banana cream.

Captain shook his head. "I'm thirty-eight years of age. I'd like to retire when I'm fifty. Speakeasy bookings already bring in solid money. Who knows how high the price goes if the kid and I can work out a permanent hitch-up with Buddy Beamer?"

"You're pushing too hard," Franklin said. "You're playing your hand like some greenhorn who just learned poker yesterday."

"Here's the thing, Daddy Warbucks. I can take the little freak out of here, scoot across the state line, and keep on providing the people with much-needed entertainment in these hard times. You won't ever find us. It's a damn big country."

"Thirty-five thousand," Franklin said. "And that's my limit."

So much money. For that, I could have a little house, food, maybe eight or ten years of freedom from the stage.

Still on one knee in front of the vanity bench and holding my hand, Loretta gave no indication that taking a thirty-five-thousand-dollar hit concerned her. In fact, she smiled at me.

I was afraid to smile back at her. I don't know exactly why. Like maybe a smile would tempt fate, and Captain would pull the knife that I knew he had, and everything would go dark from there.

"Here's a thing to think about," Captain suggested. "Say I take her out of here and quick across the state line. Say you're crazy enough to try to find us, as self-righteous as you are. You probably have enough dough to hire detectives to start looking. So say one of them tracks us down, gets some kind of court order. What am I going to do then? I don't have retirement money. My meal ticket is going to be taken from me. Maybe I'm set to do jail time. You put me in a corner like that, why wouldn't I slit her throat just to spite you?"

"Forty thousand," Loretta said. "If you won't take that offer, I'll slit *your* throat. Some night you'll go to dreamland and never wake up. Maybe they find you with your cut-out Adam's apple jammed in your mouth, pig that you are, ready to be roasted for a luau."

Well, that was sure something, the way she said it. She sounded as serious as a cold-blooded gangster. I learned much later that she was imitating a former vaudeville song-and-dance man, James Cagney, who was about to make it big in *The Public Enemy*. I wasn't scared of her because it wasn't my throat she threatened to cut, but Captain stared at her the way he might have stared at a growling Doberman. After a silence, Captain seemed to decide he preferred not to have a dream cut short by the blade of a stiletto. "You're crazy enough to pay up. But I'm sure as hell not taking a check."

Franklin said, "I'll drive back to LA and get the cash."

"No banks are open on the weekend," Captain said.

"Since Black Tuesday, we don't trust banks. Sooner or later, there's going to be a run on them."

"I'll stay here with Alida," Loretta said as she sat beside me on the bench that served the vanity.

Consulting his wristwatch, Franklin said, "It's a quarter past eight. I'll put the pedal down hard, but I might not be back before the midnight curtain call."

"The magician is on first," Loretta reminded him. "That gives you another fifteen minutes or so. If management comes looking, Mr. Farnam and I will convince them she's too sick to go on."

"Or we could do one last show," Captain suggested.

Loretta opened her purse and retrieved a small pistol. She put the handbag aside and held the pistol in her lap. She didn't respond to Captain's suggestion.

SIX

Captain's nose had swelled and acquired a purplish hue. He sat in his chair, hands on his thighs, eyes closed, like an immense toad contemplating a return to the swamp, where life had treated him better than it did here.

Prolonged and vigorous applause, filtering through the walls, sounded like rolling thunder rumbling into the city from far out at sea. After both shows the previous night, Buddy Beamer received a standing ovation. And now a third.

As the applause faded, the band launched into a lively number with an accelerating tempo intended to encourage the customers to vacate the premises so that the waiters and busboys could clear the tables and dress them for the nine o'clock seating.

Doors slammed, and the hallway grew quiet, and Captain opened his eyes. For some reason that could not have been innocent, he tried to start a conversation with Loretta. She would not respond.

After a while, the distant music of a lone piano meant Blue Mood was open for the second seating. When the band launched into mellow dance music, we knew that it was half past nine. Franklin had been gone for more than an hour, but it seemed much longer.

Captain rose from his chair, and Loretta raised her pistol, and Captain said, "Relax. I'm just going to the bar to have a couple of beers. Your husband expects to find you here. There's nowhere on the property where you can hide and hope to intercept him. I'll have a word with the guards so they won't let you leave with my girl by either the front or back doors. You got it?"

"Yes."

When he had gone, Loretta and I took turns using the half bath that adjoined the dressing room. I removed my gloves because she had already seen my hands when I was onstage. After washing up, I put the gloves on once more. I'd be going out into the world, where it was safest to conceal everything below my neck. Dixie cups were stacked beside the sink, and we drank some water as we sat side by side on the rectangular vanity bench.

Without Captain to overhear, Loretta told me where we would go first when we left Blue Mood, who we would see and for what purpose. I was amazed that already she had laid out a plan of action and was prepared to follow it as soon as I was free of Captain.

"When that's been done, where then?" I asked.

She was surprised, for she assumed that I understood what she and Franklin intended. "Why, of course you'll come to live with us. We'll adopt you. You'll be one of ours, as much a part of the family as our three children—Isadora, Gertrude, and Harry."

Such a grace seemed impossibly fantastic. My voice was unsteady when I said, "Adopt? But how? No birth certificate. No real name, only what Captain called me. The way I look, what I am, how—"

"Those are not worries you need to have," she said, smoothing my hair with one hand. "We have the best of attorneys and a lot of friends in what might be called 'high places.' Franklin will handle it all. By tomorrow afternoon, we'll be home, and you can meet the three hellions who will be your sisters and brother. In a month or two, your last name will legally be the same as theirs."

I said, "But why? Why would you do this?"

Continuing to smooth my hair with one hand, she said, "Anyone who would harm or abandon a child—'it would be better for him that a millstone were hanged about his neck and that he were drowned in the depth of the sea.' Every child deserves to be loved, sweetheart. It's a hard world, and there's not much any of us can undertake to make it right. But now and then there's a little thing that we can do. Now and then like this."

As she finished speaking, I did something that, in the interest of holding on to hope and sanity, I had not done in years. I wept. The "little thing" to her was everything to me. Such is the world.

My tears had long dried by the time Captain returned from the bar at a quarter till midnight. His movements were slightly too slow and clearly calculated, which is a strategy many tosspots embrace in an attempt to appear sober. He returned to his chair and fixed us with a menacing stare. Promptly at midnight, the band played a brassy fanfare. The floor show was about to begin.

Captain said, "I told management my star is too sick to go on. They weren't happy. These are people you want to keep happy. When you take her out of here, if anyone stops you, say you're taking her to a hospital. She's got a fever and been throwing up. Got that?"

"Yes," Loretta said.

He cocked his head and studied her. "You don't have to like me."

"I don't."

"I mean——to pass the time with a little conversation, you don't have to like me."

"I loathe you. I despise you. I'm disgusted by you."

He nodded solemnly. "That's your privilege. Truth is, I don't like you much, either. But I'm not so high and mighty that I won't talk with you."

At twenty minutes past midnight, when I would otherwise have been stepping out of the upright coffin nearly naked and abashed, to the gasps and little cries of revulsion from the audience, the dressing room door opened and Franklin returned, carrying a valise. Everyone stood. Franklin put the valise on the vanity and opened it. Captain came forward to examine the contents. Convinced everything was jake, he closed the valise and carried it to the door.

Copious beer had loosened the flesh of his face and benumbed the muscles. I expected him to dredge from the dark treacle in his pitchman heart an insincere, absurdly sentimental goodbye. Instead, he said, "Franklin and Loretta. You each spoke the other's name just once. You have a lot of money in these lean times, but you're no industrialist like Henry Ford. I ask myself what business is growing when so much else is shrinking. With so many Dicks and Janes eager to escape their troubles, rivers of coins are flowing into movie theaters. They say Greta Garbo was making five thousand bucks a week in the silents and now much more. You two have 'showbiz' polish. I don't know your last name, but I have contacts. I could find you in three days. Do what you want with this twisted little freak. Just leave me alone, forget I ever existed, and I'll return the favor." As laughter and applause for Buddy Beamer swelled in the showroom, Captain stepped into the hall and pulled the door shut behind him.

Judge not lest you be judged. I had forgiven my mother. I had forgiven all the goggling marks who passed through the Museum of the Strange. I had forgiven the leering, laughing drunks in all those speakeasies. I now forgave Buddy Beamer. However, I still could not forgive Captain Forest Farnam. I wished him dead and asked God to forgive me for doing so.

SEVEN

The headlights of the yellow Cadillac sedan cleaved the night. To the west, a rippled track of light cast by the descending moon revealed an ocean that was otherwise a vast and daunting darkness.

Loretta and I had waited in the car while Franklin checked out of Hotel del Coronado and a bellhop put their luggage in the trunk. I must have been a curious sight, robed and hooded in the back seat, and one thirty in the morning was an uncommon checkout time. The del Coronado staff were too discreet to raise an eyebrow.

My rescuers rode up front and I behind them on the way to Los Angeles. I was weary but not sleepy. I seldom went to bed earlier than two in the morning. Besides, I was too excited and too nervous about the new life ahead of me to lie down on the seat and go to sleep. Loretta had mentioned a household staff that included a cook, three maids, and a majordomo. I'd read many novels of nineteenth-century England in which grand houses on sprawling estates provided the main setting, but I couldn't imagine what residence would require such a retinue here in California, where the history of the place went back mere decades instead of centuries.

We motored north in silence, which might mean that we were emotionally exhausted, but which might also mean that we were all brooding over what this new arrangement entailed and having second thoughts. I felt that I should speak up, assure them that they could take me back to Captain. *Really, I should say, he's not as bad as he seemed tonight, he steals books for me, brings me the foods I like most, he never beats me, and in his care I'm safe from people worse than him, a world full of people worse than him, there's much to be said for being safe.* However, I didn't have the courage to say any of that. I was too selfish to give them the option of undoing what had been done. If the future to which we had committed proved to be an ordeal for them, I could slip out of their house one night and make my way in the world as best I could, go where they couldn't find me if they were compelled to search. Maybe I would find my way to the sea one night and swim out along the rippled track of light cast by the moon until the water drew me down and closed around me. The world is beautiful and enchanting, but there are many ways out of it if life becomes unendurable.

Northbound toward the city, I stared out the starboard window at the shapes of barren hills that defined the eastern horizon and rose to a universe of stars. From time to time, along the roadside, a series of eight or ten Burma-Shave signs offered an amusing rhyme, but I was too far behind the headlights to read the message that the placards conveyed.

EIGHT

After eighteen years in business, the Beverly Hills Hotel was still the most impressive establishment of its kind in that fabled city. Shortly after four o'clock in the morning, Franklin rented a luxurious bungalow. As a bellhop pushed a luggage cart, we followed him quietly, in respect of the many sleeping guests, along a softly lighted path through lushly planted grounds to our accommodations. In the barest breath of a breeze, the tall palms whispered to one another—*she, she, she.* I felt as if I were entering a heretofore secret world, an American Shangri-La, and that even the trees knew I did not belong in such a paradise.

This was Sunday, the seventh of September. Franklin and Loretta were not scheduled to return to Bramley Hall until Thursday. They said that we would in fact go home on Tuesday, after I had been prepared well for that event. I didn't know what they meant by "prepared," but I was too sleepy to ask.

The bungalow provided a charming foyer, a living room, and two bedrooms more beautifully furnished than any place I had ever seen. The air smelled faintly of spices and roses, a scent that I would later discover came from small decorative porcelain dishes filled with potpourri. Each bedroom had its own spacious bath. Although no more than ten or twelve minutes had elapsed since Franklin asked the front desk clerk if rooms were available, a night maid had been to the bungalow ahead of us to switch on lamps and turn down the beds.

The bellhop, Steven, was a handsome young man, a little cheeky for such an elegant establishment, but in a sweet way. After he placed the luggage where Loretta wished to have it, he smiled at me and winked and said, "Your outfit is very stylish, Miss Riding Hood, but you don't have to worry about wolves. They're only to be found in the early evening in a nearby speakeasy." I thought that was funny, and as Franklin tipped him, I thanked Steven for his advice as to the habits of the local wildlife.

When he had gone, I said, "He was very nice, wasn't he?"

Loretta smiled. "You'll be charmed by everyone in this town from the gas-station pump jockeys to the dolled-up shopgirls in the best department stores. They're all actors hoping to be discovered, and they think anyone they meet could be a casting director or have the ear of one."

I felt inadequate for the town, yet I was enchanted by the magical quality of it and grateful to be there. As bookish as I am, I thought that Quasimodo must have felt much like this, to an extent enchanted by the magnificence of Notre Dame and yet aware that he would always be an outsider, scorned by many and loathed by some, yet seeking the mercy that surpasseth all understanding.

My eyes burned, and I longed for sleep, but bed would have to wait. My bathroom had both a shower and a tub. The tub was clean and the water was hot and there were plenty of towels—three conditions that never occurred simultaneously in the motels where Captain and I stayed. There was a selection of soaps with different fragrances. If I'd fallen asleep in the tub and drowned in my bathwater, that would have been as fine a way to go as any.

Considering the strange and fearsome body that Nature has given me, I do not expect to have a long life. Although I have never been sick, the wrongness within me must equal the wrongness without. I have not been examined by a doctor or X-rayed, and I hope I never will be. I don't want to be forewarned that some tangled coil inside of me will one day rupture, filling me with brief pain and eternal darkness. Whatever comes, let it come upon me by surprise.

As dawn arrived, I slipped into my bed and fell asleep at once. In the nightmare, we arrived at Bramley Hall and discovered that Captain Farnam had moved in uninvited. The children were nowhere to be found. When we asked about them, the moonfaced hateful pitchman only smiled. He carried a black bag of the kind that a doctor might carry when making a house call, and he would not let us look in it. Franklin went to search the basement—and didn't come back. In the kitchen, on the gas stove, something was boiling in a huge soup pot, but Captain prevented us from removing the lid. Loretta opened a drawer to get a butcher knife with which to drive him out of the house, but the knives were all missing.

I woke with a gasp and sat up in bed, shaking so violently that it seemed the bungalow itself was being rocked by an earthquake. The blackout draperies were drawn shut, and only weak light traced the edges of them. Although the room was swathed in shadows, I knew I must be alone. The bungalow was silent. Franklin and Loretta weren't up and about. According to the bedside clock, I'd been asleep only two hours. A dream is just a dream. It portends nothing. Nothing. I was exhausted. The dream was just a dream, not an omen. I lay down again and soon slept peacefully, untroubled by Captain.

NINE

Loretta rapped on my door at eleven thirty Sunday morning, and by noon I and my new guardians were having breakfast at the round table in the dining nook off the living room. Warm cheese omelets were accompanied by aromatic bacon, crisp toast with whipped butter, and individual compotiers filled with chilled mandarin-orange segments topped with shredded coconut. Rich, dark coffee steamed from the silver-plated pot when Franklin poured it into our cups.

How magical it seemed that this lovely repast could be summoned from the hotel kitchen, each dish hot or cold as required, served on pretty china, and accessorized by a slender glass vase holding a single red rose. All of it might have been conjured by a wizard. An egg-salad sandwich from an Automat couldn't compare. I wouldn't have been surprised if it had cost two dollars or even twice that for the three of us.

The rest of the day was likewise enchanting, although I felt some trepidation when Franklin departed for the afternoon, leaving us alone, to prepare the way for us at Bramley Hall, where we would arrive the day after tomorrow. Their estate was but a fifteen-minute drive from the hotel. I thought I concealed my anxiety, but Loretta quickly read my mood and asked the reason for my concern.

"Well," I said as I perched on the sofa, "I'm sure this sounds silly, and no doubt it *is* silly, but I dreamed of Captain Farnam last night." In case she was of a mind to attribute the slightest credibility to the predictive power of dreams, I did not reveal that in the nightmare Captain had intruded into Bramley Hall and that the children had been missing. I didn't want to worry her, for surely it was foolish to believe that the nightmare had also been a prophecy. I revealed only this: "I dreamed he found us, as he said he could do if he wanted."

Loretta sat beside me and gently pulled me against her. "He is a monster, and there's nothing unusual about dreaming of monsters. Everyone does. His threat to find us in three days is just as phony as he is, sweetheart. That galumphing swine is giddy to have fallen into a payday beyond his greediest dreams, and he'll do nothing to risk his freedom now. He'll build a house on that plot of coastal land you said he owned, and he'll sit on his patio, staring at the sea and eating cake and drinking bootleg bourbon until his heart is clogged with fat as dense as the contents of a Swift's Silverleaf lard can. He's a cowardly user, not an audacious doer. He's no more likely to barge into our lives than Valentino, rest his soul, is likely to rise from the grave to remake *The Son of the Sheik* as a talkie."

Leaning against her, I said, "You sure know how to make me feel better about most everything."

"I'm not shoveling a lot of hooey at you, dear."

"Yeah, I know. It's not just what you say. It's how you say it, ma'am. You're so confident and sharp and funny."

"I'm funny, am I?"

"In a good way."

"Well, when you're in the movie business, you better have a sense of humor or you'll throw yourself out a high window."

"Is it as crazy stressful as all that?"

"The stress is invigorating. But you're swimming with sharks all the time, and sharks have no sense of humor. They especially don't like to be laughed at, even though their insatiable appetite and self-importance are pretty damn funny. Frank and I laugh a lot behind closed doors."

"I think I understand."

"I'm sure you do. You're a very bright girl. But we agreed you won't call me 'ma'am.' Do it again, and severe discipline will ensue."

"Yeah? Will you make me work in a blacking factory?"

"You never know. At the very least, I'll make you scrub floors until your knees are blistered and your fingers bleed."

I laughed, leaned away from her, and met her eyes. "That, too, is very Dickens. If you really could reduce me to such a terrible condition, you must have many floors."

"Acres," she said.

I felt something then that was new to me, that was not respect or admiration or gratitude, though it encompassed all those things. I was reluctant to put a name to it, for fear that events to come would not justify this feeling. I might prove to be engaging in assumptions that were wishful thinking. What I felt was a condition that could bring great pain if not reciprocated, so the best course was to wait and hope. Of course the word was *love*. For the first time in my seventeen years, I had someone to love, and I dared to think that she and Franklin loved me if just a little, or could in time come to do so.

Such was the fullness of my heart that I might have made a blubbering spectacle of myself if just then someone hadn't knocked rapidly on the front door of the bungalow. Even as Loretta and I rose from the sofa, Marjorie Hollingsworth Merrimen threw open the door and entered without waiting for an invitation. "*Bon après-midi, ma amie!* The valet sped off to park my new Pierce-Arrow with such enthusiasm that it is no doubt worthless wreckage with him dead behind the wheel." She stripped off her pale-gray gloves as she stepped out of the foyer and crossed the room. "Nothing excites young men of his benighted generation more than eight cylinders. Women come in a distant second on their must-have list, I'm afraid. The human race will, I swear, wither away altogether because of the automobile."

I knew who our visitor was, because Loretta had told me she would be coming and had described her to me. A tall, slender woman of about fifty, she had a somewhat long but attractive face. She was at the same time brisk and graceful, attired in a shamrock-green suit, a white blouse, a silk scarf fashioned as a necktie, and a tilt hat. She looked very chic and worldly wise. She came straight to me and framed my face with her hands as if looking at me through a movie camera. "You divine child, you are the very image of Lillian Gish, who always has been and will always remain the most beautiful actress in the history of film. You also have eyes like hers, eyes that more than see. And that glorious hair! You must never cut it short. The bobbed hair of the past decade was an abomination, and yet we still see it everywhere on those flappers in their shapeless shirt dresses. The only garment I can condone from that period is the cloche hat. I adore cloche hats. Lillian Gish as I live and breathe. You look lovely as well, Loretta."

On a few occasions, I'd been told I had a pretty face by those who would have called me a monster if they had seen me from the neck down. However, no one had ever before praised my appearance at such length as this or with such enthusiasm. Miss Merrimen put her purse on a small table and sat in the armchair beside it. The two women seemed calm, prepared to discuss the task at hand, but I lost my equilibrium. Although I was sitting on the sofa again, I felt as if I were in motion, adrift on a length of flotsam with ocean swells rising and receding under me. I couldn't know if Miss Merrimen's compliments were sincere or whether she knew everything about my deformities and, out of pity, chose to flatter me while she could, before the time came for me to reveal myself. I blush now to admit how much I delighted in her praise.

Yet every time the thought of Miss Merrimen's praise lifted me, I was reminded of the truth of my physical nature, whereupon the delight receded. Would the time ever come when, like a lowly caterpillar, I would turn into a butterfly?

Marjorie Hollingsworth Merrimen was a clothing designer and dressmaker of some renown. She worked for various studios, creating costumes suitable for the characters in the stories, for which she received screen credit. For those who could afford her services, she also made clothes for women who would never be on the silver screen but wished to look their best and make an impression. More than half of the clothes in Loretta's wardrobe bore the Merrimen label. I was to be the designer's special project.

Although it was clear that these two women were not merely business acquaintances but also good friends, I found it surprising that a person of the designer's status would come on a Sunday to wherever Loretta might be, to consider the task at hand and take measurements. As I was to learn in time, it was not always or even primarily the Fairchilds' fortune or their success in the motion-picture industry that earned them special treatment. They had made many friends who admired them and regarded them with affection that money and position could not buy. I would also eventually learn that such virtue was not common in the film world, where the sharks were numerous, voracious, and humorless.

For fifteen minutes we sat in the living room, making small talk. I understood that this was to allow me to get to know Miss Merrimen and be comfortable when she took my measurements. Early in the conversation, she opened her purse and withdrew a pack of Pall Malls, which she placed on the padded arm of the chair. I expected her to light a cigarette, but she did not.

Loretta hung a Do Not Disturb sign on the bungalow door, but she thought it best that we retreat to my bedroom before I removed my robe. Miss Merrimen brought a small notebook with a pen clipped to it, a yellow tape measure, and the pack of Pall Malls. She put the cigarettes on a nightstand.

"Now, dear Alida, with your lovely face and hair, there is no need for a hood. You might have an occasion to wear a hat, so we'll provide you with a few options. A variety of cloche hats, of course, a few berets, perhaps a knitted balaclava with matching scarf." I could not picture myself in a hat of any kind. I was certain I would look foolish, but I said nothing. "How tall are you, dear, and what do you weigh?"

"On a good day when things aren't so heavy, I'm five feet tall. I stopped growing about five years ago, although I keep trying. I weigh ninety-three pounds."

"Do you gain weight easily?"

"For the past five years, regardless of what I eat, I haven't gained a pound or lost one. I seem to be stuck."

"Darling, there are women who would pay a fortune to be so stuck. Now, if you will, I need you to undress to your underwear so I can make an accurate record of your proportions. Every woman I dress has to do this if the clothes are to be an ideal fit. I've seen Loretta in her skivvies perhaps as often as Franklin has. There's no reason to feel uncomfortable."

I thought it odd that Miss Merrimen and Loretta would imagine that I might be embarrassed to undress, considering that for years, day after day, I'd been put on display nearly naked. Loretta herself had seen me boldly presented on a stage. To my surprise, as I began to disengage the series of snap fasteners that held my robe together at the front, I grew self-conscious about how the dressmaker would react to my appearance. Loretta would have prepared her for what she would see, but there are things for which no amount of preparation is sufficient. My fingers trembled as I worked the metal snaps, and I realized that undressing in an intimate situation involved a much greater risk of mortification than parading nearly naked on a stage. An audience is a mere *thing*, a creature of many faces, none of which speaks to the heart as does the face of someone you love, as already I loved Loretta—or someone who might become a friend, such as Miss Merrimen. The sleeves of my robe were wide, but the sleeves of my long johns had been cut off because they were too tight and would not comfortably accommodate my arms. What remained of that knitted undergarment, which was a size too large for me, still concealed much of my tortured form. Nevertheless, I expected Marjorie Merrimen to be seized by horror or pity, the two reactions with which I was most familiar, the second being the worse of the two. I undid the last fastener. The robe slipped off and puddled on the floor.

Marjorie Merrimen, couturiere to the stars, neither gasped nor made that thin whimper of compassion with which I was so familiar. Her voice wasn't strained when she said, quite businesslike, "Well, we can do a great deal better for underthings than this. What I'll provide will be more comfortable and prettier. You'll feel warm but fresh. I guarantee it. I do think dresses are not the way to go. A flowing robe, duster length, is more practical. However, there's no reason why you have to be costumed like a dour monk on a penitential pilgrimage. They should be robes with shape to them, robes of quiet colors, perhaps with good lace around the collar and at the cuffs. Contrasting buttons, piping, all sorts of subtle flourishes, though not too many for any single garment. I'll make you seven different robes, one for each day of the week, and seven more as backups, so you'll always have the right choice to fit the occasion and your mood. Your gloves are—shall we agree?—rather less than elegant. May I see your hands, dear?"

I took off my gloves, and I could see at once that she was not entirely prepared for my hands. Until the night just passed, my life had been one of rigid routines, the same experiences repeated day after day, the same offenses, with no prospect of change. Therefore, I was not accustomed to surprises. Miss Merrimen's reaction to my hands indeed surprised me. She went to her knees before me and took my left hand in both of hers and kissed it, and then my right hand. She did this with such tenderness that I felt *my* eyes well with hot tears, and I required all my resources to repress them as she had repressed hers.

"Is there pain?" she asked.

"No, ma'am. It's not arthritis, just how my fingers are. They don't hurt. They work okay. And those aren't bruises or fungus. That's how my nails always are."

She looked up at me and smiled. "I will design the most amazing gloves for you, Alida. The right gloves can make even the most ordinary outfit look special. Socially prominent ladies have *collections* of gloves, and so will you. The clothes must be stylish and in good taste, but the accessories are every bit as important."

Now that Miss Merrimen had seen the challenges my deformities posed when it came to clothing, she asked me to take off my shoes and long johns so that she could make precise measurements, of which there needed to be more than was necessary with her usual clients. I did so without shame, for I knew now I was in the company of people who regarded me not as a freak but as a girl. While she employed her tape measure and recorded her findings in the little notebook, I saw her glance repeatedly at the pack of Pall Malls on the nightstand. I asked if she would like to pause for a cigarette. "My dear," she said, "when I leave here, I will quickly smoke the entire pack with pleasure. But although Loretta and Frank's teetotalist attitude toward tobacco strikes me as ill-informed and downright silly, I adore them so much that I respect their request never to smoke in their home or office."

"This isn't either one," I noted. "And ashtrays are everywhere you look."

"All true," she said. "But I'm certain Loretta will argue that the hotel is her home while she's staying here, and I have learned that I lack the intellectual capacity to win an argument with your mother. However, in a few years, when you're twenty-one, if you were to decide to indulge in the noble tradition of Sir Walter Raleigh, you and I will sneak out behind the garage and light up together."

Loretta looked cross, but I could see that she was amused and that her indignation was a pretense. "I can think of nothing more obvious and incontestable than the claim that inhaling enormous quantities of smoke will ruin your lungs."

Miss Merrimen sighed. "Darling, I will only remind you that the advertisements quote prominent doctors and scientists to the effect that smoking actually strengthens the lungs, improves circulation of the blood, and in numerous other ways improves your health."

"That is all bullshit wrapped in humbug and served on a bed of flimflam."

"I cannot believe," said Miss Merrimen, "that physicians and scientists with impeccable reputations would lie."

"Oh, now, Margie. When they see a main chance, ninety percent of them are as sly as movie moguls, just grifters in white coats, waving university degrees. For enough money, they'll tell a long chain of lies and swear on their mother's grave that every link is the pure truth."

As Miss Merrimen measured my arms and took notes, accounting for the features that snagged and tangled ordinary sleeves, she said, "Alida dear, you should ruminate on this revealing exchange between Loretta and me. Participation in the motion-picture industry tends to make people cynical not just about the movie business but also about much else. You will be spending a great deal of time with my otherwise wise and wonderful friends, Franklin and Loretta, so you must guard against being infected by their cynicism."

"Maybe it isn't cynicism," I said. "Maybe it's just a clear-eyed understanding of how the world works."

Putting on a mask of dismay, she said, "Child, I fear their influence has already led you onto a dark path."

With such banter, they distracted me during the measurement process, which could have been awkward and embarrassing. Instead, the time passed quickly and in a spirit of fun.

When she had all the numbers she needed and I was once more fully dressed, Miss Merrimen promised that she would choose the fabrics from her current inventory, cut them herself to patterns that she created, and put three seamstresses to work that very night. She would return on Tuesday morning with two sets of fine undergarments, two robes, and pajamas. The remainder of my new wardrobe was to be delivered over the next two weeks.

Looking as fresh and purposeful as when she had arrived, she kissed each of us on the cheek, asked us to pray that the parking valet was not dead in her ruined Pierce-Arrow, and breezed out of the bungalow, the pack of Pall Malls clutched in her left hand.

I used my bathroom, washed my hands and face with a soap that smelled like lemons, and brushed my hair. Although I didn't need to hide my hands from Loretta, I put on gloves as a matter of habit.

When I returned to the living room, I found that Loretta, too, had freshened up and had produced a deck of cards from her luggage. She proposed that she would teach me rummy.

Just then the doorbell rang. Startled, I whispered, "Captain," and I stood up straight, shoulders back, hands fisted in my gloves, ready for whatever might come. If Loretta heard my soft exclamation, she made no comment. She opened the door to admit a bellhop pushing a food-service cart. Sooner than later, I needed to bleach away the memory of Captain Farnam until he became a faded figure on the fabric of the past, with no power to cast a shadow on my newfound happiness.

Loretta had ordered an afternoon tea. The cart served as a table, draped with pink damask and laden with delicious little sandwiches, scones, and two-bite cakes. When this delectable production had been wheeled in front of a window and flanked by chairs brought from the dining nook, the two of us settled before a view of the gardens, to what Loretta called "a divine refection." I felt as if I were in an English novel, in a story rife with challenges and travails that would nonetheless end in justice and gladness.

TEN

Between the afternoon tea and a late dinner, Loretta taught me rummy, and we competed toward a winning score of five hundred. She won the first two games; however, I squeaked out a win in the third. Rummy was fun, although the best part of the competition was the conversation that came with it. All my life, I had been talked about and talked at, but I had seldom known anyone whom I could talk *with*. Captain spoke of little but himself, and he did not require—or appreciate—feedback from me. Loretta was witty, with a trove of fascinating anecdotes and opinions.

She was kind enough to say I was more articulate, well read, and sensible than any girl of seventeen she'd ever known. "Or most women of twenty-five," she added. I discovered that I had a thirst for praise. I had long been parched from want of it. I warned myself that I should not let her words inflate me too much, even if they were as sincere as they seemed to be. Pride comes before a fall.

She asked me when I learned to read and if Captain, of all people, had taught me. I had been reading as long as I could recall and had no memory of being taught. I must have first read Kenneth Grahame's wonderful *The Wind in the Willows* when I was four. The carnival season that year had been sweltering, the long spring and summer shaken by numerous thunderstorms. I vividly remember reading that book over and over as the sky roared and lights flickered in the Museum of the Strange, where Captain paced and ranted because the bad weather kept the marks away. My indifference to the plunging box office receipts infuriated him, so that he tore the book from my hands and threw it on the stage floor. I got off my padded stool and retrieved Mr. Grahame's treasure. As I returned to my seat, Captain approached me, one fist raised above his head as if he were master of the storm and would call down its violence upon me to make my skeleton glow visibly within my flesh and leave me smoldering. I recall meeting his eyes and holding his stare as I'd never done previously. I thought of Badger and the other brave little animals of the wildwood, and I neither looked away from Captain nor shrank from him. The walls of the tent thrummed in the wind, and the taut canvas ceiling glowed with a reflection of the lightning. He reached for my book, but I pressed the volume against my chest. His hand stopped short. While light chased shadows, it seemed as if we held that tableau for minutes, though the truth was mere seconds. As if some secret tenant living in the darkness of Captain's heart warned him that the power rocking the sky existed also—and doubly strong—within the book, he drew back his grasping hand and turned and went elsewhere to rant. By the following year, I had read, among other things, all the Sherlock Holmes stories. I loved Holmes because he was a gentleman who was never dismissive toward anyone other than fools and criminals.

Shuffling the cards, Loretta said, "Good heavens, you were a child prodigy."

I never thought of myself as such, and I denied it now. "The only thing special about me is what made me such an attraction in Captain's ten-in-one. I *had* to learn to read. Learning to read was necessary for survival. Without books, without being able to escape into the worlds within them, sitting on that stage day after day with no distraction, I would have gone stark, raving mad. You know how they sometimes throw little kids in a pool and say 'sink or swim,' and so they swim? With me it was sink or read, and I stayed afloat. That's all."

She looked at me in silence for a moment and then said, "You're really something."

"It's nice you think so. But I am just what I am, and I'm okay with that."

"No, dear. You're more than what you believe you are."

I thought that was an odd statement, but I didn't say as much.

When we were finished playing cards, we sat down to dinner. Loretta had ordered the same for each of us from room service—roast chicken, French-fried potatoes, and a sort of soufflé of eggs and corn. Every meal we ate was better than the one before, and the aroma of this dinner was almost divine enough to make me faint.

She said, "People find carnivals exciting, magical. But even when there's no attraction as tawdry as a ten-in-one, I suspect it's like life in Hollywood—little that's pretty under the glitter."

"Carnies are very tolerant of one another," I said. "They're outsiders. They don't fit in the straight world and don't want to. They have their demons and twisted histories, but most of them are no worse than people anywhere, I think. They have one another's back, aligned against the world that doesn't want them and they don't want. But no one in their world seems to get truly close to anyone else, at least not for long. I always felt there was an inescapable sadness to it all."

"How so?"

I put down my fork, my dinner unfinished. "Well, I guess one thing is . . . like how they mostly marry. There's no minister, no justice of the peace, no paperwork. After the midway closes down for the night, the carnies that are friends of the bride and groom . . . they gather around the carousel to be witnesses. The couple getting married . . . they ride together, only them, just three times around. That's it. That's all. If the night comes where one of them wants a divorce, then after closing and in front of witnesses, he or she rides three times *backward*. And so the marriage is over. I saw two divorces like that, and it seemed so sad I couldn't ever bear to see another. I went to a wedding, thinking maybe that would be better, two riding together toward the future, but it was every bit as sad. Anything that really, truly means something—it shouldn't be that easy." I picked up my fork but didn't use it. "Divorce is so sad, like a kind of funeral. Don't you think divorce is sad?"

"When children are involved," Loretta said, "I believe it's near impossible. Frank and I don't make commitments lightly. There's no carousel ride in our future, dear. If we ever got sick and tired of being married, the only way out would be to shoot each other, and neither of us is suicidal. No need to worry."

"Oh," I said, "I was just talking about the sadness of divorce in general. I didn't mean you and Franklin might ever."

Of course I had been asking about them indirectly, and she knew it. She smiled. "Is something wrong with your dinner?"

"No, no. It's delicious." My appetite returned, and I put my fork to work until nothing was left on my plate.

There was so much I wanted to know about Loretta and Franklin. This was their story, not mine. I am rather like any horse or dog for which a novel is named—only apparently the central figure, when in fact the story is about the family, about their gain and joy and loss and grief. I didn't yet know how to ask about their past, their lives, without seeming to be inquisitive or even meddlesome.

That night I dreamed. I didn't yet believe that dreams mean anything. You're lying there unconscious, doing nothing, going nowhere, so your brain gets bored. It starts making up stories to entertain itself until you get your lazy butt out of bed. That's what dreams are. If I had believed they were something more, the dream I had that Sunday night would have been disturbing. I found myself on a carousel, astride a painted horse that pumped up and down as the motorized platform and decorative cornice rotated around the inner drive. There was no music, only what sounded like heavy footfalls. For the longest time, no source of the sound could be seen. Then Captain came into view, walking in the opposite direction from that toward which the carousel turned, approaching me, making his way between the rising-and-falling horses. He smiled and said, "Welcome home," and I saw blood dripping from his scarlet hands, not the claret of his own veins, but the blood of innocents.

ELEVEN

Monday, the day before we would return to Bramley Hall, proved to be less eventful than Sunday. A previous guest had left a jigsaw puzzle in a drawer of a sideboard. Loretta and I worked it together.

By invitation of my puzzle partner, Mr. Giovanni Leone paid us a visit at eleven o'clock. In Hollywood, Mr. Leone was to shoes what Miss Marjorie Merrimen was to dresses and accessories. I protested that I had mostly worn slippers, which accommodated my unusual feet well enough. Loretta insisted that slippers would not do. "We're a walking family, honey. You'll be taking long walks on the beach with us, long walks in parks. We'll be going to San Marino from time to time to walk the Huntington estate. Henry Huntington, a dear man, died three years ago, but he left an amazing legacy. Henry was book crazy, art crazy, and simply mad about elaborate gardens. The estate is six hundred acres, and half of it is magnificently landscaped. We sometimes walk around and around there for hours."

Mr. Leone didn't merely sell shoes. He and his crew of artisans crafted them to order. All the most stylish people—women and men—wore them. Loretta insisted that I must relent and at once get on with having my feet measured. Mr. Leone's time was valuable, she said; six pairs of his shoes, suitable for a variety of occasions and activities, would cost us as much as a Ford Model A Victoria. I started to react, but the slightest curve at the right corner of Loretta's mouth and a certain twinkle in Mr. Leone's large brown eyes revealed that she was ribbing me.

I said, "If I had been making such shoes for years, I would by now have retired to a villa in Italy."

Mr. Leone smiled. "When these six pairs are delivered, I will do just that."

His voice was soft, his manner as gentle as that of a clergyman whose faith was genuine. No doubt Loretta had prepared him for what he would see when I removed my socks and slippers. However, I was touched by the matter-of-fact way he proceeded to take measurements while putting me at ease by telling sweet, amusing stories about some of the celebrities who wore his shoes. He made me feel almost as if my feet were not merely unremarkable but were also fair enough to grace a pair of glass slippers and attract the attention of a prince. By the time he insisted on putting my socks on for me and helping me into my slippers, his tenderness had brought me close to tears. I did not, however, want to become a Weepy Wanda, sobbing into my hanky every ten minutes until it shrank to the size of a postage stamp, so I counseled my heart to behave itself.

To this point in my narrative, I might have left the impression that my three-day journey from life as an enslaved freak to that of the ward of a prominent family in the film business was as smooth and joyful as what any bird might feel when taking flight from a tree branch into the heights of the sky. In fact, though a profound gladness was the greater part of it, I was often also in emotional turmoil—afraid that my ascent would suddenly become a fall, abashed by the upper-class splendor for which I was so unsuited, confused by the manners, traditions, and rules of this new world. Looking back, I can see that it was neither the wealth of my new guardians nor the prospect of freedom, not even the love with which they embraced me, that gave me the pluck and resolution to make my way forward and become what they believed I could become. More than anything else, it was the *kindness* with which they showered me, kindness without pity, that encouraged me always onward, and not just their kindness but also that of people like Miss Merrimen and Mr. Leone and so many others who were their friends. The times are mean and meaner every day, and the colony of those who make motion pictures is no less mean than the larger world it entertains, perhaps more so. Somehow, by some quality that Loretta and Franklin possessed, some quality that included probity and integrity and compassion but was not properly described by those words alone, by some quality that surpassed my understanding at that time, they had gathered around them a community of like souls, the kinder people in an otherwise mean and indifferent cosmos.

They preferred that I call them Father and Mother, but I could not. My saviors would forever be Franklin and Loretta to me, nothing less. I would have felt most comfortable using the honorifics "sir" and "ma'am," but they forbade me from doing so. I thought of myself not as one of the family but as their devoted friend. Although I was granted many privileges, I sought none. I was astonished to have been rescued, to be valued. I challenged myself to be *the* friend of the family who would never fail them.

That was the moment I knew I must soon begin to write about them and all they did for me. My material would be far different from the cruelty, narcissism, and carelessness of Tom and Daisy Buchanan and their friends that Nick Carraway had chronicled in *The Great Gatsby*. Even if the Fairchilds and their kind had been, underneath the glamor, a "rotten crowd" to equal the Buchanans and their ilk, I did not possess Nick's keen nose for moral negligence of all degrees. My seventeen years had relentlessly exposed me to the supreme depravity of Captain and his kind, which I imagined had desensitized me to the scent of lesser wickedness.

That night before we made the short trip to Bramley Hall, in the privacy of my own room in the bungalow, where I could not be heard, I cried softly. The cause was not sadness, but quite the opposite. I indulged myself for a short time and then slept. I didn't dream of Captain, and I hoped I never would again.

TWELVE

Tuesday morning, Franklin returned to the Beverly Hills Hotel to have breakfast with Loretta and me before driving us home. He was wearing a blue sport coat with a patterned display handkerchief, a white shirt with an open collar, gray flannel slacks, and black loafers by Giovanni Leone. He looked handsome. He appeared relaxed, too, as though preparing the children and the estate staff for my arrival had been not in the least stressful, though I was sure it must have been.

Marjorie Hollingsworth Merrimen and a valued associate named Selma Skolimowski arrived with the first tranche of my new wardrobe. Everything was lovely. I was more excited than I expected to be, and for the first time in my life, I dressed myself with pleasure. I had never imagined that undergarments could be so comfortable or have such high yet demure style, while covering even my difficult arms. After some dithering, I chose a sapphire-blue robe with a white Peter Pan collar, two-inch white cuffs, and a one-inch white-ribbon hem. Loretta and Franklin said I looked beautiful, but of course they would, and I knew I wasn't. I must admit, however, that I certainly felt presentable.

On the sunny September afternoon in 1930, when Franklin piloted the yellow Cadillac sedan through the estate gate and parked at the apex of the palm-lined circular driveway, Bramley Hall loomed as monumental as a palace. A chill of inadequacy set me trembling.

Loretta turned in the front passenger seat and looked back at me. "This belongs to you now, dear. All of it belongs to you as much as it belongs to anyone."

Although she and Franklin had been unfailingly compassionate and kind during the few days I had known them, her glorious promise was so extraordinary that I could not help but wonder if it might be insincere. All the good they had done for me—could it have been a deceitful scheme to lure me into a new kind of servitude even worse than I had known heretofore? No. Impossible. To think as much was to be wickedly ungrateful. My doubt arose from my conviction, instilled in me by others since early childhood, that I was unworthy of a life like those that most people enjoyed. In spite of Bramley Hall's grandness and beauty, I suddenly worried that its walls encompassed a truth yet hidden from me, a dark and terrible secret.

Franklin put down his window and spoke to someone through the call box. As the halves of the immense gate began to swing inward and as we proceeded houseward on the driveway flanked by colonnades of Phoenix palms, Loretta explained that, at her husband's insistence, the estate was named in honor of Charles and Eunice Bramley, her deceased parents. I knew there must be a story behind the naming, but I failed to ask because I was awestruck at the sight of the mansion.

The long driveway led under a columned portico that shaded the main entrance. The house was clad in limestone, but the carved features were what most impressed and intimidated me, not least of all two second-floor balconies. A three-part window bay served each, and the majestic surround included a carved cartouche and scrolls. They were the kind of balconies on which a king or a pope would appear to wave at crowds gathered below.

As he parked under the roof of the portico, Franklin said the residence had been built and the grounds fully landscaped in just a year and a half; in those days city regulations were minimal. As I marveled at everything I saw, my breath repeatedly catching in my throat, Loretta turned in the front passenger seat and looked at me and said, "This belongs to you now, dear. All of it belongs to you as much as it belongs to anyone."

Just then a man in a black suit, white shirt, and black tie opened her door. He said, "Welcome home, Mrs. Fairchild."

She took the hand he offered. "Thank you, Julian, so good to see you." He was the majordomo, Julian Symington, whom she'd told me about. *He's a doll,* Loretta had said, *although old-fashioned and more formal than I wish he would be. I've told him to call us Loretta and Franklin, but if he ever heard those names fall from his lips, he would probably have a breakdown. As you're not yet twenty-one, he'll feel comfortable using your first name.*

Julian was distinguished, fiftysomething, with curly white hair that would have been curlier if his barber hadn't used straightening cream, heat, and stern discipline to control it. Everyone seemed to know about these efforts, for every two weeks he kept an appointment with the barber and returned home with almost straight hair that, day by day, rebelled against what had been done to it, until it was almost as curly as if he had gone to a beauty parlor to have a permanent wave. Mr. Symington felt that aggressively curly hair was inappropriate for a manager of a great house and its staff.

As Loretta set foot on the pavement and Franklin came around the front of the sedan, Mr. Symington opened my door and offered his hand. "Miss Alida, I am pleased to meet you and to welcome you to Bramley Hall. I hope you will be happy here. You must feel free to call on me for anything you might need."

After years of dressing like a monk, I felt that I was modestly becoming in my new clothes—until I got out of the car, whereupon I grew self-conscious. Surely anyone could see it was not befitting of me to assume I belonged in such a grand place, among respectable people. My outfit must appear to be an ill-conceived costume, and Mr. Symington no doubt thought I was masquerading as a social equal of Loretta and Franklin in an effort to better my position. I was determined to press on nonetheless, in hope I might win his trust in time, but my voice had a tremor when I replied. "I've heard such lovely things about you, Mr. Symington. I couldn't be anything other than happy to be here. Why, it seems like one step beyond paradise."

Mr. Symington unloaded the luggage as Franklin and Loretta escorted me up three steps, across a shallow terrace, and through the front door into the foyer. The space might better have been called a "reception hall." In the event of a party, fifty people could have gathered there comfortably to have a first drink and let anticipation build for the occasion before moving on to the main venue. The floor was overall a cream-colored marble, though more colorful stones were inlaid to form a patterned border and central medallion. The walls were paneled in select mahogany of a rich red-brown hue. At the far end, two curved staircases, separated as are the halves of a wishbone, rose to a second-floor gallery.

Loretta and Franklin intended to take me on a tour of the house and grounds, but first they led me into the library, where the staff that served under Mr. Symington waited to meet me. The size of the room and its thousands of volumes excited me more than anything else had to this point. I turned in a circle, enraptured. The chamber offered five seating areas—armchairs, divans, reading lamps of elegant design and proportions. Before I could explore the shelves, there were five people to meet. They were lined up like soldiers in a reviewing line, obviously curious and all but one of them smiling.

They had not been told anything regarding the fearsome truth of me that my unconventional clothing concealed. The previous day, Franklin sat with the staff to explain that my mother had been an old friend from his and Loretta's school days. According to the script, she'd recently passed away, with no living relative to take custody of her only child. If my differences were extreme, I was fortunate to have five senses, a good mind, and mobility. He said that I was so sensitive about the tragic legacy of my conception that I should never be asked about it and no effort should be made to catch a glimpse of what Nature had made me endure, which would be an offense that could get even the most valued of them fired. There is some irony in that instruction, considering that over the years, I had been exhibited nearly naked before thousands of oglers for whom I was the most fascinating zoo animal or creature from a nightmare that they had ever seen.

The groundskeeper, Mr. Wilhelm Reinhardt, was the first to step forward. He was perhaps forty, deeply tanned, with a face that, had he been an actor, would have gotten him roles as a kindly priest and a warmhearted country doctor. He oversaw a gardening crew of five men provided two days a week by an outside service. Unmarried and childless, he worked six days a week out of love for the gardens. He welcomed me sweetly and invited my suggestions as to new flowers and plants I would like to see.

Next came the head housekeeper, Mrs. Victoria Symington, wife of the majordomo. She wore a calf-length dress the blue of robin's eggs and a white apron over it, as did the three younger women who were housemaids answerable to her. She seemed less formal than her husband, rosy-cheeked and quick to smile. She said, "Except for what the cook wants, I do all the shopping. I only need to know what you need, and it will be gotten. You're going to love it here, child, and we're going to love having you. If my mister seems a littlest bit forbidding, please know he isn't. At heart, my Julian is as threatening as buttered toast and a warm mug of cocoa."

The first of the three maids, Lynette, was a petite brunette in her thirties, as cute as the wonderful playwright Anita Loos, with such large and compelling eyes that I wondered why she hadn't become the wife of a rich man and the mother of a bevy of children as sweet to look at as she herself. Next to Lynette stood Harmony, a tall and freckled redhead who, though attractive, appeared awkwardly assembled and so full of energy that she could barely hold still. She welcomed me as warmly as Lynette had done, but she grinned broadly, as if the addition of a new member to the Fairchild family promised excitement and adventure. Beside Harmony, Anna May produced a smile as fleeting as the shadow of a bird on the surface of a pond. She was a pretty but solemn blonde. Her greeting was more reserved than those of the others, but I saw no animosity in it. In fact, I suspected that she was preoccupied with troubles in her personal life so entangling that she could not foresee a way to extract herself from them. My long experience of anxiety had trained me to recognize it in others, and I had become somewhat adept at imagining the cause. In her case, I doubted that the reason was anything other than a man; in this I would be proved prescient.

The cook, Luigi Lattuada, would be introduced to me later. He was currently making the rounds of his favorite markets in a panel truck, acquiring food for the weekend. He traveled with three large ice chests specially designed to keep a variety of goods chilled and fresh without freezing them or diminishing their quality with cold burn. "Everyone here adores Luigi," Mrs. Symington told me, and Mr. Reinhardt said, "He will frighten you at first, but don't judge him on appearances," and Harmony said, "From time to time, he'll scare you even after you know him well and understand what a sweetheart he is, but he's ever so fun, I swear he is, but never play cards with him." Thus I was primed to anticipate an encounter with perhaps the most colorful character on the staff of Bramley Hall.

As everyone departed to leave me with Franklin and Loretta, I hurried at once to the nearest library shelves to scan the titles of the volumes. "The wonderful Mr. Dickens!" I exclaimed. "You have all his works. *Great Expectations*. How could anyone resist a story when the lead character is introduced with such an opening. 'My father's family name being Pirrip, and my Christian name Philip, my infant tongue could make of both names nothing longer or more explicit than Pip. So, I called myself Pip, and came to be called Pip.' And every word thereafter is wonderful until the exquisite final paragraph."

I turned to them, so excited by the wealth of knowledge and entertainment shelved around us that I was strangely warm and felt as if my face must be shining. They regarded me with bewilderment. Loretta said, "You loved the book so much you memorized the opening paragraph? How long ago was this?"

"Oh, years and years. And this!" I slid a finger down the spine of *A Tale of Two Cities*. "It's a great deal darker than the other but every bit as fabulous in its own way. 'It was the best of times, it was the worst of times, it was the age of wisdom, it was the age of foolishness, it was the epoch of belief, it was the epoch of incredulity, it was the season of Light—"

Franklin interrupted my recitation, which was understandable because I'd hardly begun what is one of the longest first sentences of any novel. "You memorize every opening or just those of Dickens?"

"He's the best, I think. I mean over his entire body of work. There are no stinkers. But there are so many great stories just here in the *D* section." I drew their attention to *Two Years Before the Mast* by Mr. Richard Henry Dana. "'Chapter One: Departure. The fourteenth of August was the day fixed upon for the sailing of the brig *Pilgrim*, on her voyage from Boston, round Cape Horn, to the western coast of North America.'"

"Have you read this?" Loretta asked, pointing to *The Three Musketeers* by Mr. Alexandre Dumas. I said of course I had, that it was a thrilling and often humorous tale. She plucked it from the shelf, opened it, and flipped past the preface to the beginning of the story. "The first chapter has a title."

"Yes, ma'am. I'm sorry. Sorry I called you ma'am." I recited the chapter title, "'The Three Gifts of M. d'Artagnan the Elder.'" As I remembered the joy of that novel, I rushed into another recitation. "'On the first Monday of the month of April, 1626, the market town of Meung, in which the author of the *Romance of the Rose* was born, appeared to be in as perfect a state of revolution as if the Huguenots had just made a second Rochelle of it.'"

Loretta looked at Franklin, and during a long moment of silence he returned her stare. If I had to describe their mutual expression with one word, I could not do so, but I can say that it seemed to me they were both surprised and confused, though I wasn't entirely sure why. Franklin asked, "How many novels have you read, would you say? Fifty? Sixty?"

"No, no," I said. "Hundreds. Remember, Loretta, I was four when I read *The Wind in the Willows*. You can read a great many books in thirteen years when you have nothing to do all day but sit on a stage, trying not to see the marks gaping at you."

"Hundreds?" Franklin said. "You've committed to memory, word for word, the openings of hundreds of novels?"

"Yes, but—"

"The effort required would be enormous."

I was so transported by the thought of exploring the many books in the collection that I did not recognize their astonishment for what it was. I thought they were just surprised and approving that I, in spite of my disabilities and lifelong isolation, had attained an admirable knowledge of literature through self-education. "It's no big deal, no effort. Just reading and retaining like anyone does if they love books."

As I continued to read the spines of the volumes before me, the rhythm of my heart kept pace with my growing eagerness to seize the opportunities they offered. I continued to fail to properly register Franklin and Loretta's amazement. Loretta said, "Honey, do you mean . . . are you saying that . . . that you can quote every page of every book you've ever read?" Still focused on the titles of the worlds that waited to be explored, I said yes, every book, just as they could do, as anyone could do.

Franklin took *Great Expectations* from its shelf and opened it and said, "Chapter Nineteen. Do you remember Chapter Nineteen?"

I turned to him, assuming he had not read the novel—else why would he have to refer to the page to check the accuracy of my memory when he could rely on his own? I said, "Of course it's Pip speaking. The entire book is written from his point of view. 'Morning made a considerable difference in my general prospect of life, and brightened it so much that it scarcely seemed the same. What lay heaviest on my mind was the consideration that—"

Interrupting the game by flipping perhaps a hundred pages ahead, Franklin said, "Chapter Twenty-Eight."

"Oh, that follows the sad chapter where Joe comes to London to see Pip at Barnard's Hotel. Dear Joe. And Pip behaving badly toward him. 'Chapter Twenty-Eight. It was clear that I must repair to our town next day, and in the first flow of my repentance it was equally clear that I must stay at Joe's.'"

Franklin closed the book, and his hand shook as he tried to return it to its place between two other volumes by Dickens.

"God in Heaven," Loretta said. "How could so much be memorized and recalled word for word years later?"

"Oh, I didn't need to struggle to memorize anything. Just like you, like anyone, reading a book is knowing it forever. I'm no different. At least not that way."

Neither of them had been speechless before, but they seemed to be having trouble finding words. Then Loretta said, "Come sit down with us, sweetheart." She led the way to a sofa, and I sat between them, and she said, "Have you never shared this with anyone before? Surely you have."

"Shared what?" I asked.

Franklin said, "That you have such an amazing capacity for memorization."

"No, like I said, it's not memorizing. It's just reading. Like anyone who loves books. Anyway, who would I talk with about books? Captain Farnam had no interest in them. Until you, Captain was the only one I knew well enough to converse with at length, and we never talked much. He didn't really think of me as a person. I was just an asset. As he put it, I was his 'best chance for early retirement.' He gave me food, a bed. He stole books for me. But he always kept his distance, kept to himself, because he found me repulsive. When he was drunk, he said I was disgusting. That was okay, because I found him disgusting, too. I didn't have any patience for his guff. He was never not a pitchman, everything a con and all of it boring."

Loretta put her arm around me, and her voice was thick with emotion. "I thought I understood, but I wasn't close. Even with the others in the carnival, there was no one. You've always been alone."

"Not really. I had the books I'd read, all the people in them, what they said, the things they did, the places they went. They were all real to me. You know how it is. Even when Captain didn't get me new books, I had all the old ones, even after he took them away from me and threw them out, I had them, you know. I could live in them again and again. I had friends in them. I was part of them, those worlds. You know how it is."

"That's just it," Franklin said. "We don't know, Alida. Loretta and I remember books, the stories, characters—but not the way you do. We can't open them without holding them in our hands. We can't summon one like a favorite dream, summon it in every vivid detail and live in it again. No one can. What you can do is . . . amazing."

"Even that isn't an adequate word," Loretta said. "What you can do, this power of yours, is awesome, otherworldly."

They regarded me as though I was the deepest of mysteries, as though I was stranger than they had realized, stranger than they had imagined anyone could be. I was small and had vulnerabilities, but I also had *this*, which I thought was an ability common to everyone, but which evidently was unique to me. I knew too well how uniqueness can scare people into erecting barriers. Desire and despair overcame me in equal measure—a sudden desperate determination to hold fast to the life I'd had with them for such a short time, matched by the despondency that follows close upon the sense that hope is quickly slipping away. My voice broke as I said, "It's not a power, not a power over others. It's just a talent. You know all about talent, making movies. Even if I'm the only one in the world who can do it, then it's just maybe a gift . . . a gift to make it easier to be what else I am. This doesn't make me a freak twice over, not twice over, it just doesn't."

Loretta drew me tight against her. "No, of course it doesn't. Honey, you're not a freak. That's an ugly word. I don't want to hear it ever again. You have differences, disabilities, but we all do."

"We all do," Franklin said softly. "Alida, some of us . . . our disabilities aren't obvious. They're internal. In our minds, in our hearts. That's not the case with you. Your mind is healthy, and your heart . . . is pure. The freaks are those whose hearts are full of hate and anger. Yours isn't. I don't know why it isn't, how you could have avoided becoming bitter. Maybe the reason is this ability to hold books in the library of your soul—every word—and step into them when this world is too hard. It *is* a gift. A great gift."

I held fast to Loretta as she held on to me. "Then I can stay? I can stay here?"

They were genuinely surprised by my question, and they overspoke each other as they assured me that this was my home now and forever, that if I ran off, they would find me even if somehow I got halfway around the world and they had to bring me back kicking and screaming from Sweden or Italy. Unable to repress my tears, I found myself crying openly, not sobbing wildly or blubbering like a big silly baby, but crying nonetheless and for the second time in five days. This wasn't me. I wasn't a weeper. Or maybe it was me. The new me. Now that I was free from the carnival and the speakeasy circuit, from daily mortification, maybe I no longer needed to be tough. I didn't like that idea at all. My internal library was stocked with novels confirming that the world was beautiful, that life could be lived with grace and happiness, *but that life was not always easy*, so you had to stay tough, very tough, to make it through the hard times that were sure to come.

I let go of Loretta and sat up straight on the sofa and blotted my eyes with my hands, which is an effective procedure when you wear absorbent gloves. As I wiped my face, I apologized for misunderstanding and going sloppy on them. I assured them that I would never be like one of those weird women in some novels, members of the family who lived separate from everyone else, alone in a tower room, sniveling through the night over some lost love or other long-ago tragedy. "I don't even know if Bramley Hall has a tower," I said. "Probably not. A tower wouldn't be consistent with the architecture." Franklin said that if I changed my mind, if one day I wanted to be one of those sniveling women, he and Loretta would have a huge tower built to accommodate me. So that was how all the crying turned into laughter from one second to the next.

"Can this be our secret? I won't tell anyone what I can do if you won't. I don't want to be stared at for this the way I used to be stared at for being . . . a biological oddity. I just want to be someone like everybody else, just like everybody else for once."

"We'll swear an oath of silence," Franklin said, "and sign our names in blood if you want."

I smiled and shook my head. "I believe I can rely on just your word of honor."

"Then you have it. But I should warn you, Miss Fairchild, that being just like everybody else is no picnic."

"I suspect as much," I assured him. "There might not be sharks, but there'll always be ants."

Loretta got up from the sofa. "I'm sure you'd be happy to spend the day here in the library, but we've got things to do. A tour to complete, children to be introduced. Let's get on with it."

THIRTEEN

Room after room delighted me, but when I saw the kitchen, I was thunderstruck, marveling at its size and the number of appliances. Two complete O'Keefe and Merritt ranges, each with three ovens and two broilers and six gas burners, handsome works of white porcelain and stainless steel. Most amazing were the Frigidaires. In those days, maybe one in ten houses had a Frigidaire, if even that many. Here were *three* lined up side by side. Loretta explained that the kitchen could serve more than a hundred guests at a party, when a catering company would be hired to cook under the stern direction of Luigi Lattuada, their cook, who was still out shopping.

The beauty and scale of the Bram were humbling and the grounds enchanting, but it was a shadowland compared to the brightness of the children. I was anxious about meeting them, but I need not have been. Toward the back of the ten-acre estate, in the shade of lacy California pepper trees, stood a two-story bungalow in the same style as the main house. The upper floor provided an apartment for Mr. and Mrs. Symington. Half the lower level was devoted to the two rooms and bath where Mr. Lattuada lived. Only those three staff members resided on the property. A schoolroom occupied the other half of the ground floor, where the nanny and teacher, Miss Imogene Blackthorn, watched after and instructed the children five days a week.

How Miss Blackthorn knew we were approaching I can't say, but she stood waiting in front of the building. A tall, willowy woman with auburn hair and sharp but attractive features, she was dressed rather severely in a long black dress with no decoration other than a simple white-ribbon bow gathered at the collar and trailing down the bodice. Her personality belied the austere image created by her clothing. She at once favored me with a warm smile and took my hands in hers as if it were the most natural thing in the world for a girl of seventeen to be wearing black gloves on a mild September day. "I'm pleased to meet you, Alida. What do you think of Bramley Hall, these grounds? Could there be any park anywhere lovelier than this?"

"I don't have much experience of parks, Miss Blackthorn. But this seems more than that, like another world and time, where tree nymphs and fairies are everywhere, keeping just out of sight."

"Now that you've put it that way," she said, "I will never be able to think of it otherwise. You like stories about fairies and such, do you?"

"Oh, I like stories of all kinds, ma'am. Stories are the best thing we have."

"You'll get along well with the children. Their imagination gets more exercise than they do. They live in stories of their own invention as much as they live in Bramley Hall."

Loretta said, "If we're not careful, they'll end up telling stories in the movie business."

"God forbid," said Franklin. "We haven't coddled the little dears only to throw them into *that* cauldron."

"You mean because of the humorless sharks?" I asked.

"Exactly."

Miss Blackthorn said, "They're very excited about meeting you, Alida. I've warned them to be on their best behavior, but don't be surprised if they ricochet around the room a little bit."

Looking past her, I saw three faces crowding one another at a schoolroom window. The moment they realized they had been seen, the children seemed not merely to retreat but to *fling* themselves away from the glass.

As the teacher led us inside, I was nervous and self-conscious about facing this small but important class of students. Many years had passed since being displayed onstage had affected me this way. Captain and the slack-mouthed marks had not withered my sense of modesty. I still shrank from anything indelicate and from being observed too eagerly. In the Museum of the Strange and in the speakeasies, I resisted becoming as bold and decadent as the audience by developing a strong sense of reserve, holding myself aloof from my surroundings, holding back feelings from expression, refusing to communicate. I retreated into my novels, which were more real to me than the tawdry place in which I actually existed. Now I found it curious that, having had respectability bestowed on me by my new guardians, I felt less self-assured than I did as a freak-show exhibit, at least during this early stage of my new life. When you have hope, everything is so much more important and meaningful than when you don't.

The classroom was spacious, with a wall of cupboards that no doubt contained instructional materials, a large blackboard, and a cork bulletin board on which were pinned drawings and poems by the students for the admiration of all. Three desks were lined up side by side, and the children sat there, facing the teacher's larger desk, in a posture that denied they had been at the window only a moment earlier.

Each of them had been tasked with writing a special greeting in rhyme. As she was the eldest, twelve-year-old Isadora went first. A pretty girl in the image of her mother, she had flaxen-blond hair lighter than mine and lovely striated eyes neither entirely blue nor entirely green. She stood up and said, "My dear Alida, welcome to the Bram. May you be as happy here as I am. I have but one request to make. Please always let me have the last slice of cake."

Evidently, they had composed their salutations without sharing them until now, for Gertrude and Harry giggled and clapped approval.

Gertrude rose to her feet when Isadora sat down. As she would make clear at dinner that evening, she was not a child of ten, but ten and a half. Gertrude had flaxen hair, and her eyes were so blue they appeared to be lit from within. Although she, too, resembled her mother, her features were elfin, whereas Loretta's were as classical as those of a goddess in Greek mythology. Throughout her life, Gertrude would more often be called "cute" and "adorable" rather than beautiful, though she was no less attractive than her sister. Anyway, being regarded as cute and adorable is often a more winning look than great beauty, which can be intimidating. Gertrude read her greeting from an index card, which she held in both hands. It was then, as she was about to speak, that I realized her left hand was incomplete. The little finger and ring finger were missing. That might have been the consequence of an accident if not for the fact that half her palm was gone as well. Although the heel of her hand joined her wrist in a sudden swell of flesh, her thumb and remaining two fingers appeared to have full function. There was no obvious scar tissue. Indeed, in spite of what it lacked, the hand looked well formed, strangely natural. I knew in my heart that this was how little Gertrude had come into the world. In that moment, I better understood Loretta and Franklin Fairchild—the kind of people they were, as well as one reason why they were that way. Beginning in the dressing room at Blue Mood, they had inspired my love, and my love had grown, but now it began to mature into something more. At that moment there began to be devotion in it, though I am unable to properly articulate what I mean. Recognition of their journey with their daughter somehow consecrated them in my affections, made hallow my intense and tender feelings for them.

Gertrude glanced shyly at me and cleared her throat and read her composition. "Dear Alida, I'm so happy to have a second sister. My little brother can be quite a blister. Now with three of us in the Bram, we can gang up on the little lamb." This received the reaction you might expect—laughter and enthusiastic approval from Isadora, playful booing from Harry. I clapped, grateful that, though my hands needed to be gloved, they were complete in their own way.

Nine-year-old Harry thrust to his feet and shook his fist at Gertrude and waved at me. He was dark-haired and dark-eyed like his father, but with an impish quality that suggested he might be less inclined to take seriously much of what other people considered to be important. Somewhat small for his age, he nevertheless had a presence bigger than his height and weight. He'd memorized his welcoming words. "Dear Alida, violets are blue, roses are red. Be careful of my sisters. They aren't right in the head." With that outrage, it became the girls' turn to boo, and Harry replied to their disapproval with a long, wet raspberry.

"I will tolerate your rudeness to one another," Miss Blackthorn said, "because it was mildly amusing, but none of you is close to being the next Will Rogers." She pointed at Harry. "Don't you dare direct a Bronx cheer at me, young man."

With greetings completed, the children left their desks and gathered around me, unraveling questions at me far faster than I could answer them. "What do you think of the Bram?" "Do you like your rooms?" "Did you like my rhyme? I was going to call Harry a 'little ham,' because he hams it up all the time, but I thought 'little lamb' was nicely ironic. Don't you think it's nicely ironic? We just learned about irony last week." "Did you see the fountain with the stone dolphins? I adore that fountain, the way the spouting dolphins seem to be frolicking with such delight." "Did you know we have a dog?" "Do you like cats? We like cats, but Mother is crazy allergic to them and would positively stop breathing and die if we had a cat in the house."

"Wait, wait, wait!" I said with such excitement that they all looked wide-eyed at me. "Are you serious? Do you really? Do you have a dog?" I'd long yearned to have a dog, but there were none allowed in McKinsey Shows, as there were in other carnivals. Mr. Burnell McKinsey said dogs were "filthy beasts" and forbade people who were in any way associated with his operation from having such a pet. I had seen photographs of dogs, of course, many breeds, each beautiful in its way. When Captain and I were traveling the speakeasy circuit, I sometimes saw dogs, though nearly always at a distance. I had read Mr. Jack London's *The Call of the Wild*, the fine story of a noble dog named Buck, his journey from a life of abuse and suffering at the hands of men to the leader of a wolf pack, free and unbowed, as Nature intended him to be. I read *White Fang* by Mr. London and *A Dog's Tale* by Mr. Mark Twain and what other dog stories Captain had from time to time come upon in his thievery, and I had enjoyed them. I'd long thought that dogs would prove to be more loving and loyal—even wiser—than the human beings I had known. Now that fortune had brought kinder and more generous people into my life, I hoped only that any dog I came to know would be their equal.

"His name's Rafael," Gertrude said. "He's German. He worked as a shepherd before he came to us."

"He is a shepherd," Isadora clarified, "but he never worked as one. He was bred for motion pictures, and he's as handsome as Rin Tin Tin, handsome and very smart, but he can't act."

"He could if he wanted to," Gertrude elaborated. "He just can't be a phony the way actors are. He can't pretend to be afraid or vicious or dumb because he isn't any of those things."

"He's a killer," Harry declared.

Isadora had no patience for such talk. "Don't be absurd."

"Rafael is a pissafist," Gertrude said.

"Pacifist," said Isadora.

Harry grew insistent. "He could be a killer if he needed to be. If some bloodthirsty Huns came down from the hills with submachine guns to murder us all, you better believe Rafael would for sure kill them."

"Harold," Isadora said with a sigh, "the Huns were defeated twelve years ago. It was all over after the Battle of the Marne, before you were even born."

"That's how much you know," Harry said with disdain. "The Marne was in June. The Battle of Belleau Wood was in July, and nothing was close to over until the end of September, after the Battle of the Bulge."

"All right, but that was in Europe, not here."

"The Huns never give up," Harry warned. "Lots of them came to the States after the war. Some of them are up in the hills with submachine guns, just waiting."

I interrupted this discussion of recent history. "Where is this would-be killer, failed actor, and never-was sheep herder? I can't wait to meet him."

"We put him in the school bathroom," Isadora said, "until we had all met you."

Miss Blackthorn said, "He really is gentle and well behaved, but he's big and he looks a bit fierce. We didn't want to scare you. Now that you've been prepared, I'll get him."

As the teacher approached the door to the bathroom, Franklin said, "Rafael is just two, so he can still behave somewhat like a puppy. But he's becoming a responsible gentleman and patrols the perimeter on the ground floor each night before the children go to bed. He's very serious about the job. It's quite something to see."

Miss Blackthorn opened the lavatory door, and Rafael came into the schoolroom tentatively. He was God's dog, truly, too beautiful for this world, black across his neck and back and the top of his bushy tail, black around the muzzle, but otherwise a mélange of various shades of gold and copper, with here and there a lighter accent of biscuit brown. His ears were set high and erect, and the expression in his almond-shaped dark-brown eyes left no doubt that he was intelligent and alert.

He met my eyes briefly and then pretended indifference, but I knew I was nonetheless the subject of greatest interest to him. He felt obliged to make the rounds of his family, starting with Loretta and ending with Harry, sniffing them one by one, wagging his tail, allowing himself to be patted and stroked and cooed at as he made his way toward me. He stopped short and gazed up at me, his tail having gone still, his body taut. I felt that I was not only being studied but also analyzed. A dog's sense of smell is many thousands of times greater than that of a human being, and its nose brings it more information than do our five senses collectively. The children and their teacher could only speculate about the abnormalities that were concealed by my robe, but in that first inspection, Rafael came to know my physical nature perhaps more completely than did Loretta and Franklin even though they'd seen me bared upon a stage. I feared that the dog would find me too strange to trust or befriend me. Then he settled to the floor at my feet and rolled onto his back and offered me his tummy, his forepaws limp in a gesture of surrender.

Everyone laughed, and Franklin said, "Rafael, you are a very good judge of character."

"Alida," said Loretta, "your status as a member of the family is now official. You've been granted a four-paw rating."

I knelt beside my new friend. If having his belly stroked was a pleasure to him, it was a greater pleasure for me to attend him. My concern about not belonging at the Bram faded. If I were to number the best moments of my life, that first encounter with Rafael would be one of them—and not toward the bottom of the list.

When I rose and the shepherd got to his feet, Isadora asked, "Will you be joining the class with us, Alida? Miss Blackthorn is a stern taskmaster. She exhausts us. We suspect she was once a drill sergeant. But we learn so much, and we have a lot of fun."

I understood the girl's thinking. I was mere inches taller than she was and every bit as slight. Though I was seventeen, I appeared to be her contemporary. However, of all the places in the Bram where I might belong, this schoolroom was the least of them. Before I could think of a polite excuse for declining, Loretta said, "Alida isn't just seventeen. She's also quite well educated. She has other interests that she needs to pursue on her own."

Only when I saw Miss Blackthorn relax did I realize she had tensed at Isadora's suggestion that I might join the class. Her work was difficult enough, instructing three students of different ages in the same room at the same time. She might be stressed to add a fourth. I assumed the children were no longer sent to a public or a private school because sweet Gertrude had been ridiculed by those who found her hand a source of amusement. Children can be cruel. She would be safe here among her siblings, her self-esteem intact. I complimented Miss Blackthorn on her obvious talent for instruction. The children enjoyed being taught by her, and their comportment was impressive. The three were attentive and respectful toward her, but she had not repressed their youthful spirit. She seemed genuinely pleased by my words. Yet an aspect of her expression and a sharpness in her eyes suggested she was suspicious of me. Experience—and many novels—had taught me that if people regard you with suspicion when no credible reason exists to do so, they are keeping from you a secret that you need to know and that it is they who have earned suspicion.

FOURTEEN

While Loretta and Franklin attended to business matters, I found my way back to my second-floor suite, which I'd seen during the tour. Living room, bedroom, bath, and walk-in closet—they all seemed even larger than when I first explored them. A bag containing my small wardrobe—much more would be coming from Marjorie Merrimen and Giovanni Leone over the next week or two—lay open on my bed. I put things away in dresser drawers, including a long nightshirt in a soft material that was nonetheless concealing.

For a time I sat in the living room, admiring the furniture. I tested the sofa, the armchairs, the straight-backed side chairs, and all were comfortable. Nothing in the room was an expression of me, but I didn't mind. I'd never lived in a room that you could walk into and see anything that declared, *This is Alida's place.* If given license to change things, I'd have had no idea what to do. Who was I, after all, but books well remembered and memories well forgotten?

I closed my eyes for a moment's rest and saw Captain sitting on my sofa beside an albino man with long white hair. The pink-eyed albino listened intently, nodding.

I erupted from the chair. So vivid had been the image that I half expected to find unwanted company. I was alone. I must have dozed off for a minute. A little daymare. Nothing more.

Two windows provided views of the back-acre gardens, perhaps two-thirds of the property, and between them was a French door. I stepped onto a balcony and listened to birds singing in the pepper trees. I could see fountains and winding paths, statuary and a small pavilion, all the way to the bungalow at the end of the estate. I'd always lived at ground level in the carnival. When Captain and I traveled and stayed in motels, he booked us into first-floor rooms even if there was a second story, as though he believed it wise always to be able to make a quick exit. As I stood there, a strange sensation overcame me. With a wall only at my back, with warm sunlight all around and empty air between me and the limestone terrace twenty feet below, I felt at peace, as if I belonged here more than anywhere else in the Bram. If I were to climb onto the balustrade and step into the void, would I at last be in my element? This was not just a thought but also an urge. I definitely was not contemplating suicide, which is a most heinous act, selfish and blasphemous. Rather, I felt that if I better understood myself, I could step forward into a freedom beyond my fondest dreams. As I warned you, it was a strange sensation, and it passed quickly.

To properly accommodate the children and because Loretta and Franklin were often early to bed in order to meet production calls at studios, dinner was at five thirty. Having freshened up by five o'clock, I saw an opportunity to make the acquaintance of the chef, Mr. Luigi Lattuada, who was by then surely busy in the kitchen. My suite was but a few steps from the back staircase. The moment I opened the stair door to descend, I found myself in a rising draft of smells so delicious that my mouth watered. We had eaten a late breakfast at the Beverly Hills Hotel, but the day had been so busy that we'd not had time for lunch.

The clatter of cookware rose in that vertical passage, and I hurried down to meet the wizard who could conjure such wonderful aromas.

Luigi combined with Lattuada led me to believe that the chef would be as Italian as Enrico Caruso or even Ettore Boiardi, who was maybe the most famous Italian in America since launching his hugely popular canned-pasta products almost three years earlier, under the Chef Boyardee brand. Overseeing the steaming pots and sizzling pans, however, was a tall, broad-shouldered gentleman as handsome as Mr. Duke Ellington, the composer and band leader whose music was on the radio and whose photo I'd seen in a magazine. I excused myself for intruding and explained that I was looking for Mr. Lattuada of whose cooking I had heard such good things. He said, "As unlikely as it may seem, I am the highly praised Lattuada, previously of Milan and Genoa. And you must be Princess Alida, about whom one likewise hears only good things."

"Oh, I'm no princess, just a commoner who has somehow fallen down a chimney into paradise. If you don't mind my asking, what is your accent? You don't sound Italian."

"I have a British accent because my dear mother is a Jamaican educated in London, where she met my father, who is Italian." As Mr. Lattuada talked, he remained in motion, making sure no pot boiled over, peeking through an oven-door window, plucking a bottle of cream from a Frigidaire. "They moved to Italy, opened a restaurant, and created me. I grew up speaking English with my mother's accent, Italian with my father's accent, and very bad French."

"I find that fascinating," I said. "All those faraway places I will never see. Are there many like you in Italy?"

"Cooks? Oh, many cooks. Many, many. If you mean Italians who speak with a British accent—not so many."

I blushed. "That was rude of me. I'm sorry. I didn't mean to be. My manners are self-taught, and obviously I haven't been the best teacher."

"Ah, you mean are there many Negroes in Milan and Genoa. Well, not so many that horsemen wearing white sheets have been inspired to set crosses on fire."

"Ku Klux Klan," I said. "I've read about them. They're terrible people."

Stirring something with a large wooden spoon, he said, "They're *among* the worst, but as you will learn, this world provides us with a variety of worst people, each group with its own obsessions."

"I've known some of them. One in particular. He valued his own life but no one else's."

Mr. Lattuada paused in his stirring and regarded me with what might have been sympathy and surprise. "I'm sorry to hear that."

"He was, I believe, what Mr. Freud would call a psychopath, although I suspect the whole psychology thing is only the littlest bit more useful than the advice provided by tarot cards."

He put his spoon aside and adjusted the gas flame under the pot and said, "If I may be as rude as you so recently were—how old are you, child?"

"You're funny, Mr. Lattuada. I mean that in the best way. I mean you're funny if that's what you intend to be. If that's not your intention, I apologize. I'm seventeen."

"Indeed, I have a sense of humor. I am revealed and cannot now pretend to be dour and humorless like the French chefs I have known. I imagined you were at most thirteen, but as you've talked, I see my error."

"I'm small for my age. There's not much chance I'll ever be taller. From my perspective, you're enormous but not terrifying."

"Did you expect me to be terrifying?"

"It was a possibility. Mostly I expected you to be like Chef Boyardee, with a little mustache and a tall white hat."

"I tried a mustache, but I looked ridiculous. My tall white hat I left in Genoa. Now you best skedaddle, or I'll be so distracted I'll burn your dinner."

"It's been a pleasure meeting you."

"So it has. You are always welcome in my kitchen."

A butler's pantry separated his domain from the dining room. As I reached that door, I looked back at him, and he was staring after me. I said, "The Bram seems like the New Jerusalem, does it not?"

"It does indeed."

"The New Jerusalem wouldn't have even just one of the worst kind of people, would it?"

He was silent for several seconds. Then he said, "No, it should not. If ever you smell one, you pay me a visit and tell me who the scent comes from."

I gave some silence back to him before I said, "It's not you. Maybe it's not anyone. I won't pretend my nose is always reliable."

When I passed through the spacious butler's pantry into the dining room, I found that Mrs. Symington was setting the table for the family dinner. The three maids serving under her had just left for the day. When I asked whether I could help, she showed me how to fold the linen napkins so they made an impression equally as elegant as the china and silverware.

"Franklin sits at the west end of the table, Loretta at the east. Forgive me if it seems odd for a housekeeper to use their first names, but they insist on it. Now that we've four children, two of you will sit on the north side and two on the south."

"Where should I sit?" I asked as I worked with the napkins.

"In the south chair closest to Loretta. The conundrum is how we decide who sits next to you without causing a general consternation among the urchins. Each has come to me separately to insist on being your companion at table."

"Really? Why ever would it matter to them?"

"You are the newcomer, and newcomers are always mysterious and exotic. Plus I understand that you made quite an impression on them

92

in the schoolroom—and on our darling Rafael. May I suggest you be first to table and stand behind your chair, with a firm grip on it, to avoid the anticipated collisions. They will no doubt burst into the room in high competition, and the chair next to yours will be occupied by the most determined. If Loretta and Franklin want to become involved, let them take the risk, not you or me."

"When will you have dinner?" I asked.

"Certainly not this early. Happily we don't have stage calls to meet, as our employers do. Julian and I will clear the table, rinse the dishes, and stack them for Anna May to wash in the morning. Then we shall have dinner in the kitchen with Chef Luigi."

"I suspect Mr. Lattuada is a good dinner companion," I said.

"Your suspicion is well placed. He's a rare man and friend."

"The Bram is such an amazing house. Huge. It's a good thing you have such helpful ladies like Lynette, Harmony, and Anna May. Anna May seems very serious about her job. She must be a hard worker."

Mrs. Symington looked at me sideways as she placed the last butter knife on the last bread plate.

I'd been too obvious. Anna May had seemed to be anxious and perhaps preoccupied by thoughts of some trouble in her life outside of Bramley Hall. I'll admit my judgment was based on nothing more than intuition, which also told me that her trouble might in some way become mine, too.

In the carnival, the fortuneteller, Madam Zena, had for a while taken an interest in me. Her behavior had been too peculiar to be called friendship. She was strangely insistent about spending time with me, trying to instruct me in matters such as palm reading and crystal gazing, in which I had no interest. When I could not divine her motivation or intentions, I became uneasy and broke off the relationship as politely as I knew how. Sometimes I wonder if Zena might not have been the fraud she seemed to be and if some of the power she claimed to possess might have rubbed off on me.

"They're all good girls," Mrs. Symington said. "Anna May has been through a rough patch, but she's coming out the other side. If she seemed a little cold toward you, she'll warm up in time. Don't take it personally. She's a lovely person."

"I understand rough patches," I assured her, "how sometimes they come one after the other until you begin to think there will never be an end to them. It's nice of you to share as much with me. I don't need to know more. I didn't need to know even that much."

She met my eyes with a probing directness. "I believe you're an insightful girl, Alida. Insightful and thoughtful and kind. I'm pleased you're here in the Bram, and I've no doubt this will be a better place for your presence."

FIFTEEN

No experience in my life had been closer to perfection than my first dinner at the Bram. The food was marvelous, the conversation lively. The autumn twilight purpled the world beyond the windows so that the candlelight grew more magical course by course. Having won the chair beside me, Harry proved to be gracious enough to thumb his nose at his sisters only once when the appetizer was served and once again as we received the entrée. As welcome here as anywhere in the house, Rafael lay in a corner, watching us with interest, certainly not an advocate of the rule that he must never be served from the table but nonetheless obedient and hopeful. Because I had read so many English novels, I knew which fork to use for what purpose and was not surprised when the salad came after the entrée, before the dessert.

Prior to retiring to my suite, I visited the library to borrow a copy of *Barchester Towers* by Anthony Trollope. The day had been so long and tiring, so filled with event, that it seemed as if Tuesday had folded all of Wednesday into itself. After I prepared for bed and donned my lovely new nightdress, I found that I would rather dream than read. When I switched off the nightstand lamp, I turned my head to the windows and saw, beyond the pale shape of the balustrade, nothing but a sky full of stars, as if the great house were untethered from Earth and floating serenely in the vastness of the universe.

I dreamed of Bramley Hall, though my mind reorganized the order of its many rooms, changed some elements of the decor, made the big house even larger, and replaced its electric lights with candles throughout. I was searching for someone I couldn't name, but the residence seemed to be deserted. The eerie quiet was disturbed only by the click-click-click of a dog's claws on stone floors or the soft padding of paws on a Persian carpet. Wherever I looked, Rafael was not there, yet I sensed him in the shadows and somehow knew we were searching the Bram for the same person, not for any member of the family, but for someone who did not belong there. At one point, I dreamed that I woke—which had been a feature of previous dreams—and that someone stood at my bedside, gazing down at me as I lay in the pallid light of the risen moon. In a voice thick with sleep, I murmured, "Are you there?" She whispered, "No," and turned away into the darkness. "Who?" I muttered, but I knew, for even from that one word I recognized Anna May's voice. She was surely a figment of my slumbering mind. She couldn't be there, for she was not on staff at night and lived off the estate. I faded from a dream of being awake and again into the funhouse-like distortion of the Bram, searching through pulsing candlelight with unseen Rafael always nearby.

Wednesday, Thursday, and Friday were sunny settling-in days, as Tuesday had been. I familiarized myself with the estate and embraced whatever opportunities arose to interact with family and members of the staff. If this was to be my world, I wanted to know it end to end and top to bottom, understand every nuance of its operation.

The most interesting—and to a degree unsettling—conversation of that period occurred on Thursday, when I kept company with Harmony for an hour as she stalked through my quarters like a long-legged red-haired freckled stork. Among other things, she was assigned to clean my rooms and service them daily. Twice I'd made my bed in the morning before going to breakfast. Now she made it clear, gently but firmly, that I must not relieve her from any chore that was hers. "The children's parents require them to make their bed, but not the adults. It's a hard world right now, Alida, even in this golden state of milk and honey. Five million have lost work, and others will soon. Loretta and Franklin are more generous than makes sense. I will never find another job as sweet as this. You may put your laundry in the hamper yourself, if you must, but leave everything else to me." I explained I hadn't intended to put her livelihood in jeopardy, that I made the bed because I enjoyed doing so. Until the Bram, I'd never had a bed of my own, only a lumpy mattress on the floor, one sheet, and one blanket. "Well, knock me down with a mop!" she declared. "Is that true, girl?" I had no idea what she meant by the mop, but I assured her I wasn't fabricating anything. Anyway, it wasn't a hardship except when there were rats. Harmony said, "I've known rats of both kinds, the two- and four-legged varieties, but I've never had to sleep with either species. You must have quite an up-from-under story, here now at the Bram." She heard the curiosity in her voice and said, "Don't listen to me. I must have been a cat in nine other lives and still have some feline blood. Your past is yours, and I've no right to it. That's been explained to us in a most sincere fashion, and I take the instruction seriously. Five million out of work. You understand?"

"Perfectly," I said. "Anyway, I'm not keen on reliving any of it. They say the past is never really past, but I'm going to prove them wrong. I'm all about what happens next, not what happened then. I can't believe my luck, Harmony. Do you believe God is in control, and He works everything out for the best? I do. But then it seems blind luck has so much to do with it. Loretta and Franklin being where they were on the particular night they were, having the means and the desire to do what they did for me. Mr. Einstein says God doesn't play dice with the universe, and he ought to know, I guess."

As she hung fresh towels in my bathroom and I watched her from the open doorway, Harmony said, "God's got it all covered, but He has to allow luck because people have free will. People make our luck, Alida, our good luck and bad, by what they do that turns our lives one way or the other. It was the same people that slammed me with the worst bad luck ever and at the same time good luck that saved my life. It was all so stupid crazy, tragedy and comedy all twined together. It was as ridiculous as one of those movie jokes where some guy gets one foot stuck in a bucket and stomps around like a fool, hilarious as anything—but then he falls down the stairs and breaks his neck."

"Tell me. Tell me everything." Stories were what had kept me sane, taught me how to live, how to survive, how to hope. Harmony's story sounded like one I needed to hear. I wasn't the kind of person to whom stories happened. My life had been cloistered, shut in if not shut away. Stories had always been for reading. Now they were also for gathering from others that I could write of them. "Please tell me, Harmony."

"I probably shouldn't."

"You're not supposed to ask about my past," I said, "but it's okay for me to ask about yours. Nobody told me I couldn't. So tell me, Harmony. Please. I won't lose my job, and neither will you."

She said, "And what job is it you have?"

"Well, if I have one, it's to annoy the hell out of you." She laughed. I said, "Unless it's painful. I don't want to upset you."

"It was painful at the time. Devastating. But that was in 1919, a lot of years ago. The pain mostly fades when you have enough years to pore over the absurdity of the thing."

While she wiped down the vanity mirror and the sink below it, she talked me back to Boston, where she had lived in 1919.

Harmony had been twenty, a talented pianist who provided music for customers as they shopped in the city's finest department store. "I also performed livelier music in a nightclub the year before prohibition. In those days, it wasn't a thing many women would set their mind to do, but I had a bit of dreamer in me, which some called a bit of devil. I expected to secure work in one of the dance bands that were achieving success as the popularity of jazz grew."

On January 15, 1919, a Wednesday, Harmony was celebrating her twentieth birthday, having taken off work at the department store to enjoy a long lunch with her parents at a restaurant in Boston's commercial district. Shortly past noon, at the Purity Distilling Company, a fifty-foot-high iron holding tank exploded. People in the vicinity were killed by shrapnel, but that was only the first wave of death and destruction. Instinctively, Harmony broke into a run, but her mother and father halted and turned to look back.

"When I realized they weren't with me," she said, pausing in her cleaning to stare into the vanity mirror, "I stopped and turned and shouted at them to run. The explosion had killed the driver of a Purity delivery van, which came hurtling down the street, a runaway Ford, wide of my parents but angling toward me. Beyond the truck, farther uphill, something strange was happening, but it didn't make sense—what I was seeing—and the truck was my first concern. I'd passed the firehouse before I looked back, and now I dodged into a service passage between the next two buildings. The truck went past and crashed into something, so I didn't need to keep running, but panic had hold of me because of the horses, the screaming horses."

She fell silent. Although she still gazed into the mirror, I suspected she didn't see her reflection. "The horses were screaming. There were still some horse-drawn wagons in those days," she said. "Not a great many, most of them owned by businesses resistant to the cost of motorization. It's a horrible sound—the terror of helpless animals. I thought they'd been frightened by the explosion, only the explosion, and yet I didn't turn back. On some deep level, I must have begun to realize what it meant, the strange thing I had seen farther uphill, what was coming. There was a fire escape, a switchback ladder, on the three-story building to my right, and I climbed it frantically, all the way to the top."

Harmony's account of the flood was succinct but vivid. In a tremendous gush, the ruptured tank poured out two million gallons of molasses. The tidal wave was said to have been at least fifteen feet high, with the power of a freight train. A few buildings were swamped by the surge. Several firemen were trapped and buried in the sludge. Twenty-one people perished, and forty were badly injured.

"My mother and father were knocked off their feet and swept down the street and slammed into the firehouse. They died. Screaming horses, screaming people—and through all of it, the sweet smell of molasses so overwhelming you could hardly get your breath." Harmony turned from the mirror to me. "Because they believed prohibition would soon pass and their investment would be worth nothing, Purity had deferred maintenance on the tank. You could say Purity killed my folks, or you might even say it was prohibition that killed them, but however you look at it, God wasn't to blame. It was bad luck. And by their decisions and their actions, other people make our bad luck—and good luck—for us. My good luck was that runaway Purity truck chasing me out of the path of the wave, and that too was because of the deferred maintenance and the threat of coming prohibition. What do you make of all that, Alida?"

I stood in the bathroom doorway, benumbed by the one-two punch of tragedy and absurdity. "I don't know. I mean, it's so . . . so awful. How could it mean anything?"

She said, "But it does. Everything is meaningful. Everything. Even death by molasses, as silly as it sounds. But it's like what we're being told is in a language we don't know, and we have to translate it somehow, puzzle it out from a word here and there."

She took a deep breath, blew it out. "Enjoy life—that's what I learned. But stay alert. Always trust in the rightness of the world. But stay alert. Never be bitter or despairing. Life is a great gift. Love and mercy are the promise of life. But stay alert. Remember everything we do spins off good luck and bad luck for other people, so don't do what's obviously stupid or wicked. Eleven years, and that's all I've got. It's more than nothing, but it doesn't seem like much."

A few minutes later, when she had finished with my rooms, as I accompanied her to the hall door, I said, "You were a pianist. You were going to be in a big band. Why did you . . . ?"

"Why am I here instead, a housemaid? My bad luck had two parts that day, with the good luck in between. I lost my parents, but I was saved. Then on the top flight of the fire escape, I stumbled. The treads were open metalwork, and some had been partly eaten away by rust. I grabbed at a higher tread to keep from falling backward, hooked my hands through the holes. In that moment, my feet went out from under me. All my weight suddenly hung from my fingers. Three on one hand snapped, two on the other." She held up her elegant hands for examination, fingers spread, as if she were a magician assuring the audience nothing was concealed, that the imminent appearance of a dove must therefore be true magic, not a mere trick. "They look all right. They work okay, but okay isn't good enough."

My expression must have conveyed a tortured sympathy, for she smiled and said, "I'm happy, Alida. As happy as I've ever been. I refuse to be unhappy." With her red hair, green eyes, freckles, and broad smile, she seemed to emit a light of her own. "I love this family. I love the people I work with. I have a young man I love, and he loves me. Other people make our luck, yes, but we make some of it ourselves. If we're not always where we want to be, we can find a way to want to be where we are."

"I want to be here," I said. "I've always wanted to be here, but I didn't know how to find it. Then it found me."

She regarded me in silence for a moment and then said, "But?"

I nodded slowly. "I want to be here. This is where I belong. I'm safe here, happy here—but I'll stay alert."

"Stay alert, Alida." She stepped into the hall and pulled the door shut behind her.

Throughout the rest of Thursday and most of the following day, no need arose to stay alert for impending death by molasses or any lesser threat. At eleven o'clock Friday night, I was wearing my nightdress, curled cozily in an armchair in my living room, reading *Barchester Towers*. Earlier in the day, my first two pairs of custom-made shoes had been delivered by an employee of Mr. Giovanni Leone. Shaped to my feet, as soft as slippers but with firm soles, they laced up to where my ankles met my calves, giving reliable support where it seemed that my thin bones, if exposed to sudden severe strain, were most likely to fracture one day, though they had never yet troubled me. I had just turned the page to Chapter Twenty-Four when someone rapped softly on my door. Because of the late hour, I thought, *Stay alert*, and put my book aside on the lamp table.

I had long been of the habit of concealing my abnormalities when not on a stage. Those who paid to satisfy their sick curiosity deserved to have their sleep disturbed by what they'd seen, but I was careful to avoid shocking those who, quite innocently, might get an intimate glimpse of so much as my hands. Even alone in my rooms, I wore a new pair of the elbow-length gloves sewn by Miss Marjorie Merrimen, and the long sleeves of my nightdress provided double concealment. Thus attired, I arrived at the door just as the soft rap-rap-rap came again.

"Who's there?"

"Clyde Tombaugh," a girl said just loud enough for her voice to penetrate the door. "Clyde Tombaugh," said another girl, and a young boy confirmed, "Clyde Tombaugh."

When I opened the door, I was not surprised to discover that, in spite of the late hour, the Fairchild children stood in the dark hallway. They were dressed in pajamas, barefoot, obviously intent on something other than a courtesy visit. Each child held an Eveready flashlight with the lens under his or her chin so that the up light distorted facial features into a spooky mask. Rafael sat before them, facing me; he did not have a flashlight.

"We are here," Isadora whispered, "to invite you to join our club."

"What club is that?"

"The Clyde Tombaugh Club."

"Would you like to come in and tell me about it?"

"No," Gertrude whispered. "We need to get on with discovering while Mom and Dad are asleep and drooling all over their pillows."

"They don't drool," Isadora said disapprovingly.

"Well, *I* drool in *my* sleep," Gertrude said.

"Of course *you* do."

"I inherited night drooling."

"Nobody inherits drooling."

"Just because you're twelve doesn't mean you know everything."

In the manner of all long-suffering older sisters, Isadora sighed with exasperation.

I returned them to the main subject. "What do the members of the Clyde Tombaugh Club hope to discover?"

"The darkest truths of the Bram," said Harry. "Where did the suicide occur? Why is it never spoken of? Was it really a suicide, or was it murder? Is what we've seen a ghost or is it a sinister stranger living secretly among us? This is a house of a thousand secrets."

"It doesn't seem like such a place," I said.

Lowering her voice to an even softer whisper, Gertrude said, "Houses of a thousand secrets never seem like what they really are. If they seemed like what they are, why, then they wouldn't have any secrets. Isn't that right, Izzy?"

"What would I know about it?" Isadora replied. "I'm only twelve years old. I don't know everything."

Being a boy of action, Harry was impatient to get on with the night's adventure. "Are you in the club or not, Alida? Are you with us or not? Maybe you think this is just a stupid game, but it isn't. This is serious business. Our future hangs by a thread. A spider's thread. Are you with us or not?"

They lowered their Evereadys and stood in a puddle of light, staring at me expectantly. Rafael cocked his head and fixed me with his amber-brown eyes as if to say, *Well?*

I was five years older than Isadora, eight years older than Harry. Under other circumstances, that difference in ages would have been an unbridgeable gap. I was an adult, and graybeards like me could be expected to mock anything like the Clyde Tombaugh Club. But they had been told to treat me like a sister, which to a degree defined me as different from other adults. And my smallness made me seem less like an adult than like a child. To be mortared into this family as securely as a stone in a wall, I must win the trust and affection of these children. With a mind that was a library of beloved stories, I could commit to make-believe with no less enthusiasm than Isadora, Gertrude, and Harry.

He pressed me again. "Are you with us or not, Alida?"

"I'm with you," I declared.

Could it be that I was welcome in this new nest, welcome beyond my fondest hopes? Were we four children now birds of a feather, five if we counted Rafael, floating down the warm California days in a future of peace and grace?

My companions responded to my words with four smiles and one wagging tail.

"Grab your flashlight and let's go," Harry said.

"Go where?"

"Wherever the terrible truth lies," he said, for he had read his share of boy's adventure novels.

And I knew the best thing I could do was stay alert always and everywhere.

SIXTEEN

Eventually I would learn that the Clyde Tombaugh Club was named for Clyde William Tombaugh, an astronomer who'd recently discovered the planet Pluto. His achievement inflamed the Fairchild children's imagination, which had already been burning brightly. The year had introduced us to Wonder Bread, Mott's applesauce, pinball machines, windshield wipers, and the first supermarkets. But nothing could thrill youngsters more than the revelation of another planet out beyond Saturn, beyond Neptune, a new world on which they would never set foot and to which they could therefore attribute a most colorful zoology of both enchanting and terrifying creatures. They had already been embarked on a mission to uncover the secrets of the Bram, if there were any. The glory of Tombaugh's discovery inspired them to rename their group, which they had previously called the J. Edgar Hoover Society.

So it was that I found myself hurrying with my adopted siblings along the main second-floor hall as the last hour of Friday ticked toward midnight. Eventually I would learn all the rules by which successful investigations must be conducted. At that point, however, I had been informed of only two tactics. First, when running—and we would often be running when we weren't stealthily creeping—we must not leap like gazelles or charge in the manner of stampeding cattle. The cavernous spaces of the residence were conducive to echoes that might betray us even though their hardworking mother and father were said to "sleep like Egyptian dead under the ancient pyramids." To make as little noise as possible, Isadora and Gertrude and Harry were barefoot on these adventures, but I could not be seen without the concealment of shoes. Second, flashlights were essential to navigate the maze of passageways and the many chambers of abysmal darkness safely, but one must at all times keep one's finger on the switch. At the first noise—the creak of door hinges, a footfall, a cough, a stifled sneeze—that betrayed a presence elsewhere in the house, our Evereadys must be doused in an instant.

Either Rafael had been schooled in the need for quiet or canine instinct informed him of it. His nails never clicked on stone or wood, and the pads of his paws didn't thump on the Persian carpets as had been the case in my dream. He glided along as though he had studied the prowling technique of cats, and he seemed even to make an effort to suppress his panting.

By eight o'clock or so, after Chef Lattuada and the Symingtons had taken dinner together in the kitchen, they always retired to the bungalow and did not return until morning. The other employees were away at their own homes. Although there were four of us in the Clyde Tombaugh Club and though Loretta and Franklin would wake and respond if we had reason to scream for help, the Bram seemed to be a lonely place at that hour, dangerously so, like an abandoned monastery or a forsaken mausoleum. As we swarmed down the grand staircase, across the reception hall, and through a series of rooms, flashlight beams fencing with the gloom, I couldn't escape the feeling we were not as safe as we assumed we were. A mild, crawly sensation of supernatural menace overcame me, and I chastised myself for indulging it. If some threat arose, whether an otherworldly entity or a mere burglar, good Rafael had the sharp teeth and the canine courage to deal with it.

Our first destination proved to be in the basement, which had not been on the tour that Loretta and Franklin had given me. Instead of a stair-head door, access to this subterranean vault was through a legless Japanese cabinet more than four feet wide and over seven feet tall, a black-lacquered beauty lightly ornamented with a dozen butterflies rendered in gold leaf. This hulking and yet delicate piece stood against the end wall of a corridor. Isadora opened the doors, revealing a black interior with three empty shelves. She felt for a hidden release, whereupon the shelves swung away, as did the back wall of the cabinet to which they were attached. She stepped inside and was suddenly silhouetted by a light that came from the secret realm beyond, into which she proceeded. Gertrude followed her sister, and Harry ushered me after them. Beyond the back wall of the cabinet lay a wide landing and concrete steps leading down between rustic stone walls. At the bottom, a formidable oak door succumbed to a key that Isadora produced from a pocket of her pajamas. As Rafael wended among us, we passed through the door and into a chamber that was illuminated by a chandelier in the form of six little bronze men holding light bulbs shaped like candle flames. The basement did not extend under the entire house but was only about twenty by thirty feet. The walls were lined with wine racks that held hundreds of bottles of the most desirable product of France.

"Mother and father," Gertrude assured me, "are not alcoholics, and they aren't crazy-violent bootleggers either. They don't own even one machine gun."

"Maybe one," said Harry.

Dismissing him with a wave of her hand, Isadora said, "They just sometimes like to have wine with their dinner, especially when they're entertaining guests. Thinking people must not sacrifice all expressions of elegance on the altar of the Anti-Saloon League."

As Rafael sniffed along the rows of bottles as if appreciating the fine Bordeauxs and Burgundys, Isadora opened a shallow drawer in a center table. She removed napkins, various corkscrews, and a small glass aerator. When the drawer was empty, she withdrew it and turned it upside down on top of the table. A plastic sleeve had been glued to the bottom. From that she withdrew an eight-by-ten envelope and opened the clasp and spilled a few items from it.

"What is this?" I asked.

"Evidence. We hide it here so that it can't be easily found and destroyed."

"Evidence of what?"

"Evidence of the darkest secrets of the Bram," Harry said.

Gertrude explained further. "Evidence of nefesterous deeds."

"Nefarious," Isadora corrected.

"That's how snippy twelve-year-olds say it," Gertrude replied, "not how everyone says it."

With one finger, Isadora tapped a wallet-size photograph of a man in his thirties. He had curly hair, thick eyebrows, a droopy mustache, and a stern expression. "We found this in a game box, the Landlord's Game, which we like to play. It was stuck to the jail square. It had never been there before, but at first we didn't realize someone had intentionally put it there for us to find."

"Who?"

"That remains an ongoing mystery."

"And who is this guy?" I asked, indicating the photo.

"We're not sure, but we suspect he's François Le Clerc."

"Who is François Le Clerc?"

Isadora passed a one-column four-inch-long newspaper clipping to me. "Two weeks later, this fell out of Gertie's hat when she was getting dressed in her Sunday best."

"It's the prettiest hat in America," Gertrude said. "It's got blue ribbons and silver fringe all around the band, and a little yellow bird."

The clipping reported that François Maurice Le Clerc, 36, of Santa Monica, had been sentenced to a prison term of fifteen years following his recent conviction for voluntary manslaughter in the death of Martin S. Leveret. Before being removed from the courtroom, he had disparaged the judge with a series of words, none of which could be printed in a reputable newspaper. At the bottom of the clipping was the date August 14, 1929.

Harry had been studying for his role as Sherlock. "Quote—'Voluntary manslaughter—the unlawful killing of a human being without malice, either expressed or implied, without deliberation, upon a sudden heat of passion, or otherwise during the commission of an unlawful or lawful act without due caution and circumspection.' End quote. If there's malice, then it's murder, so this Le Clerc guy maybe wasn't feeling malice, but he was sure feeling something."

"Who put this in your hat?" I asked Gertrude.

"We don't know, but we're going to find out if it's the last thing we ever do."

Rafael appeared tableside and grumbled as if in agreement.

"Just one month after the hat," Isadora continued, "on October fourteenth of this year, Harry found *this* placed like a bookmark in something he was reading." She held up a small photo of a flat-faced man with an uncertain smile and the myopic gaze of someone striving to pass—but failing—an eye exam. "We suspect this might be Martin S. Leveret, the victim of François Le Clerc, though we haven't been able to confirm our suspicions."

"What book was it in?" I asked Harry.

"*The Wise Man's Poker Strategies* by Albert Roy Bluffer, also known as Albuquerque Al, published in 1872 and still in print. I'm going to be a professional poker player, chasing the game from San Antonio to

Santa Fe to Pascagoula—or maybe picking clean the gulls and grifters on paddle-wheel steamers up and down the Mississippi."

"Or a dentist," said Gertrude.

"Don't be ridiculous, Gertie. I'd never be a dentist. Who in his right mind would want to be a dentist?"

"Well, before Albuquerque Al, you were crazy about Dr. Sheldon Sarsaparilla and his book, *The History of Teeth*."

"His name wasn't Sarsaparilla. It was Solomonson."

"Whatever his name was, you carried that book everywhere. You slept with it under your pillow."

Glancing at me, blushing, Harry said, "A couple of my teeth fell out all of a sudden. I didn't understand about primary teeth and permanent teeth. I admit to being kind of scared. Not actually scared but kind of. I didn't want anyone to know. I thought they'd probably send me to the hospital and I'd never get out. I kept my mouth closed."

Isadora said, "We called that the Time of the Great Blessing."

Ignoring her, Harry said, "Once I learned all about teeth, I was okay. Dr. Sheldon Solomonson saved my sanity. But I never ever wanted to be a dentist."

Plucking a fourth item off the wine-cellar table, Isadora said, "So this was what started us on a truly serious investigation last July. Before then, we were just the dumb J. Edgar Hoover Society, running around in the wee hours when it wasn't a school night, being silly, with no real mystery, just stories we made up."

"I was never silly," Gertrude protested. "Anyhow, there was, too, a real mystery back then—the mystery of all the dead things."

"Probably that was no mystery," Isadora said, "although we pretended it was. That could maybe have been just Nature doing what she does, letting things die." When she unfolded the paper that she had picked up from the table, it proved to be about two feet by three feet. "This was a publicity sheet for a movie—*Darkmoor*

Lane. Our mother wrote it, and both she and Daddy produced it in 1928. It was released early '29, was well reviewed, did good business." One side of the sheet featured the title and a shout line: *Is it the road to happiness or a dead end?* There were credit lines for the director and producers. Below were romanticized portraits of the four featured players. "Last year," Isadora said, "Emil Jannings won as Best Actor—that new award they created—for *The Way of All Flesh* and *The Last Command*. I liked the second better than the first, and in that one William Powell was every bit as good. Clara Bow is the 'It Girl' everyone's been so gaga about. She can be very funny, but I predict trouble for her, maybe tragedy. Mary Pickford, a lovely person, can claim to be an enduring star. And Edmund Lowe is, as always, solidly Edmund Lowe."

At that point, I had never seen any of those actors' work, and in fact not one film, but I nodded along.

"The other side is what's important," Harry said. "Stop with all the name-dropping and show Alida the other side."

"What else would I do, Harold Percy Fairchild? Set fire to it instead?"

Gertrude giggled and informed me that Harry hated his middle name. "He sometimes threatens to change it to Hercules or Rex."

"It's not a threat," Harry corrected. "It's a promise."

The reverse of the publicity sheet featured a map of the route by which the fictional Darkmoor Lane wound through lonely hills from a town called Nonaville to an old, decaying windmill near the sea, with important landmarks of the drama identified along the way.

"This," said Isadora, pointing to neat red lettering next to the windmill, "is not original to the map. Someone added it to this copy."

The block lettering declared, Martin S. Leveret. dead.

"Where did you find this?" I asked.

"It was another Friday night," Harry said. "Mom and Dad had an early call for Saturday, so we were going on a ghost hunt. There aren't really any ghosts in the Bram. It was just a stupid game."

"It wasn't stupid," Gertrude disagreed. "It was fun. Anyhow, you don't know for sure there aren't ghosts in the Bram. There could be ghosts all over the place, just waiting to scare the bejesus out of us."

"When I snatched up my Eveready for the hunt," Isadora said, "it didn't weigh enough. Someone had removed the batteries, but I couldn't imagine who or why. When I unscrewed the end to slide fresh batteries into it, I found this publicity sheet folded and tightly rolled inside. This was the first clue left for us. We'd never heard of Martin Leveret before that. Since then, the other clues just keep showing up."

"We knew right away this was the start of a challenge," Harry said. "The hardest part is waiting for each new piece of the puzzle to show up. We're being taught the virtue of patience, I think."

Isadora nodded agreement. "Which is one reason we changed from the J. Edgar Hoover Society to the Clyde Tombaugh Club. You have to be clever to solve crimes, but you have to be clever and extremely patient to find a new planet."

I had felt uneasy since I was shown the photo of Le Clerc, if it was Le Clerc, and my uneasiness had grown. "Your parents can't be copasetic about this."

"They don't know. We haven't told them."

"Why on earth not?"

"We think it might probably be them. They're always telling us how important it is to exercise our imagination. After all, that's what they do. They're imagineers."

"I don't think it's them," I said. "There's something too dark about this to be them."

"If it's not them," said Harry, "then it must be someone on staff just having fun with us. We don't want to get anyone on the staff in trouble. Mom and Dad might do something rash."

"Your parents are the last people who would do anything rash." Then I thought of how they had paid Captain forty thousand dollars and taken a biological oddity like me into their home. "Well, maybe not the *last* to do something rash, but they'd be fair with whoever is doing this. No one would be fairer."

"They're very protective of us," Isadora said. "Schooling us at home, always shielding us from the seamy side of the motion-picture business. We hear things anyway. Or overhear."

Harry shook his head as if recollecting some astonishing gossip they had heard. "If you want to know, we scheme up situations where we can't help but overhear. We're not proud of it, but I'm pretty sure we're not going to stop, either."

"Don't you dare tell them, Alida," said Gertrude. "Don't you tell them how we snoop or about Martin Leveret and all that. If you tell them—I warn you, there'll be hell to pay."

"Gertie!" Isadora admonished. "No need to be so snappish. You could have said it in a nicer way, a Fairchild way."

Gertrude took a deep breath and exhaled extravagantly. "There. I blew the nasty demon out of me. He might come back, but I'm in control for now. Please, Alida, keep our secrets with us. We're naughty sometimes, but we're not downright evil."

"I would never betray you," I assured them. "Anyway, it's not my place to tell them. That's up to you. But I do think this weird stuff about Le Clerc and Martin Leveret is more worrisome than you think it is. I believe you ought to consider telling them about at least that much."

"We will take it under advisement," Isadora said.

Harry nodded solemnly. "We'll form a development committee of executives to explore the film potential of the idea."

"You can even be on the committee and have a vote," Gertrude proposed. "In fact, let's have a vote right now."

Returning the four pieces of evidence to the envelope, Isadora said, "All in favor of keeping Mother and Father in the dark about this, raise your hand." They all raised one hand. "All in favor of spoiling the fun and destroying the adventurous spirit of the Clyde Tombaugh Club, raise your hand."

I did not raise my hand. "All right, all right. Far be it from me to second-guess such a prestigious development committee. But when ruination befalls us, don't say I didn't warn you."

Rafael drew our attention with a prolonged, loud yawn. He sat in the doorway of the wine room, looking as profoundly bored and impatient as a cat.

"Okay, all right," Gertrude said. "It's time to take Alida up the secret stairs to the roof."

Harry pretended to be horrified. "You intend to throw her off the roof?"

"If I ever throw anyone off, it'll be you. But that would be pointless because you'd just bounce like a big, rubber dummy."

And so Isadora returned the drawer to the table and filled it with the corkscrews and other items she'd taken from it earlier, and we left the wine room, extinguishing the fake candles held aloft by the six little bronze men. We ascended into the Japanese cabinet and returned to the hallway. With midnight soon upon us, we flew through the dark house in pursuit of our flashlight beams, as quiet as the ghosts that—perhaps—did not exist within these walls.

Never in my life had I been as happy as I was in that moment. Maybe the Bram harbored someone with bad intentions, and maybe the "challenge" the children had accepted was something more sinister than a game. However, being allowed to indulge in girlish fun, compressing an entire childhood into a few months or a year before taking on the solemn responsibilities of adulthood, seemed not too much to ask. *To the roof!*

SEVENTEEN

I could not fathom why the stairs to the roof should be hidden from easy discovery, with the entrance through a greenhouse grotto.

The Bram had a conservatory with three tall, windowed walls and a domed glass ceiling of many panes with beveled edges through which sunlight descended as though in a rain of prismatic crystals, littering the limestone floor with geometric fragments of rainbow colors. At night, as now, it was a jungled darkness of palm trees, lush ferns of numerous varieties, rhododendrons, and more, twined through with clematis and wisteria and night-blooming jasmine. This cultured wildness drew the beams of our Evereadys into its feathery clefts and lacy lacunae, folding light away in its bowers, revealing little. Sprays of small orchids—white and pink—were the exception to the rule of gloom, seeming to glow with a radiance of their own when our electric torches revealed them.

The fourth wall was a work of cunning masonry disguised as a natural rock grotto about twenty feet wide, fifteen feet from front to back, and roughly eight feet from floor to ceiling. In the center of that space, a shallow pool glimmered with the lights we carried, like a magical lens through which we might look into a strange city extending deep beneath the Bram. At the back of this little cave, a doorless opening led to a circular staircase of concrete steps and painted walls.

Rafael appeared enthusiastic about a visit to the roof. He sprang ahead of us, taking the steps two and three at a time, at once disappearing around a turn, undaunted by a vertical race into blackness where our Evereadys could not reach. When we arrived at the top, we found him standing on a landing in front of a midnight-blue door that bore an image of a silvery moon encircled by a ring of stars, as though a mystical revelation lay beyond.

Isadora unlocked the door and crossed the threshold. I followed the others and discovered we'd come into a stair-head vestibule. As I stepped into the cool but pleasant night air, onto a large section of roof that was flat and rimmed by a parapet, I asked, "Why all this? Why not just normal stairs, a plain door?"

"Mother and Father," Isadora said, "wanted us to be raised in a place that teased our imagination and expanded our minds, a place that would be fun."

"What we all know," Gertrude added, "is they built it to tease their imagination, not just ours. They're old, smart, and busy—but they like having fun as much as we do, though they'll never say so."

"They aren't old," Isadora said. "They're just mature—though they're in love with the idea of childhood."

"That's why they make good movies," Harry said. "Groucho Marx was here for dinner last year with some other people, and he said, 'Kids, you little goats, the reason your parents make good movies is because they're basically children.'"

Isadora picked it up from there. "Groucho said, 'I don't like children, noxious little things, but I like your parents. I don't like the three of you. You're too small and far less sophisticated than I am. If you want me to like you, grow up. There's no guarantee that I'll like you, but as long as you don't become critics, there's a small chance of winning my approval.'"

Mr. Marx had made such a strong impression that Gertrude, too, remembered part of the conversation word for word. "He told us, 'I would say it's been nice meeting you, but I'm not a liar. Now stop your annoying babble. Go to your rooms. There are hungry bogeymen under your beds, and if you don't give them a chance to devour you, they'll come down here and eat *our* dinner.' He was funny. Isadora thinks he was nice. I'm not sure about that, but he was very funny."

"The thing is," Isadora explained, "Mother and Father want us to be what they weren't—and not go through what they went through. That's why the grotto and the hidden stairs and the Merlin door, which is what we call it. That's why the other quirky fun things about the Bram."

"'What they weren't, what they went through?'" I asked.

"What they've come through isn't for us to talk about. They'll tell you when the time is right, when you've settled in and all the legal hooey has been dealt with."

Even in an estate that seemed like Eden, in a beautiful house with exquisite finishes, with wonderful art and thousands of books, where there was compassion and friendship and love in abundance, a family history was likely to include dark chapters, sharp memories of suffering and even of despair. Such is the world.

We clicked off our Evereadys because the roof was bathed in moonlight. In spite of Mr. Thomas Edison's genius, which had for decades increasingly pressed back the darkness, Los Angeles and its many suburbs had not yet acquired sufficient glow to rob the night sky of its splendor. We moved around the observation deck, wondering at the sea of stars among which were planets in the millions and forever beyond discovery.

Standing beside me at the waist-high parapet, Isadora pointed to a thin ribbon of light in the west. The Bram was on an upland, and we were more than forty feet above the ground. From that high vantage point, we could see for miles, beyond all habitations, to where the moon pressed its reflection on the waters of the Pacific. "I'm going to cross all that one day," she declared. "I want to see Japan and China. I want to see India. I want to see everything."

Her ambition rendered me short of breath. I could understand the yearning to experience all that the world had to offer, but I could not imagine having the freedom or the agency to fulfill such ambition. With my deformities and limitations, the world would best become mine through books. I didn't want to see everything firsthand at whatever cost in misfortune, but instead to be safe from the many cruelties that were provided in greater abundance by new places and new people. I had been made for a cloistered life, and miraculously I had at last been delivered into the security of Bramley Hall. I was too grateful for this grace to be jealous of Isadora's ability to one day indulge in wanderlust.

The house featured pitched roofs to the north and south, attics with oculus windows, and chimneys. The only vertical element on the flat deck was in the center: a six-foot-tall obelisk mirrored on all four sides, supported by four stone balls resting on a black-granite plinth. Moonlight as pale as frost gathered on the mirrors, and the mystery of the thing was a magnetism that inevitably drew us to it. According to the siblings, the obelisk had no purpose other than to encourage them to marvel at it on a moonlit night, squint at it when it flared like a beacon in the sunshine, and fashion dreams around it, dreams that sometimes disturbed their sleep with delight and sometimes with terror. I wondered how many parents, even among those who had the financial resources, would go to such lengths as Loretta and Franklin had gone to kindle wonder in their children and fuel their imagination; I decided the answer was very few.

We didn't notice—but Rafael did—an item that had been tucked in the space between the plinth and the base of the obelisk, among the stone balls. The shepherd growled and first reared up to claw at the object with his forepaws, but then he thrust his snout into the gap and finessed an envelope out of it with his teeth. He dropped it at Isadora's feet and licked his chops. Picking up his offering, she sniffed and said, "It feels greasy, smells like bacon." Someone had assumed—or known—the children would take me to the roof during the night's adventure and had made sure Rafael would find what had been left for us by smearing it with a scent he couldn't ignore. Isadora put down her Eveready, and we focused our beams on her hands as she tore open the envelope. A label from a jar of Gerber baby food—pureed peas—slid into her left hand. She turned it over, but nothing was written on the back of it. The other puzzle pieces had suggested a larger picture that would prove sinister when complete; this message appeared unrelated to the previous four.

"Maybe," Gertrude suggested, "whoever's tormenting us is just someone who likes peas a lot."

"Nobody likes *pureed* peas," Harry said.

"Babies like them. Babies think Gerber is the bee's knees."

"Well, I'm pretty damn sure it's not some stupid baby leaving all these things for us to find."

"Don't say 'damn,' Harry."

"Ha! *You* just said it."

"This is creepy," Isadora said when she took a closer look at the front of the Gerber label. "See? The picture of the smiling little tyke? Someone blackened his eyes."

The eye sockets appeared empty, suggesting not that the chubby-cheeked symbol of the company was blind but rather that a malevolent presence lived within him, an entity with black eyes that could see as clearly in absolute darkness as in daylight.

"Maybe you should think about telling your parents, after all," I advised.

"No, no! Nuts to that," Harry said. "This isn't a threat. It's just spooky. It's still only a game. We go running to Mom and Dad, we'll look like big babies. I'm not a big baby, and I don't want to look like one. Any of you makes me look like a big baby, the wrath of Harry will crash down on you like the Katmai volcano crashed down on Alaska."

"'Wrath of Harry,'" Isadora said. "I shudder at the thought. Don't you shudder at the thought, Gertie?"

"I'll never sleep again," Gertrude said.

Harry snorted with disgust. "Why couldn't I have two brothers?"

"Relax, Katmai Harry," said Isadora. "There's no reason to tell mater and pater. Alida worries too much. That's what happens when you get to be seventeen. You start worrying too much. She's never going to tattle. She's true blue and loyal. The Clyde Tombaugh Club will find the miscreant who's been tormenting us and wring from him an explanation."

We stood staring at the label in Isadora's palm, transfixed. Like a visitant materializing from the spirit world, a great horned owl swooped low over our heads, startling us. As one, we doused our Evereadys. The huge bird, with a four-foot wingspan, soared to the steep roof of the south wing, settled on a chimney, and began to ask the eternal question of its kind. The night was crowned with stars, and the moon poured light as pale as skim milk into the mirrored obelisk. The air grew cold. Our exhalations shaped brief plumes. I sensed change of some kind coming. Rafael made the thin beseeching sound with which he expressed the need for affection, and I knew how he felt.

EIGHTEEN

Under the silence of the heavens, within the hush of the great house, having retreated to the kitchen where the Frigidaires softly hummed, by candlelight in the first hour of Saturday, the four of us gathered at the round table to eat Chef Luigi Lattuada's homemade peach ice cream. This frozen treat had been produced by a White Mountain ice cream freezer with a hand-crank churner, using ice and salt and cream and muscle. We enjoyed larger servings than the one we gave to Rafael, but he was happy with his portion and expressed his pleasure with a long sigh and an odorless fart.

Our conversation was minimal at first as we brooded about the disturbing, eyeless Gerber baby. Soon, however, the siblings were informing me about what they called the "Case of the Plethora of Dead Things," which had baffled the J. Edgar Hoover Society earlier in this same year. *Plethora* meant an overabundance, an excess. I doubted Sherlock Holmes—or especially Mr. Hoover—would have used such an uncommon word in the title of a case, but the siblings were proud of it. Isadora remained somewhat skeptical that a criminal type had been sneaking around and leaving dead creatures in places where they wouldn't ordinarily be found; she was willing to consider that it might have been just Nature in action. But Gertrude and Harry were still adamant that a clever trickster with a mysterious purpose had been behind it all, and their sister didn't rule out that possibility.

The previous March, in the first instance that suggested an evil-minded schemer at work, Gertie had been preparing for bed when she found a dead bird in the closet, in one of her slippers. She called Izzy to her room. Neither of them was able to explain to their satisfaction how a bird had come to be in a windowless space. They were mature young women, not repulsed by the tiny carcass. With respectful solemnity, they wrapped the dead bird in a lace-trimmed handkerchief, tied the hanky shut with a length of blue ribbon, and set it aside for burial in the morning.

The next grisly discovery came four days later. The Fairchild children were required by their parents to make their own beds in the morning and turn down the bedclothes every evening rather than leave those tasks to the housemaids, who were busy enough. As Isadora was preparing her bed one night, she found a dead mouse under her pillow. At that point she hadn't yet begun to wonder if this might just be Nature being Nature. Then and for weeks, she believed a villain must be in the house, engaged in skullduggery. In fact, she and Gertrude suspected their brother of being the culprit. However, because their parents schooled them in the moral imperative of having plenty of evidence before accusing anyone of anything, they remained mum, watched, waited, and plotted revenge in case it might be justified.

Five days later, Harry hurried them to his bathroom to see a dead mouse, this one curled in the water glass that stood on the apron of his bathroom sink. This exciting development gave them a yet more important reason not to report these incidents to Franklin and Loretta. Even good parents, fair and well meaning and with a sense of wonder, would take the investigation from their children and pursue it as an urgent inquisition, resolving the matter in short order. What was the fun in that? For more than a year, Izzy and Gertie and Harry had been late-night adventuring, inventing ghosts and vampires to chase down, devising dire mysteries for members of the J. Edgar Hoover Society to solve—and now a *real* mystery had sprung up around them. A drama. A puzzle. A *challenge.* Their self-respect, their integrity, their *honor* required them to pursue the truth of this situation themselves, for it was them, not their parents, on whom it had been bestowed. They could not shirk their duty.

Occasionally through April and mid-May, dead creatures appeared in unusual places. A second bird. A third mouse. Most distressing was a cute little rabbit, one of a spring litter, with blood around its nose and mouth but no wound. Then the plague ended. Bird, mouse, mouse, bird, mouse, rabbit. As time passed with no further cadavers, Isadora became more willing to conclude that perhaps no human agency had been responsible for these bizarre occurrences. If some twisted individual had been tormenting them with dead things, what was his purpose, what message was intended? No less than sane citizens, mad people had their motivations. If the purpose had been to frighten and disgust the Fairchild siblings, why stop? Lunatics weren't known for losing interest in their obsessions so easily.

Now, months later, he hadn't stopped but, after a hiatus, had only changed tactics. The Case of the Plethora of Dead Things was surely related to the recent business regarding Le Clerc, Leveret, *Darkmoor Lane,* and the Gerber's baby. The Case of Darkmoor Lane, if that's what it should be called, seemed to suggest a perpetrator who harbored a grudge or, at the very least, believed that he was on a mission to right an injustice.

As we sat at the kitchen table in front of our empty dishes and our licked-clean spoons, I knew I ought to go straight to Loretta and Franklin with what I'd been told. However, if I did so, I would risk alienating my fellow members of the Clyde Tombaugh Club for a while and perhaps permanently. From my extensive reading of novels, I well understood that even happy children lived in a condition of quiet rebellion against the world of adults and that, among those whom they welcomed into their secret society, they valued loyalty above all else. Isadora, Gertrude, and Harry had accepted me with surprising generosity, but weeks or even months would be required for the cords that bound us to become so tightly knotted that they could not be undone. I would rather deny myself ice cream and cake and books—even books, even forever and ever—than forfeit the grace of friendship and belonging that I'd found with these three bright souls. I loved their mother and father, but I loved my siblings no less. Indeed, I might have loved them more, for I recognized my own vulnerability in them and knew their fears; in a world ruled by the strong, shared weakness spawns a binding sympathy. In the years to come, considering how busy Loretta and Franklin were, I would be spending more time in their children's company than in theirs. I told myself that if the unknown tormentor meant to hurt them, he'd have done so already. I told myself that my experience of evil would ensure I'd see danger coming before any harm could be done, and *then* I would go to Loretta and Franklin. I told myself, in the meantime, I would solve this mystery, after which any risk that might exist would have been removed. I knew I was being selfish, but I did not believe I was reckless. I would heed Harmony's advice. I would enjoy life, but I would stay alert. All would be well if I remained alert.

A short while later, alone in my suite, I finished brushing my teeth. I returned the toothbrush to the ceramic caddy next to the bathroom sink and looked up to see that I wasn't reflected in the mirrored door of the medicine cabinet. As if through a window, I saw Captain in a three-piece tweed and the albino gentleman in a sharply tailored gray suit and pale-gray fedora. They were standing in a dimly lighted parking lot, next to a Chrysler convertible roadster, as a thin tide of night mist washed low across the blacktop. Captain said, "I must be crazy—paying a gumshoe this much by the hour." The pale detective said he was worth twice what he charged and would at last have what was wanted by this time tomorrow.

"He's looking for us," I said, and my words erased the image from the mirror much like a hand would wipe a film of condensed steam from a pane of glass. I had not dozed off. This vision could not be dismissed as a daymare. I did not know what was happening to me. I could only hope that it never happened again.

NINETEEN

While we are making luck of our own as best we are able, other people are making luck for us, good and bad. Sometimes luck falls toward us like dominos, bringing a series of insights, and something we have struggled to understand becomes clearer than we imagined it ever could be. The night of the peach ice cream, I slept soundly, but I dreamed of dead mice, dead birds, dead baby rabbits. This was not a nightmare, for each creature recovered from death. The birds flew out of slippers; mice scampered from under pillows; rabbits hopped out of sight into the safe concealment of verdant foliage. When I woke late Saturday morning, I felt that my subconscious, in its dreaming, had been telling me to be alert for revelations that would solve the mysteries that had baffled the children.

In the early afternoon of that sunny day, as Harry and Gertrude were playing badminton on the court behind the pavilion, Isadora and I were sitting on the rim of the fountain, enjoying the cool air that the breeze brought off the arcing streams spouted by the stone dolphins. Water spilled down a series of granite bowls, and it was on the edge of one of those that a bird landed to drink. "That," said my companion, "is just like the bird that Gertie found in her slipper and like the one we found lying in the back hall when we were chasing the ghost of Rudolph Valentino. Valentino didn't die here in the Bram, of course. He never even visited this place. But since no one has ever died here, to the best of our knowledge, we have to settle for spirits who come visiting from elsewhere."

Later, when Isadora went into the house for her piano lesson, when Harry and Gertrude retreated to their rooms to clean up for dinner after working up a sweat at badminton, I lingered in the gardens to admire the last roses of the season. Mr. Reinhardt, the groundskeeper, was trimming a low hedge that surrounded the roses. He and I began talking about flowers when a bird like the one at the fountain landed on the stone walkway. A few pill bugs rolled up tight in an attempt to avoid being eaten. As the bird pecked at them, Mr. Reinhardt answered my question about it. "Oh, *fräulein*, that pretty fellow is a purple martin. Migration season. He is passing through, *ein klein Zigeuner*, a little Gypsy. We have no great flocks of his kind at any time of year, but in summer a few families return to the Bram and stay till late autumn." He pointed at two large birdhouses atop tall poles in the northwest corner of the property. "Swallows. Mere two-ounce swallows. But they chase bigger birds out of those apartments. Tough little guys."

I wished him a good day off, for he didn't work on Sunday, and as I turned away, I thought of another question. "With the estate wall all the way around, do we have rabbits?"

"*Kaninchen!*" His brow furrowed, and his eyes squinted behind his wire-rimmed glasses. "They come in through the driveway gate and eat my flowers. No roses. No begonias. But much else. When I catch one, I put it off the property." He made shooing motions with his hands. "*Weggehen, weggehen!* I cannot kill them. They are too sweet. I put them off the property. *Danken Gott*, we have had only one hare. A hare has such longer legs than a rabbit. Catching one is a fool's errand. And Rafael is no help. He refuses to chase a bunny. He just sits and watches it and wags his tail. And the first time the one hare made a ten-foot leap, our fierce dog ran off and hid from it."

At the word *"dog,"* the bird took flight, leaving half the order of pill bugs unconsumed, as if it knew what the word meant but lacked an understanding of Rafael's gentle nature.

Assuming that the first exotic word the groundskeeper used meant *rabbit* in German, I said, "Has a *Kaninchen* ever produced a litter while inside the estate wall?"

"Once! Early last spring. A doe can have four litters a year. There were seven kittens in this one. What damage could have been done to my flowers, herbs, and exotic grasses. What devastation!"

"What happened to them, the kittens?"

He put down his hedge shears and took a plaid handkerchief from a pocket of his khakis. Judging by his expression, I thought he was going to cry, but he blew his nose. Then he said, "The kittens are born without fur. They look like tiny *Meerschweinchen.* Guinea pigs. The mother leaves them in a shallow burrow. She covers it with grass to hide her babies and returns every evening to nurse them. In ten days they double in size. They become covered in fur. In a month, they can leave the burrow to find their own food." He tucked away the plaid handkerchief and withdrew a plain one from a different pocket. He took off his eyeglasses and polished them. "A month! So tiny, they were. So vulnerable. How could I wait a month? I kept thinking—hawks, owls, and rats. *Dreckige Ratten!* Stuffing themselves on the kittens. I couldn't sleep. I moved them into my office with their mother." His office and the gardening-supply room were behind the school bungalow. "I fed them vegetables from Chef Lattuada. I built a rabbit hutch to keep them safe. When they were two months old and quick, I drove them out into the hills. Five miles from here. I set them free, the doe and six, so small in those endless fields. It was a hard thing to do. A rabbit in the wild lives only a year or two. So many predators." Having put his glasses on a low garden wall, he was blotting his eyes with the plain handkerchief. "It was hard to do, but there was nothing else."

"Such is the world," I said.

"That is very true. 'Such is the world.' So very true, Alida."

"'The doe and six.' Weren't there seven kittens?"

"One escaped the hutch. I don't know how. Perhaps when I was cleaning it, putting in fresh water, the door opened. I searched and searched but never found it. Poor thing."

As he put on his wire-rimmed spectacles and picked up the hedge clippers, I stood in contemplation of what information the day had brought to me for so little effort on my part. I didn't know quite what to make of them yet, but I realized that certain valuable facts had been laid before me like gold coins.

Dinner was another triumph for Chef Luigi Lattuada. His kitchen seemed to be a culinary wonderland where food was prepared not by the usual methods but by the application of magic formulas and rare ingredients passed down through countless generations of *sorciers de cuisine*. Over dessert, Franklin declared, "When the day comes I'm so old and feeble that I can digest nothing but pabulum, I'm sure Luigi will find a way to make it delicious."

"That could be as soon as Monday," Gertrude said, and everyone laughed, especially the children.

After the family was well fed and after the chef had enjoyed his dinner with Julian and Victoria Symington, Mr. Lattuada and Franklin retired to the music room. During the past few years, on either Saturday or Sunday night, their habit had been to take one generous snifter each of fine and highly illegal cognac while they listened to music of which both had become aficionados. The music room contained a Steinway where Isadora took lessons but also comfortable chairs and a gramophone. Franklin had a collection of 78-rpm disc records that in those days were made from a shellac compound and were heavier than the vinyl records that would come into home use years later. To encourage the children to develop a wide background in culture, the door was left ajar; though they weren't permitted to be in the music room and disturb the adults, they were encouraged to sit on pillows on the hallway floor and listen. That was my first weekend at the Bram, and I settled on a pillow between Isadora and Gertrude. They were familiar with the recordings and excited to hear them again. Isadora whispered that we might want to dance. If we did, we would have to move farther along the hall and do it quietly. So it was there—September 13, 1930—that I first heard the group called the "Hot Five" and the singer and trumpet player who fronted them. His name was Mr. Louis Armstrong, and of course everyone came to know him in time. "West End Blues," "Savoy Blues," "Tiger Rag" . . . During an amazing number called "Heebie Jeebies," he sang some verses in what they called "scat," making vocal sounds in imitation of instruments.

After listening for a while, Isadora and Gertrude could contain themselves no longer. They got up from their pillows and moved about twenty feet along the hall, where they danced together, obeying the rule of silence. Harry stayed where he was, rapt by the Hot Five but full of boyish disdain for dancing. *"Stupid girls,"* he whispered. I felt the music in my heart, in my muscles and bones, and I wanted very much to dance, but I dared not. I was neither dressed for dance nor properly constructed for it. I sat and listened and comforted myself with the promise that I would dance in my dreams.

In fact, that night I *did* dance in my dreams. I had never done so before, because I'd never for a moment considered I could one day dance either while awake or asleep. My imagination had not been able to encompass the possibility. Now it could. I did more in my dreams than dance. I explored the lush gardens of the Bram, which expanded far beyond their real-world dimensions, with new wonders everywhere I went. At all times, parades of rabbits proceeded and followed me. Small birds landed on my shoulders and sang to me. Mr. Reinhardt and

I got aboard his Ford truck and drove into the hills and found the doe with her six kittens, and we brought them home. I was dancing again when a voice came to me out of the dolphin fountain: *Alida, ask Mr. Reinhardt about mice. Ask the children about the perfect world of peace and light.* It was a woman's voice, one I did not recognize. I'd never had the experience of being spoken to directly by a disembodied voice in a dream. When the unseen speaker repeated those two instructions, I promised to do what she had asked. The fountain overflowed, and I danced effortlessly on running water, through ferns and flowers, into moonlight and stars, into darkness and quiet.

TWENTY

Mr. Reinhardt insisted on working every Saturday in his beloved gardens, but he had Sundays off. Therefore, I was unable to ask him about the mice until Monday. Even if he'd been at the Bram, I could not have spoken to him right away that morning, for we were going to church. I had never been to a church before. The prospect inspired something worse than apprehension and less than fright. I assumed that everyone would stare at me in my unusual dress, would speculate about what the garment might conceal, and would one way or another express the opinion that I did not belong there. As it turned out, no one in the congregation had any unusual interest in me. I sat with Gertrude between Isadora and Harry, and we four sat between Loretta and Franklin. The organ music was stirring, and much about the service was beautiful, and I liked the fragrance of incense. The experience was over sooner than I expected, and we left accompanied by the tintinnabulation of bells.

From there we boarded the yellow Cadillac again, and Franklin drove us to a restaurant overlooking the Pacific, where we sat at a table with a view of the sea and had brunch. There were no little food windows, as in an Automat, and we were not required to deposit nickels in a slot to obtain a meal. The ambience was very pleasant, though the diners were a noisy lot, especially considering that no booze was served in that establishment. I expected the waiter to admonish me to take off my gloves to eat. When he made no such comment, I wondered if Franklin and Loretta had in advance appealed to everyone in the church and restaurant to treat me as if I were an ordinary child. They would have needed to know all those people and would have required an inordinate amount of time to contact them prior to Sunday. I decided that was unlikely but couldn't be ruled out altogether. The food was good, though it was not as exceptional as any meal at the Bram.

When we got back to the house, Franklin and Loretta revealed that a projectionist had been hired and that we children were to be treated to an afternoon of motion pictures in the screening room. We watched silent two-reelers—Charlie Chaplin, Harold Lloyd, Buster Keaton—that elicited more laughter from me than anything other than Voltaire's *Candide*, which I had read three times. Then the siblings wanted a full-length talkie, and they agitated for *Darkmoor Lane*. They had seen the film, and I had not, but we were looking less for entertainment than for something that might help us solve the case that currently preoccupied the members of the Clyde Tombaugh Club. We found it. At the very bottom of the opening list of performer credits were the names of two actors, bit players, who appeared in the movie as "Gangster 1" and "Gangster 2"—Martin Souris Leveret, now dead, and François Le Clerc, now serving fifteen years for the voluntary manslaughter of Leveret.

Darkmoor Lane proved to be a pretty good program picture, the kind that unspooled as the second movie of a double bill. However, we had trouble sitting still until the end card. Immediately after the screening, we were expected for dinner at the kitchen table with Franklin and Loretta. Chef Lattuada didn't work Sundays and Mondays, but he stocked a refrigerator with some dishes that could be eaten cold and others that needed only to be reheated in an oven. We Tombaugh detectives ate at a measured pace and participated in the table talk as if nothing else in the world urgently called to us. After the six of us cleared the table and washed the dishes, Loretta and Franklin went for a walk in the artfully lighted gardens, whereupon I and my companions and our faithful canine sprinted for the library as though all the demons in Hell must be chasing us.

Closing the library door and standing with his back against it, Harry said, "The killing must have happened during filming. Or if the cameras weren't turning at the time, Le Clerc at least rubbed out Leveret right there on the set."

Gertrude shook her head. "We don't know that for sure."

"Maybe you don't know, but I do. It's how it had to be. The scenario requires it. Dramatic structure. How often have we heard about good dramatic structure? Like a thousand times."

I said, "Wouldn't your parents have told you if it happened on the set?"

"Definitely not," Isadora said. "They wouldn't want to distress us. They would worry that we weren't old enough to handle it."

"I just handled it," Gertrude declared. "So there."

Harry shrugged and turned his hands palms up as if to invite an explanation. "What's to be distressed about? Someone gets bumped off on the set. It's exciting, that's all."

"If they'd told us," Isadora said, "we'd have worried about them being murdered every time they went to work."

"Hey, it wasn't murder, just plain old killing. No malice. No premeditation. I explained all that."

"So you're saying we would have been all right with Mother and Father getting killed at work, just so they weren't murdered? Are you really nine, little brother, or do we have the math wrong?"

Harry resorted to a raspberry. "Okay, so they didn't think they should tell us, but now someone else is telling us. Someone thinks we should know, and now we know."

"It's more than that," I said as I paced to facilitate clear thinking. I had never paced for that purpose before. I'd always been on a small stage, in a small room, in the back seat of a car, with no space to pace. "Whoever's sending you these messages, these clues, is making a statement."

"What statement?"

"You never solved the Case of the Plethora of Dead Things."

"Thanks for rubbing it in. It feels so much better now."

"I mean that case is this case. All the same thing. Whoever's sending these photos and newspaper clippings started out earlier in the year, leaving dead things around to scare you and disgust you and get your attention. Yesterday, Isadora, you pointed out a bird like the one found in Gertrude's slipper. Later, Mr. Reinhardt said it was a purple martin. I didn't think much about it at the time because I was more interested in his story about the rabbits."

"Martin Leveret," she said.

"There's a book," I said. "I saw it the other day." With the siblings close behind, I hurried across the room to a section of shelves devoted neither to fiction nor biography, but to volumes about the natural world. The tome I wanted was thick and oversize—*Mammals of the World: An Illustrated Zoology*. I carried it to the main library table and opened it and paged through the alphabetical listings to rabbits. Three pages were devoted to the species, with several photos. The four of us crowded around, scanning the text.

"What're we looking for?" Gertrude asked.

"I'll know it when I see it," I said.

When I didn't see it anywhere in that entry, I paged toward the front of the book until I found the section on hares, another three pages with photos. The word seemed to leap from the text. "Leveret," I read aloud. "A young hare is called a *leveret.*"

"You're so clever, Alida," Gertrude said. "If my parents insist that I go to some boring college, I'll want you to go with me and do all the learning and test-taking for me."

I heard the same voice that I'd heard in my dream. *Alida, ask Mr. Reinhardt about mice.* The speaker sounded somewhat like Madam Zena, the fortuneteller in the carnival. "I'm supposed to ask Mr. Reinhardt about mice."

"What about mice?" Harry asked.

"Well, I'm not sure. A voice in a dream told me to ask him. It might have been the voice of a carnival fortuneteller I once knew." Voices in dreams, carnivals, fortunetellers—combined, they were a stimulus that caused my friends to tremble with excitement. I said, "Maybe mice have been a problem for Mr. Reinhardt or maybe it's something weirder than that. But he's not here today."

"Mr. Symington would know about mice," said Isadora. "He knows about everything Bram."

"But this is a day off for the Symingtons."

"They don't often go anywhere. They usually stay here, in their apartment on the second floor of the bungalow. They won't mind a quick visit. We can apologize effusively for disturbing them."

The one thing you could say with absolute confidence about the Clyde Tombaugh Club was that the mere prospect of adventure, however slight, inflamed its members into the reckless pursuit of it. As we were about to leave by the exterior library door, Harry clasped Rafael's burly head between his hands and met the shepherd's eyes. "We've got to avoid Mom and Dad. They're in the gardens. You know their smell. Do not fail us." The dog sneezed as if to confirm his reliability and commitment to the cause. Isadora opened the door, and Rafael went through first. We followed, avoiding the landscape lighting where possible. Ten acres equals a few blocks of ordinary backyards, allowing us to stay off the paved paths and move through planting. We remained close to the estate wall and arrived at the bungalow without having to explain ourselves to a parental patrol.

The windows were dark in the Symingtons' apartment, for this was one of the rare occasions when they went somewhere on a day off. However, lamplight warmed the windows of Chef Lattuada's quarters. Buck Rogers, up there in the twenty-fifth century, would not give up and go home just because his intended target for the night was off to Santa Monica for an evening of dining and dancing, and neither would we. The siblings believed the chef liked them all but had a special soft spot in his heart for Gertrude, not because of her deformed hand so much as because of her attitude and the way she couldn't help but often mispronounce his name as Lugenie Lanaconda. "Also," she said, "because he's kind enough to pity anyone named Gertrude." She took the front position in our little group and rang the bell.

When Chef Lattuada opened the door, I was happy to see that he was holding a novel he'd been reading, happier that it was *A Tale of Two Cities*. The final chapter of that work moves me profoundly with its honoring of self-sacrifice and its celebration of forgiveness. The last two lines always make me cry in the best way.

Even as Chef greeted us, our gaggle of amateur detectives peppered him with apologies for the interruption and with not entirely germane questions about mice and martins and hares and whether another batch of peach ice cream might be spun up sooner than later. His hands were big enough to juggle cantaloupes, and he used the bookless one to make a settle-down gesture. "If you have not come here to raid my refrigerator, I am pleased to invite you into my home. Just understand, I will defend my precious Frigidaire and its contents to the death."

His living room was not large, but cozy and welcoming. As the children and I sat side by side on a sofa, Isadora said, "We won't take much of your time, sir. We're here because we're desperate to solve a mystery." Chef Lattuada occupied one of two armchairs, while Rafael collapsed in front of the fireplace to bask in the heat of the burning logs. "Alida needs to ask Mr. Reinhardt about mice, but he's off today, and the Symingtons aren't home, as we expected them to be, so we have no one to turn to about mice except you."

"And now that it's you," I said, "I have more than mice to inquire about, if that's okay."

"Why don't we start with mice? It's an unpleasant subject and best gotten out of the way, no less so than crocodiles."

He knew how to keep a conversation lively. I smiled. "Well, I guess I need to know if we have a mouse problem here at the Bram."

"Not in the house itself, so far as I'm aware. Summer of last year and again this past spring, there were mice in the garage." The cars were kept in a building separate from the house. "It seems," he continued, "the mice were eating the insulation off the automobile wiring. Personally, that's a dish I don't enjoy, and I would never prepare it for your dinner, but rodents seem to fancy it."

"Did Mr. Reinhardt set traps for them?"

"No. He put poison in clever bait stations with entrances so small that only mice could get in to nibble at the stuff. It was so effective and quick-acting that the mice had no chance to complain to authorities."

"So there were a lot of dead mice lying around if someone had a use for them."

"Mr. Reinhardt is a kindly man who would not disappoint anyone in need, even when the people in need are seeking dead mice. May I say, Alida, you are so uncannily like Isadora, Gertrude, and Harry that you might all have come from Mars on the same rocket ship."

The siblings liked that one very much. So did I. "I believe we're done with the subject of mice," I said. "You once told me you speak

French, so I guess you might know some French people from your days in Europe."

"I speak bad French. But I knew some good people there."

"Did you ever know anyone or hear of anyone named Leveret? Is that a French name?"

"I suppose it could be. It's not French, but people adopt names that gradually become widely used. A leveret is a young hare. Some French chefs have numerous recipes for hare, but I've never cared for the game taste. I knew people named Leverrier. Levesque. That's the best I can do."

"If Mr. Leveret is French," I said, "then his middle name is likely also French. Maybe you'll know. His middle name is Souris."

"So we are not done with mice, after all. In French, a *souris* is a mouse. Evidently that's not his middle name, but a nickname he embraced."

Dead purple martins, dead mice, and a dead hare. The unknown person behind the Case of the Plethora of Dead Things was the same person who, months later, began to taunt the Fairchild children with photos and newspaper clippings.

My questions had made Chef Lattuada uneasy. Now my expression alerted him that this was something more than a foolish game. "You better tell me what's going on here."

I looked at my companions. They nodded. I said, "Someone has been sending threats to Isadora, Gertrude, and Harry. Things that didn't seem like threats at first, things maybe no one but Nature sent. Dead birds, dead mice, a dead rabbit. Now I think someone close to the family blames Loretta and Franklin for something they didn't do, for the death of a man named Martin Leveret, a bit player who was killed by another bit player on the set of *Darkmoor Lane*."

Chef Lattuada slid to the edge of his armchair and leaned toward me. "Someone close to the family. Who?"

"I don't know. I hope it's no one on the staff. Maybe someone who comes and goes, an outside service."

Sensing the tension that had arisen, Rafael got up from his place by the fire and shook himself and came to stand with us.

"There's something else." I didn't want to tell the chef that I'd been guided by a voice in a dream. Even an adult as open-minded as he would have doubts about a girl who claimed to hear a voice in her head or in dreams and acted on its instructions. I focused on the siblings. "Tell me about 'a perfect world of peace and light.'"

They were startled.

"That's nothing," said Isadora. "It's just stupid. It doesn't have anything to do with the dead things and Leveret and all that."

"I think it does. I haven't been snooping on you," I assured my fellow Tombaugh Club members. "It's just . . . I was told to ask you this by that fortuneteller we talked about earlier. I need to know what it means—'the perfect world of peace and light.'"

"It doesn't mean anything," Isadora said. "It's boring grown-up wouldn't-it-be-nice talk. It's not something that could ever be, so it's not important. We don't understand it anyway, who she's talking about, so we just tune it out."

Gertrude said, "She doesn't yammer on about it every day. Just when she's in her lemon mood, all sour in her lemon mood, her face squinched up. After a while, she hears herself, how sour she sounds, so then she's fun again, fun and nice, 'cause that's who she really is, who she wants to be."

Harry stood up from the sofa, apparently convinced that his full height must be utilized to give his words credibility. "So we never told anyone 'cause she's always so sorry how she grumps about things. She asks us not ever to tell anyone. She just wants a better world and gets angry that it won't get better. She's maybe a little crazy about it sometimes, but everyone is a little crazy sometimes about *something*.

I'm a little crazy about hating ham, how it tastes so salty and gross and hammy. You put ham on my plate, I won't eat anything else on the plate. I might never eat off that plate again. I'm a little crazy about it, see?"

Chef Lattuada's voice was tender and affectionate, with a note of sadness. "This is more than not liking ham. 'A perfect world of peace and light' is one of the slogans of a very dangerous group. I am so sorry for Miss Blackthorn that she's been made to believe the things they teach and wants to make you believe them, too."

TWENTY-ONE

On each of her five days at the Bram, week after week, Miss Imogene Blackthorn chose to wear dresses so similar to one another that they might have been the same frock. They were not the same, however, for she was fastidious, obsessed with personal cleanliness; she owned multiples of what she felt should constitute the uniform of a tutor and nanny, though the terms of her employment did not include a dress code. She laundered and ironed a garment after she wore it once, no less faithfully than she shampooed and conditioned her lustrous auburn hair every day. Only rarely did she dare use the blackboard during instruction, because chalk dust on a black dress required immediate attention with an artist's brush of soft, fine hairs that would not work the pale powder deeper into the fabric.

The morning following the Clyde Tombaugh Club's meeting with Chef Lattuada, Miss Blackthorn breezed into the schoolroom at 7:55, according to the large wall clock. Because the siblings were almost always at their desks in anticipation of her arrival, she did not glance their way as she crossed the threshold but called out, "Good morning, all, good morning," as she let the door fall shut behind her and pivoted to the freestanding coatrack on her left. She hung her purse by its straps and her coat over the purse. When she turned and saw me in a side chair brought from the main house, sitting in line with her three students, she appeared to be surprised but not concerned. "Alida! What brings you here on this fine morning?"

"The need to learn," I said. "Izzy, Gertie, and Harry were telling me about something that sounds so very smart and important. I can't believe I know nothing about it. They say the subject is over their heads, they can't explain it, so I thought you wouldn't mind having a fourth student for a day."

Rounding her desk, Miss Blackthorn said, "If it's about Albert Einstein's theory, I only mentioned it in passing, to stir up their imagination. I'm afraid I don't understand it myself, at least not well enough to teach even ten minutes on it."

"Oh, I've heard of Mr. Einstein's theory, ma'am. I don't know anything about it, zero, but I'm pretty sure I don't *want* to know anything. It sounds like brain-busting stuff. I'm not up to that. I'm talking about making a perfect world of peace and light. It's only twelve years since one world war ended, but people are saying another and bigger one is coming. I get scared when I think about it, so many people maybe dying. Something's wrong with the world, with people, how they think—and I want to know what it is that's gone wrong, how to fix it—if there is a fix. I want to live in a world of peace and light."

After a hesitation, Miss Blackthorn said, "Peace and light and plenty. That's the promise." Turning her attention to the children, she said, "We agreed you wouldn't talk to anyone about this. Some people won't let themselves understand it, and they get angry, even some people as smart and kind as your parents."

Isadora said, "We promised not to tell Mother and Father, and we didn't. We told only Alida because she's one of us. She's already one of us in every way. We can keep a thousand secrets from everyone in the world, but the four of us can't keep even a single secret from one another."

Miss Blackthorn rolled her chair from behind the desk and sat close to us. She smiled warmly at the siblings. "Sometimes, I've felt that when I talk about this, it goes in your left ears and immediately out your right ears, that none of it sticks. I'm so pleased if that's not the case. I only want what's best for you, what will make your lives much happier, make the world a better place for you."

With the full force of her elfin charm, Gertrude said, "Gee whiz, Miss Blackthorn, don't you worry about sticky. Everything you tell us is sticky. It all sticks between our ears because we trust you and love you. Izzy and I love you and even Harry loves you, though he won't admit it because he's a boy."

Harry made a sound of disgust and looked down at his desk, as if too embarrassed to meet Miss Blackthorn's eyes, as boys do when it is revealed that they have some feelings as mushy as any emotions that girls entertain.

Suddenly it seemed my three friends were natural-born thespians who could do a passable job performing in anything written by the Bard of Avon.

Miss Blackthorn's eyes filled with unshed tears. Her mouth softened. She sounded sincere when she said, "You're all so special. I'm so blessed to be at the Bram, to be part of your lives. When I'm old and gray, I'll count my life a success if I've helped you find your way through the dark times to the wisdom that'll ensure your happiness." She scooted her rolling chair closer and leaned forward, wrapping us in a thrilling cloak of high-minded conspiracy. "There are always people who think they know everything and their way is the best way. They are the Closed Minds, and the tragedy of humanity is that the Closed Minds often rule the rest of us. Thirty years ago, wiser people who understood the importance of eugenics needed to conceal their commitment to work secretly for a better world. But year by year, the cause has gained believers and become respectable. Children your age, however, remain oppressed by adults who think you're too weak-minded to be told certain hard truths."

Miss Blackthorn focused primarily on me, because I was the one who purported to know nothing about the topic, while the siblings had long been propagandized. She spoke of Charles Darwin's cousin, Mr. Francis Galton, who founded the eugenics movement with the intention of improving the human gene pool by identifying people of the best genetic stock and encouraging them to procreate. Soon eugenicists wanted to redirect human evolution more aggressively by forcibly sterilizing the "unfit" to prevent them from reproducing. This proposal was endorsed by the finest universities, the brightest journalists, the wealthiest philanthropists, and by the federal government. President Theodore Roosevelt supported it. Mandatory sterilizations began.

"Imagine, Alida, we started at last to stop breeding by the feebleminded, paupers, drunkards, criminals of all kinds, even petty criminals, epileptics, the insane . . . the blind, the deaf, the mute. They have been doing the same in the United Kingdom, Australia, Canada, especially in Germany. Many of those people who put civilization at risk by their bad behavior, their foolish theories, by their weakness, have been prevented from infecting future generations. Hundreds of famous artists, writers, actors, and educators have endorsed eugenics. George Bernard Shaw, Margaret Sanger, Clarence Darrow, Woodrow Wilson, on and on." Miss Blackthorn became a little breathless with excitement. "By 1920, four hundred universities and colleges offered courses in eugenics. In 1927, after the Supreme Court approved of legally mandated sterilization of unfit people, thirty-six thousand were no longer able to procreate. We hoped for at least a hundred thousand in 1928, two hundred thousand the year after. We could have been on our way to peace, light, plenty, a world with no crime, with a smarter population, arriving at Utopia in ten or twenty years. But there has been a backlash. For all its undeniable success, eugenics has been condemned by know-nothings of various kinds. People who understand the rightness of eugenics, the shining promise of it, are slandered. Lies are told about their motives. If we care about the future, we must never give up the struggle, but in the current environment, we need to work for our ideals behind the scenes. Wisdom, courage, and shrewd planning are required. Do you want a better world? I do. Oh, I so much want it. I want it for you. I will surely have passed away before we achieve Utopia, but I want it for you."

"A world without criminals," I said, "the poor eliminated, a lot less sickness, no foolish people doing stupid things, no bad people at all, only smart people, only *very* smart people. Who could be against that? These backlash people, jeez, they must be very dumb or wicked or maybe both. Probably both. I have just one question. One thing I don't understand. When you were listing those who ought never to reproduce, you hesitated between 'the insane' and 'the blind.' Between 'insane' and 'blind,' who did you leave out?"

Miss Blackthorn was morally adrift, perhaps morally bankrupt, in a swoon of mad ideology, a godless religion—but she wasn't stupid. The moment I asked my question, she knew that I wasn't an innocent seeker of knowledge, that I had an agenda. The list was in an anti-eugenics book in Bramley Hall's library. As her face paled, her eyes became a more intense blue. In some circumstances, silence can be a weapon; she'd decided it was the only one she possessed, and she looked as though she wished it could cut like the tempered steel of a sword. For her, the children ceased to exist; she gave them not a glance, not a word.

I said, "I've read the list, you see. Between 'the insane' and 'the blind,' there appear 'genetically unfit communities' and 'the deformed.'" I thought surely she would be tormented by at least a small measure of guilt, enough to make her glance at our Gertie's deformed hand. However, it was becoming clear that Miss Blackthorn lacked the self-awareness to imagine she was capable of a wrong thought or bad deed.

I said, "The dead birds, the mice, the little rabbit—that was to draw the children into a mystery. But then Martin Leveret, François Le Clerc, *Darkmoor Lane*—what was your point? What did you hope to achieve?"

Her pallor darkened into a blush, not of embarrassment but of righteous anger. "They need to know, don't they? Why should they grow up believing their parents are doing meaningful work, only to discover one day that it's all trash? A man died in a fight during one of their productions. Oh, yes, it was Le Clerc who did it, but they went right on filming. They released the picture and made their money. They always make their money." As a teacher, she seemed to have little regard for reason. "They always make money because they make lowbrow entertainment, not art. They don't make motion pictures with the important themes, issues, policy positions, the politics that inspire true artists. They make pabulum, the movie equivalent of Gerber's baby food, and they're blind to their lack of substance. They cater to morons, fools, the unfit, when the world needs to be rid of those useless people, not cater to them, be *rid* of them."

She rose from her chair. Perhaps she meant to leave. It was then the door to the school lavatory opened. Luigi Lattuada, there as a witness, stepped into the classroom, followed by Loretta and Franklin. The chef's dazzling smile was less warm than usual, for he knew to what "unfit" group she would assign him. The Fairchilds were not smiling at all.

TWENTY-TWO

School having been canceled, the children and I gathered in the pavilion with cold bottles of Coca-Cola, though it was early in the day for such an indulgence. Twenty-four years earlier, cocaine had been deleted from the soft drink and replaced with caffeine, but kids of all ages still speculated that traces of the drug remained in the formula.

"If you drink enough bottles quick, one after another," Harry warned, "say forty bottles, you would be jacked up."

"Or spewing like Vesuvius," Gertrude said.

Harry persisted. "And if you got that way just twice, you'd be addicted for life, a pathetic cocaine dope fiend with no way out except off a bridge."

Gertrude said, "You better drink those forty bottles right there on the bridge."

"Why would I drink on a bridge?"

"If you drink all of it here at home, then on your way to the jump, you'll have to stop every three minutes to pee. You'll never get to the bridge."

"Then I'd go on the roof of the Bram and dive headfirst into the terrace below."

Gertrude made a sound of disgust. "And who's going to clean that up? No one who works here signed on to deal with a sickening pile of pee-soaked boy jelly."

"Just to be done with this subject," Isadora said, "I promise I'll clean up the remains. It'll be an honor and a pleasure."

"Heck," Harry said, "I'd never jump off the roof and leave a mess. I'd drink those forty bottles while sitting in the Cadillac and then drive at a hundred miles an hour into a bridge abutment."

"Is that," Gertrude asked, "the same bridge you would have jumped off if you could have walked there?" She turned from her brother to me. "Sometimes boys just don't make any sense at all. Have you noticed that, Alida?"

Mr. Symington found us in the pavilion and said that Loretta and Franklin were waiting for me in his study and I should hurry along. I was so rattled by the events of the morning that I could not discern from either Mr. Symington's expression or intonation what my guardians might wish to say to me.

As I walked to the house and passed through the ground-floor rooms, I shuffled my deck of memories of the recent incident, worrying that I would find a joker, something I'd done that could be construed as being emotionally damaging to the children. After all, what did I know of families, never having had one of my own? What did I know of the traditions and shared experiences of the Fairchild family? Very little. The surface only. And yet, having been there just a week, I had engineered the dismissal of Miss Blackthorn—or so it might seem. Yes, Loretta and Franklin participated in my setup of the teacher by remaining out of sight and eavesdropping, but in retrospect, they might have found the experience demeaning.

The study door was open when I arrived, and I closed it behind me. Loretta and Franklin stood at a window, staring at the gardens. They turned at the sound of the door.

"Are you all right, Alida?" Loretta asked.

"Yes, ma'am. But I'm sorry for all the inconvenience I caused you, what with Miss Blackthorn leaving and no one to replace her."

In addition to the desk, the room provided a button-tufted sofa upholstered in deep-red leather and two armchairs with footstools. Loretta patted the sofa, and I sat. She settled beside me and took one of my gloved hands. That was when I thought I might be okay.

Franklin perched on a footstool. "Alida, dear, I have made the mistake before of valuing college degrees more highly than I should, but I'll never make that mistake again. Loretta and I finished high school. No higher learning. No money or time for that. Imogene had a degree from the finest women's college in America. That was the deciding factor, why she was hired. She graduated summa cum laude. Labored tirelessly with President Wilson in his attempt to establish a League of Nations. Took a job at *The Smart Set*, a witty intellectual magazine. After her parents were ruined in the great recession of 1920–'21 she went two years without getting a stipend from them, but then she needed a job with better pay, benefits. She seemed humble. Claimed to love children, felt the need to protect their innocence. We felt so fortunate to find her." He rapped his knuckles against his forehead as if to say it was as wooden as the head of Pinocchio. "Tradesmen who live by their skills, laborers who earn their way with muscle and hard work, farmers, salesmen, secretaries—I've never known any who surrendered their precious common sense to an ideology. But in my experience and Loretta's, a certain kind of person finds the academic world not merely prestigious but also glamorous, a throne of power. They believe ideas are more important than people. They relish the chance not to encourage young minds to be independent thinkers, but instead to grind and polish them into mirror images of the teacher's prejudices and delusions. We thought we'd protected our little brood from corrupting influences like that, but we were wrong."

Loretta gently squeezed my hand. "Miss Blackthorn's behavior was treacherous. But her blathering about eugenics meant nothing much to children as young as Izzy, Gertie, and Harry. I tell myself, at some point they would eventually take it more seriously, realize how evil it is, and come to us about it. Like most mothers, I think my lambs are too smart to be taken in by some loathsome flimflammer. But the human heart can be an easy conquest for darkness incarnate. At least one of our babies might have . . . have been lost to us forever, turned into an engine of hatred by that bitch."

"No," I said. "Not any of yours. Each of them has a strong mind. And when they're together, they're ten times stronger."

She brought my gloved hand to her lips and kissed the back of it. "You're a godsend, Alida."

"I'm only me."

She smiled. "Isn't that what I just said?"

"The kids are proficient at math," Franklin said. "Loretta and I can teach them how to apply what they know to personal finances and to managing a business if that eventually interests them."

Loretta said, "We can bring in a tutor just for basic biology and science, if that seems necessary."

"What we're about to suggest," Franklin assured me, "is exactly that—only a suggestion. If you say no, then nothing changes. You're a knowledge sponge. The kids are eager learners. You've had hard experience of the world, harder than most people ever will, and you haven't become a hater like Imogene Blackthorn. Strange as it might seem to some people, we believe the more we can educate them within the family, the better. Would you teach literature, history, and civics to our ducklings? Would that be something you'd enjoy?"

A sinking sensation overtook me. Every child inhabits both this world and one of his or her imagining. When children are entwined in a covenant of friendship, their secret worlds mesh into one. Though I was five years older than the oldest of the Fairchild siblings, they welcomed me into their private universe. For the first time in my life, I had friends. As their teacher, would I remain to them as I was now, sharing their secret world? Would distance open between us? Would I lose what had been so precious to me after only a week?

Loretta understood my silence as completely as if I had shouted my concern. "Nothing needs to change, dear. You don't need to be the stern teacher and dour disciplinarian. Just be an older sister, one of them, sparing them from the tedium of the typical classroom by sharing books and ideas that have delighted and enlightened you. Let them discover history as it really was. Help them find the truth of life, truth in a sea of lies. After that, it's up to them."

And so it was that in less than a week at the Bram, I became not just a member of the Clyde Tombaugh Club but also the big sister responsible for the education of my siblings. I was well read not just in fiction but also in history and the sciences, and I retained everything I read word for word. To my surprise, I found within myself not a teacher as much as an enthusiastic guide who offered adventure-filled excursions to exotic lands, deep into jungles of strange knowledge, across mysterious seas of possibilities. My students and I had fun in the classroom, experiencing together the wonders of Earth, studying the myriad life-forms that the planet nurtured, seeking an understanding of the human condition as the finest literature presented it. During the next two months, no distance opened between me and them, as I feared would happen. In fact, the bonds between us seemed to grow stronger by the day.

The autumn of 1930 was mild even for Southern California. The rose bushes put forth as many flowers in early November as they had during the summer. Hummingbirds lingered mid month before departing on their migration. Beginning the last Tuesday of the month, the maids and Mr. Reinhardt were given six days off for

Thanksgiving. With them went the balmy weather. On Wednesday, from the northwest, a gray tide washed across the sky. The day dimmed. The air grew cool, and a breeze rose, and the fronds of the palm trees made a sound like wire whisks being lightly stroked across snare drums.

Thanksgiving at the Bram involved everyone who lived on the estate. Franklin, Loretta, the Symingtons, and Chef Lattuada began preparations that Wednesday, all of them busy in the kitchen, each of the four amateur cooks taking instructions from the professional. They would be almost as busy on the day itself, and at dinnertime tomorrow, all would be at the table with the children and me—nine of us and, prowling the room hopefully, one German shepherd.

This tradition confirmed for me what I suspected—that neither Franklin nor Loretta had any family other than the one they had created for themselves. On the night the siblings and I had climbed the hidden stairs to the roof and gathered at the obelisk, Isadora implied that there were tragedies in her parents' past of which it was not her place to speak. *They'll tell you when the time is right, when you've settled in and all the legal hooey has been dealt with.*

So on Wednesday afternoon, with the adults in the kitchen, I was at loose ends. The lively conversation and occasional bursts of laughter suggested that the proper functioning of a culinary team required lubrication with a little wine. Elsewhere in the house, each sibling was engaged in a solitary pursuit.

I put on a jacket designed for me by Marjorie Hollingsworth Merrimen and went outside to stroll the gardens.

TWENTY-THREE

I find it hard to convey the extravagant sense of freedom that informed me during those early days at Bramley Hall. There was no Captain Farnam to obey. No show times to meet. No marks whose stares of abhorrence pierced as cruelly as the pins that fixed an exotic insect to an entomologist's specimen board. The burdensome aspects of life rested so lightly on my small shoulders that at times I felt as if I were floating through the rooms and hallways of the house and along the garden paths, my feet not quite making contact with the surfaces over which I crossed. Never having needed more than three hours of sleep, I had a few times awakened in my dark bedroom with the conviction that I was liberated from my body and from all concerns, a mind within a soul, neither in this world nor the next, but adrift in a dimension between lives. That illusion lasted less than a minute, until I could not deny that a mattress and bedclothes cocooned me, and although this experience was both disquieting and delightful, it was always much more the latter than the former.

On the afternoon of Thanksgiving eve, under an overcast sky, I set out to explore the gardens. Even by then I knew those acres and all their attractions as though I had been born within the estate walls.

Nonetheless, when alone I toured the gardens at a leisurely pace, for every enclave was no less beautiful for being familiar, and always some small details, if not new to me, *seemed* new and charming on rediscovery. In the gray light of the cloaked sun, the last roses of the season flourished, all petals intact, some blooms red, others coral pink, still others as pale orange as peaches. In spite of my intention not to hurry, I found myself moving past the roses without pausing to admire them. I took a fork in the path that led beyond the pavilion to a one-acre lawn groomed for games and dog play. In memory, I heard Harmony's voice, *Stay alert, Alida. Life is a great gift, love and mercy are the promise of it, but stay alert.*

Beyond the deep lawn stood a grove of five large well-sculpted *Metrosideros excelsa*, which Mr. Reinhardt said were more commonly known as New Zealand Christmas trees. Showy tufts of crimson flowers crowned their branches, an arresting spectacle even now and more so when bathed in sunlight. *Stay alert.* I did not know what to be alert for, but I felt that I should not delay out of excess caution. The lawn was due for mowing after the holiday. Trembling in the breeze, the grass lapped at my feet as if I were walking on water.

The trees were broadly crowned, the branches densely leafed, so the floor of the woodlet was for the most part carpeted in darkness. What little ashen light sifted between the big trees did not diffuse beyond the natural mulch on which it settled. Letting my eyes adjust to the gloom, I eased forward. Dead leaves crunched underfoot, and the breeze soughed softly through the highest branches. I did not know what had drawn me here, but I knew I had come with a purpose. Sometimes in dreams, without knowing why, we're compelled to proceed through a maze of unfamiliar rooms or wend deeper into an ominous landscape until a sudden encounter shocks us awake, some threat we cannot remember when we sit up in bed, sheathed in sweat. This felt like a waking version of that experience. I stopped tramping through the leaves, and the breeze seemed to subside. In the hush, I scanned the murk, my head cocked to the left, to the right. The faint sound was detectable less because of the volume than because of the quick rhythm. Even so, I can't rightly say my ear led me to the source. Strange as it might seem, I felt that my heart led me, for I was overcome by a sudden sense of impending loss, by pity and sorrow, that reeled me urgently through the gloom until I saw a shape of lesser darkness lying on the black ground. As I knelt, I recognized the rhythmic sound as the panting of a dog. When I put my hand on his side, I knew that he was our Rafael. His heart raced, and his breaths were shallow whiffs. At my touch he issued a thin whimper, leaving no room for doubt that he was in great distress.

Gentle Rafael, sweet Rafael, only two years old, always an eager companion on midnight adventures, member in good standing of the Clyde Tombaugh Club, known to have been frightened by a long-legged leaping hare—if he were to die, the children would be devastated. And they would not be alone in their grief. I'd known him only nine weeks or so, yet I found myself insisting, "No, no, no, no, no," each repetition as much a sob as it was a word. If I'd obeyed my first impulse, I would have run to the house for help. However, intuition argued that he would be dead by the time I brought help back here. "He's been poisoned," I heard myself say, though there was no way I could have known that to be true.

My second impulse was to comfort him, to hold him so that he would not die alone. Or at least that's what I thought I meant to do, for I was not capable of conceiving what in fact happened. I settled behind him, on my left side, and pulled him against me with one arm. I told him he was a good boy, gentle and beautiful and much loved, that this was only his first life and that the next would be in Heaven. "There must be dogs in Heaven," I assured him, "because they're better than people. They deserve Heaven more than we do." Violent tremors shuddered through him. I held him tighter, whereupon his tremors passed into me. I do not mean either that I felt them more profoundly than before or that I developed sympathetic tremors of my own. His body stiffened and his legs kicked. Each time that he convulsed, a simultaneous volcanic concussion originated in the very core of me and sent shock waves to my extremities. I was not merely feeling his convulsions through bodily contact; I was *experiencing* them as I would a lethal current if I grasped the bare wires of a frayed lamp cord. They became *our* convulsions. My thin cries and his pained whimpers were synchronized. My legs scissored like those of a hound fleeing a threat in its dreams. A smell similar to that of potent onions overwhelmed me, and with it came a flavor that was far too sweet to be pleasant. I knew, without knowing *how* I knew, that I was drawing from Rafael the poison he had consumed, and not only the poison but also the dire effects of it, the damage that it had done to his organs and tissues. He was being made right and whole again. The astringent scent swelled into a repulsive malodor. The sugary flavor became cloying. Scent and taste intensified, forming a dark cyclonic mass that turned slowly but relentlessly through my mind, pulling me down into its funnel, as if I were the sailor narrator of Poe's "A Descent into the Maelström." A roaring blackness took me.

I could not have been unconscious more than a minute or two. Rafael awakened me by snuffling loudly and licking my face. When I sat up, he backed off and stood panting, not with canine anxiety, but with the note of eagerness that expressed his happiness when he was in the thick of a late-night adventure with the children. I was not even briefly confused about what had happened. I had brought the dog back from the edge of death to full health. The *what* of it could not be denied, but the *how* beggared explanation. I was not blessed with the power to heal. If I were so gifted, surely the power would have manifested years before this when I held a bird with a broken wing as it died, when I had sat bedside as another human oddity in the Museum of the Strange succumbed to heart failure. When holding Rafael against me, I thought I had felt his convulsions becoming mine instead of his, the poison migrating from him into me. If anything like that had really occurred, I should be dying now—or dead. However, I felt in the best of health, perhaps even better than I'd felt when I set out to tour the gardens.

Although Rafael rarely barked, when I got to my feet, he issued one loud yawp, as though in approval or celebration. A meager wintry gray light sifted through the interlaced trees. It wasn't sufficient to relieve the murkiness, but it was enough to find the reflective layer of his eyes and foster the animal eyeshine that allowed him to see in the dark better than I ever could. I met his steady stare, and he met mine. I wondered if he might understand what had occurred better than I did. That wasn't a far-fetched notion, considering that I didn't understand it at all.

There was no way I would tell anyone in the family what had happened—or seemed to have happened. Whereas I had once been a freak, I was merely an oddity here at the Bram, and I treasured my newfound status. Month by month, year by year, I would seem less odd to everyone, until one day I'd fit in so well that I would be thought normal. I had no intention of doing anything to make anyone wonder if I might be some kind of spooky nonesuch. It was necessary, of course, to let the family and staff know that someone had attempted to poison Rafael. Until the miscreant was identified and confronted, Rafael remained at risk. The problem was that the shepherd appeared healthy. Even if I were to embrace the role of freak and claim to have healed him, I had no evidence to prove my story.

The shepherd followed me out of the woodlet, onto the acre of lawn. When he paused there and looked at me, I said, "Evidence. How can I tell them you were poisoned when I have no evidence? And look at you—grinning and wagging your tail, the picture of good health." I was speaking aloud to myself, not so much to him, certainly not with any expectation that he would understand the word *"evidence"* and act on it. The shepherd set off across the yard as though with a destination firmly in mind. When I didn't at once follow, he stopped and looked back as if to say, *Are we on the same page or not?*

He led me off the lawn and, by one paved path and then another, past the dolphin fountain, around the small palm-ringed amphitheater where, on birthdays, the children watched entertainers—magicians, jugglers, clowns—and from there directly through the hedge maze. When we came to the bungalow with the schoolroom, I thought of Miss Blackthorn as she'd been on that first day I'd come to Bramley Hall. A faint chill stepped down the ladder of my spine. The teacher had been dismissed more than two months earlier. She might possess a capacity for enduring hatred that the passage of time could never diminish. However, she'd shown so much affection for Rafael that I could not seriously credit her with an attempt to kill him. Her role as a poisoner was almost certainly limited to the toxin of ideology that she hoped to inject into the minds of children.

We passed the bungalow and continued to the southwest end of the property. In the corner where the western estate wall met the southern wall stood a statue of W. C. Fields that was manufactured for one of his motion pictures. He had gifted it to Franklin and Loretta because they had been among the backers of his Broadway hit, *Poppy*, which Paramount later filmed as *Sally of the Sawdust*. Fields had stipulated that the statue be set in a remote corner of the estate. "Place this hallowed effigy," he insisted, "where no casual inebriate will stumble across it and be amused to empty his bladder thereupon. Find for it a quiet corner where perchance a wandering monk will come upon it while ardently searching for the meaning of life and, on sight of it, will shatter like a crystal goblet." The statue stood on a black-granite plinth and was surrounded by a wide limestone apron on which those words had been engraved.

Rafael stopped in front of the statue and stared at a large lump of raw meat lying on the limestone to the left of the great comedian. Red meat. Perhaps beef. A good cut. Steak. Someone had known there was a dog in residence. Concerned about a confrontation with a German shepherd, the poisoner most likely hadn't come into the property but instead had tossed the bait from the top of the wall. There would have been a pound or more of steak, enough for the scent to attract the intended victim.

But why? The estate occupied an entire promontory overlooking much lower land, and there were no close neighbors to be annoyed by the baying of half a dozen hounds if the Fairchild family had been of a mind to harbor such a pack. Rafael, not being a barker and alone of his kind at the Bram, could not have done anything that would motivate a poisoner to kill him.

I tore an enormous leaf from a nearby *Gunnera manicata*, picked up the bait with it, and carried it to the house, with Rafael close behind me. Cuts had been made in the meat, and oval tablets smaller than sunflower seeds had been wedged into the resulting pockets. I counted five in what amounted to about a four-ounce chunk of beef.

The children were still engaged in their various pursuits in farther rooms, but the adults were in the kitchen where I had left them. I didn't put the contaminated meat on a counter but held it out in both hands, displayed on the large, soft, prickly-edged leaf for their inspection. I said, "It looks as though someone meant to poison our Rafael. I found this on the pavement near the statue of Mr. Fields."

If some were skeptical of my claim, they were not able to sustain their doubt when they got a close look at the bait. Mr. Symington said, "I believe those little brown tablets are a brand of rat poison, although not one that Mr. Reinhardt ever used."

Franklin grimaced at the foul meat. "To attract a dog, the villain behind this would have thrown more than a single piece of meat over the wall. Maybe Rafael already consumed the rest."

The shepherd sat alert in the nearest corner, the tip of his thick tail wagging as though he must be anticipating a treat.

I was quick to put Franklin's fear to rest. "There were three more chunks. I threw them back over the wall. It's just wild brush on the other side. If anything eats them, it'll be a coyote, which just means that a lot of little rabbits won't be killed and eaten."

Loretta gave me a look of incredulity, perhaps because it was not like me to excuse so cavalierly the killing of even a coyote, but she said nothing.

Everyone agreed that a mystery had been put before us, that we needed to identify the poisoner and learn his motive, and that until the mystery was solved, Rafael must not be outside except when on a leash. Further discussion of the issue must be delayed. Everyone had left culinary tasks unfinished. Today's preparations must be completed, for much else needed to be done tomorrow.

"A proper Thanksgiving feast," Chef Lattuada said, "is as much an act of glorious creation as it is one of grotesque consumption. I will not allow my reputation as a glutton to be diminished because, as the chef, I failed to lay a table that made gross overindulgence possible. My pride is on the line."

That night I could not easily fall asleep. I listened to Rafael softly snoring. Being a fair-minded dog in all things, he did not favor me or one of the children more than the others when it came to gracing us with his presence at bedtime. If he spent Monday snoring next to Gertrude, he devoted Tuesday, Wednesday, and Thursday to the rest of us before returning to her on Friday. He had slept alongside me on Tuesday night, yet here he was again on Wednesday. I suppose he wished to express his gratitude for being saved from poisoning. I wouldn't be surprised if he bedded down with each of the children twice before returning to me for a night.

The question of who had attempted to poison Rafael might have kept me awake all night if the shepherd's recovery from imminent death had not been an even bigger mystery that thwarted sleep. The event in the grove of trees filled me with wonder and with a vague expectation of revelations. It also gave rise to apprehension, fear of the unknown. When at last I did fall asleep, the usual settling noises of the great house woke me more than once. Always I sat up in mild alarm, breath caught in my throat. Black shadows stood in every corner of the moonlit room, and it was easy to imagine that one of them was more than a shadow. Each time, I reached out in the dark to put a hand on Rafael. I expected to find that he had never been there or, worse, that he was dead. When I placed my hand on his flank, I felt his chest rise and fall with his slow and steady breathing. Eventually all hope of further sleep was gone for the night.

Had I found my place in the world, here in the Bram, or might I be destined to belong nowhere? If I developed the ability to embrace a dying creature and make it well again, I must admit to being both a freak and a phenomenon. Fully exposed, I would simultaneously disgust and enchant people. No one in the world would be able to confer on me the normalcy for which I yearned. Any unfortunate soul who is both freak and miracle worker will be forever gazingstock. Everywhere I went would be a stage. Whatever I did would be a performance. Only isolation would provide peace. Once I might have accepted such an existence, living only through books. I have always needed people. In my former existence, those characters who lived only on paper gave me experience and sufficient fellowship, for they were all that I had. However, now that I'd known kindness in the flesh, been warmly welcomed as a friend, known a loving touch, a loving smile, a life in books alone was no longer life enough.

Lying there, I kept thinking of *A Tale of Two Cities*, mostly the inspiring last chapter. Sydney Carton, posing as Charles Darnay, goes to the guillotine in place of the other man because the love of Carton's life is Darnay's wife. I wondered to what extent Dickens might have been inspired by John 15:13. I wondered why I wondered.

Rafael woke with sunrise, yawned, and thumped his tail on the mattress. By then I decided that what occurred in the *Metrosideros* grove would remain our secret. If ever someone in my new family were to fall gravely ill and the doctors could effect no cure, I would discover at that time whether what happened with the dog was what it seemed to be, and learn if the gift I once possessed might still be with me. Common colds, mere flu, and other minor interruptions of good health would remain subject to Nature's curative power. This decision was the only one that allowed me anything close to a normal life, but having made it, I knew that one day I might be ravaged by regret. Therefore, every night since Thanksgiving 1930, my bedtime prayer has been simply "God, forgive me."

TWENTY-FOUR

My first Thanksgiving Day was everything I hoped and much more, and the fun began at eight o'clock in the morning. At breakfast, we were told that a ceramic turkey the size of a milk bottle had been hidden somewhere in the house. Nine clues to its whereabouts were provided in nine numbered envelopes. If we members of the Clyde Tombaugh Club were able to find the bird by two o'clock, we would have dinner on December 14 with Loretta and Franklin and their four guests—Stan Laurel, Oliver Hardy, and their wives. The renowned comedy team's short films—including *From Soup to Nuts*, *Perfect Day*, and the recent *Another Fine Mess*—had made them famous. Laurel and Hardy! What a fun dinner that was sure to be! The wives of the comedians, Lois and Myrtle, suggested the competition; Mr. Symington chose the place where the prize was hidden; Loretta and Franklin devised the clues. Chef Lattuada, who might have been a pretty good comedian in another life, suggested a consolation prize if we didn't find the turkey. In failure, we would not meet Laurel and Hardy. We would eat dinner alone and be escorted to the roof where we would stand in the dark and wave bye-bye to the departing guests while the chef played "So Long, It's Been Good to Know You" on the ocarina.

Obviously, these fiendish adults knew exactly how to structure a challenge so that the competitive instinct of children would be supercharged. We were happily outraged that we had been given only until two o'clock and that the consolation prize was so unfair. If we could not begin the turkey hunt until we cleaned our plates, then we would hog down our food as if we were mannerless savages. We were told we must open only one envelope every half hour, which meant that we wouldn't see the final clue until half past noon. This was of course typical—*typical!*—of the rules adults make to ensure they will get what they want, which in this case was our humiliation. We raced directly to the library, where we engaged in rebellion against the injustice of the rules by tearing open all nine envelopes. Those numbered 2 through 9 contained only blank slips of paper. Envelope number one provided a clue not to the whereabouts of the ceramic turkey but to the location of the *real* envelope number two. Mere words are not sufficient to describe the exhilarating outrage with which we responded to this shameless treachery. We took thirty-six minutes to locate the second envelope tucked among the logs in the drawing room fireplace, and it contained nothing but a puzzling twenty-word clue to the whereabouts of the third envelope.

"When I grow up and have children," Isadora said, "I will never be so cruel as to subject them to emotional turmoil like this."

I pledged myself to the avoidance of becoming an unfair adult. "On my next birthday, I'm not going to accept being eighteen. I'm going to insist on being sixteen and move backward from there."

Gertrude said, "If we have to pay a price to have dinner with Laurel and Hardy, why don't our parents just beat us with sticks? This search isn't going to go well. It's already not going well. I'm a nervous wreck.

It would be more humane to just beat us with sticks and then let us go to the dinner."

Isadora threw up her hands in exasperation. "If only it were that easy. Mother and Father aren't the kind who beat people with sticks."

"You never know," Harry said. "Kaiser Wilhelm seemed like an okay guy, everyone's friend. Then the Germans sank the *Lusitania*, twelve hundred people drowned, and the next thing you know, there's a world war and ten million people are killed. So, after all, he turned out to be the kind of guy who would beat you with a stick, and even worse."

"Whoever said the kaiser was an okay guy—those people were idiots," Isadora declared. "Anyway, Daddy and Momma wouldn't have any interest in sinking ships and ruling Germany. So what does this clue mean? We better find the third envelope quick."

As the day progressed, we didn't stop our search to have lunch. We didn't even *think* about lunch. We lived for the hunt, and Rafael was as engaged in the mission as we were. He was so enthusiastic and got so worked up that we had to put him on a leash and take him out to pee three times. When the clue in the fifth envelope proved to be crushingly difficult to solve, clever Rafael earned our everlasting gratitude by finding the sixth for us. He could make no more sense of the clue than the rest of us, but his nose eventually led him to the conservatory, among the palms and ferns and orchids, where the envelope was taped to the underside of a teak bench. We gave him two dog biscuits and hoped that he might come to our aid yet again and quickly find the remaining three, but whatever trace scent had drawn him to number six did not exist on any further envelopes. By our own wits, we acquired the ninth and final clue, which consisted of **Dad has gone early to bed**. That was the easiest clue of all, aimed at Harry, and he solved it in a minute flat. Four Laurel and Hardy shorts had been released in 1928, and *Early to Bed* was Harry's favorite of the four. Dad—Franklin—always sat in the same seat when watching a movie in the Bram's screening room. The five of us flew through the house and found the ceramic turkey eighteen minutes before the deadline, under the theater seat. A triumphant procession ensued, concluding in the kitchen, where the treacherous adults were still cooking and the air was redolent of a feast to come.

Mrs. Symington said that Laurel and Hardy had called to express their regrets for not being able to attend the December dinner after all, but members of the Clyde Tombaugh Club were too hard-boiled to fall for a razzing that obvious. Having been taught the proper way to arrange a place setting, we four set the table. We were so high on the day's adventure and on the prospect of a turkey that was *not* ceramic, the task was almost as much fun as the hunt had been. After we all freshened up and changed into our best clothes, we gathered at five o'clock for a long dinner marked by much laughter.

Here are a few things I thought that evening, now more coherent and polished than when I first thought them. On this holiday when we give thanks, we are expressing gratitude not merely for the food and drink, but as well for family and friends, for this world of great beauty and the opportunities it offers. We're giving thanks for our life, because even when life is hard, there are joys to be had in living it, even if those joys come from finding ways to escape the hard world for a while, as books allowed me to escape. Happiness and despair are choices to be made. If I hadn't embraced books and lived in the worlds within their pages, I might have sunk into despair, unable to see the light even when it shone. Had that happened, I wouldn't have survived to be brought here by Loretta and Franklin, to know Izzy and Gertie and Harry, to experience Thanksgiving and so much else. Sometimes it might seem that hope is for fools, but it is only such fools who have any chance of making it through the long night to a new dawn.

After the dishes had been washed and dried and put away, after we had said good night and gone to our rooms, I remained in a state of elevated happiness not far short of rapture, grateful for relief from evil, pain, and loneliness. I went onto my balcony. The night was cool, but I was not chilled. The overcast had begun to break up. Among the clouds were jigsaw pieces speckled with stars. The garden lights had been extinguished. With the softest lamplight at my back but otherwise darkness all around, I felt as I had on my first day here, when I had stood on this balcony in warm sunshine. I had come from slavery to freedom, a miraculous journey that had taken less than a tank of gasoline; as measured in consequences, however, it was a voyage of ten thousand miles. I could not rightly wish for more, and yet I felt that if the balcony fell away from the house and crashed to pieces on the terrace twenty feet below, I would not go with it. I would stand in midair, unfazed, and then would step forward into an even greater freedom the nature of which I could not yet imagine. As I inhaled deeply, the clouds opened as slowly as the shell of a mollusk, revealing a moon as round and white and perfect as a pearl.

TWENTY-FIVE

At a late breakfast on Friday, with just the siblings and me at the table, Harry declared that the trouble with all holidays was the next day. The next day was reliably a major letdown. "Next days are nothing days. Nothing happens. No one has the energy to do anything interesting. It makes you want to gross out everyone by eating bugs, just to get something started."

"I love the day after," said Isadora as she spread marmalade on a slice of toast. "I like to lie around thinking about where I'll go on the day after I'm twenty-one and finally grown up. I'll travel somewhere exotic the day after every holiday, somewhere related to the holiday just celebrated. I'm going to see the world ten times over. After Thanksgiving, I might go to Turkey. You know, after the fall of Rome in the fifth century, Constantinople was the capital of the Byzantine Empire for a thousand years. That's six times older than the United States. What must a city that old be like? It must be wondrous. Strangely enough, I read that Turkey raises a lot of cattle and sheep, but they don't raise any turkeys."

"You," said Harry, "are the perfect example of why I might eat an entire bowlful of squirming bugs if that would change the subject to something halfway interesting. Anyway, Constantinople is called Istanbul now. If you ever go there, just remember they were allied with the Huns in the war. You'll have to wear a tent, only your eyes showing, wherever you go."

"I am fortunate," Gertie said, addressing me directly, "to be the middle child. The first child was spoiled because she was the first. The third child was spoiled because he was a boy following two girls, so a son was a big deal. As you can see, the excess attention they received has left them both mentally ill, while I remain sane and sensible."

Harry's next-day hypothesis was not destined to be elevated to the status of a theory on that twenty-eighth of November. The hallway door opened and Anna May entered the breakfast room, not in her maid's uniform on this vacation day but in evident distress. "I didn't sleep. Not all night. I gotta spill something. Your parents gotta know. I let it go too far. I didn't mean for something like this to happen. I let it go too far because I thought he'd just give it up. But not him, never him. He clings to bad ideas like a tick to a cat. I should've known. Where are your folks?"

Isadora sprang to her feet. "I'll take you to them. They're in the study, working on a script. I believe it's a pirate picture, but they want Wallace Beery for a featured part, so it must be to some extent a comedy. I love Wallace Beery, don't you? He's such a big, bearish, goofy sweetheart."

The door to the kitchen opened, and Mrs. Symington entered. She was surprised to see Anna May on a holiday weekend. "Annie, what are you doing here?"

"She needs to see Father and Mother," Isadora said. "I'll take her to them. It's no trouble at all."

"You finish your breakfast, young lady," Mrs. Symington said, motioning for Isadora to sit down. "Annie, come tell me all about it."

Anna May followed her boss into the kitchen, and the door swung shut behind them. We four young detectives froze for a few seconds and then erupted from our chairs as though we received an electric shock. The compulsion to eavesdrop was stronger than the inclination to do the right thing and mind our own business. When we hesitated and exchanged glances, however, we wordlessly acknowledged that Mrs. Symington would expect us to surrender to curiosity and would catch us in the act. Humiliation and perhaps even punishment would follow. There wasn't enough room at the door to accommodate all our ears anyway. We sat down to our unfinished breakfast.

Isadora looked glum as she stirred a spoonful of Welch's grape jelly into her half-finished glass of orange juice. She couldn't yet set off to see the world ten times over, so she compensated by being adventurous when it came to food combinations. "So much for the idea that the day after a holiday is always dull. Something big is about to happen. Everything is going to change. We will remember this day for the rest of our lives."

"How it's going to turn out," Harry disagreed, "is it's going to be even less interesting than a cat with ticks. The 'he' she was talking about will be some pasty-faced Elmer Gantry she fell in love with, but the cad stole the church money and ran off with the Sunday school teacher."

"If you're going to be a successful Mississippi River steamboat card sharp," Isadora said, "you better learn to read people better than that. Anna May's whole life is hanging by a thread. She's ready to throw herself in front of a freight train. She has leprosy or a brain tumor, and the man she loves won't stand beside her in her hour of need."

"When I'm a writer," Gertrude said, "I for sure won't write any stories that stupid. I'm going to write stories that make people happy, stories about a talking mule, books about a rabbit whose best friend is a duck and they have adventures."

"Move over, Hemingway," Harry said.

Isadora put down her grape-jelly-and-orange-juice cocktail without tasting it. "When did you decide to be a writer?"

"Like forever. At least eight years ago."

"When you were two?"

"Two and a half," Gertrude corrected.

The siblings continued to be siblings, but my thoughts harkened back to my first day at Bramley Hall. Something had been worrying Anna May since I'd met her almost three months earlier. On that occasion, as she stood in the receiving line, her smile had been weak and brief. She had been mantled in anxiety as surely as an angel would be clothed in light. Mrs. Symington had said Anna May was going through a rough patch but was a lovely person and would warm to me in time. My first night in the Bram, I had dreamed that Rafael and I were prowling its many rooms, looking for someone who didn't belong there. At one point, I dreamed that I woke and that a shadowy figure stood at my bedside, watching me. It had been Anna May. *Are you there?* I had asked. *No,* she'd said. Of course Anna May left every day at five o'clock, and the visitor who had spoken just one word to me had been an eidolon, a phantom shaped by a sleeper's mind. As I finished my breakfast, I assured myself that Anna May's urgent visit this morning had nothing to do with events back in September. Whatever brought her here on the day after Thanksgiving had no more to do with me than it did with leprosy. My imagination had caught a fever from Isadora.

Seven hours later, as I was ensconced in a library armchair, reading R. D. Blackmore's *Lorna Doone,* Franklin and Loretta came to share with me the truth of the situation, which did indeed tie me to the worried housemaid. They sat on the sofa opposite my chair. Anna May had remained at the Bram for less than an hour after she arrived at breakfast. My two guardians had been busy in the six hours since her departure. "There's no way or reason to withhold this news from you," Loretta said, "and we don't want you to hear it in pieces from other people." Franklin assured me that I had nothing to fear. He said they were on top of things. Although Loretta was as beautiful as ever, her face had little color, and she looked fatigued. "Dear, you know there are good people in our business. You've met a few. You'll meet more, people we know and respect and trust. The tabloids claim the motion-picture industry is full of depraved people. They call it 'Hollywood Babylon.' There is some truth in that, maybe a lot of truth. Some actors and actresses aren't prepared for fame, not the level of fame movies bring, fame unlike anyone in history has experienced before—and they're showered with stupendous wealth virtually overnight. Everyone knows their faces, and millions adore them, so some are the kind who soon adore themselves. They become monsters of self-regard. Others regret the loss of privacy and don't know how to deal with adoration. It makes them a little crazy. Or they feel they don't deserve it, fear losing it and falling out of favor. Whatever their story, they often turn to the same escape—cocaine, marijuana, heroin. Sometimes, when they take up with terribly immoral people, they find themselves doing things that leave them with no self-respect, until they believe the only way out is suicide."

Anna May was not an actress, but her brother, Connor, believed he was and that he should be known throughout the world. Although he snagged a variety of small roles, stardom eluded him. According to Franklin and Loretta, Anna May had known her difficult and troubled brother was a dope runner, a go-between who drummed up business in the world of moviemaking and delivered merchandise from a major drug dealer to the customers. This income kept him in high style while he waited for his big break. The work not only brought Connor into contact with Hollywood players but also involved him with numerous hangers-on and seedy hustlers. One of those was Willy Joe Maxwell, a freelance photographer who peddled his work not merely to legitimate magazines and newspapers but also to the most lurid tabloids. Without our knowledge, Maxwell had been a threat to me since I came to Bramley Hall.

Through his contacts in the world of speakeasies, Willy Maxwell had learned that Franklin and Loretta, notable figures in the movie business, had been customers at Blue Mood in San Diego on Saturday, September 6. One of the performers that night was unconventional for the venue, a young freak who appeared onstage nearly naked. Mr. and Mrs. Fairchild were said to have "bought out the freak's contract" from her promotor, Captain Forest Farnam, and taken her away into the night. Maxwell was sold that information by a Blue Mood employee on Sunday morning, September 7. By that afternoon, he located Farnam and, without revealing what he had learned about the Fairchilds, he determined that Captain had never taken—and never allowed to be taken—photographs of the freakish girl, because no one would pay to see what they had already seen in one publication or another. That was a calculation common to carnies who owned a ten-in-one or a hootchy-kootchy show. Maxwell concluded, as would most men like him, that the Fairchild couple brought the freak into their lives for decadent purposes. He became excited by the prospect of an unusually creepy scandal that would be highly profitable for an entrepreneur of his boldness—if only he could gain access to the girl. Among his sources for stories was Connor Sizemore, who took a sawbuck or two in return for tipping off Maxwell where private parties in progress would present an opportunity to photograph a few celebrities who were inebriated or drugged past the point where they might make fools of themselves. Of the contacts in the photographer's black book, only Connor would be able to help Willy learn details about the layout of the Bram. His sister was on the household staff.

When Loretta had first sat on the library sofa, she'd plucked a small decorative pillow from it to give her more room. She held the pillow on her lap during the story she and Franklin had to tell. Now her hands tightened on it as if it were the throat of someone into whom she meant to choke some common sense. "That Monday evening when you and I were still at the Beverly Hills Hotel, Maxwell and Connor were already badgering Anna May in her apartment, trying to persuade her to cooperate. They knew we were bringing you home. They wanted to develop a floor plan of the Bram so Maxwell could find his way to your room. They wanted to know how to get into the house at night with the least risk of being caught. Maxwell intended to come here with a woman as bad as he is, someone to overpower you, perhaps with chloroform, and keep you quiet while he . . . got his pictures."

Loretta did not say that the woman would have stripped me out of my pajamas so that I could be photographed naked. However, I had no doubt that was the intention.

"Week after week," Loretta continued, "month after month, they kept digging at Anna May. She wouldn't give them what they wanted. She insisted there was nothing different about you, you were just a kid like the other kids. She thought they would give up on the idea sooner or later. She didn't tell us because she worried Connor's drug running would come to light and he would go to prison."

"Connor had always been trouble," Franklin said. "He and Anna had never been as close as a brother and sister ought to be. But she felt she should be loyal to him, protect him from himself. Then a week ago, Connor and Maxwell said, 'All right, okay, forget about it, maybe it was a screwy idea all along.' Anna May believed they had given up on the scheme. Then on Thanksgiving Day, Mrs. Symington phoned each of her girls to wish them a happy holiday. In passing, she mentioned that Rafael escaped poisoning by some unknown vile person who had thrown contaminated meat over the estate wall. Anna May knew at once that Connor and Maxwell were going ahead with the operation if by one means or another they could eliminate the danger posed by Rafael."

"Which means," said Loretta, "somehow they got a floor plan and a way into the house."

In those days, even the grandest mansions rarely had alarms. Those security systems available at the time were problematic and frustrating, issuing false alarms or ceasing to function without warning. Usually, little more was needed to guard against a home invasion than good deadbolt locks.

If Willy Maxwell and Connor Sizemore had developed a floor plan and other useful information about the Bram, there was one likely source. I said, "Imogene Blackthorn."

Loretta grimaced. "We can't know, but we *know*."

"Have you called the police?"

"Not an option," Franklin said. "They can't make arrests on the basis of intentions that aren't provable. Besides, if this ends up in court, the trial becomes not about the criminals and the crime. It becomes about you. The defense attorneys and the scummiest of the tabloids will see to that. Sweetheart, we aren't going to let you be dragged into this. Never. Maxwell thinks we're pigeons. We're not."

"We can handle him," Loretta said.

I didn't doubt that they could handle Willy Maxwell. I just wondered, "How?"

And even if the current threat was dealt with effectively, Captain was still out there. If Maxwell had found me, so had Farnam—and with what intention?

TWENTY-SIX

Willy Maxwell lived in a rented Art Deco bungalow on a residential street not far from Charlie Chaplin Studio. He was a man of the night, always on the prowl for celebrity cocaine parties and drunken revelers and middle-aged married directors squiring sixteen-year-old girls into or out of dens of iniquity. He wanted photos for which he could write stories that would sell to *GraphiC*, a Bernard McFadden rag located in New York, which paid him a thousand dollars for a piece that could support a headline like WEEKEND ORGIES OF SILVER SCREEN STARS or YOUNG STARLET WARNS OF CELLULOID ROAD TO RUIN. Many of his "young starlets" were girls who had come to Los Angeles to be famous, began to pay their bills by selling more of themselves than their acting talent, but nonetheless still dreamed of being the next Janet Gaynor. Having possessed innocence and lost it, some of them could break your heart—if you were not Willy Maxwell; for him, they were nothing more than material. He worked seven nights a week because he took so much pleasure in his profession, especially when a shocking photo and the accompanying story humiliated the subject and damaged a major career. He usually rose at eleven o'clock in the morning and took his breakfast shortly after noon at the Vine Street Diner. At half past eleven on the Sunday after Thanksgiving, before he could set out from home, he answered the doorbell and found two Los Angeles Police Department detectives. They were holding their ID for his inspection, as if they didn't have time to waste in the niceties of an introduction. Their names were Shamash and Astarte.

They were big men, about six feet four, as physically imposing as Gene Tunney, the boxer. Tunney was as handsome as any actor, but not these two. They were so hard looking that even if they played thugs that the hero beat into pulp, no audience would believe any hero ever born could survive an encounter with them. Their suits were top of the line—wide in the padded shoulders, trim-cut in the waist—and their shoes looked Italian. They wore fedoras with style, at a slightly rakish angle. Quality wristwatches. Pinkie rings. Had they been wearing cheap suits, they might have scared the hell out of Willy, but he was shrewd enough to know them for what they were—cops on the take, his kind of people. Whatever they wanted, whatever trouble they laid on him, there would be a deal to be made.

They wanted to know where he'd been between midnight and 3:00 a.m. He said he'd been around and about, here and there, wherever he heard the action was, making a living from the sadly sinful behavior of his fellow Angelenos in the entertainment business. He gave them a few addresses, but they weren't satisfied. They asked if he knew a girl named Marion McMurray, and he said he didn't, and they said his business card was clutched in her hand when she was found stabbed to death, and he calmly said that perhaps he had known her by another name. People in the motion-picture business often changed names, sometimes more than once. Shamash and Astarte didn't want to come into his house for a look around, nor did they suggest he accompany them downtown to the Robbery/Homicide Division, which was a relief. However, they asked that he take a ride to the apartment of Marion McMurray to help them interpret a few odd things about the crime scene. Shamash assured him that he didn't need a shyster. Astarte said there was a deal to be made that would be beneficial. Willy had already tumbled to the fact that they were bent. He had often done profitable business with dirty cops. He was in a line of work where, if you wanted to prosper, you took chances that most people avoided.

And so Willy Joe Maxwell got into the back seat of the unmarked sedan. Shamash drove, and Astarte sat in the front passenger seat. Their destination was an upscale apartment building at the west end of Wilshire Boulevard, the kind of place where a girl who made a good living in a bad profession welcomed men who would never hire her for a role in a movie but appreciated the conviction with which she faked orgasms. The apartment was elegantly furnished, although the bed was blood-soaked. Willy was impatient to learn why they had brought him there. The stench of gore made him eager for fresh air.

They explained that Marion McMurray wore monogrammed panties. They suggested that, when he went home, he should conduct a search of his house to find his collection of five pairs, including one caked with blood. They invited him to spend an hour searching this apartment to see if he could locate the dead woman's client book. His name appeared in it with notes about his kinky preferences. They suggested that he ought to examine the shoes in his closet at home to find the pair with Marion's blood on the soles. It was a setup. Willy had not been her client. These bulls weren't going to pin this on him, but they meant for him to understand they could send him to death row for another case whenever they wished. "Or," said Shamash, "it could work the other way. You do what we're going to ask, and if one day you knock off somebody, we make sure you're not the sucker who takes the fall for it."

Having received—and paid for—many tips from cops regarding the errant behavior of Hollywood glitterati, Willy had considerable respect for police corruption and the benefits that could flow from it.

Shamash and Astarte had delivered a threat rather than a tip, but it was a threat that came with a get-out-of-jail-free card. Willy had been born understanding the concept of quid pro quo. He said, "Whatever you want, consider it already done."

Shamash explained what Willy had been smart enough to agree to. He would never again try to kill the Fairchilds' dog. He would make no attempt to enter Bramley Hall alone or in the company of anyone else. He would never, under any circumstances whatsoever, photograph the girl being adopted by Franklin and Loretta Fairchild. He'd never come within a hundred yards of her. Furthermore, he would make no inquiry with anyone in the police department or the government regarding Detectives Shamash and Astarte; if he were to do so, they would know, and they would assume he intended to rat them out to Internal Affairs for having been paid under the table to represent the Fairchild family in this matter. Were that to happen, the next time Willy woke, he would be dead and in Hell.

Now that the three of them were players on the same team, full of mutual respect and affection, the detectives took Willy Maxwell home. They collected the five pairs of monogrammed panties that had been planted in his residence, including one that was stiff with dried blood. They showed him which pair of shoes had bloodstained soles so he could dispose of them. Willy offered each man a pint of the finest Scotch from his illegal stash, but they declined because they were on duty and because, in all good conscience, they could not violate the law of prohibition, which they were sworn to uphold.

Although Franklin and Loretta, being talented filmmakers, had created a convincing storyline and had produced it to perfection, the success of it—they admitted—depended in part on Maxwell being less hip to flimflam and bunco games than he thought he was. In Marion McMurray's bedroom, he couldn't be faulted for not realizing the bedclothes were soaked in pig blood, not human blood. Few if any surgeons would have had a sharp-enough olfactory sense to tell the difference. The badges and ID of the LAPD Robbery/Homicide Division, which Shamash and Astarte had presented to the photographer, were so accurate in every detail that any department official would have accepted them without a second glance; in 1930, the title "prop man" was new to the motion-picture business, but some of those who did the job were so talented and obsessed with detail that they could have made a living outside the law as forgery artists. Identical to the make and model that the LAPD provided for detectives in any of its plainclothes divisions, the sedan Shamash had driven was tagged with a reproduction of police department license plates; it had appeared in *Darkmoor Lane*, and Willy had not for a moment doubted that it was what it seemed to be. Shamash and Astarte, whose real names were Leonard Sharpe and Enzo Valenti, might have triggered Willy's suspicion if they'd been actors well cast for their roles. However, their faces were too ordinary for movies—not handsome enough to sell a production, not mean enough to be the faces of villains, not quirky enough for roles that provided comic relief. Nevertheless, they possessed solid theatrical techniques and the confidence to masquerade as corrupt cops because they were members of a recently created profession, stuntmen, and for a few years had spent their days on set, watching actors and learning how to pass for them successfully in the hard-action shots. Sad-case Marion McMurray was not dead. In fact, she did not exist. The apartment was owned by a young actress who was having success playing best friends and kid sisters, and who was expected one day to have top billing. Willy Joe Maxwell never had a chance.

TWENTY-SEVEN

As November gave way to December, I marveled that in all the novels I'd read, no character had experienced a more eventful three months than those that I had just lived through. From carnival freak show to Bramley Hall, from resignation to fierce hope, from a life lived in books to a life worthy of a book, from the cold regard of Captain to the love of a warm and happy family.

On the evening of Tuesday, December 2, when I was in bed with a book, Loretta came to my suite to prepare me for Anna May's return the following day. Anna May had taken a few days of vacation time after discovering that her brother and Willy Maxwell tried to poison Rafael—and why.

"I know you will be kind to the girl," Loretta told me, "but I want you to understand why kindness is especially warranted in her case. I assume you know nothing of her past."

"She pretty much keeps herself to herself," I said, putting my book aside.

Loretta sat on the edge of my bed. "Her and Connor's mother was distant, self-absorbed. The woman had no interest in her children.

Their father was a fiend for rules and a demon for enforcement. The mother never came to their defense."

"He beat them?" I asked. "For all his awfulness, Captain never beat me, though at times his self-control seemed a near thing."

"Bronson Sizemore, their father, scarred them both. Scarred them physically and psychologically. As punishment, among other cruelties, he sometimes locked them in a closet for a day or two without food or water. By the time she was an adult, Anna May sought peace and safety above all else, which meant living alone with a pistol in her nightstand and another in a kitchen drawer. She says she'll never marry, never chance a man like her father. The safest romance, the only kind she wants, is found in pulp magazines that specialize in love stories with happy endings."

"She's a gentle soul," I said. "That speaks highly of her after what she endured. Others would've been made mean by such a father."

Loretta smiled and took one of my gloved hands. "Who would know better about gentle souls? I'm sure you'll also understand about her brother. He's handsome. Has some acting talent. Wants to be a movie star. Who doesn't? But he lacks discipline. He's bitter, full of hatred for the world. He went for easy money. Drug dealing, running whiskey, providing to rich movie stars what they want and should not have. He made a place for himself because he was quicker to violence than his competitors. Yet Anna May kept him in her life."

I squeezed her hand. "I do understand, Loretta. Sympathy born of shared suffering is a strong bond."

"Now that Anna May has learned that he meant to profit from your pain and humiliation, she has at last pushed him out of her life. When she returns tomorrow, she will want to see you."

"And I want to see her."

"She blames herself for not standing up to her vicious father. She blames herself for surrendering to fear and not protecting her younger brother when they were children. Blames herself for what he has become. She blames herself for many things for which in truth she has no blame. It's etched in her heart to feel guilt merely because of an innocent association with others who have done wrong."

I shook my head. "She doesn't need forgiveness. She had nothing to do with what her brother and Willy Maxwell planned. For heaven's sake, she warned us. Because of her, you and Franklin had time to cook up Shamash, Astarte, and the ugly death of Marion McMurray."

"But she *does* need to apologize. When you accept her apology, it'll be as if a priest has given her absolution. You say you're a freak when you're not. *You are not.* She thinks she's a *moral* freak when she's an innocent. The world is full of such confusion. How sweet it would be if you convinced her otherwise about herself and, by doing so, saw yourself for the angel that you are."

For a minute or two, I could not speak, nor could she. But of course we had no further need for words just then. When we could get to our feet, we hugged each other. We held hands as I walked her to the door. She kissed my forehead, and she left.

I don't know why I expected to lie awake till dawn. Instead, I slept soundly, deeply, and did not dream. The day had left me with no anguish for my sleeping mind to resolve.

The following day, Wednesday, December 3, is one I will never forget, and not just because of my meeting with Anna May. Harmony was excited to announce that the young man she had mentioned to me back in September, the one whom she loved and who loved her—Allen Sussman—had asked her to marry him. She said yes. He had been an audio engineer and sound effects man on a radio show that dramatized news stories of the past, one of which had been the explosion of the immense holding tank at the Purity Distilling Company in 1919 and the deadly flood that followed. Recently he landed a job on a new production at a higher salary, and the program—a half-hour comedy—was an immediate runaway hit. Harmony Mintner would become Harmony Sussman in March 1931. She wouldn't leave her job because she was paid very well, as were the others on the staff of the Bram. The Fates that made her an orphan and robbed her of a career as a pianist had now brought her a husband.

At half past nine, Anna May came to my rooms. I welcomed her and brought her to the sofa. I sat, and for an instant I thought she was going to kneel before me in supplication. Mortified, I quickly patted the cushion at my side, and she settled next to me. She was trembling and not able to sustain eye contact. As a grown woman who worked for people who valued her, she knew that no discipline would be administered, yet the battered child within could not dismiss the possibility of a sudden, angry blow.

I realized then that she and I were sisters, related not by blood but by dreadful experience. Anna May's mother had been as indifferent toward her children as if they were the offspring of a stranger. My mother was gone, either dead or a misty figure who had spun so many mysteries around herself that she was cocooned forever beyond discovery. Anna May's father had been a monster as fond of violence as any predator in fevered fiction. My unknown father might actually have been a monster, considering the biological legacy he left me, and Captain was a horror in his own right.

Anna May apologized for transgressions she had not committed, and I forgave her for them as though they had been real. A haunted quality in her voice, the words she used and those she avoided, and an enduring sorrow in her eyes revealed a profound loneliness of which I knew well the texture and bitter taste. I resolved that in the days ahead I would make every effort to befriend Anna May and encourage her to feel valued as much more than a housemaid.

Even as that intention passed through my mind, Rafael padded through the open door to the upstairs hallway. He came directly to the sofa and insisted on inserting himself between us. It was as though he knew everything that had occurred because of the threat against his life, understood that we were there largely because of him, and that he expected to receive the affection he deserved as the instigator of positive change in our lives. Without success, the alchemists of the Middle Ages had sought ways to turn lead into gold. Dogs were alchemists that knew something more valuable than that elusive formula—how to turn weeping into laughter.

After lunch, the siblings and I were in the game room adjacent to the library. Of two tables, one provided for a jigsaw puzzle that could be worked for days or weeks without anyone disturbing it. The second table was for cards—today 500 rummy. Members of the Clyde Tombaugh Club had for the time being set aside the camaraderie with which we investigated mysteries. Each of us was determined not only to reach five hundred points first, but also to do so by such a wide margin that the other three would be humiliated beyond endurance.

When Mr. Symington stepped into the room to say, "Alida, the Mr. and Mrs. wish to see you in his study," my score was an even hundred points, and every one of the three card sharps was far ahead of me. If I threw in my hand, I could fairly—though not credibly—claim that I could have won if I'd been able to stay in the game.

Anticipating my intention, Isadora said, "We will all put down our cards, all four of us, and wait for you to return, Alida. There is no limit to how long we'll remain patient while the game is put on hold. Even if you were to be gone a year, we would be here when you return, wearing the same clothes, emaciated but cheerful and ready to pick up where we left off."

"Ah," said I, "and how long do you need before you've memorized the cards in the hand I leave on the table?"

"That," said Gertrude, "is what a lawyer would call character aspiration."

"Assassination," Isadora corrected.

"As if you would know," said Gertrude. "I just might become a lawyer so one day I can rub your face in just how wrong you are."

Harry said, "Go ahead and chicken out, Alida. It's a cowardly thing to do, but if you can live with the realization that you're a coward, then go ahead and do it. No one will hold it against you or think less of you or mock you. It'll be on your conscience and no one else's."

"Thank you," I said, and threw in my cards to be added to the remaining draw.

As one, my companions shouted—"Loser!"—and booed me out the door. God, I loved them.

In Franklin's office, he sat behind his desk. Loretta sat to the left, and an empty chair stood in front of the desk. A man I'd never seen before occupied a chair to the right.

The visitor wore a gray suit, a white shirt with silver-and-onyx cuff links, and a striped tie. A pair of reading glasses was balanced low on his narrow nose. He had a deep tan and white hair. His smile seemed warm and genuine. I liked his smile. His eyes were the gray of brushed steel, and his stare was sharp as he peered at me over the half lenses of his gold-rimmed spectacles. I did not like his eyes. Franklin said the visitor was Mr. Morgan Waterford. With the stately grace of a gentleman, Mr. Waterford rose to his feet, nodded in a sort of half bow, offered me his hand, and said that it was a pleasure to meet me. *Stay alert.*

He turned out to be a founding partner in a law firm that had grown until it now employed one hundred and ten attorneys, a number in which he seemed to take pride. I had read Mr. Dickens's *Bleak House,* so I had mixed feelings about lawyers. Those steel-gray eyes were ice-cold now and colder every time he focused on me. Although his smile had seemed warm, he had no further use for it as he picked up an attaché case that stood on the floor and put it on his lap.

"In spite of considerable effort," Mr. Morgan Waterford said, "I must tell you that we have not yet been able to locate your birth certificate. We have not developed any credible information on the identity of your father, although we suspect that he might have been the founder and first owner of the Museum of the Strange, which we understand, in carnival parlance, is commonly called a 'ten-in-one.' That person seems to have gone by five different names during the first two years of the enterprise before then selling it to Captain Forest Farnam, and not one of those five individuals has a true history. In other words, they are five false identities. In each case, there was a wife, each with a unique name. As none of those five women has a true history either, we assume they were the same person living under false identities. The possibility exists that this woman might have been your mother, but we have no evidence of that. We do not know who she is or where she is—or if she's even alive. Finally, Captain Forest Farnam. He earned the rank of captain as an engineer in the US Army. In 1905, he left the Army in order to work for the noted engineer John F. Stevens on the construction of the Panama Canal. He died there of malaria in 1906. No doubt about that. His name began to appear once again in various public records beginning in 1909. We have been unable to discover who your Captain Farnam might have been before he stepped into a dead man's shoes. I regret to say, young lady, in regard to the investigative aspect of our assignment, we've served you and your guardians less well than we had hoped."

"No, sir," I said. "You've told me more about Captain than I ever learned during all the years I was under his thumb."

This was followed by more lawyer talk about the laws governing adoption, which were less complicated in those days. I had spent the past three months learning the ways of the family, having adventures with the Clyde Tombaugh Club, and worrying about somehow being made to return to Captain and the Museum of the Strange. As I listened to Mr. Waterford, I began to realize that during that time, Franklin and Loretta, through their attorneys and otherwise, had used their contacts and influence successfully. The point of this meeting was not to prepare me for bad news, but to educate me so that when I signed the papers swearing I understood what the Fairchilds were offering me and what I was accepting, I would be as informed as the law required. Because I was not an infant, I legally had choices to make as to my future. And because I was not a fool, I made the right choice, accepting the incredible gift that this family had given me. When Mr. Waterford produced from his attaché the sheaf of adoption papers, I signed them with alacrity even though my trembling hand twice dropped the pen.

Included in the adoption was a name change, and not just from Farnam to Fairchild. As long ago as the few days that we had spent at the Beverly Hills Hotel, I had expressed the desire to shed both names Captain had conferred on me so that I would not think of him every time someone addressed me. Having given this considerable thought, my guardians arrived at a name that was enough like Alida for me to adjust to it, but which possessed a different meaning and inspired a different nickname. Adiel, pronounced *add-e-l*.

"*Adiel,*" said Loretta. "It might lead some to call you *Addie*, but it seems to us that's more pleasant than being called *Alley*."

"You're free to pick another name if 'Adiel' doesn't resonate with you," said Franklin.

"It resonates," I assured them. "It sounds just swell. It sounds like who I always should have been."

I didn't ask how they arrived at it or why it appealed to them, because at that moment all I cared about was signing those papers before the moment popped like a bubble and I discovered that I'd been dreaming.

Although I had been surprised that the adoption was to be finalized, everyone else at the Bram had known and kept the secret. In celebration,

Chef Lattuada had prepared a special meal. Although the food was fit for royalty, the best thing was that everyone, not just the family, sat together at the extended table. Harmony, Anna May, Lynette, the Symingtons, Mr. Reinhardt, and Luigi stayed late, quite late—thirteen for dinner. The number presented no risk of bad luck because we counted Rafael as number fourteen. There was much laughter, and I discovered that even some laughter could make me cry. I had destroyed the reputation that had been my armor. I was no longer the toughest, most hard-boiled freak of all freaks. The best thing about the event wasn't, as I had first thought, that everyone at the Bram sat down to a celebratory dinner with me. The best thing was that they *wanted to*.

TWENTY-EIGHT

The rest of December passed as if the four weeks were only one. Christmas trees were set up and decorated in the entrance foyer, the living room, the dining room, and the library. Fireplace mantels were draped with evergreen garlands that would be replaced as they grew dry and discolored. Mr. Stan Laurel with his wife Lois and Mr. Oliver Hardy with his wife Myrtle came to dinner on the fourteenth. In their short films, Laurel had been funnier than Hardy, but at the table, at least on that occasion, Hardy was the funnier of the two. Their wives were more amusing than either of their husbands—which made for a lovely evening but might have been why both marriages ended in divorce.

By Friday the nineteenth, beautifully wrapped gifts began to be arranged under the tree in the living room, and every morning a few more appeared as though by the visitation of elves during the night. On the afternoon of the twenty-first, we children gathered around the breakfast table with Franklin and Loretta to receive a status report on our individual trust funds. I was surprised that a fund had been established for me and amazed by the amount with which it had been opened. I insisted I had no need for my own money. Franklin counseled me that one day I certainly would have a use for it. More would be deposited in every fund each December. There would also be annual appreciation of the assets. Each of us was required to decide how much to give away this year. A charity was named, and we were expected to be generous though not irresponsible.

Brow furrowed and eyes squinted, Franklin said, "This court is now in order. Three of you rich little snots have been through this ritual in previous years, and Adiel will have a painful education in the process."

Gertrude objected. "I don't like being called a 'rich little snot.' I demand to be called a 'rich little booger.'"

"And I," said Isadora, "demand to be called a 'rich little hocked up glob of phlegm.'"

"I second their demands," Harry declared. "Those are perfect names for them."

"And Harry," said Gertrude, "should be called a 'stinky rich little fart boy.'"

"Your father and I," said Loretta, "will certainly take your demands under advisement later tonight over an illegal beverage. Adiel, do you have something else you'd rather be called than a 'rich little snot'?"

"I'm content with that, Your Honor."

Isadora warned, "Don't be a suck-up, Adiel."

"Okay. I demand to be called a 'rich little pus pimple.'"

The ritual, the process, and the expectation of this kangaroo court was this: As each of us children suggested a figure to donate to charity, the two judges would gently and with humor mock us for being Scrooges in the making or for mistaking ourselves as Rockefellers. Because I owned the newest fund, my suggestion of 10 percent was met with approval. As for the other three, each ideal contribution depended on the age and success of the fund—13 percent for Harry, 15 percent for Gertrude, and 17 percent for Isadora. The siblings, well versed in this ritual, howled at the unfairness.

Having money of one's own was miraculous, and giving it away was more fun than I would have imagined back when I didn't have any. "It's not a sin to live well if you've earned it," Loretta told me. "But it's shameful not to share. The two most dangerous human flaws are greed and envy. Some unfortunate people have both, and therein lies the cause of all wars, most murders, and untold suffering."

Harry said, "I object. Your Honor is preaching from the bench."

"Denied."

"I object," said Gertrude. "I'm greedy and envious, and I don't feel unfortunate at all."

"Denied."

"I object," Isadora said, "on the grounds that I'm bored."

"Me too," Loretta and Franklin said in unison. "Court closed."

During the months I'd been free from Captain, I had discovered much about families that confirmed what I learned from novels. One of the best discoveries I made at the Bram was that if everyone in the family loved and respected one another, even the dullest tasks could be fun. Of all that one generation might leave to the next, one of the most important legacies is laughter.

That night, I had a dream in which Captain appeared and said, *The two most dangerous human flaws are greed and envy. Therein lies the cause of most murders.* I woke trembling and sweaty. After an hour or so, I convinced myself it was a dream, not a premonition, and I settled back into an uneasy sleep.

The remaining days of that December went by faster than magic reindeer can fly. For the first time in my life, midway between my seventeenth and eighteenth birthdays, I experienced Christmas. It was all I could have hoped. On Wednesday, Christmas Eve, we went to church one hour before midnight for a service lit by one thousand candles. From Thursday through the following Tuesday, the family played games together, threw balls for Rafael until he surrendered to exhaustion, and set off on delightful expeditions—including to the late Henry Huntington's vast gardens in San Marino. We baked cookies together, prepared meals, and dealt with basic housekeeping because the staff was off on holiday through the first of January; none of it seemed like work because we were doing it together.

Chef Luigi Lattuada, who was vacationing at a seaside hotel in Mexico, sent telegrams for five days—December 26th through the 30th. They were addressed not to Franklin and Loretta, but to me and the siblings. As none of us had received a telegram before, the first one was flat-out magical and the next four were highly anticipated. The messages were, in the order received: having a wonderful time without you; I do not miss you at all; when I dreamed you checked into the hotel, I woke screaming; if you come here I will throw myself off a cliff into the sea; on second thought, if you come here I will throw you off a cliff into the sea. Each of the five was signed, your much-loved chef. One thing was certain—in addition to being a fabulous chef, when Mr. Lattuada was in a joking mood, he sure knew his audience.

On New Year's Eve, after dinner, we enjoyed glasses of lightly spiked eggnog in the library while listening to recordings by Duke Ellington and his twelve-piece band. At eight o'clock—eleven on the East Coast—Franklin tuned the radio to Chick Webb and his band performing in Harlem's Savoy Ballroom. There was no stopping this jazz, this swing style. If you heard it once, you knew it was going to be the music of our lives, which it proved to be throughout the 1930s and the war.

At midnight, we were in the gardens with a supply of sparklers, carving the darkness with blades of glittering light. The hissing and crackling, the gunpowder smoke, the scent of the chemicals that gave the sparks color, the minims of light like fireflies born and at once gone—it was exciting and lovely from the moment Franklin lit the first until the final encrusted length of wire sputtered away its last feeble sparks.

Loretta said it was time for bed, whereupon much groaning and pleading and general consternation arose from us. We were as awake as we had ever been! Surely we could not sleep for hours yet! The stroke of midnight brought a new day, yes, but it also closed the old world and opened a new one. We needed hours to adjust to these new circumstances. Loretta smiled and gave us fifteen minutes as she and Franklin retired for the night.

We members of the Clyde Tombaugh Club had earlier agreed to conduct a secret post-midnight ghost hunt after the adults went to bed. Previous ghost hunts had not turned up anything supernatural. The siblings were willing to consider that no one had yet died in the Bram and that they might have let their imagination spin a bit out of control. However, Mr. Reinhardt had poisoned mice and rats on occasion, mostly in and around the garage. It was disquieting to think that a horde of rat ghosts might be slinking through the house at night, looking for ways to get even with us. If that might be the case, the wise thing was to get proof of them to persuade a rodent exorcist to banish their spirits from the Bram. With that fanciful theory to build a game around, the night should have been ours.

However, as we stood in the dark gardens where the astringent smell of sparklers was slowly fading, weariness came over us quicker than we expected. The long day had been so tiring that we decided to postpone the rodent ghost hunt until later in the month. We went to our rooms, slightly miffed at ourselves for lacking the energy to fulfill our rebellious intentions.

Rafael spent the first few hours of 1931 snoring in my bed. I dreamed of a ghostly Pied Piper leading multitudes of red-eyed rat spirits through the dark rooms and hallways while we slept. When I saw the Piper's ghost was that of Captain, I began to issue soft cries of alarm. Although I didn't at once wake myself, I disturbed the slumber of the shepherd. He snuggled against me with his head on my shoulder and licked my neck until I woke with a gasp and sat up from my pillows.

After an absence of months, Captain had crept back into my dreams twice in two weeks. As before, I told myself that these visitations meant nothing. In fact, considering how long I'd lived under the yoke of the freak-show master, I should have had horrid dreams of him every night.

A small electric night-light in the form of a candle relieved the worst of the darkness. In that dim glow, I denied Captain any hold on me by calmly lying down again. I turned on my side, now face-to-face with Rafael. His habit was to maintain eye contact as long as I did. I repeatedly smoothed one gloved hand along his flank and said, "I sometimes wonder if we once traveled far together on the road from Nineveh to Media." He thumped his tail three times on the mattress, but I didn't know what to make of that.

I worried about what ill fortune might befall my new family, but the following three years were good for the Fairchild clan. We enjoyed a period of warmth and honey, even though events beyond the walls of Bramley Hall seemed always to be moving toward something cold and bitter.

Part Two
1934

The second dream in shades of blue was set in the Museum of the Strange. Rain drummed on the stretched canvas of the tent. Only two human oddities were on display. I was the sole paying customer.

The first occupied stall was crowned by a banner that declared GREED. On the stage, Captain Farnam sat at a table, spooning gold coins from a bowl and eating with ravenous appetite. His teeth broke as he ate and fell in bits onto the table, but he cared not.

The next exhibit was titled ENVY. Here Captain was dressed in a magician's tuxedo. From a top hat, he produced a dove whose wings were bound so it could not fly. Captain returned the bird to the hat, plucked flames from thin air, and threw the fire onto the dove.

Horrified, I ran back to the entrance and halted at the sight of rain. Instead of bearing the words ADMIT ONE, the ticket in my hand said COMPASSION and on the flip side REVENGE. I wiped my thumb across the latter and erased it. The old woman selling tickets took mine, and the storm stopped. I stepped outside into sunshine. The ten-in-one was gone with all the carnival except for the ticket seller. She said, "Compassion is not that easy, dearie," and she too disappeared.

—from a letter by Alida, April 17, 1927

TWENTY-NINE

During the three years after my first Christmas at the Bram, much happened in the wider world. The economy plummeted. The Empire State Building rose. Prohibition came to an end. Five thousand banks collapsed. Ten million people were out of work. Russian communists were murdering tens of thousands. Elsewhere, fascism was ascendant. War was in the wind. Fewer motion pictures were profitable. Having fallen from fame to obscurity, from wealth to penury, some Hollywood players committed suicide.

In a world full of dire drama, the smaller world of the Bram remained an island of peace and plenty, for which we were grateful. Indeed, life within the walls of the estate was so pleasant and so little disrupted by the problems of the age that, although I wrote of those days in my journal, I have decided not to include them here. Some would find them uneventful and therefore boring. Others might resent such ease in a time when multitudes were struggling, though I wonder how many people of that mind would tour a freak show when next a carnival came to town and give its human oddities no more consideration than would be given to the animals in a zoo.

By 1934, Franklin and Loretta were working harder than ever. As I would discover, they had been tempered by terror and tragedy in their youth and learned how to bend adversity into advantage. Two of their recent movies were runaway hits. In addition, they owned a piece of *The Champ*, which earned Wallace Beery an Academy Award for Best Actor in 1932, and they had an even more profitable piece of *Grand Hotel*, starring Garbo and Barrymore.

Three years meant three birthdays, which brought me to twenty, Isadora to fifteen, Gertrude to thirteen, and our Harry to twelve. Children grew up faster in those hard days, both children who lived on the fraying edge of want and those more fortunate who were taught, as we were, that prosperity was a blessing but not a promise of eternal success. Even for young Harry, ghost hunts and other late-night games lost the appeal they once had. Although the Clyde Tombaugh Club was never officially disbanded, it ceased to exist without our quite realizing that it was no more.

Isadora had matured into a serious pianist. She had been taking lessons since she was ten but never considered a career in music until the summer of 1931. That was when Harmony, now Mrs. Sussman, approached Loretta to say that, as she performed housework, she listened to Isadora practice. Because Harmony's once promising career had been brought to an end by the explosion in Boston twelve years earlier, she was distressed almost to the point of anguish to see the promise of Isadora's talent go unfulfilled.

"Her teacher, Mrs. Arnett," Harmony said, "is a lovely woman, but her own talent is suitable for little more than teaching society girls how to play recitals when they have their coming-out parties. She simply isn't good enough to perform on a concert stage or even with a first-rate band. Isadora *is* that good, maybe even great. But Alice Arnett is incapable of recognizing it and sadly unable to help Isadora reach her full potential."

Impressed with her housemaid's concern, Loretta went straight to the point. "Harmony, dear, I know what a musician you once were, what you lost, and how dedicated you are to whatever you undertake. If you say Isadora has such potential, I'm sure you're right. So will you do for her what Mrs. Arnett cannot?"

Surprised, Harmony said, "Oh, no. I'd love to if I could. But with my hands as they are . . . I could play examples of passages for her, but never as well as what a public performance requires. Not anymore."

"Music is of the heart," Loretta replied, "and technique is born in the mind. You have a great heart and a fine mind, Harmony. When playing a few bars or even more, as an example for a student, it isn't necessary for you to play well enough for Carnegie Hall. What matters is that the student should be inspired to play better than the teacher."

Harmony wanted to be persuaded, and Loretta was intent on persuading her. Soon the red-haired and freckled Mrs. Sussman, while still a valued housemaid, was offered an additional salary to serve as a piano teacher.

I have sworn to remember so many special days at the Bram that it's a good thing I have a prodigious memory. The day Harmony took that second job will always be one of them. She came to my rooms to share the news, and she seemed to be only half a step below a state of euphoria. Twelve years after losing all hope of a career as a pianist, she felt that her derailed life had been put back on track. She was such a good soul that the prospect of guiding Isadora to a life as an acclaimed musician gave her almost as much satisfaction as if she could have become a star herself. Since then, all of us in this special place had heard Isadora's playing move steadily toward the high plateau that Harmony was sure the girl could achieve.

During those three quick years, Gertrude had become a teenage beauty without losing any of her elfin charm. She turned away every compliment about her appearance as though she thought the words were mere flattery. For a while, I thought she might be so self-conscious of her deformed hand that when she looked in a mirror she couldn't see how lovely she really was. However, she seemed indifferent to her disability, making no effort to conceal the hand, frequently gesturing with it. Eventually I understood her reaction to anyone who praised her good looks; it was genuine modesty and nothing more. When asked what she wanted to be when she grew up, she had recently begun to say she intended to be her mother. "Maybe I'll write and produce movies. But they're not going to be all dark and grim like some of what Mother writes. If you knew Mother only from her movies, the noir stuff, you'd think she woke up every morning expecting to be falsely imprisoned for murder and went to bed at night expecting to be shot in her sleep. I might like to be the *real* Loretta, make comedies and romances, go for laughs and the good kind of tears. Or I could be a music critic, following Isadora around and getting even for what an insufferable older sister she's been to me."

As preposterous as it might seem, at the tender age of twelve and in spite of his rambunctious nature at times in the past, Harry had become a scholar. Oh yes, like other boys, he collected not just battalions but *armies* of cast-lead hand-painted toy soldiers, each two inches tall and with the stoic expression of one who fears not death. And yes, Harry often put the two game room tables together, re-created famous battles, and imitated machine guns, explosions, and the miserable wheezing of men dying from mustard gas. Unlike other twelve-year-old boys, however, these activities were not play, or at least not primarily play. Harry was seriously pondering alternative strategies and tactics that might have resulted in the loser winning so decisively that history would have been radically changed. He had read so much military history that he would soon know more on the subject than General John J. "Black Jack" Pershing.

His interest in the past began a few years earlier when he immersed himself in a series of nonfiction books about pirates. We often found him walking the halls while reading, shirt open to the waist, a rubber replica of a dagger clenched in his teeth, a colorful bandanna tied around his forehead, and one of Loretta's earrings dangling from his right ear. Lynette Rollins, the housekeeper who looked like the writer Anita Loos, was a favorite of Gertrude's, and with Lynette's help, the imp acquired a colorful plastic parrot. She suggested to her brother that he fix the bird to his left shoulder. Though he loved Gertrude, Harry was not amused. He was *serious* about history as he had not been about anything else. All of us were relieved when his interest in pirates was exhausted and he moved on to less flamboyant historical figures. He had recently begun to supplement his interest in military history with books about famous explorers.

As for me, I spent those three years being the best adopted child and sister that I knew how to be, while also serving as the teacher schooling the siblings. For a while, my biggest concern was that the three were being inadequately socialized because they had no interaction with other children their age. I had read Sigmund Freud and knew him to be a charlatan. Nonetheless, some of his prescriptions for mental health, especially as rebottled and sold with slicker language by his legion of acolytes, seemed to be worth consideration to ensure that my three charges would be well rounded.

I stopped worrying on a party night when the Bram hosted sixty guests. I came upon the siblings in the conservatory with Fletcher Henderson, the leader of a big band, and a marvelous young singer named Ethel Waters. Also present was a magazine writer, James M. Cain, who was working on a novel to be published the following year under the strange title *The Postman Always Rings Twice*. A lively conversation was underway. As I listened, I realized the children were neither bothering nor boring the guests. These former members of the

Clyde Tombaugh Club were wowed by the accomplished adults, and at least for the time being, Henderson and Waters and Cain were likewise charmed. The family, the staff, and the family's friends had socialized my students while I wasn't paying attention.

And so we arrived at Christmas and then New Year's Eve, which were only for family. There were games, including those with Rafael, and expeditions and movies. There were sparklers in the gardens as 1933 rolled into 1934. After three years as blessed and enchanting as perhaps anyone had ever known, I didn't feel I was tempting fate when I said sleepily to Rafael, "Three more years just like them."

Four days later, early on Thursday morning, Gertrude was taken to the hospital by ambulance, in such critical condition that she was not expected to live.

THIRTY

Having gotten up quite early, having had a brown-sugar muffin and a glass of milk in the kitchen before the staff began their day, I was reading *Look Homeward, Angel* in the schoolroom, waiting for the children to arrive for their lessons. In a state of great agitation, Victoria Symington came to tell me that Gertrude had been taken to the hospital and that her parents had gone with her, Loretta in the ambulance and Franklin in the new Cadillac. Isadora and Harry were currently in the care of Chef Lattuada, the only one on staff who could calm them. "The sweet child was so hot, Adiel. Our Gertie, she was burning up. Burning up and delirious." The housekeeper's face glistened, beads of perspiration looping across her brow. She was a sturdy woman in the best sense, a picture of good health, though not at this moment. She seemed to have been withered by having felt the terrible heat of Gertrude's fever. I dropped the book and rushed to the door, and she followed me. "We don't know why, what it is that's happened to her. It was so fast." I ran toward the house, and she hurried after me, assuming that I had not understood. "Addie! Addie, she isn't here. The ambulance is already gone." The great beauty of the gardens, the magnificence of the Beaux Arts house, the peaceful refuge of the estate—none of it would be the same without Gertie. None of it would matter. No light could penetrate this place once the shadow of her death had fallen upon it.

I crossed the terrace and entered the house by a library door, with the head housekeeper close behind me. I was breathless more from dread than from the long run through acres of gardens. My voice was raw when I said, "I have to get to the hospital. Can you take me, Victoria, Mrs. Symington? Can you take me to the hospital?" She said there was nothing we could do there, that it was in the hands of the doctors now, the doctors and God. Loretta would call with a report as soon as she had news. "No, no," I objected. "Please. You don't understand. There's no reason you would. There *is* something to be done, something I can do. I don't know how. I don't know why. But I can do it." The woman was distraught. She had known the siblings since they were babies. She and Julian were childless. She loved the Fairchild children no less than if they had been the offspring of a cherished sister, perhaps even as if they were her own. Fear and grief gripped her, but even if she'd been calm and thinking clearly, there was no reason she should make sense of what I was saying.

I thought of Anna May. Years had passed since her brother had schemed to destroy my happiness. We were friends. All wounds were healed. But she would feel an obligation to help me without having to be persuaded that what I claimed made sense. "Where's Anna May?" I asked. "I need to find Anna May." Mrs. Symington thought Anna May was in the laundry room, and I hurried across the library with the dear woman confused and trailing close after me. When I came into the main ground-floor hallway, I heard voices. I looked to the left and saw Mr. Symington talking to Lynette Rollins in the foyer. The day was cool, and Lynette was wearing a coat over her uniform. She always reported for work on time, so she must have been departing for somewhere rather than just arriving.

Intuition told me that Lynette, rather than Anna May, was my best hope of getting to Gertie in time. I called out to her as I ran down the long hallway. When I reached her, I saw tears standing in her eyes and jeweling her lashes. She was fumbling car keys out of her purse. I asked where she was going, and she said, "I can't focus on work. How could I? With all this, I can't stand it here. I need to be there, the hospital." I asked her to take me with her. I had never learned to drive. I'd never seen a need to learn. Now I felt stranded, helpless. "Get a coat, Adiel. Hurry." I had no need of a coat. All I required was to be on our way. I threw open the front door and hurried down the steps of the portico. The employee parking area was near the head of the circular driveway, on a wide lay-by concealed behind a tall hedge. We arrived together at Lynette's 1930 DeSoto coupe. As she started the engine, she said, "I don't think I can take this again. I really can't. I'd rather it was me."

The car was small, the compartment tight. Lynette drove fast but well, although sometimes she had just one hand on the wheel as she blotted her eyes with the sleeve of her coat. The hospital was in West LA at least half an hour from the Bram unless she jammed the pedal down. I asked if she could go faster. She put on more speed, though she said, "I want to be there, but not to say goodbye. God help me, if that's the way it has to be, then I'd rather get there after it's too late for goodbye. Holding her hand when she slips away, the horror of it . . . I don't have the courage for that." The tremor in her voice and the note of dismay that bordered on despair suggested she was tormented not just by what might be coming but also by what had occurred somewhere in her past.

Perhaps it is a consequence of having read hundreds of novels through which I have been propelled by an abnormal curiosity, but when my interest is piqued, I can't repress it. Lynette's need to tell was equal to my need to know. I asked whose hand she had been holding when death had come.

After a hesitation, she indicated her purse, which stood on the seat between us. "Photos. In the picture windows of my wallet."

The wallet held six snapshots of a dimpled girl of ten or so. Her winsome smile, which would have charmed in life, could in memory devastate.

"Her name was Elizabeth," Lynette said shakily. "She wanted to be called Libby. Her father was the worst, walked out on us when Libby was three, but she . . . she was the very best. There was no meanness in Libby, never a tantrum or a pout. She was always upbeat. She had a strong sense of herself, the way Gertrude does. But like Gertie, she was self-aware and could be so funny. She was never bullheaded. I was seventeen when I brought my baby into the world and . . . and only twenty-seven when she left me. It was 1918. How old were you then, Addie?"

"Four," I said.

"So you won't remember much how it was. A million of our men were fighting the war in Europe. Meat, wheat, and sugar were all rationed. There was plenty of work for women, work men had done before they went overseas. Like so many others, Libby and I adapted. Life was challenging, but it wasn't hard. We had each other. We were happy. And then came September."

That autumn, I'd been too young to understand events occurring in the wider world. Even then I was in a freak show, displayed in my own stall, though not yet the star. I was too young to know why carnival season was cut a month short. I read about the crisis in later years. The nation had been ravaged by the Spanish flu, for which no cure existed. One out of four people had come down with the illness. Many thousands of adults and children died.

"My Libby was hit hard by the contagion and confined to an influenza ward with more than a dozen other children. If she had been eighteen, in an adult ward, isolation rules would have barred me from visiting her. But the hospital was dealing with a severe shortage of nurses, many felled by influenza. Because children often got more desperately ill than adults, requiring closer attention, anybody willing to risk infection by properly attending to a loved one was granted dispensation from the rules if they seemed competent for the task."

I could speak only in a whisper. "You were with her when . . ."

"Yes. I could have been nowhere else." All these years later, racing to Gertie Fairchild, Lynette felt as if she were reliving the greatest tragedy of her life. "All those years ago. Sixteen years. Seems like yesterday. Seems like today. Gertie's not in the same hospital as Libby was. If it was the same, I'm not sure I could do this. Gertie's like a niece to me. No. More than a niece. I don't know how to say it except . . . God, I love her. I love them all so much. I took this job when Izzy was three and Gertie was a baby because I knew I'd never have another of my own, never dare risk it . . . the loss, the pain. I wanted to die after Libby passed. I considered all the ways I could . . . check out. But if there's a world after this world, she'll be there, and maybe if you take your own life you don't get the next one. One day I want to see her again."

"You will," I said, as if I knew anything about it. But what else could I say. "You will."

"So if I couldn't leave," Lynette continued, "then I wanted to be around children, help them grow and prosper in whatever small way I could. Two little girls, and then Harry. It's been so lovely all these years. So safe. So safe here in the Bram. Shelter from . . . from everything. And by the end of this year, it would have been even better. But it's like Harmony says—"

I finished her sentence—"Stay alert"—as she swung the DeSoto onto the approach road to the hospital and was forced to slow down behind drivers on less urgent business than ours. I asked, "Better by the end of the year?" She revealed that the Symingtons recently decided they were ready to retire to a little house they owned in San

Clemente. Franklin and Loretta felt that Lynette, with her two-year degree in accounting and having successfully managed a small hotel when Libby had been alive, could take over as property manager of the Bram and hire new housekeepers to fill the positions she and Victoria would be vacating. She would move onto the estate, into the apartment now occupied by the Symingtons. She wanted nothing as much as being fully in the embrace of the Bram and the Fairchild family.

"So why didn't I . . . in all these years, why didn't I realize if you love them and lose them, it doesn't matter a damn if they're yours or they're someone else's babies? Why didn't I realize it rips you up just the same if you love them so much?"

As she sought a parking space in the crowded lot, I said, "Why? Because maybe then you would never have taken this job you so much wanted. Maybe you wouldn't have gotten past thinking about all the ways to check out. You wanted to live. For Libby. Sometimes, to go on, we have to wrap ourselves in a little self-delusion until we don't need it anymore."

She pulled into a parking space and switched off the engine. "Adiel, I don't want to go in there."

"You're going. Come on. *Come on.*"

Together we hurried across the parking lot. The low winter sky was a seamless white from horizon to horizon, as blind as the eye of some merciless carved-stone god last worshipped five thousand years ago. The day had gotten colder since we'd come out of Bramley Hall.

When we stepped into the hospital lobby, Lynette took my gloved hand and held tightly to it as we got Gertie's room number from the woman at the information desk. She continued to hold my hand all the way to the third floor, letting go only when we stepped out of the elevator. I thought she would halt, but she stayed at my side as we followed the main hall, reading the room numbers.

Franklin came out of 332 looking ghastly, as though he'd stared into the Pit and the Pit had stared back. He seemed not to recognize us for a moment. His voice was tortured, as if he hated not just the words he spoke but also hated himself for speaking them. "There's nothing to be done. It's over."

THIRTY-ONE

Gertie didn't like to ask for help. When she'd been a toddler and trying to dress herself, she didn't want to be shown which was her left shoe and which was her right. She struggled with footwear morning after morning until she understood how the subtle curve of the shoe matched that of the foot. When it came to such mysterious implements as forks and difficult garments as zippered jackets, she wanted to be shown just three times, often only twice, and then be left to solve the problem herself over days or weeks. As a result of her insistence on self-sufficiency, she mastered the challenges of the toddler years faster than either her sister or brother. She was still a preschooler when she expressed contempt for crybabies. If she sustained a minor cut, she washed it herself, swabbed it with iodine, and applied a Band-Aid. If later one of her parents noticed the bandage, Gertie explained her failure to involve them by saying, "It wasn't even a boo-boo. It was just a so-so." She put great value on self-sufficiency and physical stoicism, which in nearly all cases contribute to a better and happier life. Once in a while, however, bad luck has its way, bad luck and tragedy.

Tuesday afternoon, Gertie had come down with what seemed to be a cold. She went to her room, put on her pajamas, and got into bed with a selection of magazines. She had no elevated temperature yet. Her mother placed a large carafe of orange juice in an ice bucket at bedside and a box of Kleenex on the nightstand. In the event that Gertie developed a sore throat, Loretta had tucked a bag of honey-lemon lozenges in a nightstand drawer. She had wanted to sit for a while with her daughter, but Gertie said, "It's a silly cold caused by a stupid virus. I'm smarter than any virus. I'll be over this in no time. You have work to do, Momma. You and Daddy have to keep us in diamonds and furs." When Loretta dryly noted Gertie possessed no diamonds or furs, the girl said, "But if I wanted them, I could have them one day. I could talk Daddy into it. When you *can't* have what you want, you want it more. That's when the big trouble starts." Loretta assured her that Franklin was no more likely to buy her diamonds and furs than he was to buy her an elephant. If she wanted diamonds and furs, she'd have to work very hard or marry a husband foolish enough to spoil her. "No problem," Gertie declared. "One day when you see a woman wearing a white ermine coat and an ermine hat and fifty pounds of diamonds, walking her elephant, you'll know who she is."

The decline was slow. By dinner, Gertie still had an appetite but wanted only chicken noodle soup followed by ice cream. Chef Lattuada brought the soup and half an hour later homemade chocolate-cherry ice cream. When Loretta and Franklin came to say good night, Gertie had already fallen asleep. Rather than wake her to take her temperature, Loretta pressed a hand to the girl's forehead. If she felt the slightest bit warmer than normal, it was not enough to be called a fever. Later it would be determined Gertie woke in the night with a nosebleed, an annoyance that bothered her two or three times a year. She got out of bed, went into her bathroom, and used a wad of medical cotton to plug her left nostril, which was the source of the flow. She most likely sat up in bed for a while, head tilted forward, before lying down to sleep once more. The cotton stopped the bleeding, but it also prevented nasal discharge from escaping the left nostril until she removed it just before she had a light breakfast in bed at nine o'clock the next morning. A thermometer revealed a one-degree fever, nothing to be concerned about, though no one could know that the events of the night just past all but ensured a mortal crisis.

As the day progressed, Gertie suffered a headache that came and went, watery eyes, congestion she could not fully relieve without risking another nosebleed, chills, and mild fatigue—nothing that suggested a condition worse than the common cold. Her appetite improved from breakfast to lunch but declined during the afternoon because she'd developed a sore throat. She was being treated with aspirin, which relieved the headache, and was drinking a lot of fluids. At bedtime, her father helped her ease into dreams by providing a shot of Scotch in a cup of milk. Loretta looked in on her twice before midnight, but the girl seemed to be sleeping peacefully.

The decline was slow—but then fast. Gertie wasn't battling a mere common-cold virus. She had a sinus infection caused by a strain of staphylococcal bacteria. The damaged blood vessel in her nose was small; nevertheless, it provided bacteria access to her circulatory system. Staph can produce toxins leading to septicemia, also called "blood poisoning." When Loretta checked on her daughter shortly before six o'clock Thursday morning, the girl was sweating and yet shaking from chills. Her fever had risen to 104 degrees. Her heart raced. She gasped for breath. She was mentally confused and too weak to get out of bed. By the time the ambulance transported her to the hospital, her fever had reach 105 degrees, and her blood pressure had fallen to 80 over 50. The medical team administered intravenous fluids to maintain her blood pressure at 90 over 60, intravenous penicillin and other antibiotics to combat the infection, and oxygen to raise her blood oxygen level. The urgent purpose was to prevent septicemia from becoming septic shock, which leads to death in more than 60 percent of the cases and sometimes leaves survivors with severe disabilities. Within an hour of Gertie's admission to the hospital, it was determined she was already in septic shock. By the time Lynette and I arrived, in spite of the aggressive treatment the girl was receiving, her temperature had risen to 106. Although her blood pressure mostly remained stubbornly at 80 over 50, sometimes it dipped to the mid 70s over high 40s. Widespread blood clotting had perhaps begun, and kidney failure might be imminent.

Franklin always seemed to be a man who could handle any trouble that came his way. No difficulty, no disappointment, no setback, no threat could disrupt his calm nature or long diminish the optimism that was as much a part of him as his love of making movies. This Franklin before Lynette and me was not the one I knew. He was a gray shade of pale. The architecture of his face, previously so pleasing, seemed to have undergone a shift in its substructure. Horror and grief robbed him of handsomeness. He appeared tormented, insecure, too lost to be the leading man of any motion picture, which once he could have been. If our Gertie was alive, even with her vital organs fast failing, there was hope. I carried that hope like a mystical light in a mysterious vessel, lacking understanding of it but certain of its power. I wasn't confident, however, that I could penetrate Franklin's anguish, convince him of what could be done, and quickly gain his cooperation. I asked Lynette to stay with him, and I went into room 332, a two-bed unit with only one patient.

In a white hospital gown under a white sheet, Gertie looked no less white than her bedclothes, eyes closed and deathly still. At the sight of her, my heart mispaced itself, chasing each incomplete beat with the premature start of another so that I could feel the hard palpitations of the extrasystolic rhythm knocking in my breast. A nurse was in attendance on one side of the bed. Loretta held fast to the railing on the other side, eyes fixed on her daughter, lips moving as if she must be silently reciting a prayer. I went to her and gripped her left hand, which was clenched around the bed rail. Though she was unable to speak, her eyes were such pools of misery that no words were necessary to convey her pain and fear.

I spoke softly, presuming that the nurse must be too busy to eavesdrop. "This is important. I didn't tell you at the time, when it happened. I didn't want to seem like even more of a freak. Willy Maxwell didn't just try to poison Rafael. He succeeded. I found the dog almost dead. I held him. I held him and . . . you saw. I don't know why or how I did it, but I did." In Loretta's anguish, she was not clear-minded enough to understand me at once. To encourage her, I drew from memory the opening sentence of a classic novel and invested it with an urgency the author never intended. "'Dorothy lived in the midst of the great Kansas prairies, with Uncle Henry, who was a farmer, and Aunt Em, who was the farmer's wife.' That's how it starts. It ends like this." After rapidly reciting the last fifty-one words of Chapter Twenty-Four, I said, "If you want every word of *The Wizard of Oz*, I've got them. You know I've got them. And so much more. If that, then why not Rafael? And if Rafael, why not Gertie?"

Loretta was a screenwriter, a fine storyteller. She believed in a world of possibilities. An innocent character could be sent to prison for killing her lover and find herself sharing a cell with the real murderer. The same character might instead win the lottery with a ticket that a sudden breeze blew in her face. Or she could discover that a street-corner Santa, ringing a bell for donations, was the real deal, doing a little were-you-good-or-were-you-bad research. However, though she knew that I was weirdly gifted, too much was at stake here for her to accept at once that real life could be as strange as anything in a work of fiction. She said, "Honey, if that's what happened with Rafael, maybe it was a one-time thing. Maybe it was just for dogs. What if you try with Gertie—and you can't?" I understood her worry. When hope is gone, daring to hope again only to be disappointed makes the loss doubly painful.

"Mother," I whispered, using that sacred word for the first time with her, for the first time with anyone. "Mother, let's do this. Let's do this together."

After she searched my eyes, after I met her stare with more confidence than I felt, she kissed my brow. "If it's not like Rafael, it won't be your fault. Never your fault."

With that, she knew what needed to be done. The nurse—Teresa—must not be present, and Franklin needed to join us. If some new treatment existed that might be tried or if Gertie were responding to her current care, Teresa might have been reluctant to leave the girl unattended in critical condition. But when Loretta requested private time for family prayer, Teresa responded with sympathy. She said she could be summoned with the call button. She stepped out of the room and sent Franklin in to join us.

I called him Father and asked him to trust me, and although he appeared as bewildered as he was grief-stricken, he said of course he trusted me. "Lynette should be here, too," I told them. "She's got to be. Not just because she's going to be property manager or anything like that. She's lived a long time with sorrow since Libby died. Nothing can lift that from her. But maybe, just maybe, this will make it a little less heavy to bear. She dearly loves Gertie. I'm sure she can be trusted with secrets. She knows what matters and what doesn't—and trust matters."

The four of us gathered around the bed. I put down the railing to have better access to my sister. Climbing onto the bed to lie beside her would have been awkward, and I could not have drawn her against me without disturbing the intravenous line, the oxygen tube, and the lead from the EKG monitor. There was no reason to suppose that I had to fold her in my arms as I had done with Rafael. I could put one hand on a hand of hers, my other hand on her head. Perhaps that would be enough contact. When Rafael's affliction had passed out of him and through me, my physical reaction had been such that I would have fallen if I'd been standing. I asked Franklin to stand behind me and provide support if I required it.

A short while ago, I had raced away from Bramley Hall with an urgent sense of purpose and arrived at the hospital with the firm conviction that I could do for dear Gertie what I'd done for Rafael. More accurately, I believed that what had been done for the shepherd *through* me, by some power I could neither name nor understand, would now be done through me for my sister. As I leaned against the bed and placed my hands on her, a cold shadow of doubt fell over me. A nervous flutter passed through my chest and stomach. If a clock had been within my line of sight, I would not have been surprised to see its mechanism frozen by the intensity of my sudden irresolution. Who was I, after all, to assume I possessed the power to raise anyone from near death to health and life? Who was I but a carnival freak, long exhibited nearly naked on a stage, mocked and cursed, to whom normal people responded with horror and disgust and sometimes pity? Luck had lifted me—or call it *grace*—from the mire of a sordid life into an Eden of plenty and respectability, but I had done nothing to earn or facilitate this elevation. I was clothed and fashionable in my own way, but I was still a freak. I attended dinner parties with the rich and famous, but I was no less a freak than I had been in the Museum of the Strange. At the Bram, my walk-in closet featured a full-length three-way mirror that revealed to me always and only the same thing. I was a kind of chimera as in the ancient myths, a human head with a human face, and otherwise a deformed composite that no one could explain. Who was I to save a girl when I could not save myself? There at sweet Gertie's bedside, I was shaken by a waking nightmare inspired by doubt: *From the shores of death, my sister returns to life with shocking suddenness, erupting off the mattress, the body of a child with the head of a rabid dog, foaming at the mouth, eyes red and pitiless, full of the terrible rage that is love turned to hatred, all because I don't know what I'm doing.*

Just as I thought failure was inevitable, a calm settled on me, and the shadow of doubt faded with the waking nightmare. Gertie's fever became mine, beads of perspiration bursting across my brow and streaming down my face. Her headache came with the fever, wave after wave of pain seeking a shore on which to break. I became aware of the patterns of blood vessels throughout my body, arteries carrying poisoned blood away from the heart into narrower arterioles and into capillaries, tiny venules carrying poisoned blood into veins and back to the heart. The stench of toxins. The nauseating taste of bile. My heart, which had been racing, abruptly slowed and my blood pressure fell to match Gertie's, fell and kept falling. My vision began to fade; everything before me fractured into shapes composed of fewer and fewer pieces. I passed out and collapsed backward into Franklin's arms.

Later they told me that I was unconscious less than a minute. Franklin lifted me, turned, and put me on the vacant bed. Loretta and Lynette hurried to me. Franklin said they should summon the nurse, but Loretta saw problems with that, awkward questions that would have to be answered. Fortunately, they hesitated. I had only fainted. I rose toward the sound of my name and opened my eyes and saw their faces hovering over me. I was weak and a bit disoriented, in a peculiar state of mind, part of me still wandering through the book from which I had quoted to Loretta. Harking back to Chapter Eight of that story, I said, "'They carried the sleeping girl to a pretty spot beside the river, far enough from the poppy field to prevent her breathing any more of the poison of the flowers, and here they laid her gently on the soft grass and waited for the fresh breeze to waken her.'"

As you might expect, my companions stared at me as if I had called into question my sanity, Lynette frowning with even greater bafflement and concern than the other two. Their worry evaporated not because I smiled and said, "End Chapter Eight," but because their attention was drawn to the success of our effort when, in the first bed, Gertie sat up and said, "Hey, why am I tangled up here? Where am I? In a *hospital*? If this is supposed to be funny, it's about as funny as Abbott and Costello on the radio without Costello."

THIRTY-TWO

The doctors didn't want to admit their diagnosis could have been so wrong. They couldn't believe a child as apparently ill as Gertrude could so suddenly return to good health. Yet Gertie stood now before them, out of her hospital gown and back in her pajamas, her vital signs normal, her usual ebullient self. Her parents and I and Lynette worked hard to quell whatever suspicion might evolve in the wake of the girl's recovery. We pretended bafflement even as we celebrated what had occurred. We pressed for explanations after the doctors insisted they had none. We worried aloud that septic shock, once cured like this, might return. The physicians explained that septic shock simply could not be cured as quickly as Gertie seemed to have been cured, but once cured it didn't just come back like a temporarily interrupted sneezing fit. We mispronounced the names of illnesses and generally portrayed ourselves as medical ignoramuses, which is what they wanted to believe we were. When their amazement at Gertie's recovery occupied them less than frustration with our silly questions, Loretta distracted them further from consideration of our role in this event by saying she believed in miracles and that this was for sure a miracle. She asked the doctors if they believed in miracles. They said no, but the nurses said yes, which annoyed the doctors. By the time that Franklin paid the bill, the physicians were eager to put the whole episode behind them. They were grateful no one spoke of legal action due to a misdiagnosis.

Although baffled by events, Gertie was excited to be taken home by her friend Lynette. She'd never been in a DeSoto before. And to satisfy the urge to snack while driving, Lynette kept a bag of Frito corn chips in the car, a recently marketed treat that Chef Lattuada had not yet added to the pantry at the Bram.

I rode in the Cadillac with Loretta and Franklin so that we could decide how to manage the revelation of my gift. We quickly agreed there would be no revelation.

"If the children know what I can do, we won't be able to go on as we were. We won't ever be the same with one another, equal and growing up together. I don't want to lose that. I treasure that."

Franklin's astonishment affected his driving. Several times, when he realized he was half on the shoulder of the highway, he pulled onto the pavement with a warning to himself—"Whoa, whoa, whoa" or "Watch it, watch out." He glanced at the rearview mirror, in which my face was framed. "You've known since that day with Rafael and the poisoned meat?"

"I suspected. I was pretty sure. I couldn't be certain."

"It was too much, wasn't it?" Loretta intuited. "Too much to handle. It would've been if it were me."

"Yes, ma'am. I don't . . . I can't walk on water. I'm only what I am—just a human oddity. No one should think I'm something more. If I thought I were, I would be condemning my own soul."

Loretta's chief worry was that of a mother who knew well the ways of children. "If our rascals think of you as a miracle worker, they might be careless. If some reckless stunt might be fun, why not risk a broken arm when it can be mended with a touch?"

226

I agreed. "Just because maybe I can sometimes help heal the sick, that doesn't mean I can restore vision to a damaged eye or reattach a severed foot. I'm sure I can't. I'm sure the dead stay dead. Even if I could call someone back from that far shore, would it be them who returned? Or something else. I wouldn't dare."

We were silent for a mile or more.

Then Loretta said, "The estate staff can't be told. Lynette will have to be warned about that."

"We can trust her," I said. "I'm sure we can. She'll realize how my life would be destroyed if tens of thousands of people sought me out to change the destiny that disease shaped for them. How could I say no to them? But what would the unintended consequences be if I laid my hands on thousands? What if I spared a murderer, so then he went on murdering?"

This silence was heavier than the previous one, much as the air thickens in advance of a thunderstorm.

"We owe you everything," Franklin said, his voice breaking.

"*I* owe *you* everything," I protested. "You owe me nothing. What happened wasn't my doing. Not really. The healing was accomplished *through* me by a power I don't understand."

No one was more grateful for—and humbled by—what happened than I was. I loved them and their children more than I could put into words. A world without Gertie would not be a world to which I could resign myself.

Loretta thought she and I should sit together later in the day to talk of cabbages and kings. I agreed, for no other day in my life had raised more serious issues needing discussion even before the sun reached its zenith. She would come to my suite at four o'clock.

I'd not had breakfast. Yet if lunch had been imminent rather than two hours away, I would not have sat down to a plate of Chef Lattuada's most delicious creations. I was overcome by weariness unlike any I had previously experienced. My mind remained sharp. Yet the fatigue was not exclusively of muscle, tendon, and bone. I felt as if I had been hollowed out or that some vital substance had in part been drained from me, so I would need to let that reservoir refill before I could be myself again. In the living room of my suite, I settled in an armchair. On the lamp table beside me, a copy of *Look Homeward, Angel* waited. For the moment, however, the story I was living had more interest for me than I could find in any book.

I remembered how Gertie's illness passed out of her and through me, causing my vision to fail before I fainted. I was not quite the medical ignoramus that I'd pretended to be when I'd been trying to scam the hospital personnel. I knew the collapse I experienced was a vasovagal attack. When blood pressure drops too low, the brain can't get enough oxygen to maintain all the functions it regulates, so it resorts to a brownout to keep systems operating at half power until blood pressure rises. With Rafael, I thought I had opened a door and let his illness escape him. But I now realized, with Gertie, I took the sickness from her and into myself. It didn't pass through me in an instant; for a short time, maybe a minute, I suffered from septic shock, *my* blood poisoned with staphylococcal toxins as potent as those that nearly killed Gertie. By some trick I wasn't consciously aware of, I expelled the bacteria and toxins, recovering from the shortest case of septic shock in history. With this realization came a revelation I knew to be true: Each time that I spared someone from death, my life was shortened by weeks or months, or years. This was by the design of some authority I couldn't name, according to a law I could never challenge in any court, for a purpose as mysterious as the reason why I was born as I am. I cherished life and the people who made mine meaningful, but I wasn't afraid of death. I'd long known that every gift worth having comes with a price. The cost is not a burden; the cost, not in money but in sacrifice, tells us what we ought to value most. Gertie was alive. *Alive.*

At that moment, I had what a Zen master would call a *satori*, a sudden enlightenment. Others might say the understanding was a grace bestowed. The gift had always been mine since the day I was born; however, it remained unopened because the person I had been for seventeen years had not yet been a girl whose heart had fully formed. In spite of all the wonderful books that had shaped me, I had never developed the degree of empathy that would compel me to recognize and use my healing power. I had been unloved and unloving while in the company of Captain. Love was the key that unlocked my gift. My love for this family—my family—and their love for me had brought my misshapen heart to its full and intended form, first for the benefit of Rafael when he'd been poisoned and now for Gertie. In a sense, they had healed me with their love, making it possible for me to heal them.

Although exhausted, I was also exhilarated. That one such as I, a miscreation twisted into existence by indifferent Nature—so long a monster, a laughable grotesquerie, an object of pity—should find myself in possession of a noble purpose and the power to fulfill it seemed to confirm that even fallen sparrows did not live in vain.

A memory came to me of Chef Lattuada opening his door to the Clyde Tombaugh Club, holding a copy of *A Tale of Two Cities*. I must have been half-asleep, because it was not an accurate recollection, but was part memory, part dream. Instead of asking about the purpose of our visit, he said, "You know very well why you came here. John fifteen, verse thirteen. Now would you like a piece of pie?"

I slept in my chair.

In a sleeper's fantasy glazed with a faux frost of moonlight, I was on my balcony. I climbed onto the balustrade. Purple martins slept in the trees. White rabbits dreamed in their burrows. Defying gravity, I stepped off the balustrade and walked through the night above the gardens, heading east, away from most of the clustered suburbs. No vehicles traveled the roads below me. The land above which I drifted became ever more remote, with here and there a farm and crops in growing season. I knew I was no longer in California. Ultimately I descended toward a family farm that had seen more prosperous times. A sway-backed barn, a leaning silo, a stable and two-story house so weathered and paintless that they were silvered by moonlight. I ghosted across a meadow toward the house but halted when a pale horse and pale rider raced toward me through the tall grass. I wasn't seen because I was there only in spirit. The horse, wide-eyed and screaming in terror, was ridden by a long-limbed figure that seemed now like a lanky boy, now like a mantis. The rider bit the screaming horse on the neck.

THIRTY-THREE

Two days after Gertie's recovery from septic shock, Loretta sat with me in the parlor of my suite and spoke of her long-ago losses and how she met Franklin. Whether I was just a friend of the family or her daughter by adoption, her story was part of mine, as mine was part of hers. It was added to the shelves of my inner library.

She had known much terror and more horror than she would ever reveal to Isadora, Gertrude, and Harry. She and I were bonded now by the secret of Gertie's recovery, which encouraged her to share more with me. However, she had another reason for being forthcoming.

I will include here only the bare essence of what she told me, bleaching the terror and horror into pale facts.

Before Loretta was born, her father and mother—Charles and Eunice Bramley—immigrated to America from England. He was a skilled tailor. She was a talented baker. Opportunities in their homeland were so limited that they needed to build their future half a world away, in San Francisco. Loretta was born on March 14, 1897, three years before her folks purchased a home in the heights.

On April 18, 1906, the quake struck at 5:13 a.m., shortly after she dressed for school. It was 8.3 on the Richter scale. The house was badly damaged, but she escaped without injury. Her parents had already left for work. When she stepped outside, the smoky streets were crowded with wailing, bleeding people. Hitched to wagons, injured dray horses were dying—or dead and stiff-legged—in their traces. Clusters of corpses had spewed forth into the street with the shattered substance of the hotels and apartment buildings.

Loretta needed more than an hour to make her way down through the broken city as isolate flames began to join in great tides of fire. She arrived at the bakery where her mother had become the manager—and saw the woman's battered corpse being loaded onto the bed of a horse-drawn wagon filled with the dead.

Now, taking advantage of a lap blanket draped over the arm of her chair, Loretta pulled it around her to ward off the chill of memory. She said, "Hundreds, if not thousands, were dead. The city needed to spare itself from the worst diseases that would be spawned from legions of cadavers, so some were buried in communal graves. Often there was no way to identify the bodies and no one to make a record of them. I never knew where they interred my mom. The tailor shop where my dad worked was ashes. Perhaps nothing of him remained but bones. I never found out."

I began to understand how she had become the woman she was. Hardship had not broken her; it tempered her as a sword is tempered by heating and quenching. She was lovely and gentle, but she was also steel.

She said, "I headed back home, though the house was damaged. I didn't know where else to go. The city had grown dangerous. Looters. Drunks. Men who, in the face of Armageddon, no longer had moral reservations regarding rape. As the afternoon faded into evening, the noise grew noisier—shouting, laughter, drunken singing. Screams in the distance were those of women, children. Structures continued to fall—roaring, rattling, echoing across the hills."

Being a child with no living relative of which she was aware, with no inheritance pending, Loretta became a ward of the state. South of San Francisco Bay, the community of San Jose suffered some damage, but a state-operated orphanage there agreed to accommodate her and other children in her circumstances. The court commended her to Mercy Village until her eighteenth birthday.

As I listened for more than an hour, I had moved forward on my chair, until I sat on the edge of it.

"Mercy Village," Loretta said, "was merciless, but that's a story for another time. I've told you all this and brought you to the orphanage so you'll understand what I'm about to share. It's something I've found strange and wonderful since we walked out of Blue Mood with you more than three years ago, but after what you did for Gertie, it's stranger and more wonderful than ever. Two things got me through those ugly years at Mercy Village. One was Franklin, who also had been taken there, but that's for him to tell. The other was a future that I imagined for myself. I spent hours every day elaborating on it. That future was the hope that sustained me. I imagined I'd fall in love with a fine man. We would take on the world together and never back down. We'd *be* something, build a business to ensure we never wanted for anything. There would be children, a family so strong that nothing could tear it apart. Of course that man became Franklin. And here's the strange, wonderful thing, Adiel. This family I imagined would include a girl whom we adopted. She would be a girl who, like me, had lost everyone and everything. We would embrace her as ours no less than the children we made together. That was my childish bargain with God, Adiel. If I promised to save a girl as miserable as I was, swore I'd give her all the world has to offer, then God would be obliged to give me the future I wanted. Bargaining with the deity is wrong and silly. It reduces Him to an old rug merchant or used-car salesman. Of course, it's what children do. And not just children. Sorry. I'm babbling."

"Not at all," I disagreed. "I believe in miracles. You saved me from Captain. You are my miracle."

Years had passed since I'd thought about what Captain might have done after Loretta and Franklin paid him off, what my few little "daymares" might have meant. Having mentioned his name, I found myself wondering what fate had befallen him. He surely hadn't built the small retirement home on the oceanside lot. He would have realized that sitting on a porch and staring at the sea for the rest of his life wasn't for him. He needed to feel important, respected, feared. Holding power over others gave his existence meaning. I pitied whoever was currently his chattel, and I was grateful that he was out of my life.

THIRTY-FOUR

The economic depression grew worse in 1934, but the state of the economy was not the only thing that shaped the times. For one thing, it was also a year of great music. Early big bands continued to introduce Americans to a sound they didn't know they wanted until they heard it. Formed that year, the Dorsey Brothers Orchestra came on strong. Instead of three trumpets and two trombones, the Dorseys used one trumpet and three trombones. The sound was huge.

After three years with Harmony Sussman as her teacher, Isadora had become, in her family's opinion, a musical genius. She could play a romantic piece like Liszt's "Dream of Love" and follow at once with a piano sonata by Haydn in high style. However, on those occasions when Izzy smiled while at the keyboard, she was playing a number by Duke Ellington or the Hot Five, or a tune Chick Webb's band performed on a broadcast from the Savoy Ballroom.

On Saturday, April 14, almost two weeks after Easter, she heard the Dorsey Brothers' "Stop, Look and Listen" just once on the radio and hurried to the music room the moment the number ended. Relying on memory, in little more than two hours, she adapted the orchestral arrangement into a piano solo. Throughout that process, I sat toward the back of the room, listening to her with admiration just short of amazement. In four years, she had become an accomplished young woman and seemed to have found her passion.

The following Monday, at three o'clock in the afternoon, Chef Luigi Lattuada and I were standing on opposite sides of the center island in the kitchen, having coffee, when the subject of Isadora came up somewhat indirectly. I said, "This is really good coffee."

"I add a little chicory root when I brew it."

"Chicory root," I said. "I'll have to remember that."

"Yes, a day might arrive when your life depends on remembering chicory root. You never know."

"Is the difference only chicory root?"

"I also add a little cinnamon. I hope remembering both that *and* chicory won't tax your memory too much."

"This is really, really good coffee."

"Even though I take great pride in my coffee, such pride that I would kill any man who spoke against it, forgive me if I suspect you came here to talk about something else."

After the siblings rushed out of the schoolroom at the end of the day's instruction, each hurrying to the object of her or his fascination, I had wandered the gardens with no conscious purpose. I was in a state of mild melancholy that I could not explain. In truth, I didn't desire to understand the source of it. I wasn't a moody person and didn't want to slide into being one.

Perhaps I had wandered into the kitchen because the analysis and advice of a chef seemed far less likely to damage my psyche than would the diagnosis of a trained psychotherapist. Were I to praise Chef's coffee a third time, I would appear insincere; though superb java, it wasn't so good that he could justify murdering anyone who spoke ill of the brew, and we both knew it. When I began to discuss my melancholy, I realized I knew the cause of it after all. "Isadora is sixteen. She's finding herself, her talent, her purpose so fast that in a couple years she'll be off on her own. And a couple years after that, Gertie will go, and then Harry. It'll all fly by as if it were a few months. What will the Bram be like without them?"

Chef deeply inhaled the fragrant steam rising from his mug and sighed with pleasure. "It will still be the Bram in every way that matters," he said, as if he could discern the future from the aroma of a particular cup of coffee as reliably as phyllomancers could predict events by studying tea leaves. "What comes next surely could be less charming, though we might be surprised. Franklin and Loretta built this place for the love of family and to delight children. A place that's built for such reasons, whether grand or modest, will always inspire love and provide delight. We just have to be patient and see how it works out. Baby birds shed their eggs for a nest and then the nest for the sky. But these baby birds won't ever shed us, Adiel. They have been inoculated against every cold affliction of the heart. They'll be warmhearted all their lives, and they'll love us as much as we love them. Family is important to them, to us all."

When birds leave the nest in which they hatched, they make a new nest elsewhere. A nest provides safety, high above the reach of most predators. Bramley Hall was the only nest that I had ever known, and I didn't have the instinctive skills to build a new one. Franklin and Loretta made me a beneficiary in their wills, promised me a life in the Bram, and it was their nature to ensure that every promise they made was ironclad. I was not afraid of being put out of Bramley Hall to forage for myself. I was not worried that Franklin and Loretta and my three siblings might go away. However, by the power of some unpredictable calamity, they might be *taken* away—leaving me the last of the Fairchild family and alone.

There is less to fear when you have nothing to lose.

Following Gertie's crisis in January, Franklin and Loretta had been swept back into a troubled film project that he described as like an ocean vortex, whirling ever faster, pulling everyone—cast and crew—into oblivion. Time passed, and the shoot wrapped, and they marveled that the film was "less embarrassing than expected."

Late in the afternoon of the third day of July, Franklin was sitting in a lounge chair, under a patio umbrella, on the deck by the swimming pool. He was casually but smartly dressed. In an hour, he and Loretta were having dinner at a restaurant on the beach in Santa Monica to celebrate the completion of the picture.

I settled in the chair beside his. "You look as handsome as that new guy—Cary Grant."

"You're a terrible liar, Addie. No one but Cary Grant is as handsome as Cary Grant. He's going to be the biggest thing ever."

"Well, he's always well put together. In that outfit you're as well put together as he is."

"I'll accept that much. I'm more a Buster Keaton type who can dress like Cary Grant."

Six months had passed since Loretta recounted what happened to her in the earthquake of 1906. She'd left it to Franklin to tell me about Mercy Village, the orphanage to which they had been committed separately.

Now, as the sun painted ripples of orange light on the swimming pool, he said, "Mercy Village isn't worth the time it takes to damn its name." Franklin was not given to anger often, perhaps because anger is said to be, after pride, the most lethal emotion to the prospects of the soul. Now his voice was marked not by rage but by impersonal displeasure at unworthy acts, a cool indignation. "I was sent there on the same bus with Loretta. I had more low experience than she did. I knew right off that the place was a sewer. I knew what risks a young girl took by being in the care of the couple who owned the place—Nigel and Marigold. Loretta was so innocent. I had to look after her. We became friends, though we never imagined where our friendship would one day lead."

Two iridescent ruby-throated hummingbirds were busy in the day before us, hovering in feathered splendor and then abruptly darting to another flower to sip what it offered.

I asked, "How long were you kept in Mercy Village?"

"More than three years. By then Loretta was almost thirteen. I was fifteen and could pass for eighteen. Those days, less than half of kids graduated—or even attended—high school. There were no laws against child labor. Everywhere kids our age were working for low wages, pitiful wages, but they were on their own and eager for it. We knew how hard it might be. Many children worked twelve hours a day. But some prospered. If we stayed in Mercy Village, we had no hope of prospering. It was a rough-and-tumble time."

"The orphanage just let you walk out?" I asked.

"We didn't ask, Addie. We just left one night. The next four years, through 1913, we did piecework in the garment industry."

Word by word, his voice grew softer. He stared past me at the house, his mind conveying him to another time. Considering how well his life had gone these past two decades, I might have expected a modest smile, a suggestion of quiet satisfaction. But his face composed itself into a somber expression.

When he returned to the moment, he said, "President Wilson was promising peace while ensuring World War I, meanwhile imprisoning his domestic adversaries without trial. American troops deposed the president of Mexico. That same year, Loretta and I were married. Cecil B. DeMille's movie *Squaw Man*, the first full-length picture, was a huge hit. Motion pictures were exploding in popularity. I was twenty. My bride was seventeen. We needed to get out of the threads-and-needles business and find what we wanted to devote our lives to. Back then, the choices seemed to be either working for a company that made guns and bullets or one making movies."

I said, "You're not a guns-and-bullets guy."

"I'm not," he agreed, "but I'm glad they exist. Without them, the only movies we'd be making would be about what a great, kind man Kaiser Wilhelm was. Anyway, Loretta and I didn't have much to offer Hollywood other than energy. Loretta was as pretty as they get, and she had writing talent. I had nothing more than a line of bunkum, hokum, and humbug. But Hollywood usually treats a fast-talking guy with a good-looking girl on his arm as if he's a genius and she's pretty damn smart in her own right for recognizing his potential. It's pathetic, but that's how it was, is, and probably always will be. So we faked our way into low-level crew jobs and bootstrapped each other out of the trenches and into the executive suite."

The expression that had persisted since he'd alluded to World War I suddenly gave way to a far more cheerful aspect. His eyes were done with melancholy in favor of warm satisfaction. The arc of his smile was as good a definition of *affection* as any in a dictionary.

I followed the direction of his stare and saw Loretta standing on the terrace, outside the library, casually but smartly dressed for dinner at the beach, a radiant figure in the oblique sunlight. She waved at us.

Franklin and I got up from our lounge chairs, and I said, "I'm amazed to be here. I can never repay you or find the words . . . the words to . . ."

His frown was not of disapproval but of dismay, and it lasted only an instant. Perhaps he saw that I might break into tears and that breaking into tears was the last thing I wanted to do. He said, "Listen, kid, the truth is we brought you here because we're selfish Hollywood narcissists who ruthlessly use people, use them and use them until they have nothing more to give. We do so without shame or regret, and in fact with wicked glee, so you had better continue to give more than you get or you are *gone*. Is that clear?"

He had managed to transform my pending tears into laughter. Hugging him, I said, "Yes, sir, it's very clear. I've seen Mr. Max Schreck in *Nosferatu* in your very own screening room, so I know the kind of creatures I'm dealing with."

"Good," he said. "Now, I'm going to dinner with my wife, where we can spend a few hours scheming against not only you but also our other children. It falls to you to have dinner here and to pretend to Chef Lattuada that you enjoy his food."

He kissed my brow and headed up the garden path toward the house. Loretta waved again, at me this time, and I waved back.

And so, after spending some time in the gardens, I went into the house and lied to Chef Lattuada, assuring him that dinner was marvelous when in fact it was so much better than that.

THIRTY-FIVE

The remaining months of 1934 passed without surprises but with many moments of joy. There were birthdays to celebrate, including Rafael's sixth, and holiday parties. Mr. Groucho Marx and his lovely wife, Ruth, came to dinner. He said, "On this one occasion, I will tolerate children at the table in order to convince my better half that the two we have at home are more than enough. Ruth, dear, as the chaos and mayhem unfold at this table, keep in mind that these Fairchild hellions, though terrible, are better behaved than other children who are allowed to assemble in groups." Gertie decided Mr. Marx was, after all, both funny *and* nice.

On the afternoon of Saturday, the third of November, I found Harry in the game room, where he had combined the two tables. With scores of miniature war-blasted trees that he crafted himself and stones that represented boulders, he had laid out an approximately accurate portion of Belleau Wood in France, where a critical moment in that famous battle had played out. The smaller detachment of cast-lead soldiers wore painted-on German uniforms, and the others were American Marines. Some were lying prone, some kneeling, others standing erect, sheltering as best they could behind whatever cover the landscape provided. Harry was sitting on one of four stools that provided him with various perspectives on the scene, alternately studying the tableau and consulting a book of military history.

I perched on another stool. "So you still haven't won Belleau Wood? You've been on this one for—what?—two weeks now?"

"It's not a game you play and finish in an afternoon, Addie. It's not a game at all. Probably there's no way to figure out how to win it faster than they did in 1918."

"I'm not patronizing you, Harry. I know it's more than just play to you. If it was just play, you'd have been done with it ages ago. You've been studying one battle or another most of the year."

He put aside the book but continued to study the arrayed infantry. "A brigade of Second Division Marines figured to clear Belleau Wood of Jerries in maybe eight or ten hours. It took them twenty days. They were *Marines*, the toughest fighting force in the world, and still it took them twenty days."

I studied him as he studied the battlefield. Eventually, I said, "How many Marines died in Belleau Wood?"

"Five thousand and two hundred. The German general, Ludendorff, positioned hidden machine-gun nests behind pretty much every boulder and fallen tree. Our guys were slaughtered."

For a while, I thought about that number before I said, "Are you going to be a Marine?"

"I just turned thirteen, Addie. Anyway, there's no war now. And there won't be another. Counting civilians and military, ten million died in the last war. Nobody is ever going to be crazy enough to start another one."

What history I knew was from good novels, like *War and Peace*. Tolstoy had written that one seventy years ago. Technology raced forward, but the human heart was as it always had been. "If you ever try to go off to war, Harry, you'll have to deal with me first."

He looked up from Belleau Wood and grinned. "You'll do what—shoot me in the foot so I'm disqualified by a limp?"

"If I have to. But that won't be necessary. I'll just tell the Marines your middle name is Percy."

"What a wretched thing to do."

I returned his grin. "You have no idea how vicious I can be."

That night I dreamed of Harry going off to war at the age of thirteen, wearing a uniform sized for a grown man, the pant legs and sleeves rolled up, the helmet pressing down over his ears. It ought to have been a funny fantasy, but it had no amusement value. He was making his way through a dark wood filled with the rattle of machine guns and the screams of dying men. I tried to pull him behind the cover of a tree, but I recoiled when I realized he was covered in blood. *Save yourself,* he said, and he whidded away through darkness relieved only by the brief flashes of grenades and mortar fire.

A month later, on Friday, December 7, the family and staff were decorating Christmas trees in five rooms. Gertie and I were assigned to the library, provided with cartons of ornaments, and threatened with a dinner of just a soda cracker and a stick of celery if we didn't dress the tree to the highest standard by five o'clock.

Among a family of lively talkers, Gertie was perhaps the most loquacious. By the time we'd hung only half the ornaments and none of the garlands or tinsel, we'd discussed at least a dozen subjects and had come to Isadora. "I'm worried about my sister. Oh, not you, Addie. My other sister. You're as put together as a Pierce-Arrow. Not that you're a machine. You're not a machine. If you were a machine, however, you'd be as put together as a Pierce-Arrow. When I'm old enough to drive, I don't want to drive anything but a Silver Arrow fastback coupe. That car *jumps.* The thing is, our Isadora is old enough to drive, but she doesn't care at all about that. What she cares about is getting out there and doing what she knows she was born to do, which is not play Mozart in a concert hall."

Inserting wire hangers in a dozen red ornaments, I said, "She wants to be a jazz pianist, swing style, a big band behind her."

"Yeah, that's part of it. She wants to burn up the keyboard, kick the audience into high gear, but not just that. Maybe not even mainly that. You need to talk to her. I could tell her how to get past what she's dealing with, but I'm the little sister, don't you know. When it comes to something this serious, big sisters don't think little sisters know what the hell they're talking about. Of course, in spite of being younger than Izzy, I've often been the big sister in this relationship. I've got my weird hand, and those of us with weird hands tend to grow up faster, but she doesn't understand that. It's all about chronological age with her. I love the crazy old bitch, but I can't help her. You can. Help her, Addie. Help her before she develops a bleeding ulcer and one night vomits blood all over the dinner table. That'll traumatize Chef Lattuada, and the dear man doesn't deserve to be traumatized."

So two days later, on Monday morning, I followed the last notes of a Beethoven sonata to the music room, where Izzy was practicing alone. In a brief silence during which she most likely rolled her head to stretch her neck and flexed her long-fingered hands, I came to the end of the hallway, where the door was ajar. As I stepped into the room, she went from Beethoven to Chopin as if she had been possessed by the spirit of Ludwig and now by Frédéric François. She played the B-flat Minor Sonata with such grace and nuance that, if you didn't know better, you might have thought she had composed it. I stood out of the way, enchanted by the music. When Izzy saw me, she terminated the sonata with seven inappropriate notes that most people would translate into the words *shave and a haircut, two bits*.

When she called my name and patted the piano bench, I sat beside her. "Chopin would want to break your fingers for that joke."

"Not at all. He was a darling little man with a sense of humor. Amantine Lucile Aurore Dupin—who was the Baroness Dudevant before her divorce and called herself George Sand after it—was his lover for ten years. She wore men's common clothing with a contrasting top hat. She smoked foul cigars. She cheated on him with several other men. In spite of all that, she could make him laugh, and he loved to laugh." Izzy sighed. Her gaze traveled the length of the keyboard as if she were playing an imaginary series of broken chords in one long arpeggio. "I doubt that I myself will ever have a lover."

"Of course you will," I declared. "You'll sweep some man off his feet, and he'll sweep you off yours, and I'll cry my eyes out with happiness at your wedding."

She shook her head. "Men aren't attracted to depressives. They want lighthearted girls, frolicsome and coltish, vivacious, sunny."

"You're all those good things, Izzy. For sure, you're never a moaning depressive."

"Not yet, I suppose. But I will be. How else could I end up now that I've set my heart on being something I can never be? Most big bands coming up, they don't even have pianos. Trumpets, trombones, saxes, a clarinet, a bass. If there *is* a piano, it's usually the instrument of the bandleader. Otherwise, the closest thing you'll find to a piano is a xylophone, and I'm not going there. Besides, jazz bands are entirely men except for a girl vocalist. And if the vocalist matters at all, if she's not just decoration, then she's got to be as good as the musicians, which is very damn good."

"There are a few all-girl bands," I reminded her.

Isadora covered her face with her hands and spoke through her fingers. "None is half as good as all-guy bands. It's embarrassing. Why don't they try harder? They could knock it out of the park. Why settle for selling glamour at small venues, for smaller audiences?"

I shrugged. "They figure it's stacked against them. You could be the first, Izzy. You've got the talent and the drive."

"Harmony would be devastated. She's spent so much time with me. She thinks I have what it takes to do what she couldn't, what was taken away from her."

"You've got Harmony wrong. She just wants you to be the very best you can be. She wants to see you shine. Deep down, she doesn't care if that's classical music in a concert hall or big band swing in a hotel ballroom."

"Yeah? You think so? What about this? She saw Rachmaninoff is going to be in town. She was so excited she told my parents. Daddy and Mother have a lot of contacts, people who owe them, people who don't owe them but just like them—and some know Rachmaninoff. So now they're trying to figure out how to get him to the Bram to hear me. That's totally coconuts! Sergei Rachmaninoff! I might as well throw myself off the roof right now. If I play as well as I can and he thinks I have a little something, even the littlest something, then I won't be able to get off the track to Carnegie Hall whether I'll ever be good enough to belong there or not. But if I don't play my best, if I fudge it—that's a form of lying. My parents will know that I embarrassed myself—and them!—on purpose."

We shared the piano bench in silence for a minute or two. Izzy hunched over the keyboard in a state of misery while I searched the library in my memory to consider how a few of my favorite novelists might have handled this. I drew a blank.

"So what if," I said, "you can't get past the prejudice against women musicians in the big bands? What if you're every bit as good as anybody, but the guys-only tradition doesn't change? As you said, not every swing band has a piano in the first place. What if you could have been in Carnegie Hall but instead you're not anywhere?"

She made fists and appeared about to pound the keyboard in frustration, but then she opened her hands and sat looking at her palms as if reading her future in them. "I love the piano, Addie. But I love this new, special music even more. I love swing, the culture that comes with it, the electricity of it, the *lift* it gives me. If I can't be a part of it with a piano, there's another way."

"What way?"

"Sometimes you've heard me sing while I played."

"You're a very good singer."

"I'm better than you think. Better than very good. That sounds conceited, but I've earned it. I haven't just been singing at the piano. Whenever I'm sure no one's going to use the screening room, sometimes after midnight, then I go in there to work on my voice. It's soundproofed. No one can hear me unless they're right outside in the hall. I don't have the piano, but I can hear the music in my head. I sing a cappella, never miss a note. I work on my technique. I'm developing my own style. I can do it, Addie. Maybe the singer only gets up and takes the microphone every fifth number. But even when she's not front and center, she's sitting on a chair right there with the band. Right there with the music."

"You really want this, don't you, Izzy?"

"I really do. And I'm getting close. My voice will be ready by the time I'm seventeen. It might be ready now. That's the problem."

"Which is?"

"Will Daddy and Mother say I'm just a child until I'm twenty-one. Even if they say eighteen, it'll be forever until I find out if I can make it as a singer."

As often happens, the book in my memory library most applicable to the situation occurred to me when I had given up trying to recall a volume and a scene that might be helpful. "Do you remember Winnie-the-Pooh and Piglet, when they set a trap for a Heffalump?"

Isadora regarded me as if she might be justified in asking if I'd visited the wine cellar. "I recall something about a deep hole with a honey jar at the bottom for bait. But what was a Heffalump? I don't remember. And what the heck does that have to do with this?"

"Having given little thought to what a Heffalump might be like, Piglet panicked when he thought they actually caught one. Might a Heffalump be fierce with pigs? Surely it was a monster. But after much fretting and fear, Piglet discovered the beast at the bottom of the trap was just Pooh with his head stuck in the honey jar. There was no such thing as a Heffalump."

Isadora cocked her head as though to suggest there must be more I meant to say. When I only cocked my head in response, she said, "You've been a great teacher, a lot better than Miss Blackthorn, but I must have been daydreaming in class. Are you drawing an analogy? I don't see anything analogous between a nonexistent Heffalump and my parents. My parents—our parents—they're real, and they make the rules. So your point is?"

"You're worried that Franklin and Loretta will be Heffalumps and thwart you just when it matters most that they understand you and approve of what you want to do with your life. But that won't happen. You're worried about nothing. They love you, Izzy. They'll trust you, and they'll find a way to feel safe about you leaving the Bram and going out on your own."

She frowned. "How can you be so sure?"

"There's a perfect argument to be made in your favor. They're too fair and self-aware to resist it."

"What argument?"

"You leave that to me when the time comes. You just work on your voice, your technique, and tell me when you're ready to ditch this dump. Now play that new Cole Porter song for me."

Porter's hit musical on Broadway was rich with compositions in his unique, literate style. The title song was a little risqué, but it had an irresistible swing to it. Having heard it once, Isadora was able to play it note for note—"Anything Goes."

The following night, two weeks before Christmas, I had the same dream—with a few variations—that disturbed my sleep on the fourth of January, nearly a year earlier, on the night of the day Gertie recovered from septic shock. In the glow of a dream moon, I walked above the works of Nature and humanity as though on a bridge of glass. Southwest lay the lights of suburbs. As before, I drifted eastward until the sway-backed barn and leaning silo appeared. I descended to the earth, crossed the lush meadow. This time no horse appeared with or without a monstrous rider. I ghosted through the walls of the weathered house. The living room was furnished in the odds-and-ends style of items acquired cheaply at country auctions. After a silence, Cole Porter's "Anything Goes" swelled through the house, but not as I'd heard Isadora play it. This version was distorted, sinister, suggesting impending violence. Intuitively, I knew whose voice would give new and ominous meaning to Cole Porter's words if there were to be any lyrics in this rendition. Only one person from all the days of my life was wicked enough to match the menace in the music. I felt that if I heard his voice, I would be inviting him back into my life. I heard myself say, "Home," as one might evoke the name of the son of God to ward off a vampire, and I sat up in bed, free of the dream place, safe in the Bram.

I wasn't able to return to sleep. Because the Clyde Tombaugh Club had ceased to engage in post-midnight adventures, I was reading more books recently. And I was doing a lot of thinking about what I read but also about the meaning and purpose of my strange life and gifts. I once believed my limitations allowed me no purpose other than to endure, but that philosophy no longer made sense. My life was rich with experience of the Darkness that isn't just an absence of light and of the

Light we feel but cannot see. I was beginning to understand my reason for being. Fulfilling my purpose required paying a high price. For that price, I was grateful. Anything of great value will have a daunting cost whether we pay in money or in any of the many other currencies with which we settle the debts we owe one another. The essence and impact of my life was to be a friend of this family and never to leave them in times of trouble, to repay their love twice over, to pay with my life if necessary. I got out of bed and went to a window. Gazing at the sea of stars, I marveled that a miscreation like me could be granted a purpose as fine as this and perhaps the power to fulfill it.

And so December laid down its days on the way to Christmas and year's end. Having officially retired on December 22, Julian and Victoria Symington spent two days with us as guests rather than as employees, for an early celebration of the holiday, before leaving for their new home in San Clemente. Although I had known them only four years, it was hard to say goodbye, harder for Franklin and Loretta and the siblings than for me.

Before she and her husband left on the morning of the twenty-fourth, Victoria came to the library, where I was reading Thomas Hardy's *Wessex Tales*. She settled in an armchair served by the same Tiffany floor lamp that shed light on my book. As I put *Wessex Tales* aside, she said, "We already said our goodbyes last evening, but I can't leave it at that, Addie. There's something I need to know if it can be known. It's not just curiosity, dear. It's . . . I guess I'm hoping you yourself might somehow be proof."

"Proof of what?"

Instead of answering, she said, "That first day at the Bram, you met Anna May and you knew."

"Knew? What did I know?"

"That she was troubled."

"Well, ma'am, anyone could have seen it."

"Not everyone did, child. But you knew at once. And all that with her brother."

"I didn't know about Connor. I just saw she was anguished about something and repressing it."

Mrs. Symington nodded as if I had agreed with her. "You also knew about Miss Blackthorn when no one else did."

"The children said something. I realized what it meant, what Miss Blackthorn was doing. That's all."

"And then there was Rafael."

I said nothing.

"You brought that poisoned chunk of meat to show us."

"I was worried an intruder wanted to kill him to clear the way. A burglar or something. And of course it turned out to be Connor's friend, Willy Maxwell."

Her voice and manner were not those of an interrogator. She impressed me—at this moment, although never before—as being a melancholy but still hopeful seeker of something that her heart needed and her mind resisted providing. "Addie, did you really throw those other chunks of tainted meat over the estate wall?"

"I didn't mean to poison coyotes—or anything else."

"But did you throw the poisoned meat over the wall?"

"I suppose I should have brought it to the house and disposed of it properly, but the sight of it disgusted and infuriated me."

She regarded me thoughtfully. "That's not an answer. That's an evasion. So you didn't throw it over the wall." She gave me a chance to lie; I could not. "When you found the meat, there was only the one chunk you brought to us as evidence, not three."

Although I had lied about finding all the poisoned bait before Rafael had eaten any of it, my deception harmed no one and was for the purpose of keeping the secret of my newfound gift for healing. Nevertheless, a blush of embarrassment warmed my face.

"Rafael ate the first two," Mrs. Symington surmised.

"But then he would have been poisoned. He would have died."

"*Should* have died," she agreed. "Just as sweet Gertie should have died. But Rafael didn't. And neither did she."

I tried but failed to find a way to deflect the arrow of her inquiry. "Obviously, ma'am, you've read at least as many Agatha Christie novels as I have."

"I love you, Addie. I don't want to cause you trouble. What you tell me will go no further. I'm here only because . . . because I've been waiting all my life for some sign."

"Sign?"

"Evidence. Proof. A reason to believe there's more to the world than what we can touch and see. Maybe it's you, the evidence."

"It's not me."

"Did Rafael die?"

"No." Mrs. Symington's gaze was a starving beggar's gaze, and her face a portrait of spiritual yearning that would have served as a poster advertising the radio broadcasts of Bishop Fulton J. Sheen. I had never seen this aspect of her. I couldn't pretend to be what she wanted me to be. I also couldn't disrespect her desire to find meaning in the weave of the world. I gave her the truth to make of it what she would. "Rafael wasn't dead, but gravely ill and dying."

"And you, did you . . . ?"

"Yes. I brought him back."

"How?"

"I don't know. I held him."

"Just held him?"

"And he stopped dying."

"This has happened before?"

"No."

"You were surprised."

"Very."

"You told no one."

"Not then."

"Until Gertie . . ."

"Until Gertie. I was afraid I'd fail her."

"You held her like you held Rafael."

"Yes. The infection passed from her blood to mine."

"But here you are."

"I don't know how or why."

"It's because you aren't of this world."

"But I am. I wasn't born on Mars."

"That's not what I meant."

"I know. But I'm not heaven-sent, either."

"What else could you be?"

"I'm a freak, Victoria."

"Don't say that."

"From a carnival freak show."

"Where we're from is not what we are."

"People paid to see the monster—me."

She bit her lip, shook her head.

"They never wanted their money back. I was every bit as much a monster as advertised."

"Hush. You're a beautiful child."

"And you're sweet. I will miss you."

"It's only true. You're lovely."

"The marks pitied me, feared me."

"No one could."

"The sight of me sickened others."

"I'll never believe that."

"I was billed as 'the horror with a pretty face.'"

"Carnival foolishness."

"For years, you've laundered my underthings."

"They aren't that different."

"They are. You haven't wanted to think about it."

"Monsters don't raise the dead."

"And neither did I. Rafael and Gertie weren't dead."

"Raise the dead, heal the dying—it's the same."

I rose from my chair, went to her, and held out my right hand, which was as always in a custom-made glove. She got up and took my hand. I led her to a window with a view of the gardens.

Across its breadth, the noon sky was cloaked in clouds as dark as ashes marbled with soot. The air pooled so still that even the laciest trees with the most delicate leaves did not tremble.

Although I knew the answer, I asked, "Why do you insist on my being something that I'm not?"

"Maybe you *are* what you think you're not."

"That's not an answer. That's an evasion."

She smiled, aware that those were words with which she had earlier chastised me. "Why do I insist? My stubborn heart. I have no faith in anything until I'm given evidence faith is warranted. I was married to Julian years before I could believe he loved me. Life has taught me to require proof or suffer the consequences of blind belief in anyone or anything."

Her inbred and all but implacable doubt in all things saddened me even as I understood that it was a reasonable response to this world of deceit. I said, "If I could command the clouds to roll back and the sky to be blue from horizon to horizon, I would do it for no other reason than to change your stubborn heart forever. But I can't do that because I'm not a citizen soul of New Jerusalem come down to Earth on a holy mission that might also make a nifty storyline for a Paramount movie. I'm just a freak both physically and in some ways mentally. If you'd rather call me an oddity, a nonesuch, a weird duck—that's okay.

I won't be offended. I've come around to calling myself a freak without dismay. To deny that humbling word would also be to deny the talents and the gifts that came with my physical deformities. It's all part of my birthright. Do you see?"

"I do *not* see. Why should you be born with terrible burdens, even if you're willing and able to live with them? And why should Julian and I be unable to have children in a world full of them?"

Every person is a puzzle. I had just been given a corner piece of the puzzle that was Victoria. I let go of her hand in order to hug her. "When you get bored with retirement, please come visit me for as long as you like. Me and the children. Everyone will be so happy to see you. As long as there's a Bram, you belong here. And as a guest, you won't have to make your bed."

Her heart might have been stubborn, but it was not hard. She kissed my cheek. She couldn't speak. In silence, we walked together through the house. As we entered the foyer, she found her voice. "It will be a blessing to sleep in late, never again be required to herd you little savages to breakfast and off to school."

As I opened the front door, I said, "We'll miss being able to exasperate you to the point where you sputter."

"That sounds like an admission. I always assumed the morning chaos was the consequence of an excess of youthful energy. Am I now to understand that it was scripted?"

"We often stayed up well past midnight, planning every detail. Precisely timing each spill. Deciding exactly when the door would be left open to entice a squirrel into the kitchen. Determining which of us would roll a piece of sausage across the floor to send Rafael on a wild scramble that would incite the maximum disruption of your routine."

"Hellions," she said as we descended the steps to the driveway.

"And proud of it, ma'am."

Everyone in the Bram had said their goodbyes earlier. Only Julian waited by their Ford. He helped Victoria into the front seat and closed the passenger door. He half bowed toward me. "Miss Adiel Fairchild, it has been one of the greatest pleasures of my life."

I offered him my hand. "Mr. Symington, sir, the pleasure has been all mine."

He took my hand. "I did not bother to tell the family that from now on you are the majordomo who will keep this place from tumbling down. I was sure they already understood." His voice broke only when he said, "Goodbye, dear," and shook my hand precisely three times.

I watched the Ford dwindle down the palm-lined driveway as thunder rumbled and rain began to fall.

It was Christmas Eve. We would be going to church in the rain. The staff was on vacation. Chef Lattuada left us a week of feasts. On New Year's Eve, with sparklers, we would paint bright but short-lived patterns on the darkness.

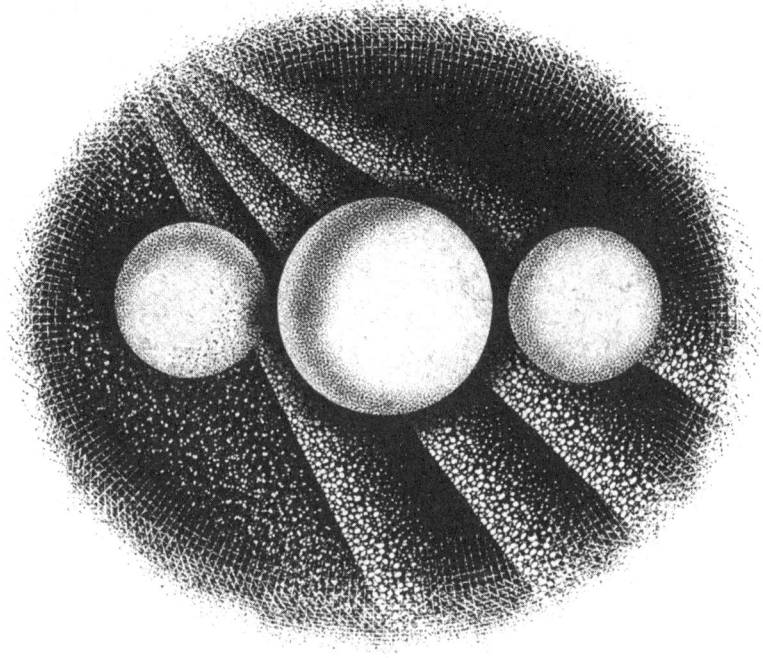

Part Three
1938

In the third of four blue dreams, I wandered in an open forest at night. The light by which I found my way came from three glowing spheres the size of a fortuneteller's crystal ball, one off to my left, one to my right, and the third ahead of me. I was searching for someone, perhaps for several people, but also for a place. I did not know any names of the people or what they looked like, for I had not met them yet. And I worried that the place I sought existed for others, not for me.

My dream quest began with an expectation of wonder and good fortune somewhere ahead, but during my long fruitless wandering, exuberance faded into a doleful longing. At last I came to a stop when a wolf crossed my path and spoke as animals do in fairy tales and fables. "If you find what you're seeking, what makes you think it will last forever when nothing else in this world does?"

In answer, I said, "There is one thing that lasts, and you know it. Tell me no more lies." After that, I walked and walked through vast colonnades of trees, walked until I woke.

—from a letter by Alida, April 17, 1927

THIRTY-SIX

In the wider world, the three years following Gertie's crisis were marked by the false promise of imminent economic recovery and by the very real threat of war. Japan attacked China. In Munich, the European allies betrayed Czechoslovakia to placate Hitler.

In the smaller world of the Bram, Lynette Rollins proved to be a superb estate manager. She had hired a woman named Leda Zentner to take Victoria Symington's place as head housekeeper and a younger woman, Peggy Powell, to assume the position from which Lynette had been elevated. Leda and Peggy adapted to the Fairchild universe as though it had all the same habits and quirks as their own families. Three years had passed without significant drama.

The new year, 1938, continued to flow forth days as lacking in turbulence as the waters of a stream with minimal slope. Yet, for no reason I could define, with increasing frequency, I warned myself to *stay alert*. By the middle of June, the siblings had all celebrated their latest birthday; Isadora was twenty, Gertie eighteen plus, and Harry seventeen. Two years earlier, I'd ceased to be their teacher, not because of their age, but because they were autodidacts and each was obsessed with a subject that I knew less about than they did.

On the last Monday evening in June, the entire family, minus one, plus the estate's seven employees and two of their husbands (Harmony's Allen and Peggy Powell's Tommy), boarded a chartered bus to be taken from the Bram to Los Angeles for dinner and a special treat. The owner of the Palomar Ballroom billed the place as "the largest and most famous dance hall on the West Coast." It was a restaurant, a bar, a nightclub, a dance hall, and a concert hall all in one, providing seating for ten thousand. Although you might think a nightclub would remind me of my speakeasy days and conjure bad memories, I was excited and eager to see the fabled Palomar.

When we arrived, our driver angled to the curb in front of an illegally parked Cadillac limousine. Two passengers exited the limo to greet us—Cary Grant and Katharine Hepburn. They had starred in a pair of hits that year—*Bringing Up Baby*, which had been released in February, and the recent *Holiday*. They had come because they were friends of Loretta and Franklin; however, they were also here for a higher purpose.

In the twilight, the immense Spanish Colonial building glowed as if it were made of translucent alabaster, and signal lamps shone at the top of up-lighted minarets. Here, in 1935, Benny Goodman's orchestra broke through the wall of bad luck and pop arrangements that had hampered it and went full swing. Their one-month booking was extended to two months, leading to their ascendance thereafter.

Two formidable men in suits and ties, Pinkerton security agents arranged by Franklin, waited for us at the VIP entrance, which was well removed from the hundreds who stood in line to receive tickets at the box office. The two agents were in possession of passes provided for the Fairchild party by the developer-owner of the property. Pinkerton's finest, each as intimidating as the former heavyweight champion Max Schmeling, shepherded us into the Palomar. A brief objection by the door attendants was quieted with a *try-me* glare from the agents and by the doormen's sudden realization that Mr. Grant and Miss Hepburn, already Hollywood royalty, were with us.

Four tables were roped off to separate our party from others on the palm-lined Palomar Terrace. We had direct access to the dance floor, which seemed as big as a football field, although we weren't there to dance. Directly across the room from us, the stage waited for the big band, while a house trio provided welcoming but far from hot music. The Moorish decor featured lighting both dazzling and romantic. Two-thirds of the tables were already occupied. Glasses clinked. Flatware rang against china. Young women's laughter trilled through the arches between the columns that framed the dance floor. I'd lived so many years in the smoke-free Bram, the cigarette haze was more pungent to me than to those who produced it, but it also possessed an exotic quality that enhanced the Moorish atmosphere.

Although I was as small as ever I had been, I could prove I was twenty-five, and although I seldom indulged in alcohol, I ordered a dry martini. Gertie, only eighteen, knew how to use her beauty *and* her deformed hand to forestall any challenge from the waiter when she ordered a grasshopper "with plenty of hop." Harry was okay with a Coca-Cola. If he'd been eighty, he would have been content with a cola. His continuing interest in military history and history in general seemed to have conferred on him a gravitas that would rule out intoxication even when, in four years, he reached the legal age to indulge. If the waiters or the management would have challenged any of us, they would have focused on Chef Lattuada, for at that point in its history, the Palomar enforced a strict color policy. The developer of the ballroom retained a partial ownership position, and he owed a series of favors to Franklin and Loretta, so he gave us VIP passes even knowing others in the management would not have done so as long as our Luigi was with us. Chef would have stayed home without a fuss, but there was no way in hell we were going to see Isadora perform without her much-loved honorary uncle here to share the moment.

Two years earlier, after a dozen auditions with California-based orchestras failed to get her work, Izzy was more driven than ever to be part of the jazz scene. She was a Fairchild, after all, and Fairchilds were motivated by rejection as much as they were inspired by success. Although the big band sound swept the nation, the heart of the scene was the East Coast, which provided more posh hotels, nightclubs, dance halls, resorts, and suitable venues than the rest of the country combined. Scores of bands stayed within that fruitful territory, though the best toured coast to coast. The Northwest birthed some good musicians but wasn't a flashpoint for new sounds that excited the nation. After doing research through music magazines, Izzy packed and moved, at eighteen, to Seattle, where it was said that most local bands avoided ballads because they couldn't find vocalists who were equivalent to national sweethearts like Doris Day and June Christy and Helen Forrest. She was hired by a ten-piece band that had steady bookings from Seattle to Spokane and south to Portland. Four months later, she was approached by Tommy Dorsey, whose band was in Seattle on tour. Soon she sang with Dorsey when Edythe Wright had the night off and on other nights did a duet or two with her. Tommy, "the Sentimental Gentleman of Swing," created moods with music that made his orchestra one of the best of all dance bands and the very best for ballads. However, Edythe had—and had earned—billing, while Isadora was an "also appearing" named only from the stage; her opportunities were limited.

This night, we were at the Palomar to witness what might be Izzy's big break or at least the beginning of a slow move to bigger things. This was also her first appearance close to home, and we Bramleyans were determined to be there in full force to support our girl. Only Rafael remained at home, and we would have brought him with us if we could have figured out how to disguise a ninety-pound dog as Izzy's grandmother.

Tommy Dorsey's band was a great one, and Bob Crosby's was near great at times. The orchestra was owned by its musicians and run by Gil Bowers, the pianist. Bob, the brother of Bing, was the likable leader and singer. They had gone through a series of girl vocalists during the previous year, but they signed Izzy as the only female singer for the length of this tour.

We had spoken on the phone with her earlier in the day, between rehearsals. She had been excited but surprisingly composed. She no longer sounded like the girl who left the Bram for Seattle little more than one year ago. Of course I recognized her voice, but she seemed more than just a year older. She sounded like a grown woman. Hearing her, I missed her more terribly, not solely because she had been away but also because I had not been with her to see her evolve from one Isadora to another. She was most pleased that she'd become self-supporting. Her parents had been sending her a monthly stipend, but in the Fairchild tradition, she'd needed to make it on her own, prove herself to herself rather than to anyone else.

As dessert was being served, the house trio concluded their session. Minutes later, the MC introduced the Bob Crosby Orchestra. The curtain rose, revealing all fourteen musicians ready to swing. They broke into "The Big Noise from Winnetka," a signature song of theirs. At least two thousand people poured onto the dance floor, which the management claimed could accommodate four thousand couples. Neither the music nor the dancers quite exhilarated me, but then I saw Izzy, and I could feel my heart pounding. The piano stood to the left of the orchestra, with Gil Bowers at the keyboard, and Izzy sat to the right of the piano, left of Bob Crosby. She looked beautiful and sophisticated, recognizably the young lady who had left home for Seattle but not much like the girl who led the Clyde Tombaugh Club on its late-night adventures. The band played three more swinging numbers, and I could not recall ever having been more impatient in my life.

Then Bob Crosby introduced "our lovely Isadora Fairchild, who has a voice of smoke and steel and a way with the keyboard that even our Mr. Bowers says he envies." She rose from her chair. She wore a peach-colored satin dress cut on the bias, with a low back and a form-skimming floor-length skirt that flared slightly at the bottom. She graciously acknowledged the light applause by briefly putting her right hand to her heart, and then she slid onto the piano bench, hitching up the flared bottom of her dress to keep it from getting in the way of the three pedals. She dared to segue from the band's arrangement of "Stompin' at the Savoy," which had been fast enough to encourage the jitterbug, to "For All We Know," one of the most beautiful ballads ever composed. Of those who stayed on the floor or ventured onto it for a slow dance, some came to a stop after eight or ten bars and stood listening, rapt. Izzy and the band then played a neat trick by allowing no time for applause, launching fast out of "For All We Know" into a serious up-tempo version of "The Scat Song," which had the Palomar rocking.

When Izzy and the band hit the last note, I stood up without realizing it, beating my gloves together, my face stretched in a grin. Everyone at our section of roped-off tables had sprung to their feet, but it was not strictly a family-and-friends reaction; half the people in the joint felt that a standing O was warranted. In my exuberance, as Izzy took a bow, I turned to Gertie and grabbed her by the shoulders and declared, "That was my sister, my *sister!*"

"I *thought* I recognized her!" Gertie said. "The crazy old bitch probably still doesn't know how to pronounce 'nefesterous,' but she sure as hell can sing."

As the band struck up a vigorous "South Rampart Street Parade," Harry joined us in a circle hug, and we put our heads together, and he raised his voice to say, "You know what this means, don't you? A year or two from now, we three won't have names anymore. I will be 'Isadora Fairchild's brother,' and you will be 'Isadora Fairchild's sisters,' and the only way we'll ever get our names back is to commit the crime of the century."

Later in the show, Isadora sang two duets with Bob Crosby. He was a good singer, but he was no Bing. We didn't stay for the second set but left when the band took a break. The staff of Bramley Hall had been given tomorrow off to recuperate. However, Loretta and Franklin had early appointments. Merely by their presence, Mr. Cary Grant and Miss Katherine Hepburn had done a good job of convincing uncounted bigots that Chef Luigi Lattuada must not be a person of color. They had exchanged phone numbers with him; he called them Archie and Kate, and they called him Weegee. We all expressed our gratitude to them, especially Gertie and I did, especially to the dreamy Mr. Grant, whom we hugged with much affection.

At that late hour, the ride in the chartered bus from Vermont Avenue to Bramley Hall took just half an hour. Everyone aboard was as invigorated as though midnight must still lay hours ahead; if we weren't all talking at once, it sometimes seemed that way.

As the staff who lived off site departed the estate in their vehicles, as Lynette went to her apartment and Luigi to his, Rafael responded to the family's noisy entrance with a sorrowful look of condemnation. Waiting in the foyer, lying on his left side and as limp as though expiring from loneliness, he withheld the wag of his tail to impress on us that leaving him alone for five hours was a grossly inconsiderate act. Gertie and I knelt beside him, gradually reviving him by effusively praising his beauty and devotion. Soon his tail motor switched on, and he began panting not from exertion but with delight that his family—his pack—had found their way back to him, putting an end to his long, lonely ordeal in the wilderness.

At the dog-treat jar in the kitchen, Gertie and I bought forgiveness with a generous penance of biscuits, while Harry stood gazing out a window, softly whistling "The Big Noise from Winnetka," waiting patiently to put a leash on our pooch and escort him to the backyard for the final potty session of the night. A year or two previously, he'd begun insisting this duty must be his after sunset. "Nature," he said, "assumes a different personality than she has in daylight, as do men whose hearts are secretly savage." Gertie and I joked that he had been reading too many pulp magazines in the men's adventure genre, tales of brawny heroes no doubt written by pale, scrawny young men who dreamed of becoming the next Hemingway. In time, we would come to realize that ingrained in Harry was a sense of responsibility to innocent people who were weaker than he was. Sometimes we have difficulty recognizing the hero in a young man whom we knew when he was but a foolish boy. When he proves his mature nature, we suddenly take greater pride in him.

Harry took Rafael outside, into the maelstrom of monsters and mayhem, while Gertie and I went to our rooms. After I had changed into my nightdress, brushed my teeth, and washed my face, I settled into bed—and got out again when I heard Rafael mewling at the door to the suite. We boarded the king-size bed from different sides and met in the middle. I didn't switch off the nightstand lamp because part of my mind remained in the Palomar and was reluctant to leave. I sat up, propped against a pile of pillows, and Rafael chose to lie beside me with his head on my thigh.

Perhaps I don't need to recount my thoughts when I sat pillowed in bed, a softly snoring dog at my side, on that June night in 1938. But that was a golden moment, that entire evening, and I cannot help but dwell on it. As a girl, Izzy's greatest desire had been to see the world from pole to pole and ten times over; now she had become a young woman whose greatest desire was to hone her talent and make herself into the best singer and pianist she could be. Her earlier ambition was not ambition at all; seeing the world was a passive intention to be taken places and shown things. She had transformed herself into an *active* woman with goals that required commitment, hard work, and humble self-assessment. That transformation thrilled me, because I loved her too much to see her squander her life as a perpetual tourist. Furthermore, her voice and piano work were pure, without forced sentiment and other cheap tricks; the way that she presented herself was enchanting but clean, wholesome.

I was self-aware enough to know that in my heart of hearts I wanted to believe I had the littlest something to do with who Izzy had become and that by such a contribution I had somewhat redeemed myself. During my time in the family, if I had to any meaningful extent influenced Izzy to become the woman I'd seen at the Palomar, my years of tawdry exhibition in the carnival and speakeasies would weigh less against me in any judgment that I made of myself or that a greater power might one day hand down against me from a higher court.

Great happiness often causes insomnia. The human mind prefers to bathe in joy rather than to trade the bright, waking moment for sleep and all the alternatives to joy that it might bring. On this occasion, however, I exhaled myself into sleep with a sigh of deep satisfaction. In the first and better phase of the dream, I floated in the night sky, above a mountaintop observatory where astronomers studied the stars and planets. As if the air were water to me, I dove toward the 200-inch lens of the telescope. As I passed through that enormous disc without shattering it, I knew this must be the Mount Palomar Observatory, and I fell into a chair at a table for six. Izzy and her piano floated high over the dance floor. She was playing and singing. The song was "For All We Know." Her voice and the piano music were ethereal. Except for me, no customers sat at the tables, and not one couple made use of the dance floor. I rose from my chair, walked through an archway between two ornate Moorish columns, and called up to Izzy, "Where is everyone?" Rather than answer me, she and her piano rose higher, higher. This Palomar Ballroom had no ceiling. Izzy's voice and the piano music faded until she ascended out of sight into the stars, whereupon the scene became as silent as a mortuary basement. I stood at the center of the vast dance floor. As I turned in a circle, seeking someone who could explain the evacuation, I saw the weathered farmhouse had been transported from the middle of America and set down here on the vast dance floor, without an accompanying barn, silo, and stable. Pale light shaped its windows, and a strange shadow swooned from one room to another. I started forward. A sound halted me, a rustling like ten thousand dead leaves swept up in a gust of autumn wind. Beyond the columns and the archways, the Palomar dining terrace lay almost lightless, though I saw baroque forms, tall and thin and pale and angular, quivering and stilting among tables. They crowded into the archways to peer at me and proved to be grotesque praying mantises the size of people, with protuberant, polished black eyes. Movement at the periphery of vision returned my attention to the house, in front of which stood a cradle holding a baby, over which a mantis loomed, flexing its powerful raptorial forelegs that featured pincers to grip its prey, working the mandibles that would devour what it captured. Mantises were quiet predators, scaring off their enemies with a snakelike hissing, but as the insect reached into the cradle for its succulent dinner, all those crowding the archways shrilled with fierce excitement. Someone put a hand on my shoulder, and I pivoted. Towering over me, Captain Farnam smiled and said, "Have you missed me as much as I've missed you?"

I woke in a cold sweat, with a sense that Death himself had entered the room. I didn't cry out, because I'd fallen asleep with the lamp on and could see that all was as it had been and should be. Some psychologists say that the more naive your life is, the more frightening your dreams will be; the subconscious tries as best it can to shake you and wake you to the truth that the world offers countless harbors in which evil individuals hide and scheme. You might think I've had so little experience that I must be naive. But naivete is the goodness that comes from having no knowledge or even thought of evil, and I am well educated in the subject. This was the third time I'd dreamed of the farmhouse and the first replay in more than four years. I took this repetition to mean it was predictive, a matter of clairvoyance. On each occasion, the scenario had grown more frightening, which suggested that the event I'd just seen—the murder of an infant—was the key event and drawing nearer, perhaps imminent. I had no idea whose child was at risk. Most disturbing at the moment was why my mind should cast a praying mantis as Death, when no insect that large existed, but I felt sure the explanation would be obvious when the threat to the victim became manifest.

At my side, Rafael slept undisturbed. His paws twitched as if he dreamed he was racing across Elysian Fields, drawn by a fragrance as mysterious as it was irresistible. Now and then his tail thumped the mattress a dozen times or so. I watched him with envy. Whatever he had learned about evil was a tiny fraction of what humanity knew of the subject.

THIRTY-SEVEN

Maybe you believe in patterns of luck. Many intelligent people do, some who are mathematicians, many who work in other respectable professions. There are true stories of gamblers who, sitting down to a blackjack game or taking a stand at a craps table, had such a high percentage of wins over six, eight, or ten hours that they broke the bank at Monte Carlo.

However, all patterns of luck—good and bad—begin with an end date that can't be known or reliably predicted. I endured a run of bad luck that lasted seventeen years. Following my encounter with Franklin and Loretta, I had for eight years enjoyed a streak of the best luck for which anyone could hope. I had no reason to believe that I would have nine more years of good fortune to balance my first seventeen ill-starred years on Earth. Indeed, if my dream of the infant and the praying mantis was predictive, the greatest maker of misfortune, Captain Farnam, was going to reenter my life sooner than later.

Beginning July 11, the Bob Crosby Orchestra had a break before resuming their tour in San Diego, and Izzy came home to the Bram for three days. The reunion was lovely, often joyous, but I could not escape the realization that our roles were changing in relation to one another. Izzy was twenty, five years my junior, but because she was out in the world doing cool things, I seemed to be still a girl while she had become a woman. Gertie, a strong personality, could hold her own with her sister; as I watched them engaging with each other, I saw Gertie, too, was fast becoming a woman, or already had done so while I'd been looking elsewhere. Harry possessed the kind of good looks that would always lend him a boyish quality, but his immersion in history and military history, which might have made another boy seem geeky, gave him a certain gravity. It was easier to see the man he would be than the boy he had been. I loved them as they had been and as they were becoming, and they loved me; at this precious time in our lives, we still would rather have been with one another than with anyone else. We seldom stopped talking except to laugh. Those were three of the best days I'd known, in part because I was aware that the drift of time and our different interests would ensure that such days became ever more rare.

Early Thursday morning, Izzy left for San Diego to spend the day in rehearsals for a Friday opening. I was afraid for her. She was twenty. She was talented. She was nobody's fool. She knew right from wrong. She had no illusions about evil; she knew it was real, that it walked the world in human dress but also in a form unseen. However, a well-balanced sense of reality and the human condition, accounting for the seen *and* unseen, wasn't a guarantee of safety. Evil's intentions are as limited as those of an animal with minimal intelligence, but its strategies and tactics are of such dazzling variety as to suggest genius. Even in a person as fundamentally good as Isadora, the heart is deceitful above all things—mistakes are made; consequences must be endured.

When Izzy left, Harry went directly to his room and his history books. I don't think he had yet given any thought to what he would do with his life. On the other hand, he did believe that the future was shaped by the past, that tomorrow was to be found in yesterday, so maybe he was getting ready for life in his own way. Gertie said goodbye to her sister and, before the tears that gathered in her eyes could spill, she hurried to her room. I didn't have to follow to know that she would go straight to her typewriter. Soon the keys would be clacking under her six quick fingers. She was a voracious reader, and though she was not as obsessed with books as I was, she felt driven to write.

Although my life had been largely lived through novels that took me places a freak otherwise could not go, I'd never considered *writing* fiction. I'd read authors who were moral monsters and who seemed not to realize it. I feared that if I revealed more of myself in a story than intended, I might discover I was not just a physical monster. Besides, Captain Farnam would never have provided me with a typewriter. If I had proved to have any talent for composition, it would have been a key with which to unlock the chains of slavery.

Gertie had begun writing two years earlier, when she was sixteen. Everyone assumed it was a passing fancy spawned by a novel she admired. Instead, she had kept at it with increasing enthusiasm, producing short stories and novellas she said were "practice for the real thing." She forbade anyone to read her work. It was an honored rule in the family that any demand for privacy, if reasonable, must be granted. If you violated such a vouchsafement, you were brought up before the family court to be embarrassed, shamed, and assigned punishment. I had no experience of that, nor had I seen it happen to anyone. But soon after I came to the Bram, Izzy admitted she had broken the rule when she was ten; the experience was so mortifying, neither she nor her siblings had ever again violated another's request for privacy. If a request for privacy was never made, then snooping was all but required—or otherwise there would never have been either a J. Edgar Hoover Society or a Clyde Tombaugh Club.

The week after our trip to the Palomar, before Izzy came to visit, there had been a four-day period when Gertie took her meals in her room and vanished from family life. Her typewriter rattled at all hours. When she at last emerged and came to my living room and threw herself onto the sofa as if she were a distressed damsel in a Pearl White silent serial, I asked if she'd found her career, if she might become a writer. She said, "I'm only eighteen, Addie, still in my damn cocoon, going through the pupa stage. I don't know if I'm going to be a butterfly or just a moth. Or maybe I'm an inferior pupa that just withers in the cocoon and never becomes anything."

"You're not an inferior pupa," I assured her. "You're a pupa of the finest kind. You're an amazing pupa."

"Yeah, well, when I read what I've written, it looks brilliant, and five minutes later it's just crap. Now beautiful, now crap, now beautiful, now crap. Maybe I'll have a career if there's a market for beautiful crap."

"Maybe you just need feedback."

"Hell no. At eighteen, nobody can benefit from being given writing advice. You have to kick your own ego around until it's scarred and dented, and *then* maybe you're ready for feedback. Maybe that's when you're twenty. Twenty-five. How would I know when? I'm only eighteen."

"Some famous writers—not many but some—were writing pretty good work at eighteen."

"No, don't tell me their names! Envy is a terrible thing. If they're dead, I'll want to desecrate their graves. If they're alive, I'll want to put them *in* their graves."

"Maybe the form of fiction you're struggling with—short stories, novellas—isn't right for you. Maybe you should try screenplays."

"What—and throw myself into the family business? No way." She grabbed a decorative pillow and pressed it to her breast, as though to ward off arrows. "Even if I was the greatest screenwriter ever, they'd say I got to the top because of who my parents were and because with my weird hand I couldn't do anything else but ride on the family name. It would always be seen as a combination nepotism-pity career. I want to write novels that *crush* you when you read them, that shake your heart half to pieces, so no one even notices my weird hand. Or if they notice it, they want to have a hand just like it because they love my books so much that a weird hand has become cool."

"Well, that's a perfectly reasonable ambition."

She sighed. "No it's not."

"It's not?" I said, feigning disbelief.

"Not the part about everyone wanting a hand like this. But I really do want to crush people, totally crush them emotionally, and shake their hearts to pieces, figuratively speaking. Oh, and make them laugh, too, and love the characters."

"Then am I right to think it's your intention, in spite of all this violent crushing, to make your readers want to live?"

"It would be difficult to build an audience if what I wrote caused them to kill themselves." She put the pillow aside. "I came in here being a drama queen, didn't I. Pretend this never happened."

"Honey, you've been pounding away at this for two years. Maybe it would help to hear a reader's opinion. Writers write to be read not just by themselves but by other people."

"Where did you get that? I'd never thought about it that way. Is that Shakespeare?" She sighed and shook her head. "Don't listen to me. Well, listen to me, but don't take anything I say to heart."

"Did someone just say something?"

"You know what it is?" she asked. "Izzy's out there, singing with a band, living her dream, and I'm spinning my wheels."

"She's coming home for three days next week. We could fall upon her in the dead of night and beat the shit out of her."

"Mother and Father won't approve of violence in the Bram."

"We know where she'll be staying in San Diego after she leaves here. You've got a driver's license. You can use one of the family cars anytime you want. All we need is a baseball bat."

"I doubt that'll make me feel better. After all, I love her." She scooted to the edge of the sofa and leaned toward me. "Maybe it would help me if I had some feedback."

"Why didn't I think of that?"

"Could you read a novella and give me an honest opinion, tough and true, without coddling me at all?"

"Yes."

"If it's crap, will you pull no punches?"

"If necessary, I'll eviscerate you."

"Really?"

"Really."

"That's wonderful. After you've hammered me with the truth, *then* you can coddle me just a little."

"Unless the story is so good that you don't need any coddling."

"Wouldn't that be an amazement?"

"What's the title of this novella?"

"I've written several. I'll have to decide which one. I'll need to read them all again and think about it. Give me a few days. Give me a week. I want to pick the right one. The least crappy one. Give me a month."

I leaned forward in my armchair, rubbing my hands together like a malevolent witch in a fairy tale. "Izzy will be leaving here next Thursday morning. I will accept a manuscript from you no later than dinner Friday. If you fail to provide the promised novella, then when you return to your room, you will find a very large pile of dead rats, which you must spin into gold for me."

"Hmmm. It's usually straw."

"Yes. It's usually straw. But this time it will be rats. Large, juicy, moldering, dead rats."

The week passed. Isadora came for three days and left for San Diego on Thursday. When the five of us arrived in the dining room for Friday dinner, I made a show of looking under my chair until Loretta asked if I had dropped something. "No. I thought I saw one of Rafael's toys, the thing that's like a squirrel or maybe it's a rat. But nothing's there. It was just a shadow."

As we settled in our chairs, Gertie said, "If you're looking for a pile of rats, don't bother looking in my room. I have no need for a pile of rats."

Loretta said, "Why on earth would Addie be looking for a pile of rats?"

"Do we have a rat problem?" Franklin asked. "We've had mice in the garage but never rats, and certainly not in the house."

Our salads were already plated before us, and as Gertie picked up her fork, she said, "There weren't any rats left in Hamelin after the Pied Piper lured them into the river. He's my hero."

"But when he didn't get paid," said Harry, "he hypnotized all the children with music and drowned them in the same river. That's not a hero in my book."

"Well," said Gertie, "if you had a contract to spin rats into gold and the task disgusted you, maybe you'd cut him some slack."

I said, "Perhaps there aren't any rats in Hamelin now, but there are plenty in California. Finding a pile of them is easy. Finding a magical spinning wheel might be harder."

Speaking so quick after me that her parents had no chance to express whatever confusion they were experiencing, which was the point of the game, Gertie said, "A person who expects to come into a fabulous rat gold fortune will be disappointed when she discovers the very thing she thought impossible is waiting to be found under her bed pillow."

"Franklin," Loretta said, "the children have evidently spent the day in the wine cellar."

Franklin said, "The girls are talking in code concerning something they don't want us to know about. Anyway, I hope that's what they're doing. Psychiatrists charge a fortune."

"I don't know about any code," Harry said.

"That's okay, son. Eventually you'll learn half of everything women say to each other is in code, to prevent us from realizing they rule the world."

"From now on," Loretta said, "the only talking in code allowed will be between your father and me. And there will be no talking at all about rats when we're at the table."

"You're taking all the fun out of dinner," Harry said.

"Chef Lattuada wouldn't want to hear that," Loretta said. "And he's the only one with the power to make it happen, just to teach you a lesson."

After dinner, I went directly to my suite. In my bedroom, under my pillow, a manila envelope contained a sheaf of typing paper. On the envelope, in Gertie's neat printing, were ten words: ONLY THE TRUTH WILL HELP ME. WAITING TO BE EVISCERATED.

The novella was titled *Backward Down the Staircase*. Seventy-six pages of double-spaced text. The first page carried no byline, as if she didn't want to admit to having written the piece until someone confirmed that it wasn't an embarrassment.

One of the drawers in my vanity was the size of the paper on which the story was written. I pulled it out and carried it into the living room and put the pages in it so that they wouldn't slide around while I was reading. I sat in my armchair with a decorative pillow on my lap and the drawer on the pillow. As I finished each page, I intended to put it on the small table beside the chair. I didn't have a pen because I had no intention of reading critically or making notations on this first pass.

I hesitated to begin. I was eager to read the story, to know whether she had been blessed with talent. However, of the thousands of books I'd read, what I'd thought of them had mattered to no one but me. Never before had the author been waiting a few rooms away, eager to know my opinion. Never before had the author been someone whom I loved more than I loved myself. I had promised her an honest response, and Gertie knew me well enough and was perceptive enough to detect the slightest inflation or evasion of my true evaluation of her work. I sat there with her heart in my lap, her heart as she had exposed it on seventy-six pages, and I almost became paralyzed as I considered the wounds I could inflict even with the tenderest of rejections. Any of the arts—and writing fiction is one—can be approached casually, as a hobby or a test of one's creativity, and in such a case, the result might occasionally be an enjoyable work of good craftsmanship but rarely a work of art. The intensity with which Gertie devoted herself to writing suggested that she would, in the short term, settle for being judged at best a good craftsman, but only if it could fairly be said that the pale possibility of art haunted the otherwise common chambers of her novella and that with unrelenting effort she could surely conjure it into flesh in her future writings. My hesitation to begin reading lasted perhaps half an hour, until I reminded myself that Gertie, although in one sense a child of privilege, was also one of my kind—designed by God but produced by his chosen manufacturer, Mother Nature, and coughed out incomplete during a partial breakdown of her machinery. Gertie was not a delicate crystal vase that could be shattered by a singer's sustained high note. Experience had tempered her, as it had me.

And so I read her novella with nervous expectation. I read the seventy-six pages again with relief and growing delight. The third time, I forced myself to read in a solemn search for subtle flaws that I had overlooked. At one thirty in the morning, I reorganized the pages and hurried down the hall to her room, intending to wake her. The door stood ajar and light shone beyond. She was sitting in bed, propped up by a mass of pillows, with a double-layer box of bonbons in her lap. She said, "I've finished more than half these chocolates waiting for you. I thought by the time you finally came I'd be as fat as Oliver Hardy. Why are you carrying a drawer? Did you throw up in it? Couldn't you get to the toilet in time? Was it the plot or the prose that nauseated you? Was it both?"

Rounding the bed, I said, "Oh, shut up, you silly genius. I'm coming up there. Don't stuff yourself with more chocolates. I need my share to drown my jealousy in sugar." I clambered onto the bed with the vanity drawer containing the manuscript. She'd anticipated my visit and had piled more pillows beside hers. Between her and me were two boxes of Kleenex. "We're not going to need those. Let's get right to it. Kid, your craftsmanship is superb. I would never have imagined you knew more than rudimentary English, enough to converse with Rafael and contribute childish observations when the rest of us are engaged in sophisticated banter, but you have proven me wrong."

"You sure know how to lift a girl's spirits."

"I was mocking your misplaced self-doubt."

"Yeah, it was hard to mistake your intention. Is it really any good, Addie? Any good at all? Don't coddle me."

"Your craftsmanship is really excellent. Twice you thought the subjunctive mood was required when it wasn't, and once you misused a semicolon."

"The hell you say!"

"You're succinct. The prose flows, flows so smoothly."

"Diarrhea flows. Vomit flows."

"Fortunately, you didn't write anything like that in this fine novella. Check yourself in the future when the impulse arises. Your style is quite another thing from your proper use of English."

"How badly does it stink?"

"Oh, it stinks like a rose. Your phrasing, pacing, similes, metaphors, all the rest of it. It's unique. It's yours. It's you. It's not a fully mature style yet—"

"The hell you say!"

"Not fully mature, but for a girl of eighteen—"

"Eighteen plus."

"—it's amazing. I'm serious, Gertie. I'm not jazzing you. Would you like me to go through it with you, page by page, to note the strongest and weakest parts?"

"I assume that discussing the strongest parts will take until Monday."

"At least until late Sunday afternoon," I said, "as long as you don't waste too much time preening over every compliment."

She handed me the box of bonbons. "Better fortify yourself."

Half an hour later, as I finished what I had to say about page seventeen and took it out of the drawer and set it aside, Gertie put her hand on mine and squeezed gently. "Do I understand what you're trying to tell me?"

"Honey, that's too sweet a setup for a funny put-down. I won't stoop to it. What do you think I'm trying to tell you?"

"I'm almost afraid to say it."

"Let's find Rafael. Maybe you can write it on a slip of paper and he can read it to me."

Her sweet face, so smooth with youth, grew smoother still as her eyes widened, as if the prospect that occurred to her was so restorative that it erased what few marks the years had left on her. "Addie, are you trying to tell me . . . Do you mean . . . Is it really possible that you think this novella is publishable?"

"In spite of this rotten economy, not all magazines have gone out of business. Quite a few come out every month, and many of them publish short stories, novelettes, and novellas. I would guess more than a few would pay to have this."

Gertie regarded me as though I had just fallen out of the sky, crashed through the roof, landed in bed, and announced that I was Peter Pan. She let go of my hand, fell back against her mountain of pillows, stared up at the ceiling, and said, "Whoosh."

"I want to read everything else you've written these past two years. This novella can't be a fluke. Maybe it's the best thing you've done, but I suspect not."

She said, "Even if everything . . ."

I waited and then said, "If that was a complete thought, I need a translation."

"Even if everything I've written and rewritten and finally feel is finished . . . even if it were all publishable, would I?"

"Would you what?"

"Publish it."

"Why not?"

She turned her head from the ceiling to me. "Did the story at any point crush you? Did it half shake your heart to pieces?"

"No. But it moved me. It greatly entertained me and moved me close to tears more than once. That's something any writer would be pleased to have achieved with a reader."

"But if I start publishing before I can knock the reader on his or her ass, just flatten them emotionally, won't I be labeled as a particular kind of writer before I've become the kind of writer I most want to be?"

"Look, sweetie, I know you're really into violently assaulting readers, breaking their hearts so hard they need a cardiologist and they ruin the book they're reading by sobbing into it so much that the pages are a soggy mess. But maybe you should just back off that psychotic impulse a little and settle for leaving them traumatized for life."

"You are a terribly sarcastic person, Adiel Fairchild."

"And you love it. I'm just saying everyone starts somewhere."

She sat up from the pillows and crossed her legs yoga style. "Have you forgotten I'm a rich little snot?"

"As I recall, for the purpose of your trust fund and being a beneficiary of your parents' will, you preferred to be called a 'rich little booger.'"

"You really do remember everything, don't you?"

"It's not entirely a blessing."

She plucked a piece of candy from the box, popped it into her mouth, and sat chewing. After she swallowed, she said, "My point is, if I really do have talent and you're not just lying to me for some sinister reason, why should I be in a hurry? With the confidence you've given me, with the unconscionable privilege of being a rich little booger, why shouldn't I take my time to write the kind of thing I most want to write? And at novel length."

"That's your choice, of course. It's not a bad plan. But I still want to read everything you've finished so far."

"I want you to. And be honest. I'll put together the whole pile of crap right now and help you carry it to your room." She scrambled out of bed. "Are you sure, for the purpose of the trust fund and will, I didn't want to be called a 'rich little phlegm wad'?"

"You're recalling Izzy's request. And it was a 'rich little hocked up glob of phlegm.'"

"Wow. Colorful. Maybe she's the real writer in the family."

Her body of finished work to date consisted of six novelettes and nine novellas, each in a manila envelope, totaling 364,000 words. I carried the vanity drawer and the box with what remained of the bonbons and Gertie carried the stack of manuscripts to my suite. We hugged and kissed each other. She said I shouldn't read all fifteen stories in what remained of the night, not in my badly ensugared condition, speed-reading in a diabetic frenzy. I promised to go straight to bed and sober up.

However, when she was gone, I read one of the novellas. It knocked me on my ass and flattened me emotionally. Really. Gertie possessed a gift that the world sorely needed. In my own small way, against all odds, although I was just a freak wholly dependent on the kindness of others, I had become the smallest part of something important. I was the supportive sister of someone with the potential to bring joy and hope to great numbers of readers. And then there were Izzy and Harry, whose lives I might have impacted as they had mine, all of us together perhaps making good luck for people we knew and others who would always be strangers to us. In those early hours of that Saturday, I had never been happier. And in that moment, I had forgotten the most important advice Harmony had given me. I had stopped being alert.

THIRTY-EIGHT

The remainder of that weekend and through Monday, I was lost, lost to the world in which I'd been born, having become a citizen of the world of Gertie's novelettes and novellas. The world of her fiction was our world in every respect, but it was made better and more interesting by her perspective on it. There was much honest sentiment in her work but no sentimentality, compassion without the indignity of pity, forgiveness that required penitence, righteous indignation but not acidic anger regarding those who were foolish or ignorant. Three of her stories were brilliant. Seven were very good. The remaining five suffered not in the quality of the writing but in their conception, although even they were readable, engaging, and most likely publishable.

I promised Gertie a full day of feedback, just the two of us, sandwiches in her room, not even Rafael allowed to interrupt. She was excited about what she called the "Bramley Hall Conference of Pretentious Little Rich Snot Writers." Although I had none of her talent, I'd read thousands of novels and thought deeply about them. I was excited to imagine I might be able to share some thoughts with her that might in some small way give her a little confidence boost and maybe even help her refine her style from 99 percent perfect to 99.5

percent. I wanted to read every story again and again before talking about them, so we set Wednesday as the day we would claw each other in the literary catfight of the century.

At ten o'clock Tuesday morning, having settled on my sofa with the manuscripts six hours earlier, I was unaware that Captain Farnam had come calling with a purpose that he declined to reveal until I was included in the discussion. Loretta came to me to say they could have Captain thrown out or even call the police to deal with him if he refused to leave. However, considering that he had made no effort to intrude in our lives for nearly eight years, we would be wise to consider he might be desperate. Desperate men do reckless and stupid things if granted no consideration. She promised that he would not get what he wanted if what he wanted would compromise my future or diminish my happiness. She assured me there was no reason to be afraid of him, that she and Franklin would not let him near me.

"I'm not afraid Captain will hit me," I said. "I never was. He's a coward. I sometimes worried he would drive me to some remote place and abandon me in the bitter cold and dark, where I'd have little chance of surviving. And I feared one day he would stop stealing library books for me. But fear *him*? He himself? Never."

"He insists on talking outdoors where no one can overhear us. He thinks we can record any conversation occurring in the house, for God's sake. Considering the life he's led, maybe he has good reason to be paranoid. Lynette and Mr. Reinhardt are setting up folding chairs on the great lawn. He didn't even trust the pavilion, as if Pinkerton agents might be hiding in the airspace under the floor."

She held my hand as we walked from the house, through the rose garden, and out to the center of the one-acre lawn. Three folding chairs were arranged in a line, facing one chair that stood twelve feet away from them. Captain waited in the lone chair. In eight years, he'd lost some hair and gained weight, but he was as pale as ever. When other men pack on the pounds, they look soft. He appeared as bone-hard solid as the mineralized skeleton of a dinosaur fossil. As ever, he wore a three-piece tweed suit, which he felt conferred on him some respectability. Although this was a warm July morning, not one bead of perspiration lent a human aspect to his face.

As we sat facing him, he said, "Nice dress. Does the job. Some might say it's odd, but they'd never guess what's hiding under it."

"Enough of that," Franklin said, "or you can leave right now."

"I'm not insulted," I said. "You can't be insulted by a skunk when it sprays you. It's just a scared little animal that has no weapon but its stink."

Loretta smiled and put a hand on my shoulder. "My girl."

Captain remained expressionless. He loathed giving anyone the satisfaction of seeing that either condemnation or praise affected him. "Whether you're kind or unkind matters not at all to me. This isn't personal. I'm a dealmaker, a businessman. I've come to make an offer that will spare you from a tragedy. If we reach an agreement, I'll keep my end of the bargain. If you choose not to do the right thing, the consequence will be of your making, not mine."

"What offer? What deal?" Franklin demanded. "I can conceive of no business we could have with you."

"That's okay," Captain said. "I've already conceived of it for you. I require one hundred thousand dollars. Because the banks have stabilized in recent years, I imagine you no longer keep the largest part of your assets in cash, which is how I need to receive it. But surely you have at least a hundred K in your home vault."

"You're out of your mind," Loretta said. She rose to her feet and took two steps toward him before she seemed to realize she had sprung into motion. She halted, looking down at him with contempt. "We paid you forty thousand to pry you away from Adiel. She never belonged with you. We adopted her almost eight years ago. She's not yours, and she never will be."

He held up both hands, palms toward Loretta, as though advising her to calm down and give him a chance to explain himself. "I have not come here to lay claim to Alida—or Adiel, as you call her. I am well aware the adoption is legal. I've no rights to her. Sit down, please. Gather yourself so we can handle this like businesspeople."

After a hesitation, Loretta returned to her chair with some reluctance.

Franklin's hands were fisted on his thighs, but his voice was quiet and measured. "Do you have photographs of her? You swore you didn't. If now you're suggesting you'll publicly embarrass her, if you're demanding money not to do it—that's extortion. A felony."

"I am not a cruel man," Captain said. "I've been a good friend and generous benefactor to many poor, deformed creatures from whom most people would turn away in disgust and fear. I have no photos. Your money would not be extorted from you. You would be paying an insurance premium to guarantee the girl's safety."

If words had weight, "safety" would have fallen to the lawn with a solid thud.

When I looked away from Captain, not fearful but outraged, I became aware that the day had grown eerily quiet. The Bram usually was graced with birdsong, but not now. The sky often presented a ballet of swallows and phoebes, but currently offered not one bird in flight. The dog was keeping his distance, watching us from within the pavilion, his head between two of the balusters. All of Nature's own seemed to have retreated in recognition that Evil had come into these gardens.

"We can deal with you," Franklin said. "This is the closest you will ever get to her—and live."

"Again," Captain said, "you attribute to me a criminal capacity I do not have. I could never commit the slightest physical harm to Alida

Adiel. You would be buying insurance to protect her from an individual with a more violent nature than I possess."

"And where would this threat come from? Who would it be?"

Captain smiled and nodded. "One does not sell insurance without specifying the threat against which the client is buying protection. I will explain. After receiving your forty thousand in 1930, I sold my interest in the Museum of the Strange for a tidy sum and as well my oceanside lot in San Clemente. I realized I now had sufficient funds to pursue investments that, in a few years, would ensure a far more luxurious retirement than I'd been anticipating. Indeed, I did quite well in spite of the economic crisis—until 1935. My mistake was in believing that our government would be competent enough to set the financial ship aright long before then. I structured my investments to pay off by '35. Foolish of me. Here we are in 1938, no better off, and no one in Washington wiser about how to fix the situation. For the past three years, I have been bleeding dollars, the worst illness I've ever known. Month by month, I thought more often of the Fairchild clan sailing through the Depression on their fine estate. I learned what I could about your family. I couldn't see on what basis I could encourage you to do business. Then all my years running the Museum of the Strange brought me the answer."

As Captain talked, there was no mistaking how smug he was, how certain of his position and his power over us. I knew him to be a man who brought to his business—in fact to every aspect of life—the shrewdness of a poker player who occasionally might lose a hand but rarely lost the game. Although Loretta and Franklin knew him less well than I did, they concluded he had a valid reason to be smug; in spite of their anger, they didn't interrupt him.

"When you're running a ten-in-one, there's often a problem of staffing. Many human oddities have serious health problems and don't live so long. They're always dying on you. Those who're odd enough—genuine freaks—they don't just come to you and apply for a job. You've got to discover them, and they aren't standing around on every street corner. You need to develop contacts in certain medical communities, among reporters for the lurid tabloids that fill their pages with everything weird and decadent. I want you to understand how, when a tip pays off, it's expensive. Maybe you think I'm greedy here, but I have expenses. I have to be generous with the tipsters or I'll lose them. I have to negotiate with the parents or whatever institution has custody. If the freak is intelligent enough to know he has value, I have to cut him in on the take. They don't come to me as young and helpless as Alida did. When I owned the Museum of the Strange, I was fair with everyone. That's why, though I've been out of the business, I still receive tips from contacts. This tip was most timely. My need for fresh capital has become severe. I was getting a bit depressed about finding a way to convince you that buying insurance on Alida Adiel was a necessity. Then suddenly fate brought me a tip about the weirdest ten-in-one attraction I've ever seen. He's a very good boy with me. Very good and grateful. But when I tell him to be bad, he can be very bad indeed. He so enjoys it. If he were very bad with your girl here, I would be far away, my alibi well established. If he were somehow to be caught, he can never be tied to me. And he won't be taken alive. Even if he were caught, he knows me by a name that isn't mine. And the name he knows is not the name that I live by these days. Since purchasing my boy, I have so diligently separated myself from my past and from everyone I knew that a hundred Pinkerton agents could never find me. So. Have I set up the situation properly? Do you understand the risk against which it would be wise to acquire an insurance policy?"

Loretta took my hand to comfort me, though the contact was also intended to comfort her. "You're threatening murder, Mr. Farnam."

"Not a threat, Mrs. Fairchild. It's a friendly advisement."

Although not disbelieving, Franklin was at least suspicious. "What is this—'The Murders in the Rue Morgue,' with you in the role of the sailor who owns an orangutan that slaughters people?"

Captain looked genuinely puzzled. "Orangutan?"

"He's not a reader," I said. "He's not faking us with rehashed Poe. If this boy of his is real, he's no orangutan."

I doubt that I can convey how grotesque it was, sitting on that manicured lawn, under a blue and birdless sky, as if a butler and maids would shortly bring a table to set between us and Captain—a table, a tea service, a small arrangement of flowers, and an array of exquisite pastries. The white rabbit hadn't yet arrived, but the Mad Hatter was definitely with us.

"Orangutan?" Captain said. "Well, of course he's not any such thing. I wouldn't have traveled a thousand miles to make a deal to acquire a monkey, as I traveled to get my boy."

Perhaps Franklin was thinking of deceitful studio executives with whom he had done business. He said, "How do we know that this 'boy' exists at all?"

With his interlaced hands propped on his ample belly, Captain looked like an editorial cartoon of a self-satisfied robber baron contemplating foreclosing on the homes of a million widows. When his veracity was questioned, he manufactured a sad expression and for a long moment stared at his hands as if they were folded in prayer for the soul of the doubting Thomas who was his host. At last he raised his head and made eye contact. "If you haven't sufficient faith in my word alone to take a life insurance policy on this young lady, then I'll provide my bona fides. My boy will pay a visit to Bramley Hall one night and leave irrefutable proof that he was here and is everything I've told you. Proof that you will regret having insisted upon, proof that will cause you grief. Then for all my trouble, the price of the policy will be raised to one hundred fifty thousand. Of course, you're wondering, if you pay, how often might I want you to renew the policy. I don't deny I'm a man of many faults, but greed isn't one of them. This single premium will buy insurance for life."

Franklin was exasperated, but he maintained his composure. He seemed to speak almost with admiration. "Captain Farnam, you are an amazing piece of work."

"Thank you, sir. I regret it is such a hard world that we are at times required to be hard ourselves in order to survive in it."

Loretta tried to match Franklin's calm demeanor, but her voice had an edge that his did not. "I believe I speak for my husband when I say there will be polar bears and penguins in Hell before we give you even one dollar. I'd rather we spent everything we have making the Bram impenetrable and hiring a platoon of security men."

"Agreed," said Franklin.

Captain smiled and nodded as if, being an experienced insurance salesman, he was accustomed to customer resistance. "I understand your petulance, and I'm confident that, as successful entrepreneurs, you'll get past your displeasure and approach this in a businesslike manner. I must tell you, no matter what extraordinary steps you take to fortify your estate, it's the nature of my boy, a function of his very freakishness, that he can't be kept out. And as to your concern about future premiums, this is the one and only, even if I wished otherwise. The boy is the instrument that makes it possible for me to do what I've advised you I will do if not paid. For now, he sees me as his savior and is pleased to obey me. But in time, he will become less . . . manageable. Even now, he frightens me, though I dare not let him know. Once he has paid his first visit to your lovely home and you realize that a hundred fifty thousand is a small price to pay to ensure he won't return, once I have my money, I'll kill him. Certain things he does . . . how he looks at me . . . I'd be crazy to think I can control him and use him long-term."

If Franklin had been ready to hustle Captain off the estate, he was given reason to hesitate by the quiet note of dread in the man's voice and a supporting anxiety in the set of his broad face. Loretta seemed likewise affected. Captain was a pitchman, wickedly effective at selling the exaggerated qualities of a thing with superlatives that he could make ring true. However, he was not competition for the great actors of American theater. I could see he wasn't faking. He was profoundly afraid of this boy of his.

Loretta was aghast. "Kill him? After you use him, you kill him? You share your intention with us as if it will put us at ease—when what it does is make us morally complicit in murder."

Captain waved his hands as if to brush away her concern. "It won't be murder. Killing in self-defense isn't murder. In addition to his physical abnormalities, the boy is a stone-cold psychopath. If we knew everything that he's done, I'm sure we would all feel that execution would be warranted."

"You're sure, are you? You call him a boy. How old is he?"

Captain promoted himself out of an undignified slump into a better posture. The folding chair was a credit to its manufacturer; it neither bent nor creaked in protest. "Mrs. Fairchild, you've no need to know anything more. I've put the proposal before you, and you either value this girl's life or you don't."

"Actually," Franklin said, "it's not that simple. The way you speak of this boy, I'm beginning to think he might exist and might be as dangerous as you claim. You've spooked me to consider your terms seriously, though a minute ago, I was prepared to dismiss you as a fraud. However, just being told this creature exists isn't good enough. A hundred thousand dollars requires that I be *certain* he's out there somewhere. I need to be convinced. How old is he? Where does he come from? Why are you sure you can control him even now?"

Under less fraught circumstances, it would have been amusing to watch Captain pout. Wisps of fine yellow hair, age lines having been smoothed away by a new layer of fat, legs seeming too short by comparison with the bulk of his torso——he reminded me of an enormous baby even before he sealed the image with a thick-lipped pout. He flexed his hands as though searching for an object to throw in a tantrum. "I won't tell you names, places, not anything you can take to the police to use against me or to have the boy taken away from me before I'm done with him. Bare bones. That's what you'll get—the bare bones of his story. If then you still don't believe he's real, God help you and this girl." As a priest takes courage from his faith, Captain found new strength of purpose in anger, which geysered in his heart and mind, bringing pastel color to his face. That pity-me pout flattened into a score line almost as thin as a scalpel cut. Although his cheeks were pink, his compressed lips were bloodless. When he was able to control his rage enough to continue speaking, his voice had become half sneer and half snarl. "I need that money. If I can't have it, then you can't have her. My boy will take her. And maybe not just her."

I knew too well the version of the world in which Captain lived. His dark universe had "neither joy, nor love, nor light, nor certitude, nor peace, nor help for pain." There was for him no right or wrong, only desire and what he deemed necessary to fulfill his desires. Our only hope depended on learning more specifics of the threat Captain lodged, an unintentional revelation he might make.

"Convince me the boy is real," Franklin said, though by now he believed. "You've said so little about him. If you'd been pitching me a movie with such a character, I would have had no interest in the project. The loss of a hundred thousand won't materially affect our lives, but my sadder experiences in the movie business have made me sensitive to con jobs."

And so Captain told us what he was willing to reveal about the dangerous creature in his control. He called the boy Jack, though that was not his name. Jack was the first—and only—child of a farmer and his wife in a remote corner of a state in the Middle West. Jack was born at home with a midwife assisting. The parents and midwife alike were shocked by the appearance of the infant, but they weren't horrified. In addition to being poor and hardworking, they were Christians. They believed things happened for a reason, that every child, regardless of appearance or disabilities, deserved to be loved and nurtured. Because such a special child added to the mother's duties, her sister and sister's husband—call them Sam and Sarah—came to live there and help work the farm. Jack's father and Sam, with the assistance of members of their church, built a small house for the newcomers.

Eight months later, Sarah gave birth to a son; call him Bobby. The boys were homeschooled, grew up together, and were best friends. To the family, as strange looking as Jack might have been, he was nonetheless just Jack, never to be feared, a smart kid with a sense of humor for which he sometimes had to apologize when one of his pranks went too far. However, because others recoiled from him with visceral disgust, the boy was never taken into town; his world was the farm and the woods beyond.

The family were fundamentalists. They raised young Jack and Bobby with strict discipline and fear of God. On rare occasions when Jack misbehaved, when his sense of humor revealed a dark side, when he was caught in a lie, he was remorseful and tearful. He didn't have to be told to ask God to forgive him; he retreated to his room, left the door open, and spent an hour or two on his knees, praying aloud.

One Saturday, the four adults drove into town to shop and have a café lunch. Bobby usually went with them. This time he preferred to stay home with his best buddy. When the adults returned in the late afternoon, Jack was distraught, shaking. Bobby had saddled Buttercup, one of the family's two horses, and had taken her for a ride. When he came back home, as he was approaching the stable, a rattlesnake startled the horse and Bobby, too. Buttercup reared and panicked and threw her rider. The horse was grazing calmly now. The snake was gone. And Bobby was dead. He'd been thrown onto the cast-iron hand pump that stood on a concrete pad to provide water for the stable. He crushed his skull against the three-inch-diameter pump spout and died almost instantly.

In this rural territory, the county sheriff ran a small shop with fewer deputies than needed. The coroner made a living primarily as the proprietor of a funeral home; he had never received training in forensic medicine. No one had time or resources to investigate deaths that appeared to all intents and purposes accidental. A month after Bobby's funeral, as Jack's mother was turning out the pockets of his jeans before washing them, she found a penny that had been placed on railroad tracks and flattened to twice its normal size under the wheels of a locomotive. Bobby's uncle had given it to him, and the boy had carried it—his "lucky penny"—at all times. No one had thought to retrieve it before the body was transported to the funeral home. At first, Jack said Bobby had given it to him, but then claimed he had taken it off the corpse as a remembrance of his friend. Over the next few days, his parents were dismayed that he more often than before broke the family rules. When he took the Lord's name in vain repeatedly at a Sunday dinner and showed no remorse, it seemed that something had happened to instill in the boy a defiant attitude and a shameful pride. His parents suspected what that "something" had been, but they didn't want to believe it. The county where they lived provided no mental health service, but after making inquiries, the parents were put in touch with a government psychologist in the state capital. We'll call him Dr. Mephisto. He did contract work for the Department of Health and the attorney general's office. He arranged for Jack's parents to bring their son to the Mephisto Clinic and leave him for a three-day evaluation.

Dr. Mephisto was a graduate of a renowned medical school, but his success as a scam artist was a result of natural talent. He would bill both the health department and the attorney general's office for his treatment of Jack, who was then just thirteen, and he would report twice the number of hours of counseling that he actually provided the boy. On the telephone, the parents described their son as having grievous physical deformities that medicine could not fix, that would be lifted from him only by divine grace. This led the good doctor to hope the boy might provide him with a third source of income. Fifteen years earlier, he had discovered the world of carnival freak shows. With considerable dedication, he had made contact with the operators of several ten-in-ones and as well with thirty psychologists and psychiatrists all over the country who had established clinics roughly analogous to his. Among the patients those specialists treated were occasional individuals with disabling deformities who were depressed or acting out their anger in perilous ways. They were usually wards of the state or clients of faith-based welfare agencies, in either case poorly served. Most proved not to be misbegotten enough to thrill the marks on a midway, neither monstrous nor amusingly malformed. Seven or eight times each year, however, one or another of Dr. Mephisto's associates sent to him, by express courier, photos of a candidate who was a sure thing. If the miscreation resisted the prosperous future that was offered, there were drugs and certain threats that resulted in a concession. To the ten-in-one operators, the doctor provided photos and a bio of the performer, along with a required finder's fee determined by the degree of freakishness of the person being offered. The money was substantial. In extraordinary cases, bidding ensued. Mephisto split each finder's fee with the associate who introduced him to the human oddity. Cash. Beyond the observational capacity of tax authorities. Jack's parents brought him to the clinic, ostensibly for a week of psychoanalysis and counseling, and Mephisto saw his patient for the first time. The good doctor's heart soared with delight.

Perhaps Jack saw something in Dr. Mephisto to which he could relate, for he never became obstreperous or engaged in deceit, and he cooperated with the analysis. As for the counseling, it amounted to little more than an explanation of the workings of a ten-in-one and an accounting of the average weekly gate that would be shared with the ten exhibits. Jack was excited by the prospect of being freed from the boredom of the isolated farm and from poverty, by being a valued star rather than an embarrassment to his family. He said, "No more Jesus this and Jesus that all day long." His smile was so wide that it briefly alarmed Mephisto. There was no question that young Jack was a psychopath, although not as extreme as his strange face suggested he might be. He had a potential for violence. He admitted to killing Bobby, but not intentionally. His cousin had been in a mood that day, taunting Jack relentlessly, finally picking a fight. "I wish it hadn't happened," Jack told Mephisto, "because of all the trouble it's caused me. But I'm not sad. Bobby always got the best of everything. He lorded over me." To cover the facts of the killing, the boy had saddled Buttercup, turned her out in the yard, and invented the story about the rattlesnake.

Jack was self-aware enough to know that only he had the power to destroy the opportunity Mephisto laid before him, that his future depended on him controlling his dark side. Nevertheless, the best ten-in-one operator for the boy was Captain, who possessed a knack for charming the most difficult oddities out of their bad behavior. Mephisto sent him four photographs, a short bio, and a price. The day he received the mail, Captain called the doctor to say he was coming by car and would be there in two or three days to "adopt" the boy.

Jack's parents had not completed elementary school. Mephisto overwhelmed the couple with a diagnosis that terrified them even though they didn't understand it. By phone, Mephisto assured them that Jack was "a psychopathic, schizophrenic, cyclothymic, paranoid, lycanthropic, idiomorphic, devil-worshipping kleptomaniac who will—not might but absolutely will—kill you in your sleep. His secret fantasy is to behead you and offer your heads to Satan on an altar. The attorney general's committee on homicidal maniacs intends to sue you tomorrow for custody of the boy and place him in a high-security asylum where he will no longer be a danger to himself and others."

When Jack's parents declared their loathing and distrust of pettifoggers and worried that legal fees would bankrupt them, Dr. Mephisto agreed all lawyers were shysters, but he explained their other option. They could choose not to contest the decision by the committee on homicidal maniacs (which did not exist), sign a document transferring parental rights to the state, and be released from all criminal and financial responsibility they would otherwise face when their son inevitably raped and murdered young women. The father wanted to know where to get those documents. Mephisto said, "I'll drive the hundred thirty miles to your place as soon as we hang up." The mother wanted to know what to tell people, how to explain that she and her husband had conceived a mad child. "How about this," Mephisto suggested. "You don't tell them any such thing. You print a note from him. He ran away, says he's going to Canada where people like him are treated better."

Now, under the birdless sky, on the birdless lawn of Bramley Hall, Captain said, "The papers they signed were nonsense. Mephisto didn't leave copies with them. Back in his clinic, he burned all of them. When I finally got there, the boy was ready to go. I dropped more cash than I can afford, but the second I saw him in the flesh, I knew he was worth it. He wore a hooded jacket when we stopped for gas and checked into motels. The past three days, where I live, I've made sure he eats what he wants, better than he's eaten before. For the first time, he can listen to anything he wants on the radio. I bought him some under-the-counter magazines with pretty girls, and he's more grateful than you can imagine. We talk about the new ten-in-one I'm going to open, what it's like in the carnival, how much money he's going to make. Maybe he'll hold himself together and be a star for me. But like I said, I know that look he gives me, what it means. In the end, it's only blood the boy wants, and he can't help himself. Anyway, he and I worked out how to make sure you all suffer if you don't come through with the hundred-grand stake I need. You did it before. Why not again? So now you tell me how it is."

Franklin rose from his chair and surprised me just a little by saying, "I believe the boy is real and he's what you say he is. It's half past eleven Tuesday. I can have the money for you by the close of business Thursday. Just this once and never again."

"What shit is this?" Captain demanded, thrusting to his feet so violently that he knocked his chair over. "You've got that much here and now in that home vault of yours, the same from which you got the forty thousand eight years ago and brought it to Blue Mood."

"Be sensible, Farnam. These are far different times. Back then, thousands of banks were failing. We didn't trust them. That part of the crisis is past. We have our money in investments, certificates of deposit. I need a little time to wind down some things in such a way that we don't lose another hundred thousand in addition to the one I'm paying you."

"Like hell. There's still a depression. Maybe worse than ever. You've got end-of-the-world money piled up here in Bramley Hall."

"You're right about things being bad, but stashing cash in the mattress is the way to make it worse."

"He's telling the truth," Loretta said as she and I got to our feet. "The economy needs investors to take big risks and get the country's engine started again. The government sure hasn't been able to do it. We can get the money, Farnam, but it'll take a few days."

"I'm not begging for a loan, a bank check, and a payment book," Captain said somewhat incoherently. "It's got to be cold cash."

"Which we can't have until Thursday," Franklin insisted. "Do you want to take a few valuable paintings for ransom, a silver tea service, maybe the living room furniture? Be reasonable, sir. You have spooked us into giving you what you want—*as soon as we can.*"

Captain's face had paled once more during his long story of the origin of the psychotic boy. Extreme frustration brought some color back to him. However, the rosy blush was confined to his bulbous nose, which seemed to glow like a reminder light that the time for his midday nip of the bottle had arrived. "Very well. But let me tell you something, Daddy Warbucks. Better not call any bastards with badges, better not think you can track me to where I live. I parked my car in town and walked two miles out here. I'll walk back. I've got a sharp eye for shadows. If I see one, the deal is off. This girl you wanted so bad to rescue from me—you won't have her anymore. I don't like surprises. If you've got one for me, just know I've got one for you already, a surprise just waiting to spring."

"Four o'clock Thursday," Franklin said. "I'll bring one hundred thousand wherever you want. Now I'll see you to the front door."

He led our visitor across the lawn and up the garden path toward the house, as nonchalant as if Captain wasn't the kind of man who would stab him in the back. When they'd gone far enough to reassure Rafael, the dog descended the pavilion steps and raced toward Loretta and me. Suddenly crows strutted through the grass, pecking for lunch. Birds began singing in the trees. I didn't know for sure exactly what to make of all that—although I had an idea.

Loretta pulled me against her. "Are you all right, sweetheart?"

"Yes. Are you?"

303

"Better with him gone."

"Captain doesn't scare me. Not him. But . . ."

"What is it, Addie?"

"I saw that farmhouse in dreams."

"Dreams plural?"

"Yes. In one of them, I saw the boy riding a terrified and screaming horse in the moonlight. I believe he bit it on the neck."

"Bit the horse?"

"Yes. All this was at a distance. I can't say what he looked like, except that he was strange."

"Your dreams are not just dreams."

"Some are more. I used to deny it."

"Do you know where this farm was?"

"No. But in another dream, it was on the empty dance floor of the Palomar. And there were praying mantises."

"Mantises?"

"As big as people. Everyone on the dining terrace was a mantis. And a mantis came out of the farmhouse there on the dance floor."

"The boy?"

"I guess it represented him. He's not a mantis, but the mind shapes dreams in metaphors."

"The subconscious."

"It's a strange animal, the subcon. The mantis that came out of the house made its way to this cradle."

"Cradle?"

"With a baby. A human baby. The mantis lifted it out of the cradle to eat it."

"I don't think I could handle your dreams."

"They're never boring. I woke up before it devoured the baby. I don't think I could let my subcon show me something like that."

With Rafael keeping us company, we walked toward the house, into which Franklin and Captain disappeared.

"So," I said, "whatever the boy is, he's real. Subconscious foresight, intuition, clairvoyance—whatever you want to call it—I've learned to trust what it's trying to tell me even though the messages need interpretation." We walked in silence for a moment. As we were passing the dolphin fountain, I said, "You're going through all this because of me."

"Not you, sweetheart. Not you at all. Because of Farnam."

"If not for me, Captain would never have been in your life."

She halted on the terrace. "If not for you, Gertie would have died of septic shock."

"We can't know that for sure."

"I know it."

"What I mean is—there's no such thing as inevitable fate."

"On my darkest days I wonder about that," she said.

"When one big thing changes in your life, everything after that changes, too. If you'd never met me, so many days after would have unfolded differently. Gertie might not have gotten a nosebleed, or if she got it, she might have come to you instead of packing it the way she did."

"So you're the cause of nosebleeds now?"

"You know what I mean."

"If you're the cause of nosebleeds, prove it. Give me one."

"I'm not going to give you one."

"I demand you give me a big, wet nosebleed right this minute."

I shook my head. "You're being silly."

"I don't think it's silly to accuse you of false advertising. You claim to be able to provide a service, but when you're asked to do so, you pretend to have made no such claim."

"A nosebleed is a service?"

"No less than the service Danny Dutton provides when he comes each week to clean the swimming pool and add chemicals to the water. What would you think of him if he just went for a swim and left, no cleaning, no chemicals, a complete swimming-pool-service fraud?"

"You're trying to make me laugh."

"If that's what I'm doing, it seems to be working. But what I'm really doing is trying to get the damn nosebleed you promised."

"I might just give you one."

"Ha! You talk big, but it's all talk. Look at my schnozzle. Not one drop."

"Your nose is perfect. No one would call it a schnozzle."

"I'll call my nose anything I want to call it—schnozzle, snoot, snout, beak, Fred."

"You don't call your nose Fred."

"Yes I do. I have a masculine side, but it's all in my nose."

So we sort of collapsed together on a terrace bench and held each other until I stopped laughing.

Loretta said, "Never ever again say we'd have been better off without you or I'll give you a nosebleed you'll never forget. You're a blessing, pure and simple. Captain Farnam is a mosquito. We'll swat him away."

"What about the boy?"

"Addie, Addie, Addie. Since when has a Fairchild ever been afraid of a psychopathic, paranoid, lycanthropic, devil-worshipping kleptomaniac?"

"Since never?"

"You said it. I'm pretty sure I know how Franklin intends to handle this—the same way that I want to handle it. Honey, by four o'clock Thursday afternoon, Captain Farnam will be in jail, charged with extortion, and the boy will be in whatever institution can help him, if in fact he can be helped. Easy peasy."

Loretta and Franklin had triumphed over so much misfortune, so many reversals, and were toughened by experience. I thought maybe a scheme like Captain's, for all its evil and potential to result in horrific violence, might nevertheless be countered and defused in ways that he lacked the sophistication to predict. As it turned out, the surprise he promised to spring if Franklin crossed him was not an empty threat. What seemed easy peasy would be anything but that. Such is the world.

THIRTY-NINE

Less than three hours after Captain walked out of the front gate, six Pinkerton agents arrived in two vehicles. They parked under the portico roof and entered the Bram carrying valises and larger metal cases full of supplies and equipment. They were dressed in stylish dark suits, varied in size from medium height and weight to junior giants, but every one of them had the look of a PI in a movie and appeared capable of knocking the jujubes out of any thug who made the mistake of taking a swing at them or questioned the virtue of their mothers. Two met with Loretta and Franklin in his study to be briefed on everything Captain had said during his visit. The other four spread through the house to assess its vulnerability to invasion by psychopathic human oddities and the carnival pitchmen who buy them dirty magazines.

All the windows were of bronze with muntins that couldn't be as easily broken as wood, and individual panes were far too small to admit an intruder if the glass was cut out. Most operative windows were the casement type with two tall halves that could be opened from the inside only with a hand crank. The handles were detachable so that no one could break a pane, reach inside, and laboriously crank the halves apart. The thumb-turn latches on the double-hung windows were replaced with keyed locks. All the exterior doors had mortise locks on the stile above the knob. The agents drilled the butte stile to add a keyed deadbolt on that side as well.

After an hour and a half, the two agents who met with Loretta and Franklin left with numerous though fragile leads to follow in search of Captain. The other four men expected to be in-house, securing the perimeter, until nine o'clock that night. Chef Lattuada provided them with a selection of hearty sandwiches, thick slices of pecan-cherry pie, and plenty of coffee to wash it all down. The consensus among the Pinkerton guys was that they might require longer than expected to complete the job and might be there for breakfast. Of course they were gone at 8:40 that evening, leaving the Bram locked up tighter than ever. They would return in the morning, Wednesday, to install concealed trip wires and associated battery-powered alarms at several outdoor sites.

Beginning tomorrow night, four agents would be stationed in the gardens, and six would patrol the interior of the Bram, although no trouble was expected until twenty-four hours later. We hoped Captain and the boy would be located and detained for police before four o'clock Thursday, when he intended to phone with instructions as to where the hundred thousand dollars should be taken and whom he expected to deliver it. If his whereabouts remained unknown at that time, things could get dicey. When he learned that there had never been any intention of meeting his demand, that Franklin and Loretta had been buying time either to find or prepare for the cousin-murdering psychopath, *that* was the moment when I would be in real danger. The crisis would escalate through the days ahead until Pinkerton could bring an end to it. So this Tuesday night might be the last in which we would know peace and quiet for a few days or maybe weeks.

During the busy afternoon and evening, when my thoughts might be expected to remain focused almost entirely on metaphoric mantises and a boy who liked to bite the horse he rode, I nonetheless lost myself in Gertie's manuscripts as I reread them with a critical eye. Maybe my easy immersion was in part because I had spent so much of my life living inside fiction written by others that I'd come to feel more at home and safer in the worlds within those pages than in the real world with its plotless chaos and frightening momentum. But it also—and perhaps primarily—was a testament to Gertie's talent.

Because of all the activity in the house earlier, dinner had been a grab-what-you-can affair. I had made a meal of only one of the sandwiches the Pinkerton crew enjoyed so much. By 10:45, I was in need of further fortification, including a slab of that pecan-cherry pie. I used the dimmer on the hallway and stair lights, so I didn't have to go from the soft revelation of a reading lamp to a brightness that would sour the mood in which Gertie's writing left me. Passing by the open doors and doorless archways of dark rooms, I felt as safe as if I were aboard a luxury liner miles out on a gently rolling sea, far from the shores where robbers robbed and rapists raped and armies clashed by night. When I pushed open the swinging door between the butler's pantry and the kitchen, I was surprised to find Chef Lattuada wiping off the center island in bright light.

"Wow. You must have an amazing breakfast planned," I said, "if you're already starting to prepare it."

"I cleaned up before nine o'clock, after I thought the last of the gumshoe guests had gone. Wasn't much debris. I was impressed that Pinkerton agents were neater than the ladies of the Community Aid Society when they visited for tea. I went back to my apartment, but later, when I stepped out to smoke, I saw the kitchen lights were on."

"Smoke?" I pretended to be appalled. "No one has permission to smoke on the estate."

"As I'm well aware. Did I say it was a cigarette?"

"A cigar would be worse."

"It wasn't a cigarette, cigar, or pipe."

"Well, you clearly weren't on fire yourself."

"It was a peach."

"A peach?"

"Yes. A lovely ripe peach."

"And you smoked it."

"Essentially, yes."

As there was not much I liked better than fencing with Chef in this fashion until one of us could no longer keep a straight face, I said, "I'm curious. When one wishes to smoke a ripe peach before bed, how does one light it and keep it burning, considering its juiciness?"

"I chose the wrong word. I should have said I stepped outside to *flambé* a peach before bed."

"How inconvenient. You'd have to bring with you not just the doomed peach but also a flambéing pan, a bottle of brandy, a source of flame, and whatever other ingredients make your peach flambé as unique as I'm sure you'd want. Why not do it in your kitchen?"

"It's no trouble outside. Anyhow, it's a sacred tradition."

"Flambéing a peach outside before bed is a family tradition?"

"Not just family. It's a national tradition."

"That would be Italy?"

"Yes. Precisely. We are a peach-loving people."

"You're telling me everyone in Italy steps outside before bed and flambés a peach?"

"Not everyone. Perhaps eighty percent of our people. There are always those who rebel against tradition. Communists and the like."

"You'll excuse me if I find this hard to believe."

"Is that so? Have you ever been to Italy?"

"I'm of half a mind to go there tomorrow."

"I suggest you wait until Mussolini and his ilk are thrown out of office, Addie. Then you and I can go together to the annual *Festa del Pesca*, the Festival of the Peach. Tens of thousands gather in plazas and parks to simultaneously flambé peaches. It is a beautiful and moving sight. The golden light of myriad brandy flames dances over the facades of the buildings and glows in the smiling faces of the celebrants, as the fragrance of all those warm peaches fills the night. It is the experience of a lifetime."

I surrendered and laughed. "I'm so glad you've never quite grown up."

"That is a fate I have tried to strenuously avoid."

"So, I came all this way for an enormous piece of the pecan-cherry pie that I should have had with dinner. Don't tell me some hungry hawkshaw got his mitts on it, so now I'll have to settle for a smoked peach."

Chef gave me two thumbs up. "I was prepared for the equivalent of a plague of locusts. I made four pies. The fourth remains safe in the third Frigidaire. If you wish, indulge yourself until you fall violently ill. For whatever reason, the malingering sleuth rummaged through two Frigidaires but not the last one."

"Rummaged?"

"As you know, I keep the contents of my refrigerators better organized than a lawyer's files. Everything was where it shouldn't be. He sat at the center island to eat and left a mess."

"If anyone in this family left a mess," I said, "they'd have to answer for it. They'd clean up after themselves because they'd know what the punishment is for slacking off."

"And to think, starting tomorrow night, there will be even more Pinkertons pinking around than there were today."

"Tell Lynette about this. She would have had to let him out, the hungry malingerer, so she'll know which one he was."

Chef Lattuada shrugged. "They're here to keep you all safe. I don't want to make them feel unwelcome—not even if one of them is a sloppy slacker." He opened the third Frigidaire and withdrew a pie. "I can give you the whole thing and a fork to take to your room."

"You're a gentleman, a true friend. But if you'd just cut a piece for me, I'll pour a glass of milk. I'll eat at the island and clean up after myself. You need to go back to your place and get a good night's rest. You'll have a lot of cooking to do. If some of the same agents come back, you've raised their expectations just like you've raised all of ours over and over again."

He smiled. "You are a charmer, Addie."

"Thanks. I've been called worse. I'll let you out."

"No need. I've got my old key for the old locks and my new key for the new locks. I hope that's the end of more keys. My dad had so many responsibilities, fourteen keys on his key ring, way too much to think about. The fewer keys, the clearer your mind, the better your life. Good night, Addie."

"Good night, Luigi. I won't forget that promise to take me to the *Festa del Pesca* when Mussolini's gone."

With his hand, he drew a cross over his heart. He left by the kitchen door, locked both deadbolts, waved at me through the French panes, and followed the lamplit garden path to his apartment.

If ever I get to sample the ambrosia that the gods of classical myth were said to eat, I'm sure I will find it inferior to Chef's pecan-cherry pie topped with a scoop of vanilla ice cream. Not for the first time, I was grateful that, since arriving at my current weight long ago, I never gained or lost a pound regardless of how much or little I ate. Over the years, I'd given hardly more thought to that curious actuality than to the fact that I breathe. Likewise, as I hadn't once been ill, hadn't experienced as much as a single head cold, concerns about my health never troubled me. Because of the radical deformities that made me a star attraction as a freak, I would never marry or have children, never be able to pursue a normal career or don a swimsuit for an afternoon at the beach—and

313

therefore I spent no time fantasizing about my future or lamenting about what I could not have. As I served myself another and smaller slice of pie, I realized with some surprise that my limitations and my lack of options comprised one reason why I could clear my mind to such an extent that I became immersed in a novel, experiencing it as if the characters and events of the story were real, and hold it in memory. I was not prepared to believe that a pie, no matter how delicious, could inspire in me the greater self-awareness I'd just achieved, so it must have had something to do with Chef Lattuada and our conversation.

By the time I finished the second serving and cleaned up after myself as the rogue Pinkerton man had not done, our current drama here at the Bram began to seem much like a sequence from the eerier fiction of Robert Louis Stevenson or that of Wilkie Collins. With an uneasiness new to me in this house, I turned off the kitchen lights, passed through the dark butler's pantry, and crossed the dining room in the palest of moonlight admitted by the tall windows. Stepping into the long main hall lighted by the sconces I had dimmed earlier, I thought of the house named Manderley in the new novel by Daphne du Maurier. Manderley was a grand yet subtly sinister house because of the portentous housekeeper, Mrs. Danvers, who was also a keeper of secrets. We had no one in the Bram with a wicked spirit like hers, and there were no baleful secrets here that were likely to lead to a fiery finish. However, as I passed dark rooms and darker rooms that lay beyond those nearer chambers, the beauty and grandeur of the Bram seemed to have been the *mise en scene* of a light fantasy that was now concluded, with a new and fearful story waiting only for the curtain to rise or the cameras to start turning.

In the foyer, as I approached the main staircase, I thought I heard a murmuring voice so indistinct that I couldn't tell what was being said. I halted, listened, but failed to determine from where it came. The library? The main drawing room? Far back in the hallway along which I'd just ventured? It might even be whispering down the stairwell from the second floor. Although I was at first certain that what I heard must be a voice and that the speaker was peevish if not angry, I began to wonder if I might instead be hearing an oscillating vibration of ductwork related to the air-conditioning system. The sound abruptly stopped, and I waited, but the murmuring did not resume.

Novels of all genres and levels of ambition engage readers with one degree of suspense or another. When a person has been immersed in fiction more hours than not and has been shaped by what was read, as I have been, there inevitably are moments when you find yourself in a situation that recalls scenes akin to many with which writers have entertained you, and you tend to act as did the characters in those stories. As I continued toward the stairs, something click-click-clicked as though a handful of pickup sticks had been cast across a floor. Then silence. Having been present when Captain made his threats, being now alone on the ground level of the mansion, moving through lightless or dimly lighted spaces where every deep shadow might be something more than it seemed to be, with everyone else asleep on the upper floor, a character in my position would usually resort to one of two reactions. She might cry out at such a sudden creepy sound, waking everyone. Or if she were the spunky but not reckless type bent on preserving her dignity, she would race up the stairs, return to her room, close the door, lock it, and assure herself that she'd heard nothing more than mice in motion behind the wainscot. I took the stairs two at a time.

The upper floor was laid out like the letter *I*, with one long hallway intersecting shorter hallways at each end. My suite was off the shorter hall at the west end. The Persian carpet runner softened my footsteps. I hurried but did not sprint, and I knew better than to glance back to see if anyone was following me. In spite of the severely dimmed sconces, when I came to the end of the main hallway and turned left, I saw a figure in the gloom.

A bright beam pinned me. Harry whispered my name, switched off the Eveready, and quickened to me. Though my vision was compromised by the sudden glare, I had seen that he held the flashlight in his left hand and a pistol in his right. The gun was his. He was expert with it. His reading of history these past few years taught him a lot, not least of all that humanity repeats the worst mistakes of previous generations and that every free, prosperous civilization will eventually be destroyed by that small fraction of its people who find no satisfaction in anything but anger. Their ceaseless complaints eventually escalate into histrionic violence producing mostly symbolic damage, but that excites the worst thugs among them to commit brutal assaults, then murder, and then mass murder. Soon civilization dissolves in war; the violent bear it away. That was the argument Harry had made to his parents when pressing the case why he also, not just they, ought to be armed to protect the family and the homestead. He was only seventeen but as responsible as any adult when Loretta began taking him to a shooting range to earn the right to have a gun stored safely in his room.

"The pistol. What's happening?" I whispered.

We stood in the junction of the west and the main halls. He continuously scanned both corridors. "I heard someone talking in Dad's office."

That home office was under Harry's room. If asleep, he would have heard nothing. He'd been lying awake, on his bed but still in his daytime clothes, wondering if maybe he would enjoy a career as a Pinkerton detective. The voice was that of a man. Not Franklin. But Franklin was the only man in the house at that hour. Unable to make out what was being said, Harry could nevertheless hear anger and urgency—or perhaps eagerness—in the cadences of the speaker's voice. Because there were no audible responses during those moments when the intruder fell silent, it had become obvious he was on the telephone. Especially after the events of the day, no circumstance existed in which a stranger should be in the Bram at that hour. Harry had gotten off the bed, quietly gone into his walk-in closet, and retrieved his pistol from the locked gun safe. If he had called out a warning to his parents, whose suite was toward the east end of the main hall, he would have alerted the intruder. My quarters and Gertie's room were in the west wing, near Harry's room. He'd decided to collect us and take us quietly with him to his parents.

The mess in the kitchen that Chef complained about had not been left by a lingering Pinkerton man. The intruder must have raided the Frigidaires after the Pinkertons were long gone, after all of us had retired to our bedrooms for the night. If my lust for pie had sent me roaming an hour earlier, I might have entered the kitchen while he was wielding knife and fork. I didn't think it likely that the security specialists overlooked a door or a window or other point of entry, nor that a ragged hobo carrying his worldly possessions in a bindle had wandered into the house through the one gap they had failed to notice. Even before being further secured, the Bram had been a place that required a concerted effort on the part of anyone scheming to enter uninvited.

The boldness of the kitchen raider suggested three things. First, he didn't care if one of us caught him at his meal; he had no fear of arrest—or of how an encounter would end. Second, he had been hungry, famished, perhaps because he'd been hiding in the house since morning with nothing to eat. Third, he came here with Captain and scaled the estate wall while Farnam's unexpected visit had drawn everyone's attention to the front gate; he slipped into the house while we were in negotiations on the great lawn, in the absence of birds. He must be the boy whom Captain called Jack. The boy who murdered his cousin Bobby for a train-flattened lucky penny. The freak whose appearance frightened people too much for his folks to take him into town. The psychopath who was Captain's obedient puppet—until he didn't want to be. No doubt he'd hidden in the Bram to report to

Captain about whether the pitchman's demands were being met. He must be extremely clever and gifted in some way that made it possible to elude the Pinkerton agents hour after hour. Now he knew Captain was not going to be paid the ransom. That was surely whom he had called from Franklin's home office. That was why he sounded angry and eager. In my mind's eye appeared the moonlit meadow from my dream—the screaming horse, the pale and long-limbed rider.

As I hurried to Gertie's room with Harry, a sudden and sharper anxiety spurred my heart and pinched my breath. Depending on the ruthlessness of the author, fraught moments like this in novels often led to the targeted girl—me—being abducted to encourage swift payment of the ransom that a mere threat hadn't yet pried loose from her parents. There was a lesser chance that the enraged intruder would murder her. Sometimes in dire moments, life mirrors fiction as much as fiction reflects life, and then we speak solemnly of the "human tragedy."

This was not a situation where etiquette required a polite knock and a soft-voiced query. The door to the master suite was not locked. This was still the Bram. As long as the exterior doors were secure, there had never been a need to lock a room door, and habits were hard to change. The bedroom lay in deep darkness, for the moon was low in the eastern sky and the windows were untouched by its ghost light. Harry eased the door shut behind us before switching on his Eveready. My heart quieted a bit and breath came to me when I saw that Gertie was asleep in clean, bloodless sheets.

When I spoke her name, she woke and sat up and squinted into the light and yawned and said, "I thought we were done with that Clyde Tombaugh stuff years ago."

"Ssshhhhh," I warned. "Someone's in the house."

"Someone dangerous," Harry clarified.

I whispered, "We'll go to your parents and barricade their door while they phone for help."

Gertie turned back the covers and got out of bed and slid her feet into slippers. She yawned extravagantly, her manner languid as she pulled up her pajama pants and straightened the rumpled collar of her top. "I suppose there's no time to put on a suit of armor."

"I've got a gun," Harry said.

"That's why I'd like armor." Her slippers didn't match the feet they were on, so she sat on the floor to use her hands with them.

"Are you awake?" I asked.

"I used to be. I'm sure I will be again."

Harry looked at me. "How can she be half-asleep and still hit us with good smart-ass lines."

"Why," said Gertie, "can Satchmo always blow such a hot horn?" She threw aside her slippers. "To hell with it. I'll go barefoot."

The journey from Gertie's room to Franklin and Loretta's suite didn't entail a trek as long and arduous as the one that Gary Cooper braved through in *Fighting Caravans* or the one John Wayne undertook in *Stagecoach*. Nevertheless, we felt we needed a basic strategy on which we agreed before leaving this room, where we had a sense of safety that was comforting though entirely false. The idea was to go from here to there without calling attention to ourselves in case the monster from the Middle West was prowling for prey. Gertie would bring her Eveready but switch it on only if, in a crisis, our Harry shouted, *More light!* I would carry his Eveready so that he could have both hands free for the pistol, but I wouldn't turn it on until he required it. Harry would lead with Gertie at his side. I would follow, walking backward to be sure we couldn't be surprised from behind. Except for the call for more light, we would not speak even if a really good smart-ass remark occurred to one of us.

Devising a strategy was meant to give confidence, but in some cases, such as this one, the fact that a strategy was necessary could exacerbate one's sense of danger. As we moved out of the room and took up our positions in the hallway, though I was a freak and had known other freaks who gave me no cause for alarm, I was afraid of Midwest Jack. He who murdered for a penny. He who would slaughter whomever Captain told him to slaughter. Why would my subconscious, which sometimes showed me what was to come, portray him as a mantis that would take a baby from its cradle and devour it? I was afraid for myself, but my greater fear was for this family that had been so kind to me. Midwest Jack was here because of me. By sheltering me, the family became vulnerable to Captain's greed, to his rage at being rejected, and to something horrific that had come into their home. I heard the pitchman's voice in memory: *In the end, it's only blood the boy wants, and he can't help himself.*

Harry, Gertie, and I crept warily along the west-wing hallway, where the sconces were so dimmed that shadows owned more than half the territory. Any one of the closed doors of rooms to the left and right might pop open like a jack-in-the-box lid and spring Midwest Jack among us. As we reached the junction with the main hall, even those gauzy lights went off, and a blackness equal to that at the bottom of an oceanic abyss washed around us. We could have ventured forward in the pitch dark by staying on the carpet runner until we judged that we were opposite the master suite. However, the lights had not gone off on their own, and the possibility that the freak of freaks was approaching us seemed to be just short of a certainty. "More light," Harry ordered. Gertie and I clicked on our Evereadys and let out our held breath when we saw that Captain's proxy loomed neither before nor behind us.

To hell with strategy and caution. We hurried to the master bedroom door. Harry knuckled it with three quick raps and then three more, a minimum courtesy. We entered without waiting for a response. Either Loretta and Franklin had been unable to turn off their minds and get the rest they needed, or they were able to shake off dreams faster than Gertie could. They were out of bed even as our lights lanced the darkness, fumbling with switches on their bedside lamps, which availed them nothing. Rafael, roused from sleep, romped this way and that in expectation that this sudden late-night confab was sure to be great fun. Our elders sought flashlights in nightstand drawers while asking what was wrong, what was happening. "Someone's in the house," Harry said. "I sort of heard the guy talking to someone on the phone, probably to Farnam. Now he's shut down the lighting system."

"He's been here since this morning," I said as Gertie engaged the simple lockset. I put down my flashlight and braced the headrail of a chair under the doorknob, wishing there were a deadbolt. "He must have been told to monitor you and be sure you were getting the hundred thousand together. Instead, Pinkerton showed up."

Most people would not cope well when informed that a murderous creature like Midwest Jack was loose in their house, as frightening an entity as any in the creepier films by Fritz Lang. Most people would either panic and take ill-advised action likely to get them killed, or they would be paralyzed by the prospect of imminent death and be unable to confront the mortal threat effectively. Franklin and Loretta were not those kind of people. His mother—afflicted by Munchausen syndrome by proxy—had poisoned his sister to death for the sympathy it got her; Loretta lost her entire family in an earthquake; both of them survived an orphanage run by grifters. More to the point, together they swam through the swamp of corruption that was the movie industry in their time, yet they had held fast to their principles and an admirable moral code. After all that, a monster in the house was more of an inconvenience than a terror.

Even when Franklin tried to call the police with the telephone on his nightstand and found that it, like the house lighting, had been sabotaged, he said only, "Of course," and returned the handset to the cradle. He and Loretta agreed that it was impossible to be certain whether this threat might be Captain's attempt to intimidate them into paying up or in fact an expression of bitter vengeance and a plot to commit murder by proxy. In either case, the wisest course was to stay together, stay put, and stay alert. Each of them kept a pistol at bedside, and Harry was armed as well. Whatever Midwest Jack might be, whether mere human oddity or true monster, he could bleed and die. If we waited here until dawn, morning sun would light the Bram better than four Evereadys. At seven o'clock, the entire staff would arrive, and there would be safety in numbers.

We had much to ponder and discuss, and there was no need to confer in darkness. If our strategically placed flashlights failed, a full box of spare batteries was stored in a bottom bureau drawer. Enough chairs were provided when we brought two from the bedroom retreat and the bench from the vanity. Rafael fairly divided his attention during the next two hours, lying asleep on one person's feet for a while and then moving on to the next of us for an ear scratching. Even in these circumstances—or perhaps I should say *especially* in these circumstances—I was very proud of Franklin and Loretta. He was handsome, and she was beautiful, and they were both as self-possessed as if we were gathered here for no reason other than the pleasure of one another's company. From time to time, one or both of them would pace as they listened to us or contributed their own insights to the discussion, not as if they were pacing worriedly but as if movement lubricated their thoughts. Wearing silk robes over pajamas, they were casually elegant, and because they had not lost their sense of humor even now, I was reminded of William Powell and Myrna Loy as Nick and Nora Charles in *The Thin Man*.

I thought that if I had been born as well formed as they were in body and mind, I would almost certainly have led a less admirable life than they had. The thousands of books that I carry in my memory reveal a nearly infinite number of ways even well-meaning souls can go wrong. From that collection of mistakes, I have no difficulty identifying scores of grievous errors I might have made if given the opportunity of a normal life. The limitations and humiliations a freak endures might well have saved me from being more like Captain than I dared to consider.

The biggest question occupying our discussion-by-flashlights was how Midwest Jack could have moved through the Bram for eight hours, monitoring every act of the Pinkerton agents without being seen or heard. Even at this moment, he must have been listening to us, amused by our speculations, for suddenly he solved the puzzle by letting us know where he was. With one instrument or other, he pounded so hard on the ceiling of the room below us that the floor vibrated underfoot. "The service mezzanine," said Franklin. The explanation was not as supernatural as we might have been imagining. In a house as immense as the Bram, architects often included a five- or six-foot-high level between main floors. Ventilation ductwork, electrical wiring, phone lines, and plumbing were run through this space, which also housed the gas furnaces, air conditioners, and other equipment that maintained the residence. This interim level, with its own plywood floor and work lighting but no windows, was accessed through a large trapdoor in the ceiling of a storage room on the ground level; ugly mechanical systems were tucked out of sight, and repairmen could easily service them. The estate manager—first Mr. Symington, now Lynette Rollins—dealt with all contracted services and was thus kept aware of the mezzanine. Franklin and Loretta visited that space once, during construction, and had no further business with it. They had put it out of mind just as owners of standard-size homes soon forgot where the clean-out traps were located and which wall concealed the chase for a specific water-supply pipe. Captain must have learned of this interim floor by visiting the building department to review the architect's plans, which were in the public records.

Now we knew how Midwest Jack had spied on the Pinkerton men—and the family. Every grille-covered heating-cooling vent in every room had brought their voices to him. It was creepy to realize that he must be at that moment staring up toward us. But he couldn't get at us through the floor, which was the mezzanine ceiling. Why had he revealed his whereabouts? What would happen next?

The bedside lamps came on. Franklin went at once to the phone, but our nemesis had not flipped a switch to restore that service. A knock on the door startled everyone and focused our attention. "My dear friends," Captain said, "since you screwed me, I can't resist telling you how I've screwed you in turn. You might feel that my delight in this reveals a shortcoming in my character, but I would say that people like you have no damn character at all. Only grifters make a deal with the intention of reneging on it as soon as the mark turns his back on them. I'm no damn mark. I'm no damn rube. The architect plans on this joint don't show a vault, but knowing your view of banks, I was sure there must be one. I never did find one on those damn plans, but I saw what I thought must be a hidden room. Once my boy, my special boy, heard you were hiring Pinkerton for their door-and-window service, his job became getting from the mezzanine into that hidden room. Not so goddamn hard. There's a three-foot-square air-exchange grille in the ceiling."

Captain was so high on himself that he salted his language with other words far worse than "damn," but I will not repeat them here. I quoted as much as I did only to give you the flavor of his rant, so you could see that, even as bad a man as he had always been, he had gotten worse. To save time and avoid further offense, I will condense his abusive tirade to its salient points. Lynette Rollins had left a set of the new house keys in a vanity drawer in Isadora's room for when she visited home at the end of her tour with the Bob Crosby Orchestra. Midwest Jack had retrieved those keys and used them to let Captain into the Bram once everyone had gone to bed except for me, as I was in the kitchen with a slab of pie. The murderous boy was excited by the prospect of being the star and a partner in the new ten-in-one that was to be set up with Fairchild money. He had shown Captain how to operate the hidden door to the secret room that served as a vault and then went off to monitor the family and be sure they didn't interrupt the looting. As insurance against future bank collapses, the vault contained $225,000 in hundreds and twenties. Captain scooped that fortune into a laundry bag he'd brought with him. Thereafter, he spent time conducting an inspection of a few rooms by flashlight, looking for small items of value that he could add to his haul—a Tiffany vase and the like. His bag was full. His car was parked along the highway less than half a mile from the Bram. According to plan, the boy would remain in the house to ensure we "dumb damn rubes" didn't try to alert authorities. Captain would drive straight back here to pick up his special boy, and anyone who tried to follow Midwest Jack would have his face torn off. Through the door, he said, "You thought you were so smart that Einstein should kiss your ass. Now you can kiss mine."

Captain was pleased with himself—"very damn pleased"—and wanted to assure us that his new identity had been so well crafted that a thousand Pinkertons could never find him. He was so euphoric and getting such pleasure from belittling us that, as he ranted on, he became more enfevered and less judicious about what he said. I was pretty sure the "little freak who was not born but was puked up instead" must have been a reference to me, but that was not what got him in trouble. He said Pinkerton and the FBI and "Jesus Christ Himself" could spend eternity searching for him in "every carnival there ever was or will be anywhere in the world" and would fail to find him. This seemed to imply that he had no intention of using the money to create a new ten-in-one. You might infer that he did not, after all, mean to return to the Bram to pick up Midwest Jack after carrying the loot half a mile and loading it in his getaway car. That was certainly the inference Jack made. Jack evidently believed that he no longer had any hope of being a freak-show star, would never be a partner in a lucrative enterprise, and would never have enough money to buy even an hour with one of the girls in those under-the-counter magazines. We all know how sad and frustrated we become when someone we trusted, someone who made a solemn promise, proves to be a liar. We can only imagine how much more intense are the emotions of a psychopathic, schizophrenic, cyclothymic, paranoid, lycanthropic, idiomorphic, devil-worshipping kleptomaniac who has been called ugly all his life and then realizes that he also has just been played for a fool. In all the years I had known Captain, I had never heard him scream. Yet I had no doubt that the screamer in the upstairs hall, on the far side of the bedroom door, was my old keeper from whom I'd been liberated eight years earlier. I do not wish anyone a painful death or any kind of death at all, so I was badly shaken even though his scream did not last long.

Although the six of us bearing the surname Fairchild (which included Rafael) were no less the victims of Captain Forest Farnam than anyone else, Midwest Jack had arrived at the conviction that we and Captain were seven of a kind, all of us aligned against him. Shrieking at us, his language even more disgusting than that of the man he had just murdered, he pounded the door with such force that it seemed he possessed Thor's hammer and would split the wood. His voice shrill with fierce glee, he promised to kill us all and swore he wouldn't break his promise as our kind did. With unrelenting maniacal ferocity, he tore at the doorknob until metal squealed and cracked. Such strength! The knob on our side fell out of the door. Key parts of the lock assembly rattled loosely against one another, and the latch bolt retreated from the striker plate in the jamb. As Jack threw himself harder against the door, we heard the joints of the bracing chair begin to splinter.

Their pistols in a two-hand grip, Loretta and Franklin shouted at us to get behind them. They needed the door to be thrown open, to see the target. That was a reasonable response, although Harry had a better one: deal with the threat before it got into the room where, even wounded, it might kill one of us. Our Harry, amateur historian and military buff, knew the accuracy of his weapon, knew how much punch the cartridges in the magazine would deliver, and was sure they would penetrate the door. He squeezed off seven rounds in quick order, grouping them in the middle square of three recessed panels. Every round passed through, but I cannot know how many still had lethal velocity on the far side. Whatever the number, it seemed to be enough, for Captain's proxy fell silent, his voice replaced by the fading roar of gunfire that echoed along the hallway and down the stairs into the ground-floor rooms. Harry didn't assume he'd dealt a fatal blow to the boy who was no mere boy. He judged that the situation didn't merit hesitation. He kicked aside the half-broken chair and pulled the door open and stepped onto the threshold and fired his last three rounds into a crumpled figure on the floor.

I will not sicken you with a description of the scene in that upstairs hallway. There are only two things you need to know. First, this family into which I had been welcomed was in many ways as warm and cuddly as the March family in Louisa May Alcott's *Little Women*, but at the core of each of them, there was something harder than bone, stronger than muscle. They knew loss and failure and hardship, but they did not know defeat. They ventured into the carnage of the hallway, stepping with care so as not to soil their feet, quickly discussed what must be done: reactivate the telephone system, call the sheriff, recover the laundry bag containing the money, close the door to the hidden room if Captain had left it open, brew a large pot of coffee for the tedious hours ahead, lead curious Rafael away from the cadavers and keep him downstairs. They hugged me, one by one, and said not a word because they knew how this episode must have affected me and understood that words were unequal to a loving embrace. Confident that the thick walls of the house and the length of the gardens combined to ensure that neither

Chef Lattuada nor Lynette Rollins, in their apartments, had heard the gunfire, the members of the family went their separate ways to attend to the tasks awaiting them. No one needed a pill to settle the nerves.

The second thing you need to know is what Midwest Jack looked like. Perhaps you do not want to know what it meant to me when I saw him dead on the hallway floor, but I intend to tell you anyway. I'll start with his appearance. He wore a black T-shirt and shorts. He was tall and lean, with ropy muscles suggesting uncanny strength. In some way I could not define, he seemed more animal than human; no one who encountered him in low light or a lonely place would think of him as a boy. His long face was malformed in a way that explained the metaphor that my inadequately clairvoyant unconscious employed to warn me about him in dreams. Exceptionally wide brow. Sharp face narrowing severely toward the chin. His mouth, frozen in a death grin, revealed teeth like the beveled edges of chisels. His somewhat protuberant eyes were set farther apart than they should have been, enhancing the vague but unmistakable impression of a mantis face.

I feared him when he was alive. In death, however, he became a subject of sympathetic pity, at least to me. He might have been born with the capacity to love, as I had been. There was no reason to suppose he had been born evil, though the possibility could not be ruled out. Maybe he had come into this world with the ability to be formed by experience into what a child of God should be. If so, he'd had the bad luck to be in the care of parents who might have *wanted* to love him in spite of his appearance but who lacked the compassion to take him into their hearts.

In their defense, life on an undercapitalized farm was without exception a hardscrabble existence of exhausting physical labor and endless worry about destitution. A sweet-faced baby could bring with him hope for the future, thereby inspiring love. An infant who looked like Jack required an effort to love and might seem to be an omen of the family's imminent destruction.

Before I discovered my uncanny talents, my good luck had been a sweet face and a good mind. My bad luck was everything else about my body. My bad luck was to have been placed in the care of Captain; my good luck was that I made money for him, so he became a source of books for me. This person, Midwest Jack, was a financial burden in a home where books were not valued. My luck had been better than his. It was incumbent upon me to recognize that and be grateful. "Rest in peace," I said. I went downstairs to do my part, wondering about luck and divine grace and nature's role in the way of all things.

The events of that day could have been a media sensation, with the sleazy tabloids and cheesy mainstream press competing viciously to sell the most extreme version of what had transpired. Before it was all done, the public might have been led to believe that Jack was actually Franklin and Loretta's freakish child whom they had chained in the attic all these years to prevent him from tarnishing their squeaky-clean reputation and glamorous image. Once again, the good will with which they had treated others was repaid.

The county sheriff, Emmett Oates, was a World War I veteran who lost his left leg below the knee while engaged in fierce resistance to the Germans at Château-Thierry. When Emmett had run for office in 1928, the sheriff at that time, Robert "Big Bob" Burnside, was so corrupt that behind his back people called him Bobby Boodle. Big Bob ran a mean campaign focusing on Emmett's "incapacity" and claiming that the war hero had actually *shot himself* in the calf in order to be sent home from France just *before* the battle at Château-Thierry. Franklin and Loretta not only backed Emmett's campaign financially; they also used the skills they learned selling their movies to design his advertising, which was so successful that people kept asking when the "bio flick" was coming to theaters. Sheriff Oates ended bribery in all county offices; he had been a friend of the Fairchilds ever since.

In the matter of Midwest Jack and Captain Farnam, they didn't ask Emmett to break any laws, only to guide them as to how best to minimize the likely mad-dog barkfest in the tabloids and other press. At 1:40 in the morning, he came to the Bram alone, no siren and no flashing lights. He had known my story since the Fairchilds first brought me home with them. They suspected Captain might not be out of our lives, in which case the sheriff needed to know the pitchman's name if in the future he got a call about some kind of confrontation at Bramley Hall, though back then no one could have imagined anything as bizarre as what happened on this night in 1938.

Sheriff Oates went upstairs with Franklin to view the scene of the homicide. The condition of Captain's corpse was such that no one but Midwest Jack or a like creature could have torn into him in the various ways he had been ripped, gouged, and bitten. It was as if the fictional universe of director Tod Browning's movie *Freaks* had intersected with our universe for a few horrific minutes. Captain's murderer was dead and beyond the reach of the law. Midwest Jack's executioner, our Harry, acted in self-defense; therefore, he had broken no law. Sheriff Oates said, "There's not a whole hell of a lot here for the law to do except waste taxpayer's money and fritter away time we could use to chase down bad guys. Besides, if we let the press in on this, then our more excitable citizens will be so frightened by mantis boy, they'll get it in their heads how there must be legions of monsters skulking through the county. Then one egg-sucking fool or another will shoot the innocent paperboy when he cycles around before dawn, delivering the *Los Angeles Times*. My best advice is we clean this up and no one talks about it until I've been shot dead in the line of duty or been carried away by cancer to my mansion in the sky."

And so, with a key taken off the dead pitchman, Harry went out in search of the vehicle Captain had said was parked half a mile away, along the county road. He drove it to the Bram and parked it under the portico. Having had experience searching corpses in a variety of disgusting conditions, Sheriff Oates finessed Captain's wallet from his trousers; it contained authentic-looking driver's licenses in three names, none of which was Forest Farnam. Because it provided nothing but false leads, the sheriff returned it to Captain's pants pocket. He and Franklin then rolled the cadavers into painters' tarps to contain bodily fluids during transport to the car. Outside, Captain and his "special boy" were unwrapped, tumbled into the back seat, and left in whatever posture they assumed. The tarps were carried to the employee parking area behind the high hedge south of the driveway, where they would be hosed off.

With the sheriff leading the way in the squad car, Franklin donned gloves and chauffeured the dead passengers fourteen miles, to a remote stretch of unpaved back road along a canyon in the county adjacent to ours. In Southern California, there were many steep-walled canyons of great depth. Only grass and scrub brush grew on the slopes of this chasm, but heavy vegetation flourished at the bottom, where rushing streams formed in heavy rains and the water table lay near the surface. Franklin stopped the car crosswise on the road, facing the abyss, and turned off the engine. With the vehicle in neutral, he and the sheriff pushed it over the brink and listened to it rattle through the brush until it came to a stop far below. Emmett used a handheld spotlight that was part of his car's equipment to search the depths. The runaway car with its grisly occupants seemed to have disappeared into the dense green canopy perhaps a thousand feet below.

By the time Franklin and Emmett returned to the Bram, Loretta had hosed off the tarps, which had dried quickly in the warm night air. They folded them and returned them to storage cabinets in the garage. As Loretta had dealt with the tarps, Gertie and I had been at work on the second floor. A series of four Persian carpet runners lay end to end along the upper hallway. Together, we rolled up the soiled rug from in front of the door to the master suite and secured it in that compact form with lengths of coarse binder twine. Only a thorough cleaning by a carpet specialist could restore the runner. However, we felt it would be reckless to try to explain the amount of blood caked in the fibers. Sheriff Oates would take it away and dispose of it at the county dump.

As the six of us gathered in the foyer, where exhausted Rafael was deep in sleep, Sheriff Oates said, "There's still the door full of bullet holes."

Franklin said, "Lynette will take it down in the morning and adapt a door from another room to serve temporarily, until we can have a carpenter replace it."

"What will she say about the bullet holes?"

"If I don't mention them, she won't."

"That's quite something. Are doors around here that often riddled with bullets?"

Loretta shrugged. "It's just that everyone at the Bram respects everyone else's privacy."

Emmett Oates considered that for a moment. "It's a good thing this is largely a law-abiding brood. If you'd taken the Ma Barker path, you'd have been an unstoppable crime family."

"We thought about it," Gertie said, "but we were concerned that Rafael would be traumatized by the endless violence."

So many friends of this family were huggers. I was never sure if they were huggers before they met the Fairchilds or if the habit came upon them after, like a communicable infection. Sheriff Oates had to give each of us a hug before leaving. When he hugged Loretta last of all, she asked if there was anything we could ever do to thank him. If she had offered him cash, he would have arrested her for bribery.

"If it's not too awkward," Emmett said, "maybe you could invite Laura and me to dinner next time Groucho Marx is here. For that, I'd help you dispose of as many corpses as you're ever stuck with in the years ahead—as long as it's not you who murdered them."

"Keep the Friday after Thanksgiving open," Loretta said. "Mr. and Mrs. Marx will be here then."

After the sheriff departed, we went to the kitchen, and Rafael bestirred himself to come with us. Loretta prepared a large pot of coffee while the rest of us dressed the breakfast table with place mats, napkins, china, flatware, and juice glasses. A short while later, as dawn was about to break, Chef Lattuada arrived and was surprised to see us sitting on stools at the center island, having coffee spiked with Baileys Irish Cream.

"Mass insomnia," he asked, "or did the Parcheesi game run long last night?"

Harry said, "We were discussing those new inventions everyone's excited about—Teflon and Fiberglas—and we lost track of time."

"Well, if you're all so starved you can't wait, I can provide you with buttered toast and prune juice."

"We'll wait," Franklin said, "for you to exercise your culinary brilliance. After we eat, we're going to sleep for ten hours and then dress for dinner."

"If your majesties would like dinner in bed, I can arrange it and spare you the need to groom yourselves."

"We might do that," Loretta said, "if we were sleeping in our usual room. But we'll most likely be shifting to a guest room for today, and that's not as accommodating for dinner in bed."

"The door to their usual room is riddled with bullet holes," I said, "and will have to be replaced. You know how it is."

"Of course," Chef said. "Well, I better get crackin' or you'll hire another Jamaican-British chef from Italy."

That was maybe the most fantastic breakfast I have ever had, for more reasons than I have the space to write about here. Suffice to say that the best things about it were my amazing family and then the food.

Part Four
1941–1944

Last night I dreamed of a meadow as vast as a continent, under the blue light of a moon as strange as any. In the center of the field, a lovely lamb stood tethered to a stake. The night was alive with the howling of wolves, though as yet the wolves themselves had not appeared. I made my way to the lamb, kissed its brow, and freed it from the stake. As it gamboled away, it vanished as if through a curtain into a parallel world of safety.

I tied the tether to my wrist and sat on the ground. My heart was full, not of fear and grief, but of joy. The wolves fell silent as they arrived, their eyes silvered by the moon. I reclined full length upon the grass so that they would know there was only flesh to feed on, not also human terror and regret. Having lived among men and women born of Adam and Eve, I had no dread of wolves. If they crossed the meadow to what I offered, I do not know, for I woke.

And so I've had four blue dreams, all in four nights. Somehow I know there will not be a fifth, just as I know that these have been more than dreams. If they are visions, they are not the revelations given to saints, for I am no saint. I wonder, however, if I am meant to be guided by the blue dreams as my life unfolds—and one day find the freedom and deep happiness that have thus far eluded me. I think it best never to speak of them, but write about them in a letter to myself, seal it in an envelope, and hide it very well. Such precious dreams are fragile and may turn to dust if shared.

—from a letter by Alida, April 17, 1927

FORTY

Enjoy life but stay alert. Always trust in the rightness of the world. But stay alert. Never be bitter or despairing. But stay alert. Life is a great gift. Love and mercy are the promise of it. But stay alert.

Without revealing my project to the family, I've written pages of this memoir every year since I arrived at the Bram. It will be my gift to them one day, a book of memories. I suppose it isn't much of a gift, but it's all I have to give. Most people forget much of the past. I do not. I like to believe they will regard the memories I leave in this volume as a worthwhile history of our time together or at least as a volume of that guilty pleasure called nostalgia. No life, certainly not just thirteen years of a life as lowly as mine, can justify a thousand pages. Therefore, from time to time, I have reread what I've written and condensed it. Furthermore, I've limited my recollections to the years that seemed, in retrospect, to be those in which events of greater significance occurred. Between those years I have focused on, eight others were full of love and mercy and joy, years during which I remained alert without cause. How wonderful my life has been—by now almost three decades—blessed in both the good years and those not as good. The promise of it has been kept to an extent that allows no complaint.

However, a new reality began for us on what we expected would be a peaceful Sunday devoted to preparations for the coming holiday.

We had gone to an early church service because we intended to have breakfast at home, rather than brunch at a restaurant. Most of the day would be spent decorating the usual five Christmas trees as well as fireplace mantels, door surrounds, and other architectural elements that cried out to be given a more festive appearance. After changing from our Sunday best into casual clothes, we'd taken longer at breakfast than we should have, because Harry entertained us with a highly amusing presentation of a movie he was writing.

For the past two years, much to Franklin and Loretta's surprise and delight, their son had set himself to learn filmmaking and the financial ins and outs of the motion-picture industry, inspired by the prospect of making history as interesting to large audiences as it was to him. The current project, if it got off the ground, was a comedy based on a period in the life of one of the least funny of American presidents, Andrew Jackson. In 1791, when Jackson was Tennessee's state prosecutor, he married Rachel Robards, the former wife of a major landowner, Lewis Robards. Ah, romance. Then it was discovered Rachel and Lewis might never have been legally divorced. Scandal! Jackson was a hothead who'd been involved in a number of brawls over the years. The press was adversarial to a fault; they hated Jackson. Lewis was befuddled. Rachel was shy and retiring but capable of cleverly manipulating the press and Nashville's elites. "The film is like a British farce," Harry said. "The basic facts are true, but the opportunities for hilarity are countless."

Isadora was home for the month. She had completed a six-week guest singer stint with Tommy Dorsey's Orchestra, performing solos but also singing duets with that new young sensation, Frank Sinatra. After four years of short-term contracts with various bands, she had gained enough admirers in the business that she had just signed a recording contract with Brunswick, which was a top-tier label that boosted Duke

Ellington among others. "It's a slog," she said, "more than half the year on tour with one band or another, the rest of the time bouncing around from one short gig to another—but, God, it's fun. If I burn out before anything really, really big happens, it'll still be worth it."

"If you crash like the *Hindenburg*," Gertie said, spreading lemon marmalade on a slice of toast, "you can always have a job as my amanuensis."

"So you think, just because I'm a big band bulbul, I don't know what an amanuensis is. What exactly would you need a secretary for?"

"For when I make the move from short fiction to novels and the fan mail comes pouring in. You'll need to answer it for me, sharpen my pencils, correctly read my *gribouillage*. And a bulbul is an Asian songbird, a nightingale, often mentioned in Persian poetry."

"Huh." Izzy raised her eyebrows. "Little sister can probably even pronounce 'nefarious' these days. '*Gribouillage*' is French. It means *scribbling*." They were grinning at each other throughout these exchanges. "By the way, that novella in *Collier's* was a knockout."

"I had a teacher who worked me half to death, mocked me for my errors, then called me 'honey,' as if she really cared about me."

"She pulled the same trick with me when I was trying to write my own songs and the lyrics weren't right. She'd work me so hard I'd be in tears. She'd hand me a Kleenex and say, 'Before you spend the day sobbing, you should look at how much a box of these disposable hankies costs, sweetheart.'"

I said, "I love you little darlings, too."

"There she goes again," Gertie said. "Anyway, sis, I heard you on the radio doing a duet with that Sinatra guy. You were fabulous, but he shows a little promise. When you cut your Brunswick records and everyone knows your name, you might want to give him a hand up."

After that long breakfast, we'd hardly begun decorating the trees when Chef Lattuada, having come to the main house from his apartment on this day off, hurried room to room in evident distress, urging us to turn on the radio. A General Electric jewel-box-style Bakelite radio was placed conveniently in every major room, for we were a tuned-in family. Most of the usual Sunday morning religious and inspirational-music programming had been wiped aside by the broadcasters' news divisions. The Japanese had pulled off a sneak attack on Pearl Harbor, destroying a significant percentage of the United States Navy's warships, killing hundreds if not thousands of sailors and others. Meaningful details were slow to come and not easily winnowed from a harvest of misinformation. The shock we felt wasn't merely emotional but also physical—a pressure in the chest, a greasy turning in the gut. Initially, the mental trauma was more severe than the fear of what was to follow the treachery of that December 7, but as the shock abated, the fear was sustained.

We didn't abandon the task of decorating for Christmas, because the holiday was about hope, peace, and the defeat of evil. However, what would have been a day of laughter was bereft of it. The work went slowly, for inanimate objects now possessed the power to resist whatever we wished to do with them. The wire hangers didn't want to be hooked through the wire loops in the necks of the blown-glass ornaments. Tangled strings of colorful lights insisted on not being untangled. An angel placed atop the tree repeatedly took flight and had to be returned to her rightful perch.

We finished what was usually a one-day effort in two days, by late Monday afternoon, when the radio was still reporting new and more disturbing details about Pearl Harbor by the hour. President Roosevelt asked Congress to declare war against Japan, which it did in six minutes. Japan's allies, Germany and Italy, declared war on the US. Days would pass before we got a picture of the devastation in Hawaii. The navy reported two thousand men killed and more than seven hundred wounded in the two-hour attack. The Army and Marines lost over three hundred, and more than four hundred were wounded. The president called the seventh of December a "day of infamy," and certainly it was, though many days of infamy had occurred in the history of humanity, and many more were sure to come. By Christmas, Japanese forces, committing atrocities that many thought would never occur again after the abominations of World War I, had taken over Guam, Hong Kong, Wake Island, and the Philippines.

There were things that ordinary citizens could do as the costs of war were brought home to us—organize paper and rubber and scrap-metal drives, volunteer at hospitals, donate care packages of candy and paperback books and other items to remind the troops of home and keep their spirits up. Those of us at the Bram, family and staff, were getting involved in those activities. Franklin and Loretta were in consultations with the Department of War and other government offices, donating their time, skills, and resources to recruiting films, propaganda aimed at the enemy, and movies designed to lift the spirits of the American people.

On December 26, with the whole family gathered at breakfast, Harry informed us that he'd signed up for the Marines four days after Pearl Harbor and had passed his physical on December 22. He had scored high on the armed forces qualification test, guaranteeing him training in any specialty he chose, but he didn't want to be in a support position. He wanted to be a grunt, trained to fight and given every opportunity to fight. He expected to be told to report for boot camp after the new year. "I didn't tell you," he explained, "because I didn't want to cast another shadow on this Christmas." He was twenty, saturated in history and military lore. We'd known he would seek to serve, but we hadn't asked him what his intentions were. I suspect, in our hearts, we hoped he would pursue a military exemption in order to work with his parents on their Department of War projects. Of course that could never have happened. That was not Harry. For all his enthusiasm for such things as the adventures of the Clyde Tombaugh Club and his quickness to engage in silly banter, there had always been a somber side to him that he did his best to keep from us in the interest of being the fun brother that we wanted him to be. We didn't get teary-eyed at that breakfast, because he wouldn't want that reaction. We were proud of him, and it was our job to express our pride without embarrassing him. In a time of war, the pride you feel for someone you love, someone willing to make the ultimate sacrifice, inevitably comes tangled with other powerful emotions—fear, anger at those who broke the peace, choking disquiet at the unpredictable nature of life, and a tenderness without pity, a tenderness so intense that I have no words to describe it.

I cried in bed that night. I cried, but not in excess, for it seemed that indulging in too much sorrow would tempt fate to punish my intemperance with a better reason for grief.

On December 29, Harry received his notice to present himself at the induction center on the morning of Wednesday, January 14, 1942. Isadora had canceled a two-week gig in San Francisco to be with us. In his remaining days at home, Harry wanted no special treatment, only to have every breakfast and dinner with all of us, to play cards with his "three sisters," and to watch some films with us in the Bram's screening room—a little Chaplin, a little more Harold Lloyd, the Marx Brothers, Laurel and Hardy, W. C. Fields, and Abbott and Costello in *Buck Privates*, which had just hit theaters in '41. He spent time with Loretta and Franklin, brainstorming propaganda films aimed at the nation's enemies overseas and those at home. Rafael received his share of attention, chasing tennis balls on the great lawn and splashing with his "brother" in the swimming pool.

The weather was mild for January. On his last weekend, Harry carried a chair through the jungle in the conservatory, into the grotto, up the hidden stairs, through the midnight-blue door with its silvery moon ringed by stars, past the six-foot-tall mirrored obelisk, and placed it at the western parapet, where he could sit with a view of the suburbs beyond these hills and the great city that seemed to go on forever. He spent time there every evening before he went to bed.

On his last night at home, I was waiting in a chair of my own, which I'd placed beside his. As he sat down, I said, "Do you mind?"

"Mind your company? Yours is far better than mine, Addie."

I said, "It's beautiful, isn't it?"

"The city? Yes. More beautiful at a distance than close up, but that's true of a lot of things, including most movie stars."

"You never sat up here like this before."

"Because I thought the city would always be there."

"Won't it be?"

"It's not going anywhere anytime soon. But I am. So I'm just sort of storing up the sight of it."

"I wish you wouldn't go."

"It's okay, sis. I'll be home in eleven weeks, after boot, for a visit. When this thing is won and over, I'll be back for good and bore your butt off with my war stories."

"If your stories are really boring, Gertie can polish them for you. She's going to be something."

"She always has been—and so have you."

After watching the moon shed a cloud, I said, "Maybe Izzy will do USO tours and one day be in a show at some overseas base where you are."

"Wouldn't that be something. But I'd rather she keep on doing what she's been doing here. She moves you out of yourself when she sings, and you forget what had you down. People stateside are going to need that every bit as much as anyone."

Although the night was calm there on the roof, wind flowed at higher altitudes, reclothing the moon.

"Everyone has something important to give," I said, "but all I've got is putting together care packages."

"You've already done more than anyone, Addie. Maybe not for the war effort, but for all of us at Bramley Hall."

"That's lovely of you to say and sweet to hear."

He fixed me with his starlit eyes. "Those aren't just pretty words. It's true. None of us would be who we are if you had never come aboard."

"Aboard. The Bram *is* something like an ocean liner, isn't it? A big beautiful ship that makes every day feel a little bit like a holiday."

"And it almost sank one day in 1934, but for you."

His words briefly perplexed me, but then I was discomfited when I realized to what he must be referring. Pretending ignorance in order to avoid a lie, I said, "Oh, yes. The day I ate only my share of Chef's pastries rather than half of everything he baked."

He reached out with his right hand and took my left. "Gertie really is something, and she's going to become something even more wonderful. Because you gave her the chance."

"How do you know about that? I mean, if there's anything to know about, which I'm not saying there is."

"I never knew until this past September. There's one day every September when I take Lynette flowers from the garden and we sit talking for a while."

I said, "The anniversary of the day that her daughter died of influenza."

"I never knew about *that* until the day the Symingtons left and Victoria told me, the day Lynette became the estate manager. Libby has been gone twenty-three years, but every year on the day of, it seems to Lynette that the loss was yesterday. Evidently Gertie much reminds her of Libby. For some reason, Lynette was more emotional this year than usual. As she reminisced about Libby, she began also remembering things Gertie had said and done—then suddenly she was talking about you and that day at the hospital. I know she swore to keep your secret, but I'm so glad she opened up to me. Don't blame her, Addie. She said you were afraid if people knew about your gift, you would be a freak twice over. It half broke my heart to hear that. You're not twice a freak. You're not a freak at all. You're one of my three sisters, each of you unique, all three of you the best. I promise to keep your secret, but only because you're my sister and you want me to."

I don't know how long I was unable to speak. He held my hand and waited. What a good man he was already, at twenty. What a fine Marine he would make, devoted to the protection of others. At last I found my voice. "I don't know how I did it, only that I could. I felt less like the cause than like the instrument through which some other power was working. At the time, there were several important reasons why it seemed I should keep it secret. Seven years later, the only one that matters as much is Gertie. I don't want her to know that she would have died in that very half hour. I don't want her to feel she owes me anything. I want her to hit me with those smart-ass comments that make me laugh. When I make a suggestion about one of the stories she writes, I don't want her to take it just because she thinks of me as Saint Adiel or something. I want her to feel comfortable saying, 'Stuff it, Maxwell Perkins, and go edit your boy Hemingway's work into ruin.' You understand, Harry?"

"Yes. Of course. My lips are sealed, but in return for behaving with more discretion than is my nature, may I ask, just this once, after all these years, if it doesn't make you too uncomfortable, may I ask to hold your hand without the glove between us?"

"It won't be pleasant," I warned him.

"As a young boy, I sometimes held the hand of my teacher, Miss Imogene Blackthorn, whom you may remember. Although she turned out to be a eugenics enthusiast and generally nasty piece of work, I somehow survived. You flatter yourself to think you could be even five percent as repulsive as she was."

"Miss Blackthorn was not a star of the Museum of the Strange. For you, dear brother, I'll deep-six the word *freak*. But we can't ignore the fact that for many years I was boldly billed as a 'human oddity,' and no one ever accused Captain of false advertising."

I took off my glove and counted on the low light of the moon to minimize the visual impact if not the tactile shock. He took my hand once more and held it for a moment and said, "Well, thus far I have survived."

We sat there for more than another hour, each of us with much to say before Franklin and Loretta drove him to the induction center in the morning. Sometimes, depending on the subject of discussion, we held each other tighter than at other times, but not once did he recoil from my touch. When the time came for him to go to his room and pack what little he was permitted to take to the training center in San Diego, he kissed my hand and released it.

As I worked my fingers into the glove, Harry said, "You are in fact a human oddity, sis, but for one reason only. You're far more human and humane than ninety-five percent of the species."

I slept that night, but restlessly. In the morning, Harry had left for the induction center in Los Angeles.

FORTY-ONE

In those early months of the wars—one in the far Pacific, the other in Europe—every day was so busy even for civilians committed to the cause that there was little time to dwell on fear of defeat. And though we slept well through the first half of the night, worry often troubled our sleep during the second half.

Our Harry came home from basic training on Saturday, April 4, the day before Easter. Of the sixty recruits in his platoon, he had excelled above all others. His physical fitness score was 290 out of a possible 300, best in his series—a series being four platoons undergoing identical training at the same time. On the rifle range, he held the series record at 234. On his first try, he had qualified as an S-3 swimmer. His special drill instructor, Staff Sergeant Detwiler, designated our Harry as the honorman "for his outstanding leadership qualities and overall performance" and awarded him a meritorious promotion to Pfc. His achievements were recognized on graduation, when he was the only recruit in his platoon presented with the Dress Blue uniform. Others had the option of buying one like it later. S/Sgt Detwiler suggested to Harry that, under these circumstances, returning home to his family to await orders was an occasion for which Dress Blues were appropriate.

After coming north by train, Harry took a cab from the Los Angeles terminal. All of us at the Bram, family and the extended family that was the staff, gathered in the portico to welcome him home. He presented such a picture when he stepped out of the taxi with his seabag that, to a one, we were briefly left speechless by his transformation. He wore the high-necked navy-blue jacket with red piping and brass buttons, sky-blue trousers with a red stripe down each leg, and spit-polished black shoes. His white barracks cap with navy-blue bill featured a brass quatrefoil, and though the face below it was recognizably Harry's, his features were chiseled as never before. I thought no one in the wide world had a brother handsomer than mine. We grievously wrinkled that fabulous uniform by the time we had all hugged him sufficiently.

He dressed in a civilian suit for church on Easter Sunday. The service, as all of them had been since December 7, was more solemn than those we were accustomed to before the war. However, by the time we returned home, we were determined to embrace a spirit of celebration not just because He was risen, but also because Harry was home and because we knew he would not be home for long.

Just four days later, April 9, seventy-six thousand exhausted American troops on the Bataan Peninsula, on the primary island of the Philippines, were forced to surrender to the Japanese. Grim news. Already the singular brutality of Hirohito's army was well known. Much later we would learn that, during the 65-mile forced march to a Japanese prison camp, ten thousand of our troops were bayoneted, shot, or beheaded. Thousands more died of dehydration, starvation, and other preventable causes. World War I, the "war to end all wars," taught only one lesson to despots—victory required greater savagery than any known before in history.

Harry had been home just two weeks when he received his orders to report to naval operations on Coronado Island, in San Diego Bay. His ultimate destination was not revealed in the notice, and when eventually he would learn it, military rules of secrecy forbade him from telling us. He promised to write frequently, and we promised to send him packages of Chef Lattuada's best cookies whenever we knew where he was stationed and that he would be there long enough to receive them. Although I'd had some experience of the pain of separation when he went off to basic training, I was not prepared for the terrible anguish of this more solemn goodbye.

Faithful to his word, Harry wrote often during the year and a half that followed, several times during each of two R&R leaves in Australia. His letters consisted of only observations he made about nature and people, never about combat, which we took to mean that he must be seeing a lot of action. He wrote about fellow Marines with whom he served and had become fast friends, using only their first names. Now and then, a letter had a melancholy quality for a paragraph, but mostly he seemed to be in good spirits, and always he sought to give us a few laughs in each missive.

The war in the Pacific had gone badly in the beginning but gradually began to turn around, starting with the Battle of Midway in June of '42, though there were still setbacks from time to time. On the home front, we were so busy with war-related work piled atop the conduct of our personal lives that I found less time to devote to this memoir. My habit had been to write as if keeping a diary and then to edit it twice a year to carve away the mundane material. Our family life was filled with interesting and amusing developments even during the months that Harry wasn't with us, more amusing as America and her allies made steady progress in battle and the cloud of totalitarianism began to lift. I had no chance to edit those pages in '42 or '43; they just kept piling up.

Then came Tarawa. Tarawa was an atoll of small, strategically important islands that lay like a necklace around a lagoon that was the sunken crater of a long-extinct volcano. Betio was the largest island, though only a half mile wide and three miles long. Twenty-six hundred Japanese manned heavily fortified, often concealed concrete pillboxes that were thought to have been largely destroyed after three days of bombardment. When the first wave of LVTs—amphibious, tracked landing vehicles known as "amtracs," each carrying twenty-four Marines—entered the lagoon with the intent to capture Betio, they encountered fierce artillery, mortar, and small-arms fire that they had not expected. Although many Marines lost their lives in that initial assault, the 500-yard-long pier was secured. The subsequent waves of LCVPs, which had a deeper draft than the LVTs, made it into the lagoon but got caught on the coral reef several hundred yards from shore and could not advance. The Marines aboard had no choice but to jump into the waist-deep water and wade to shore through a storm of automatic weapons fire. More than five hundred died in the surf.

The battle for Betio and the Tarawa atoll began on November 20, 1943, and ended late on November 22. Second Lieutenant Harold Fairchild did not die in a landing craft. He did not die in the bloody surf. He reached the beach with 70 percent of the men who served with and under him, some of those about whom he had written in his letters. From pillbox to pillbox, they moved along the strand and near twilight rejoined their commanding officer, Colonel David Shoup, who, in spite of a grievous leg wound, led others of the Second Marines to take the pier and move inland. Harry died late the next day, November 21. Nine hundred and eighty-four Marines were killed in action, and more than two thousand were wounded.

The chaos of war and the staggering number of deaths in this world war in particular made accounting for casualties a difficult task for the military, and the notification of the family was often delayed for weeks. The bodies of some of the heroic men who perished at Tarawa were claimed by changing tides and carried out to sea; the deep waters became their grave. Proof of death wasn't always easy to come by. No one in authority wanted to rush to inform a family that a loved one perished, only to discover the man said to be deceased was aboard a ship in transit to his next game of tag with Death.

Thanksgiving that year was on November 25, four days after our Harry moved on from this world, but we did not know we had reason to grieve. As always, the family and the staff prepared and ate dinner together on that special day. Among those in the large and festive gathering, the topic of conversation was frequently Harry. Indeed, Gertie and Izzy and I each read aloud an amusing paragraph from one of his recent letters. Prayer at table included the usual thanks for the food before us, for the good fortune granted us, for the love and friendship that we shared. As we joined hands with those sitting beside us, Franklin concluded with an invocation for Harry's safety and for his return before another Thanksgiving was upon us. During those war years, worry was such a constant that sometimes it could wear out; for a short while the heart would not countenance anything but hope, as on that Thursday, November 25, 1943—Thanksgiving.

We learned of Harry's passing twenty-three days after the fact, on December 14, as the war in the Pacific grew ever more fierce. The special nature of the messenger who brought the news and what else he had to say made the announcement both more devastating and more bearable. A telephone call preceded his arrival, and it came to the main house number, which Lynette Rollins answered. She knew what the visitor must have come to the Bram to report, yet she had the fortitude to gather everyone in the library without hinting at the reason either by her words or demeanor. I believe we all knew but were in denial, each of us concocting a reason of his or her own for the gathering, to delay even the consideration of the truth.

When, last of all, Lynette brought Major Talbot Collings into the library, we could no longer doubt that the worst was to be laid before us. He wore Dress Blues. Judging by the battle streamers, the unit citation ribbons, and the commendation medals that were worn on the left breast of his jacket, he had been in combat often and served with such distinction that it was a rare honor for a Marine of his caliber to be the one to perform this service to the family. We held up better than I expected. We had no choice. Harry did not shrink from duty, even kept a sense of humor when he wrote us from between his experiences of hell on Earth, and we could not dishonor him with a public collapse of our own courage. Major Collings came with a letter from Colonel David Monroe Shoup, under whom Harry had served through four campaigns. As he read it to us, most of us were weak in the legs, but none of us sat down. In that crisp, direct, unsentimental, and yet somehow deeply moving prose with which the best military leaders speak of the valor of their comrades, Colonel Shoup praised Harry for his intrepid actions, valiant achievements, and selfless devotion to duty and to his fellow Marines. Such was the gallantry of Second Lieutenant Harold Percy Fairchild that the lives of many others were saved by his sacrifice of his own life, extraordinary bravery that the colonel witnessed. Consequently, he was recommending that our Harry receive the Navy Cross, an award second only to the Medal of Honor for valor in combat.

Lynette had been wise to ensure that the news was delivered to us as a group, for we are a species that has more fortitude in the company of friends than we have alone. If Major Collings had told Franklin and Loretta in private, it would have fallen to them to tell Izzy, Gertie, and me. Receiving such terrible news is hard, though being the bearer of it, loved one to loved one, is harder still, for one has to suppress one's own grief to deliver such information with compassion. I would never have had the resolution to be the first to say to anyone, *Harry is dead.*

The days—weeks—of mourning that followed are fixed as vividly in memory as the books I've read and everything I have experienced in my strange yet blessed life. I am not able to escape the perfect recollection of them, but I won't write about any of that at this time or possibly ever. Grief can never be adequately described, and every effort to do so diminishes it. The best of novelists tell us that grief will in time subside from painful, excruciating anguish to enduring sorrow that takes a more modest toll of the heart. As I write this, a month after Major Talbot Collings delivered the news and the colonel's letter, grief is anchored in me, and mere sorrow is not in sight.

The expectation of receiving Harry's body, even in a closed coffin that would remain closed, was anticipated by all of us with both dread and longing. Most bodies of men who die in war are left in circumstances that make retrieval impossible or require burial in foreign graves, some well memorialized and others anonymous. We were given to understand that our Harry's body—along with those of certain others—was in transit and soon would be in our care. This, too, was not to occur. The transport conveying him was attacked and sunk by a Japanese submarine in the near Pacific. Remains are not the person, only the flesh he wore when among us. Nonetheless, some comfort can be had by visiting the plot where a carved stone marks the resting place of cherished bones. Perhaps that is because many of us believe that one day, when reality as we know it rolls up like a scroll and a new reality is unfurled, body and soul will be sewn together again, as if the threads between them were never broken.

With no reason for a funeral and interment, we held a small memorial service. Gertie wrote and delivered the eulogy. Izzy sang so beautifully. I found the courage to say a few words, which I took from "The Marines' Hymn" while changing just two pronouns. "In many a strife they fought for life / And never lost their nerve / If the Army and the Navy / Ever look on Heaven's scenes / They will find the streets are guarded / By United States Marines."

In the days that followed, whether still in grief or moving toward sorrow, we got on with our lives. Such is the world.

FORTY-TWO

Throughout January and February of 1944, Gertie worked harder than ever, at last focusing on a piece she expected to be of novel length when completed late that year. As I suspect might be true of many novelists, writing was her consolation. She found much solace in eight- and ten-hour sessions at the typewriter. Often when she gave me pages for comment, she would say, "I think I would have gotten a good laugh out of Harry with that paragraph," or "Harry probably would have teased me about that metaphor, but I think he would have come around to liking it." I approved of nearly all she did; she was maturing as a writer faster than I would have thought possible.

On the night of March 2, a Thursday, I was sitting in bed, reading one of Gertie's chapters that sparkled even as it darkled, when Rafael padded into the room. He stood staring at me with that expression that I took to mean, *Am I welcome? If I'm not welcome, I'll be devastated. Am I welcome? Whaddaya say?* I patted the bed, and he sprang onto it as if he were only seven in human years. He stretched out beside me, his head raised on a pillow so he could watch me, and he thumped his tail against the mattress half a dozen times to let me know he was happy just to be there and snooze. If he had wanted to cuddle, he would have signaled his desire by lying on his back, baring his tummy, and letting his forepaws go limp. He was sixteen, old for a shepherd, but still spry, free of all illnesses and infirmities since that day in 1934 when he was poisoned. Now and then over the years, I'd given some thought to his health and vigor, but I always decided the explanation which occurred to me couldn't be proven and that I was too full of myself just for considering it. Perhaps ten minutes after Rafael put his big head on the pillow, he thumped his tail again, thrice this time, and let out the longest canine sigh I'd ever heard. When I looked at him, his eyes were closed. When the sigh concluded, he was still; his mouth remained open. I held a hand before his nose, but he expelled no breath.

Although it would seem that, having grieved so hard for Harry, I would not be anguished by the death of a dog, such was not the case. The relationship with a good dog is closer to perfection than that with another human rarely manages to be. They are innocent, and we are not. They ask so little of us, but give so much. Rafael had been a member in good standing of the Clyde Tombaugh Club, a fellow adventurer, loyal pal, and confidant. I drew him against me, pressed his mouth closed, smoothed the fur of his beautiful, noble face. I told him that he was the best dog ever, that I loved him. I wept.

Mr. Reinhardt dug a resting place in a corner of the great lawn, and we buried Rafael in a bed of red rose petals. A small headstone with his name was ordered, to be installed in a few weeks. My reaction was not unique. During the days that followed, I found one or another of my fellow Bramleyans laying a flower on his grave or sitting nearby on the grass, taking comfort from the memory of him.

Dreams are conversations with ourselves. We speak to ourselves in metaphors and symbols about subjects from which we shy. One night I dreamed of encountering Luigi Lattuada at Rafael's grave. The chef was carrying a copy of *A Tale of Two Cities*. He said, "John fifteen, verse thirteen. It's all you need to know, Adiel. It's what you are—presented to

357

the world in a form that tests our comprehension and our souls." Then Rafael came out of his grave, unmarked by death, and he ran across the lawn with Luigi Lattuada. As they ran, the chef became a boy, and the boy was Harry, and the darkness became daylight, and the birds flew from their night roosts.

After that dream, I found myself revisiting the theory that previously seemed to be unlikely and—I could now admit—unnerving. I'd drawn the effects of the poison out of Rafael and had spared him from death without realizing what was happening. Was it possible that, in so doing, I had also more or less vaccinated him against all illness and disease by some power unknown and unknowable? What if he ultimately died not because he was sick or worn out, but only because, in this world of layered mysteries, there is a time for all things and a countdown clock that can't be stopped? I couldn't bring the dead back to life; Lazarus would have been out of luck with me. But Rafael's long and always healthy life begged serious consideration.

Had I been at Harry's side when the bullets cut him down in an instant, I couldn't have brought him back. But if he'd never gone to war, and if one day I'd had a visitation by some radiant being and been told that I could spare my brother from all forms of ill health for the rest of his life by passing to him, by touch, a portion of my years on Earth, would I have declined the sacrifice? Declined and left him vulnerable to disease? I who had spent the first seventeen years of my existence, used and humiliated, yearning for a purpose that would make me feel clean? The answer was clear, the opportunity exhilarating. Since that rescue from Blue Mood and the ride north through the night, I'd felt that my meaning would be fulfilled by being a friend of this family, by doing for them some grace that I could not yet comprehend. And now here I was, the moment upon me.

To bestow the grace that I hoped, surely no magic words, no "abracadabra" or "Hola Nola Massa" was required. With apologies to

Jiminy Cricket, I had no need to make a wish upon a star. I was a human oddity not just from the neck down. If I was not deluded, the most freakish thing about me was an amazing power that I possessed but did not understand, that I had long lacked the confidence to explore. But how could a mere freak be a healer? A freak ought to know her place and keep to it, shouldn't she? A freak who thinks too highly of herself might well expect that she'll become a target and that bad luck will cast her back into another ten-in-one.

No. All those fears were errors of reason and faith. Luck was not evidence of frivolous Fates at play. Luck was what evolved for us from the actions of other people and from our own actions—tides of molasses and runaway delivery trucks. This family shaped my luck by doing what their code of right and wrong required of them. Their unfailing sympathy and kindness might be traced back decades to an earthquake that killed thousands and revealed the moral virtue or depravity of the survivors, a grim orphanage run by grifters, and long hours of piecework in a sweatshop. If kindness that surpassed understanding could be born from so much suffering, then so could it be inspired by the humid sawdust-scented air and fly-infested depths of a ten-in-one. By the mockery and insults of marks who needed to feel superior to someone. It could evolve—couldn't it?—from being forced to stand nearly naked on a speakeasy stage in the company of exquisitely formed showgirls, while a drunken audience roared with laughter at the antics of a crude comedian to whom a young girl with deformities was nothing more than a prop to be poked and tickled and threatened with terrible violations. The Fairchild family made my good luck, and now I had the chance to give back to them. It seemed to me, but not to them, that the debt I owed was greater every year. I was going to repay love with love to an extent that they would refuse to accept if they knew what I intended. The meaning of my life became clear, and it was thrilling.

My experience with Rafael when he was poisoned and with Gertie when she nearly succumbed to septic shock was that healing took a toll of me. Intuition told me that the gift of lifelong health, if indeed I could give it, would not only temporarily exhaust me, but would cost years of my own life each time that I bestowed enduring strength and vigor on someone. This did not concern me. During my days in the Museum of the Strange, I had not expected to live to be thirty, and I could never have imagined that thirteen of those years would be joyful, as in fact they had been here at the Bram. To want more seemed to be to want too much. The lacerating grief I felt at Harry's death might mature into a less terrible if enduring sorrow, but I could not harbor many such sorrows and still find life to be a journey of joy. If I lost others as I'd lost Harry, the years before me would be worth living but would never be as blissful as those I had known since September 1930. My love was great. Millennia ago it was written, "Greater love hath no man than this: that he lay down his life for his friends." John fifteen, verse thirteen. The sentiment was no less true if you substituted "woman" for "man" and "she" for "he" and "her" for "his." Nor did it make a difference if the "she" was a human oddity. Anyway, the price of this gift might not be as steep as I expected. But if it required everything of me, that was just a way to grieve and in the process bring an end to grieving.

I hadn't much extended myself when I spared Rafael from poison or relieved Gertie of septic shock; what I now proposed would drain me more profoundly. Because I didn't know how high the toll would be when the gift was given or how quickly the cost would mount before I could pay it no more, I felt I needed to attend Franklin, Loretta, Gertie, and Izzy in the same day, with as little time between them as possible. Following the news of Harry's death, Isadora canceled her public performances for six months and settled for a time in the Bram. At the moment, she was in Los Angeles, recording four songs, three of which she had written. In the past year, her two records, released four months apart, had received a lot of radio play. The first broke into *Billboard*'s top forty, climbing as high as thirty-seven. The most recent release had gone to number thirty. I was in a family of overachievers, and I loved it; their every success pleased me as much as if it were my own. Izzy would return home in two days, Thursday, March 23. I was prepared to cast my spell, so to speak, on Friday.

Our songbird came home near midnight and was so exhausted that she went directly to bed. I'm sure she enjoyed a sound sleep. In my room, however, I could not sleep at all. I was as excited as I had ever been. I wandered through the vast library in my mind. Novels can show us ways through dilemmas that we might never have thought to follow if left to our own devices. Fiction can introduce us to ideas that seem exotic until we consider them long enough, whereupon they become obvious wisdom; some ideas might even repulse us until we realize we are reacting with a bias that we should want to shed. Of all the novels I'd read and that I revisited during that night, the better ones offered themes and observations that reinforced the decision I had made. Some books by bitter cynics and misanthropes aggressively challenged every value that I embraced; however, the emptiness of their arguments also assured me that I was doing the right thing—which no doubt would have infuriated their authors.

Although I had no doubt that I possessed the power to do as I intended, I lacked certainty as to how to pass the gift of perfect health, of lifelong strength and vigor. No words had been necessary to heal Rafael and Gertie. In the dog's case, I had not even had a conscious intention of saving him. There was no need to shout, *Heal!* No white-robed and hand-clapping hallelujah choir would increase the likelihood that I would succeed. As in all things, humility seemed to be the best approach. I was a freak, the veteran of tawdry stage shows, who came from nothing and *seemed* to have come from nowhere—unclaimed by a father or a mother with blood ties to me. My power was as mysterious as how my twisted body was able to function. If I did nothing but placed both hands on someone with the intent to pass my gift, surely it would be received.

When I'd drawn the effects of poison from Rafael, I apparently conveyed to him the very benefit I wanted to transmit to my family. I might have done the same with Gertie in the hospital. She had not suffered as much as a cold since then. However, I didn't want to take the chance of leaving her unprotected.

That night, the hours I spent scheming how best to inoculate everyone without making them curious about my odd behavior was time wasted. In the morning, when I went downstairs for breakfast at the kitchen table, Izzy arrived simultaneously. It was the most natural thing to stand tiptoe, embrace her with my hands on her shoulders, and kiss her cheek. I felt it happen then, like warm currents of air passing through me, out of me, into her. If she was aware of it, she felt less than I did. Her eyes widened for a moment, and there was a catch in her voice, and then she continued greeting me.

Gertie stood at the center island, watching Chef Lattuada pour coffee into a mug for her. I embraced her as I had Izzy. Once more I felt the transmission occur. She frowned. "What just . . ."

I said, "Just what?"

"What was that?"

"That?"

"Yeah, that."

"What that?" I asked.

Cocking her head, looking puzzled, she said, "Addie?"

She was a writer, after all, a novelist in the making, so it was not surprising that she would be more sensitive to events than anyone else. "I don't know what you're asking, Gertie."

After a hesitation, she shook her head and sighed. "Neither do I, amigo. I've been up half the night, revising those chapters you haven't seen. I'm done with them, as done as I can be for now."

"Gimme, gimme."

"That's them, the golden pages," she declared, pointing to a stationery box on the counter. "Be vicious."

"You can count on me."

As I spoke, Franklin and Loretta entered the kitchen. This was a hugging family. The bacon was still sizzling on the griddle by the time I had passed to them the same gift I had given to my sisters.

When I got back to my room after breakfast, I found that the stationery box contained the 280 pages that Gertie had written—and polished, polished, polished—to date. I didn't start with the two most recent chapters but began rereading from page one, as attentive as her prose required. Although mentally alert and captivated again by the novel, I was physically exhausted. I suspected the legacy I passed to the four of them had cost me every bit as much as I had thought it might. After I finished reading and made notes on the two new chapters, I phoned the kitchen to ask if Chef would send dinner to my room, just a sandwich and a split of cabernet. After I ate, yet again rereading the two new chapters, I brushed my teeth and went to bed with my diary, forcing myself to record the events of this day.

I have just now finished that entry and feel sleep stealing over me. And something more than sleep. Some change is occurring that I never anticipated. I have removed my gloves. How can this be? Whatever this is, it is not death. I'm not afraid, only tired. So tired. I can't hold the pen any longer. I am . . . becoming . . .

FORTY-THREE

How strange this night has been.

For several hours, I twisted and writhed in bed, drenched in a cold sweat, hallucinating as do those gripped by malaria in novels of the tropics.

When the torment passed, I was barefoot on the balcony, letting the cool breeze dry my nightdress. The sky was clear. The moon was in the west. The stars seemed to invite me. I don't know what I mean by that, but the stars seemed to invite me.

Before I realized what I was doing, I'd taken off my nightdress and the underclothes that Marjorie Hollingsworth Merrimen designed for me and still produced for me annually.

In all my years at the Bram, I had never been naked elsewhere than in my private bathroom. Yet there I stood on the balcony with all revealed.

I felt so light. I have always been a small person, five feet and very slender. But never before had I felt so light. Through all my years on Earth, I had felt heavy, so heavy. But now I felt very light.

What I thought happened next could not have happened. It had to be a waking dream, hallucination, proof that my mind must be deteriorating. I will not embarrass myself by writing of it.

I had become shameless. I left my clothing on the balcony and returned naked to my room. After a life of shame and humiliation, I was shameless.

I found my diary and pen beside the bed and wrote these last words. I thought they were my last. I knew I had not long to live.

Then a knock came at my living room door. I hadn't strength to get up from the edge of the bed, where I sat writing.

I called out, "Come in, Mother," for I knew who was there. My voice was weak, but she must have heard me, for she came to me.

Stepping into the bedroom, she said, "Oh, my darling girl," and she rushed to me, and I wrote these words about her coming to me, my mother.

She kneels before me as I sit here on the edge of the bed. She is weeping, as she should be, for I am naked and shameless.

"What . . . what's happening, Addie? For God's sake, what's happening to you?"

"Something," was all I said, for I was a stranger to myself.

"What's that you're writing?" She seems not to know what she should do. That is not like her. "Put it aside. Let me take care of you, Addie."

"I'm writing in the diary. That's what I always do first. Then I edit when I type it. I type it carefully, without errors. Then I put it in a ring binder. For you. All of you. For when I am gone. Writing is what I do. It's why I am."

"Why you are? What do you mean, sweetheart?"

"I write about my family. I tell the story of my family. It's what I can do. The story of my family."

"What's happening?" she asks again. "You're . . ."

The words of Captain ballyhooing on the pitchman's platform came to me, and I spoke them. "'See the strangest freaks on Earth. Pay fifteen cents for ten priceless astonishments. All visitors must be fourteen years old or older.'" The last lines of Mr. Dickens's novel also came to me, lines I had long loved, and I spoke them as well. "'It is a far, far better thing that I do than I have ever done . . . a far, far better rest that I go to than I have ever known.'"

"You aren't a freak. Addie, you never were. Never. You are so beautiful."

"Am I? If I am, it's as if I always could have been if I'd known how."

"What can I do?"

"There is a time for all things."

Mother's voice is breaking. "What can I do?"

"Let me write this last bit. Then just . . . just hold me."

"I love you."

"I love you too, Mother, so very much," I say, and this will be the last thing I write, for nothing that could be said after "love" would be worth saying.

FORTY-FOUR

LORETTA'S NOTE

I am adding this to the back of Adiel's ring binder. If Isadora and Gertrude should bless us with grandchildren, we want them—and however many generations might follow—to know that this exceptional person not only graced our lives for fourteen years but also shaped the future of the family with a selfless sacrifice that will have ramifications in the lives of all our descendants.

Today is June 24, 1944, three months since Addie passed away in my arms. I couldn't bear to write of that night until now. Gertie and Izzy are even more devastated than I. Franklin sometimes speaks of Addie in the present tense, for he had not anticipated her death as he had Harry's. The Bram seems to be haunted, not by a ghost but by the memory of her blithe spirit, the like of which we will never know again. We lost a son and daughter in less than six months, and they were both heroes, Harry in his way, Addie in hers.

Neither "freak" nor "human oddity" applies to her. I don't know any titles that do—other than "daughter" and "sister."

When she asked for dinner in her quarters that night, I thought little of it. I knew she was reading Gertie's manuscript and making suggestions. I had been busy all day long, but by bedtime I was not the least tired. In fact, my energy had not diminished at all—which has since been explained by what we read in her diary regarding the sacrifice she decided to make in her grief over Harry. Her gift to us. We would have rejected it if we had known. Franklin was full of energy, too, and when he couldn't sleep, he went downstairs to his office. I sat in our room, reading until I thought I heard distant silvery bells, which I had never heard in this territory before. I went out onto the balcony. What I saw shook me as I had not been shaken since the San Francisco earthquake of 1906.

I needed a quarter of an hour to compose myself and to decide how to deal with what I'd seen. Indeed, I needed some of that time to convince myself that I had in fact seen it.

Only when I went to her room did I discover that the situation was as dire as it was fantastic. Dread and tenderness do not seem to be companionable emotions, but I was at once in the grip of both. She was intent on writing what transpired in those last minutes, as much as she could before she became too weak to hold the pen. *It's why I am,* she had said. *It's why I am.*

In her bed, I held her in my arms. She was as naked as when she had been born, though she was no longer as she had been on that Blue Mood stage where we first saw her.

Out of respect for Addie, I will not dwell in detail on the deformities with which she was born but provide enough for you to understand why she would have a place in that hateful Museum of the Strange. Her legs and arms were so slender that it seemed she must be disabled, but the muscles were far stronger than their thinness implied. Her torso was asymmetrical, as if cruel Nature had given her a hard twist before sending her into the world, but the seeming misalignment of her clearly defined ribs, while disturbing to the eye, in no way inhibited her movement. Her knuckles were sharp, her fingers long, her nails as black as ebony and in constant need of a blunting file. Excess skin sagged from her arms in shallow loops like hastily furled flags. The vile comedian on that speakeasy stage said that the contrast between her splendid face and afflicted body confirmed that her mother had been a showgirl and her father had been a bat. Many in the audience found her horrifying and disgusting in an entertaining way; others were amused by her; some pitied her but were too fascinated to look away. The last thing she deserved was pity, for even used in that barbarous and mortifying show, she held fast to her dignity and answered the comedian's gross lines with a look that seemed to say *she* pitied *him* even as she held him in well-deserved contempt. Her gravity and self-possession ennobled her. She inspired in Franklin and me no pity at all, but sympathy and a powerful and moving sense of kinship in a world of strangers where like spirits seem to be rare.

And so, in those predawn hours of Friday, March 24, as I sat in Addie's bed and held her, the stunning change in her, which occurred overnight, suggested that the girl's real life, a new and glorious life, had just begun. She had spun no cocoon, had not retreated for a cloistered season. No science could explain her transformation, nor could any denomination of any faith known on Earth. Although she was still small and slender, her body had reformed like a withered sponge swelling to its ideal form. She might have been a child of twelve, but for the wings that graced her now that the half-furled and sagging flesh on her arms and sides had unfurled. Her skin had the peachy color that sometimes develops between the red of sunburn and the soft brown of a tan, so that she seemed to glow with an inner light. She gazed up at me, and for a moment those blue, blue eyes seemed to be windows on an eternity unlike any that I had imagined or could even now comprehend. She was the most beautiful creature I had ever seen.

When she looked past me toward the bedroom door, I saw that Franklin, Isadora, and Gertrude had come, their faces informed both by astonishment and bewilderment, as if they had been drawn here by a haunting song they had never heard before, for a purpose they had not known until it was revealed.

Adiel smiled at them as they gathered at bedside, all of them speechless, as if they understood that no word was worthy of the moment. Our girl closed her eyes.

She whispered to me, "Mother, there is a letter I wrote years before I knew you. Earlier tonight, I put it under my pillow. So that you will know it has always been coming to this and that I have no regrets. My life has been perfect." I felt her heart stop. Her smile did not fade with her life.

I imagine miracles are real, but I can't say for sure this was a miracle by the usual definition. I have not believed in magic, but one does not have to believe in something for it to be a fact.

To my family, *her* family, gathered here before us, I said, "She flew. I saw her from my balcony. She was laughing, a soft sound like silvery bells. She flew."

For most of us, the purpose of our lives remains elusive. Her voice came to me in memory: *I tell the story of my family. It's what I can do. It's why I am.*

We did not know where she came from. Neither did she. We did not know what her birth name was. Neither did she. We called her Adiel, which is Hebrew and means "an ornament of God."

As I held her body, the illusion of inner light sustained, if in fact it was merely an illusion. Her origins were unfathomable. Why we, of all people, should cross her path in the Blue Mood at the height of her mortification at the hands of a soulless comedian was a synchronicity that could never be explained. We exist now as we have always existed, as everyone now alive exists if they dare to admit it—forever in a mystery so strange and so profound that it cannot be solved.

Such is the world.

ABOUT THE AUTHOR

International bestselling author Dean Koontz was a senior in college when he won an *Atlantic Monthly* fiction competition. He has never stopped writing. Koontz is the author of *The Forest of Lost Souls*, *The Bad Weather Friend*, *After Death*, *The House at the End of the World*, *The Big Dark Sky*, and seventy-nine *New York Times* bestsellers, fourteen of which were #1: *One Door Away from Heaven*, *From the Corner of His Eye*, *Midnight*, *Cold Fire*, *The Bad Place*, *Hideaway*, *Dragon Tears*, *Intensity*, *Sole Survivor*, *The Husband*, *Odd Hours*, *Relentless*, *What the Night Knows*, and *77 Shadow Street*. Hailed by *Rolling Stone* as "America's most popular suspense novelist," Koontz has published books in thirty-eight languages and sold more than five hundred million copies worldwide. Born and raised in Pennsylvania, he now lives in Southern California with his wife, Gerda, their golden retriever, Elsa, and the enduring spirits of their goldens Trixie and Anna. For more information, visit his website at www.deankoontz.com.